W9-ANM-214

Devil's Delight

"I've had all I'm going to take from you. Now move away from that door," Kate told Clint in a steady voice.

Suddenly Clint took a dive at her and knocked her onto the bed. To make matters worse, Clint was now on top of her.

"The word is *please*," he said softly, his lips brushing hers as he spoke. "If you wanted me to move from the door, you could have said please instead of ordering me."

"I'll not say please to any man."

Clint heard her intake of breath as his hand cupped her full breast. "Then I guess you want to stay."

"Please," Kate blurted out.

"Please what? Please don't stop, or please let me go?"

Other **AVON ROMANCES**

THE HAWK AND THE HEATHER *by Robin Leigh*
ANGEL OF FIRE *by Tanya Anne Crosby*
WARRIOR DREAMS *by Kathleen Harrington*
MY CHERISHED ENEMY *by Samantha James*
CHEROKEE SUNDOWN *by Genell Dellin*
DESERT ROGUE *by Suzanne Simmons*
RENEGADE LADY *by Sonya Birmingham*

Coming Soon

LORD OF MY HEART *by Jo Beverley*
BLUE MOON BAYOU *by Katherine Compton*

And Don't Miss These
ROMANTIC TREASURES
from Avon Books

LADY LEGEND *by Deborah Camp*
RAINBOWS AND RAPTURE *by Rebecca Paisley*
AWAKEN MY FIRE *by Jennifer Horsman*

Avon Books are available at special quantity discounts for bulk purchases for sales promotions, premiums, fund raising or educational use. Special books, or book excerpts, can also be created to fit specific needs.

For details write or telephone the office of the Director of Special Markets, Avon Books, Dept. FP, 1350 Avenue of the Americas, New York, New York 10019, 1-800-238-0658.

Devil's Delight

DELORAS SCOTT

AVON BOOKS NEW YORK

If you purchased this book without a cover, you should be aware that this book is stolen property. It was reported as "unsold and destroyed" to the publisher, and neither the author nor the publisher has received any payment for this "stripped book."

DEVIL'S DELIGHT is an original publication of Avon Books. This work has never before appeared in book form. This work is a novel. Any similarity to actual persons or events is purely coincidental.

AVON BOOKS
A division of
The Hearst Corporation
1350 Avenue of the Americas
New York, New York 10019

Copyright © 1992 by DeLoras Scott
Published by arrangement with the author
Library of Congress Catalog Card Number: 91-92443
ISBN: 0-380-76343-5

All rights reserved, which includes the right to reproduce this book or portions thereof in any form whatsoever except as provided by the U.S. Copyright Law. For information address Ruth Cohen Inc., P.O. Box 7626, Menlo Park, California 94025.

First Avon Books Printing: July 1992

AVON TRADEMARK REG. U.S. PAT. OFF. AND IN OTHER COUNTRIES, MARCA REGISTRADA, HECHO EN U.S.A.

Printed in the U.S.A.

RA 10 9 8 7 6 5 4 3 2 1

Prologue

Wyoming Territory, October 1869

Dear Sister,
   It has occurred to me we share a mutual problem. We suffer from an unfulfilled desire to see grandchildren before we meet our maker.

The frail, elderly woman laid her pen down, pulled open one of the drawers in her secretary desk, and withdrew a small picture. She couldn't remember when her sister had sent it.

Mattie Whitfield gazed at the faded photo. She hadn't seen Clint Morgan since he was a young boy. Was he still as handsome? Cora said he was. More mature and a perfect gentleman, she had stated.

A sudden, warm breeze blew through the open window, momentarily catching Mattie's attention. Am I doing the right thing? Mattie wondered as she watched the lace curtains flutter. Then she thought of her stepdaughter, Kate. Such a beautiful girl, with silver-blond hair and large green eyes. Mattie clicked her tongue. Unfortunately, Kate preferred men's clothing over more feminine attire. Were it not for her lovely face and full bosom, she'd look like most of the other hands on the ranch. She even acted like them. Mattie had to admit that having to run a ranch didn't allow Kate much time for feminine ways, but still . . .

Mattie released a tired sigh, her thoughts turning to her son. If only Lucas had Kate's fortitude. Then he could run the ranch and let Kate be a woman.

Again she looked at the picture of Clint Morgan. Yes, she assured herself, I'm doing the right thing. She replaced the picture of her nephew in the drawer where it had been resting for over ten years, then dipped the pen in the inkwell and continued her letter.

After much thought, I have devised a rather daring plan that will hopefully take care of our dilemma. Admittedly, the final results will be in God's hands.

In your last letter, you mentioned Clint will soon be returning home. I ask that you strongly request he stop by Whitfield on his way. You can make up some story about concern for . . .

Mattie paused. Yes, a man who had lived the polished life of a gentleman was a perfect offset for Kate's unladylike mannerisms.

Chapter 1

Nebraska, May 1870

Hidden by a line of bushy shrubs, Clint Morgan lay on his belly, his Winchester rifle aimed, and silently waited. It had been a short winter, and even though it was still early morning, the sun was already sweltering. The dirt clinging to his sweaty face attracted flies like honey, but he couldn't take a chance on shooing them away. He tried licking his lips, but his mouth felt like it was full of dry mush. Fortunately, the renegade Indians he'd been watching had the rifles they'd come for, so it was just a matter of time before they mounted their ponies and rode off.

A crooked grin stretched his chapped lips as his gaze fell on the two white men standing by the wagon. It had taken eight long, grueling months, but finally, saddle worn and weary to the bone, he'd caught the man responsible for supplying rifles to the Indians. Now it was just a matter of collecting these two henchmen and his job would be finished.

Hearing the snap of a twig nearby, Clint rolled onto his back, taking the Winchester with him. A brave was headed straight for him, tomahawk raised. Clint had no choice but to pull the trigger,

3

the bullet hitting the brave right between the eyes. The Indian toppled to the ground, his tomahawk embedded where Clint had been lying only seconds before.

At the sound of the rifle blast, the small band of Sioux turned in unison. Their high-pitched war whoops suddenly filled the air as they ran in Clint's direction. Clint cursed his bad luck. Not only were the Indians coming for him, but the two men he'd been tracking had jumped on the wagon and were now headed in the opposite direction.

After pulling off a few more shots and killing two of the closest braves, Clint jumped to his feet and made a dash toward the trees where he'd left his horse. In the few seconds it took to cover the distance, the renegades had loaded their new repeater rifles, their bullets peppering the ground around Clint's feet.

Clint made a running leap onto the horse's back. The gray stallion was already in a hard gallop before Clint could shove the dusty toes of his boots in the stirrups. Though he had to do some fancy riding to keep the stallion moving in a zigzag pattern to avoid the onslaught of bullets, Clint managed to escape unscathed.

It took another three weeks of tracking before Clint caught up with the two wanted men again. He entered the dilapidated saloon on the outskirts of Dodge City, then stepped away from the swinging doors, standing so that the wall was the only thing behind him. His gaze traveled from the shabby men standing at the bar, to the bartender, and finally to the two men seated at a back table, facing the door. They weren't hard to recognize. One had a long scar running along the side of his nose. The other had flaming red hair. As Clint started forward, both men looked up. Jumping from their chairs, they went for their guns. Clint drew, pulling the trigger twice before either of the pair could get off a shot.

Clint delivered the outlaws to the marshal, both men strapped over their saddles, faces down, eyes permanently closed.

June 1870

Covered with a layer of dust from the top of his black wide-brimmed hat to his boots, the tall, broad-shouldered man stepped down from the stagecoach and took his first look at the small town of Whitfield. The journey by railroad from Topeka to Denver, then from Denver to Cheyenne and on to Rawlins had been long, but at least tolerable. The eight-hour passage by stage from Rawlins had been jarring all the way.

After his trunks had been safely deposited in a room at the Whitfield Hotel, Clint Morgan took a stroll to familiarize himself with the surroundings, an old habit after spending ten years as a hired gun for the United States government. However, the afternoon sky was peacock blue, the sun was dazzling, and the long stagecoach ride had left a definite need to stretch his legs.

The size of Whitfield came as a surprise. Somehow, Clint had expected it to be nothing more than a weigh station. The town, named after his uncle, the legendary Sam Whitfield, was nestled in the foothills about forty miles from Rawlins and six thousand feet up. It was going to take a while to get used to the thin mountain air, especially after spending the last three years on the prairie.

Clint discovered that the main street of town stretched for three blocks, with stores on each side and groups of neatly kept white houses at either end. A long road led up to a sawmill situated on a rocky plateau. The name Whitfield was painted in bold white letters across the front of the

wooden building. Clint surmised that it was probably the lumber that kept the town alive, that and
business from the various ranches scattered over
the big, fertile valley he'd traveled across. He even
found a park with plenty of cottonwood trees and
a gazebo. A small white church sat two blocks
over. There were ready smiles on people's faces
and they greeted him with nods of hello. A nice,
cozy little town, he decided.

Dusk was quickly approaching by the time Clint
made his way back to the main street. Half a block
from the hotel he heard the hard thud of horses
galloping down the street behind him. The thin
air was suddenly shattered by the sound of guns
firing, followed by god-awful yipping and yelling. Thinking the town was being attacked by Indians, Clint whipped around, his Colt already
drawn. But instead of Indians, it turned out to be
six young cowpokes, obviously drunk. Their faces
were sweaty, their hats askew, and they were
sliding back and forth in their saddles, finding it
difficult to even remain atop their mounts. Fortunately their guns were pointed toward the sky.

As the men galloped their horses by, Clint
watched a pair of mangy dogs take out after them.
They barked and nipped at the horses' hind legs,
causing an even bigger commotion. Women
screamed, their long, brightly colored skirts flying
up as they ran to clear the road; a baby began
crying; a team of horses pulling a buckboard suddenly bolted with the driver trying desperately to
get the runaways under control; and several
young boys skedaddled to the side of the walk,
laughing, pointing, and enjoying the spectacle.

When the cowpokes reached the last of the
stores, they yanked their lathered horses around
and headed back, still bellowing and shooting.

Two of the riders moved their horses up and
onto the boarded walk, sending men and women

darting into the various shops to escape being run down. Though it went against his grain to interfere in something that was none of his business, Clint decided to put an end to the hell-raising before someone got seriously hurt. Certainly none of the other men in town seemed inclined to do so.

Holstering his gun, Clint found shelter in front of a millinery shop and waited. When the first of the two riders was close enough, he began hollering and waving his arms in the air to spook the man's mount. Then he watched in amusement as the startled animal reared, causing the rider's head to crack against the store eaves overhead. When the horse came down, it leaped onto the street, bucking and snorting. The rider reminded Clint of a Mexican jumping bean as he bounced about on the saddle. It only took a few hard bucks before the drunken cowpoke went flying through the air. He landed so hard on the dirt of the street that it knocked him out cold. Or, Clint thought, he'd passed out from too much to drink.

The other riders brought their horses to a halt and stared bleary-eyed at the fallen man. One of them dismounted and staggered over to his companion. Again the dogs charged, but this time it was at the cowpoke's boots. The red-faced man tried kicking them, but missed.

"I don't know who you are," the drunken cowpoke said, looking directly at Clint, "but you're a dead man!" Having issued his warning, he leaned over and attempted to lift his partner to his feet. The barking dogs weren't helping matters. Finally he called to the others, "Ain't one of you gonna get down and help?"

Seeing there wasn't going to be any more trouble, Clint continued on toward the hotel. As he passed the local residents, the smiles previously offered now disappeared; backs were turned, and children snatched up. He'd seen it happen in other towns. Everyone smelled trouble in the air, and it was centered on him, the stranger in town. They definitely didn't want to get involved.

It was nearing midnight when Clint finally drifted off to sleep. Moments later he was snapped awake by the clicking of the lock. He raised the Colt from his chest and pointed it toward the door. As the door slowly, silently opened, he swung his legs over the side of the bed and turned up the lantern on the bedside table.

The heavy scent of cheap perfume filled his nostrils as a woman wearing a bright green dress stepped inside, her painted face looking garish and haggard even in the dim light. She was by no means in the spring of her youth.

"Stop right there!" Clint ordered. The fact that he didn't have a stitch on didn't bother him any more than it seemed to bother his unwelcome guest. "Drop the key."

The large key made a clunking sound as it hit the floor. "What do you want?" he asked impatiently.

Her red lips became a slit of a grin. "Name's Violet. I was sent with a message."

"And?"

"You're wanted out front."

Keeping an eye on his visitor, Clint stood and moved to the side of the window to look down. It was pitch-dark outside, but he could still make out four riders waiting in the middle of the street. One, possibly the leader, sat astride a big white horse. "Why do they want to see me?"

Without answering, the woman darted out, closing the door behind her.

"What the hell's going on?" Clint muttered to himself as he reached for his pants. "It's probably that damn cowpoke coming back for trouble." He quickly pulled on his pants and boots. Gun in hand, he cautiously opened the door, glancing to his left, then his right. Assured that no one was waiting for him in the dimly lit hallway, he moved to the stairs, then down to the vacant lobby.

Again checking to be sure it was safe, Clint stepped out onto the boarded walk, moving out of the light coming from the hotel. He wanted this over with as quickly as possible so he could return to his room and get some sleep. He lowered his gun. If they were planning on shooting, the bullets would already be flying. He tried focusing on the shadowy figure atop the white horse, but it was too dark to see more than an outline. Curious, he stepped down onto the street. "You wanted to see me?" he asked.

A loud snap split the night air. Before Clint could react, the whip snaked around his ankles, yanking his feet out from under him. His elbow hit the ground, sending his revolver flying. When the whip loosened, Clint scrambled back to his feet, fury heating his blood. Three of the men leaped from their horses and ran toward him. Clint swung at the first one. His fist connected solidly on the man's jaw, sending him to the ground. Clint heard the whip crack again. This time it went around his neck, allowing him to grab hold and pull. He easily yanked the rider from the saddle. The man released a loud grunt as he hit the ground. Clint jerked around, ready to sock the next man, when he was struck hard on the back of the head, and he collapsed like an accordion. A couple of hard kicks to the ribs followed. Dizzy, he rolled onto his back, but someone immediately slammed him onto his stomach and a hard boot was planted in the middle of his back.

"No one takes advantage of a Whitfield!"

The voice sounded like it was coming from far

away, even though Clint knew it was the person standing over him. His arms were twisted behind him, and he could feel the bite of the coarse rope as it was tied around his wrists. He tried to struggle, but his head kept swimming, sapping his strength. His legs were jerked up to meet his hands, and likewise tied. Within a matter of seconds, he resembled a calf ready for branding. His fury was all-consuming. "You damn bastard," he accused, trying at the same time to spit the dirt from his mouth. He was picked up, carried to the entrance of the alley, and dropped.

"Let this be a warning. Get out of town on the first stage!"

Clint heard the four horses ride off. In an effort to relieve his strained muscles, he rolled onto his side. Blood ran from his nose and the side of his mouth, and he could smell the dirt already caked on his face. "Whoever you are, you'll pay for this," he swore through clenched teeth.

Clint lost all track of time, but eventually the dizziness subsided. He cursed himself for not putting on a shirt before he'd left his room, because it was getting cold as hell. He could hear noise coming from the saloon across the street and down a ways. He tried yelling, but there was no response, and at this time of night, no one seemed inclined to head in his direction.

A good three hours had to have passed before Clint heard someone shuffling up behind him. His body tensed as he waited, wondering if he was finally going to be freed or if more trouble was on the way.

"What you doin' down there, boy?"

The man's words were slurred, and though Clint couldn't see him, he could smell the strong odor of cheap whiskey.

With his muscles in knots and his arms and legs feeling as if they were being pulled out of their sockets, Clint had to force himself to keep from snapping out at the man. "I'm damn sure not out here for my health," he replied in an almost civil tone of voice. "How about untying me?"

The man was silent, but Clint knew he hadn't left.

"What's in it for me?"

Clint was in no mood to bicker price. "A twenty-dollar gold piece. It'll buy you a hell of a lot of red-eye."

"You got that much money?"

"Yep, and it'll be in your hand as soon as I can get to my room." Clint wasn't about to tell the man the money was in his pocket.

"Twenty dollars! God damn!" the drunk said gleefully. "You got yourself a deal, mister." He dropped to his knees and began untying the rope.

Chapter 2

The large Whitfield ranch compound was located about six miles from town between the Medicine Bow and Sierra Madre mountains. From the seat of his rented buggy, Clint cast an appreciative eye over the majestic scenery, forgetting for a moment that after last night, he felt as if he'd been drawn and quartered. Every movement of his body, as well as of the buggy, caused his muscles and joints to scream in protest.

Snow-capped mountain peaks soared toward a clear blue sky, their rugged contours broken only by the occasional slash of sheer rock cliffs that dropped dramatically to the valley floor. The North Platte River flowed through the center of the valley, churning and plunging over boulders in some places and moving peacefully in others. Stands of cottonwood trees were scattered along its banks and on small islands midstream, adding to the beauty. The long, wide valley narrowed as Clint approached the homestead. He figured it to be only about twenty miles across at this point.

The homestead itself consisted of a large two-story house surrounded by various barns, corrals and outbuildings. Whitfield had created quite an empire, Clint thought, as he parked the buggy and approached the front door. There was plenty of water and grass for cattle, and the foothills and mountains supplied forests of Engelmann spruce, lodgepole pine and alpine fir for Whitfield's profitable lumber business. The man even had his own Union Pacific spur out of Rawlins, providing easy transportation of the lumber and stock.

An older woman of undeterminable age answered Clint's knock.

"Please inform Mrs. Whitfield that Clint Morgan is here to see her."

Clint stepped into a large foyer. He caught a glimpse of a dining room to his right before the woman motioned for him to follow her into the spacious parlor on the opposite side.

"I'll tell Mrs. Whitfield you're here," the maid said.

Clint nodded. While he waited for his aunt, he strolled about the room, surprised by an opulence he hadn't expected this far from a large city. An expensive, dark-flowered rug covered most of the floor and the rest of the room was filled with well-polished Victorian furniture. He wondered if the furnishings reflected his aunt's personality. Would she be as prudish and prim as the infamous Queen Victoria? He hoped not. He hadn't seen his aunt since he was a boy, way before she'd become the second Mrs. Whitfield. Though he'd never met any of the other Whitfields; through correspondence and occasional visits back home his mother had kept him well informed about the family. Sam had had a daughter by his first wife, then he and Mattie had a son.

Footsteps sounded in the hallway. "My dear Clint," a voice called out. "Why didn't you let me know you were coming?"

Clint turned as the small, frail woman entered the parlor. Her resemblance to his mother amazed him. She had the same heart-shaped face, warm blue eyes and light brown hair well-streaked with gray. However, at sixty-three and the older of the two sisters, few lines marred her delicate face.

"Goodness!" Mattie gasped. "What happened to you? You look as if you've been in a fight."

"A horse threw me. It's nothing to worry about." There was no reason to bother his aunt with what had happened, at least not yet.

Mattie came forward and embraced him warmly, then stepped back to peer up at him. His black waistcoat, white ruffled shirt and gray trousers were of fine material and perfectly tailored. *Cora was right*, Mattie thought excitedly. *Clint is indeed a perfect gentleman.* "Even with all those cuts and bruises, you're still a fine-looking man. So tall and strong. And to think I used to bounce you on my knee. You have your papa's black hair and gray eyes, but I must admit, if it weren't for the picture your mother sent, I wouldn't have known you."

Mattie motioned toward the tapestry-covered settee. "Come, let's sit and you can tell me all about your trip from Kansas. Cora told me in her last letter that you were finally returning to Maryland. Wasn't Wyoming Territory a bit out of your way?" she asked with just the right touch of innocence.

"My mother has no conception of distance or the direction of anything outside of Maryland and Washington." Clint eased down onto the settee, wincing as his battered body protested the action. "As of late, Mother's letters have expressed concern about your well-being. She suggested I pay you a visit."

Mattie's eyes widened. "Now, why would she be worried about me?"

"Indeed," a deep, gravelly voice boomed out. "I'd like to know the answer to that myself."

Clint turned toward the doorway. He hadn't heard the wheelchair approaching, yet there it was. The grizzled old man sitting in it eyed him from across the room. This had to be Sam Whitfield. Never having met the man, Clint couldn't even think of him in terms of being an uncle. Clint rose stiffly to his feet, taking a moment to study the white-haired old gentleman. Sam Whitfield. A man who had built an empire and lived by his own laws. Alert green eyes looked out from a deeply lined face that had been weathered by age and sun. Despite the summer heat, a wool blanket covered his crippled legs. Years ago, a loco steer had hooked Whitfield's horse in the flank. Sam had fallen, but his foot got hung up in the stirrup. The horse dragged him for almost half a mile. The accident had left him paralyzed from the waist down.

"Can't you answer my question, young man? Why would you be concerned about Mattie?"

Clint bristled at Whitfield's abrupt tone, even though he knew it wouldn't be advisable to make an enemy of the man. "Sorry. I'm not trying to be rude, but it's not often I'm in the same room with a legend." He watched Sam's chest swell with pride. "Mother hadn't heard from Mattie for some time and insisted I pay a visit."

"Samuel, You didn't give me a chance to introduce my nephew, Clint Morgan. My sister Cora's son."

Sam raised his bushy eyebrows and released a grunt. "It's my understanding you do some kind of work out of Washington."

Clint nodded. "Unfortunately my job keeps me from spending much time there." He was certain the false story he'd told his mother over the years about being a fort inspector had filtered down to Mattie.

"Where you stayin', boy?"

"At the Whitfield Hotel. I arrived yesterday."

"Yesterday?" The old man regarded him

keenly. "You wouldn't happen to know anything about an incident that took place there yesterday afternoon? My son, Lucas, was knocked out."

Clint didn't bat an eyelash. Because Whitfield owned the lumber mill and probably most of the town, it explained why the townsfolk hadn't wanted to get involved in the scuffle. "I didn't know the boy was your son."

"Accordin' to Lucas, some man charged him from behind for no reason. The boy wasn't even armed. You know anything about that?"

Hearing anger in Whitfield's voice, Clint decided to keep his story simple. "That's not exactly the way it happened. Your son and several of his cronies were drunk and rode through town shooting their guns in the air. When Lucas and another man jumped their horses onto the walk, I decided to put a stop to it before someone got hurt. Lucas's horse bucked him off and *that's* how he got knocked out."

Sam slapped a weathered hand on the wooden arm of the wheelchair. "I knew it!" He looked at Mattie. "Your son, madam, is about the most worthless thing on this ranch. He can't even be relied upon to tell the damn truth, does nothin' unless he's ordered, and runs around terrorizing the town. Then he has his friends back up his lies. As if that isn't bad enough, he can't even stay on his horse!"

"Samuel, I'm sure he has a perfectly good—"

"I don't want to hear it, madam." Sam wheeled his chair around. "Alma!" he yelled. "Where is that damn woman?"

"She'll be here in a moment," Mattie soothed.

"She's never around when you want her. Alma!"

The plump woman who had let Clint into the house came rushing in.

"What took you so long?" Sam bellowed at her.

"Have someone find Kate and Lucas and see that they're sent to my office."

Alma nodded and scurried away.

"You'll stay here, Morgan," Sam ordered. "Family shouldn't be at some damn hotel."

"Thank you, sir," Clint said with a crooked smile. "I have to pick up my things and return the buggy I rented, so I'd appreciate it if someone could meet me in town later."

"It'll be taken care of." Having said his piece, Sam wheeled his chair toward the doorway.

"I'm eager to hear news of your mother and sister," Mattie said after Sam left the room. "Let's go outside and sit under the apple tree. It's much cooler."

Taking Mattie by the elbow, Clint escorted her to the wide porch, then down the steps. Clint was still amused at how, in his anger, Sam had referred to Lucas as Mattie's son when Sam had sired the boy. Clint deduced that Kate, whom Sam had ordered sent to his office also, had to be Mattie's stepdaughter. Clint wondered if the girl was as conniving as her half brother.

"I want you to see my apple tree. I tell you, Clint, it produces the sweetest fruit a body could ever want."

As they crossed the yard, Clint saw a white stallion tethered to a post near a large windmill. Because of its size and color, Clint knew it was the same animal the man with the whip had been riding last night. "That's a fine-looking mount," he said casually, though he itched to seek out the owner. "Who does he belong to?"

"Kate."

"Oh? Who rides him?"

"Only Kate. He's a hateful horse. Tries to nip anyone else who gets near him."

Clint moved aside to avoid a pesky bee. The horse didn't have a sidesaddle on its back, and he found it hard to believe a female could even control such a powerful beast. "Are you telling me a girl can handle that stallion?" he asked doubtfully.

"She's not exactly a girl. Kate is twenty-three, soon be twenty-four. She can outride and out-shoot just about any man, and she runs this ranch. She's best, however, with a whip." Mattie didn't notice the look of shock on Clint's face. "Sam has raised Kate more like a son than a daughter," she commented sadly.

Clint found it hard to accept that Kate had been the rider on the horse last night. No wonder she had been so easy to pull from the saddle. Not that it really mattered. The corners of his lips slowly curved into a wicked grin. This wouldn't be the first time he'd had to deal with such a woman in his line of business. They were as mean as any man—often meaner.

When they reached the tall, sturdy apple tree, Mattie took her place on the glider swing and motioned for Clint to sit on one of the chairs across from her. As soon as he was settled, she said, "I want to apologize for the lie Lucas told. Such a terrible way for you to meet your cousin. But try not to be too angry with him. You know how boys are. They all lie to get out of trouble."

"It's not important," Clint replied, even though he didn't consider youth an excuse for lying. He'd known outlaws a lot younger than Lucas. "I'm sure Mother will be relieved to know you're in fine health."

"Dear, Cora. I must write her a letter this afternoon. I had no idea she was worrying so. In her last letter, she said you're retiring from your government job and returning to Baltimore to take over the family business."

"Actually, I'm taking a long leave of absence to decide just what I want to do. Joseph has managed the Morgan Shipping Company quite competently since my father died four years ago, so I'm really not needed.''

"Joseph. That's your sister's husband, isn't it?''
Clint nodded.

"Do they have any children yet?''

"No, much to Mother's sorrow.''

Mattie smiled. "I do hope you're planning on staying with us for a spell. At least until the fall.'' She waved her lace handkerchief to shoo away a fly. "Oh, here comes Kate. Now you'll be able to meet the last member of the family.''

Clint tensed as he turned to get his first real look at the woman who had arranged last night's reception. He was shocked to discover she was nothing like he'd expected. Kate Whitfield was an extraordinary beauty. There was a willowy quality about her that didn't quite fit the picture of a woman who ran a ranch, or rode that white stallion. Wisps of pale blond hair appeared from beneath the floppy-brimmed hat she wore. Was her hair short or long? he wondered. His gaze traveled to her red shirt that did little to hide her high, full breasts or a waist so small he could easily span it with his hands. Her denim britches, held up with suspenders, were a tight fit, outlining long, shapely legs. His gaze paused at the blacksnake whip coiled over her right shoulder, then moved on to meet her large green eyes. Clint felt a swift, hot tug of desire. Unwanted, definitely unwelcomed. Kate Whitfield didn't hold a trace of resemblance to the women he was normally attracted to. And, she *was* his aunt's stepdaughter, something he'd do well to remember.

"Kate, dear,'' Mattie said in her soft voice, wishing the girl were dressed differently, "how nice of you to join us. I'd like you to meet my sister Cora's son, Clint Morgan. Clint, this is—''

"So,'' Kate interrupted, "you didn't take my

advice and leave town." She was determined he wouldn't see how he affected her now that she had a good look at him. His hard ashen gray eyes didn't alter the fact that he was good-looking as all get-out. Sinfully, temptingly so. The wild flutter of her heart told her this man could be trouble—the kind of trouble she didn't have the time or inclination to deal with. Damn!

Clint was amused at the way Kate looped her thumbs over her gun belt, then brazenly scanned him from head to foot.

"I'm surprised you didn't tuck your tail feathers between your legs and cluck your way out of here after last night."

Clint wasn't about to let her rile him. Her voice was low, with a pleasing, husky quality to it. That explained why he hadn't realized last night that it was a female who had bamboozled him. Of course in the condition he'd been in, he doubted he would've recognized any voice. But he was a man who always appreciated a woman's . . . qualities, whether she was good or bad. And this woman certainly had some fine qualities.

Mattie looked from one to the other. "What are you talking about, Kate?" she demanded. "Clint is our guest. You owe him an apology!"

"I'm not about to apologize for what happened. Lucas told me he was unarmed, and that this man had taken unfair advantage of him. I did what I thought was right."

Mattie's mouth dropped open. "Are those cuts and bruises on his face your doing?"

"It's nothing to worry about, Mattie," Clint answered smoothly. "Kate learned last night that it's not always wise to continue holding on to a whip. You should have seen her go flying out of the saddle. In fact, she let forth a healthy grunt when she hit the ground. She probably has a few bruises of her own."

Kate's face turned scarlet.

"Why I'd even wager that when her men returned to the bunkhouse they had a big laugh over it."

"Sam's made me your watchdog, Morgan," Kate hissed through clenched teeth, "and he said I'm to make sure you don't get your tail into any more trouble. He said nothing about us having to be on friendly terms." Her green eyes flashed with anger, but she said evenly enough, "If you need or want anything, let me know. I'll ride to town with you, just in case some of the men haven't gotten the message to leave you alone. We've been having problems with rustlers. Besides, I need to pick up some plaster of paris at the feed store. How long are you planning on staying?"

"I haven't decided."

"Well, I hope it won't be long. I'm not pleased about having to watch over you like some sick heifer. I'll be at the house when you're ready to go."

Like father like daughter, Clint thought. He watched her walk away, wondering if she even realized how seductive, how totally feminine, that sexy little fanny looked tucked into those tight jeans.

"I can't believe what I've just heard!" Mattie said worriedly.

Reluctantly, Clint turned his full attention back to his aunt. "It's nothing I can't take care of." He reclaimed his seat.

"When I visited Cora in Maryland a couple of years ago, she indicated you travel a lot. Would it be all right if I informed the others about your work at the forts?"

"Most assuredly."

"I wasn't sure. Cora acted as if it was all very secretive."

"My mother has a vivid imagination."

For a good thirty minutes, Mattie talked with Clint about his family back east. When she thought her nephew was well relaxed, she decided to broach the subject dearest to her heart. "Clint, I was wondering if I could prevail on you to do your dear aunt a favor."

Dear aunt? Clint wondered. He was a boy the last time they'd seen each other, and as far as he was concerned, she was as much a stranger as the rest of her family.

Mattie took a deep breath. "This is such a difficult request. I don't know of any way to present it other than to just come right out and say it."

Clint cocked a black eyebrow. "Please do."

"During your stay, I was wondering if you could teach Kate the joys of being a woman."

Clint stared at her in disbelief. Was she actually asking him to give Kate a toss in bed? No, he thought, his aunt certainly didn't take after Queen Victoria.

"Being the gentleman you are, perhaps you could talk her into dressing properly, fixing her hair in a more becoming fashion, and that sort of thing."

Clint was glad she'd followed with an explanation. Nevertheless, he was a man with a healthy appetite, and he knew exactly what something like that would lead to. He'd do better to wash his hands of the matter.

"She certainly hasn't listened to me over the years," Mattie continued. "Her only concession to all my badgering is to wear a dress to supper. Perhaps it would work even better if you courted her."

Clint was so taken aback by the absurdity of the request, he started coughing.

"Let me explain before you say anything." She fidgeted with her lace handkerchief. "Sam has always felt his children should be as tough as he is.

Lucas has done every dirty job there is to do on the ranch, and Sam treats him just like any other cowhand, although Sam would tell you differently.

"When Grace, Sam's first wife, died of cholera, she left him with a baby girl. From the beginning, Sam raised Kate as the son he thought he'd never have. By the time Kate was two, Sam was already teaching her how to use a whip. By the time she was four, Sam and I were married. We had a happy home, and Kate was pleased to finally have a mother. Then Lucas came into the world." Mattie bowed her head, remembering how difficult the labor had been at such a late time in her life. She was convinced that was why she'd never been able to have another child.

Shaking off her momentary sadness, she continued. "As the children grew, Kate could take what Sam dished out, Lucas couldn't. Horses frightened him, the whip kept nipping at him instead of the target, and he hated the sound of guns. Sam tried to get the boy to learn, but Lucas would just stand in one spot and scream until Sam walked away, or he would run behind my skirts and hide. Sam would get so angry, I knew he wanted to thrash the boy. He just couldn't accept that Lucas wasn't like him. The boy was just very sensitive. But Sam became obsessed about the boy needing to overcome what Sam called cowardly fears. Then, when Lucas was about eight years old, Sam did a terrible thing. He told Lucas that if he ever expected to inherit a thing, he had to learn every job on the ranch, everything from tanning to horseshoeing.

"Well, Lucas isn't afraid of horses or cattle anymore. He rides well and can shoot a gun accurately. Although, to tell you the truth, he never has mastered the whip.

"So, the children have grown up to be what

they are today. Kate's the strong one, running the ranch and being her father's eyes and legs. And Lucas? He refuses to take on any responsibilities just to spite Sam. It's the boy's lack of interest in the ranch that angers Sam the most, and Lucas knows it. But Lucas just turned nineteen and still has a lot to learn about life. I'm sure you'll see what I'm talking about now that you'll be staying with us. Don't get me wrong. Lucas is a good boy. I know when he grows older he'll run the ranch and do a fine job of it.

"Kate is an entirely different matter." Mattie shifted to a more comfortable position. "I love Kate as if I'd given birth to her, and I know she loves me. But it's very difficult for Kate to show it. I'm worried that she'll end up a lonely spinster. She should be married and settled down with a family. That's why I want you to take her under your wing and remind her that she's a woman. Maybe then she'll find herself a man. So you can see why this is so important to me. Your mother has told me so many wonderful things about you. For instance, I know you're strong-willed, but at the same time considerate and gentle."

Clint almost broke out laughing at that comment.

"And that's exactly what Kate needs. When I saw you standing in the parlor, I just knew if anyone could properly handle such a delicate situation, it would be you." Mattie smiled gently. "After all, you are family. It won't be easy. Billy Jim, a former ranch hand, tried courting Kate. He ended up with a bloody nose just because he tried to kiss her. Like her father, Kate thinks love is a sign of weakness. She has been brought up with the understanding that the ranch comes first, Whitfields second, and all else a lowly third."

Clint glared at the woman. He'd thought his

mother was the most naive woman he knew, but
Mattie was certainly right up there beside her. She
apparently couldn't even see the possible ramifications of what she was asking. She would certainly be singing a different tune and would take
off like a scared doe if she had any inkling how
many men he'd killed, or what it took to track
down outlaws from one end of the country to the
other. He combed his fingers through his black
hair, suddenly suspicious of the whole scheme.
"Mattie, you've obviously given this a lot of
thought. Did you and my mother work out a plan
to get me here?"

"Of course not."

"You realize I may only be staying a short
time."

"Perhaps it will be long enough for Kate to
learn."

Clint rose to his feet. "I'll think about it. Now
if you'll excuse me, I still have to return the buggy
to town and pick up my things."

"I'll walk with you." Mattie stood and daintily
smoothed out her gingham skirt. She was absolutely positive that her and Cora's planned alli-
ance between Kate and Clint was going to work
out perfectly. Clint was such a fine gentleman.

Thirty minutes later, Clint was driving the
buggy back toward town. Kate followed with the
buckboard, a sandy-haired cowpoke by the name
of Paul riding on the seat beside her. Clint had
rented the buggy to alleviate his sore body, but
as the wheels continued to bounce over clumps
of the dark green grass, he regretted his decision.
At the slow pace they were traveling, it would
take a couple hours before they arrived at the hotel. Of course, the hard-mouthed buzzard bait of
a horse pulling the vehicle didn't help matters.

Upon arriving at the Whitfield Hotel, Paul took

the buggy back to the livery stable while Kate went to purchase supplies.

When Clint entered his room, he found it in shambles, his belongings strewn everywhere. Even his mother's letters had been rifled through and probably read. He felt sure Kate had to be .the culprit. She had to have ridden into town while he was at the livery getting the buggy, or he would have seen that white horse of hers. He was suddenly curious about whether she'd again brought some of her men along to make sure he'd followed her order to get out of town. Six miles wasn't far on horseback, so she could have arrived back at the ranch before him or while he was talking to Sam and Mattie.

Clint reached under the rug and pulled out the envelope from Washington. That was one thing Kate hadn't found.

Within thirty minutes, Clint had his belongings packed, and paid for the room. A short time later, Kate and Paul returned. Paul put Clint's trunks in the back of the farm wagon and climbed in beside them. The moment Clint sat down on the front seat, Kate flicked the reins and headed the team of horses toward home.

After traveling a couple of miles with no words being exchanged, Clint decided to break the silence. "Mattie was telling me you run the ranch. That's quite an undertaking for a woman. How long—"

"You can stop right there, Morgan. I don't take to small talk.. Why not say what's really on your mind? You gotta be plenty angry about what happened last night. I'd at least have a little respect for you if you just said you're mad as hell and determined to get back at me. Not that I give a damn. You may be considered family, but as far as I'm concerned, you're not blood."

Clint pulled a cigar from his vest pocket and lit it. "You know," he said between puffs, "now that you've brought up the subject, I do have a question." He took a long drag on the cigar, then let the smoke trail back out. "Just what the hell is your problem? You don't know me, or anything about me, yet you act as if I'm your worst enemy. And for the record, I don't like the idea of having a watchdog any more than I like being one."

Kate skillfully guided the team around a pine tree, more aware of the man beside her than she cared to admit. Maybe it hadn't been such a good idea to bring up last night. A weaker man would have been easier to ignore.

"What? No comment?" Clint studied the cigar resting between his thumb and fingers. "If it'll make you feel better, I have every intention of paying you back for what you did. But the difference between you and me is that I don't jump to conclusions. So if I were you, I'd watch my backside."

Kate flashed her green eyes at him. "If you think some city dude is going to scare me, you've got another think coming. I could pop my whip around you faster than you could blink an eye."

Clint had always admired a woman with fire in her eyes. Kate's were an inferno. "We'll just have to see about that, won't we?" He grinned, resting his back against the seat and crossing his arms over his chest. "I never found my Colt forty-five last night. Did you take it?"

Kate saw his cocky grin. Anger twisted her gut, along with something else she didn't want to dwell on. "Yep."

"Do you plan to return it?"

"Nope."

"Why?"

"It didn't do you any good last night and you

have no need for it now. Besides, you probably don't even know which end goes in the holster. I wouldn't want you to end up shooting yourself. Mattie wouldn't like that at all.''

Clint's grin widened. ''There you go, jumping to conclusions again.'' He dropped the cigar on the footrest and smashed it out with the toe of his boot. ''Tell me, why did you buy plaster of paris?''

''Rats, Mr. Morgan. You put equal amounts of plaster and flour in one bowl and place a second bowl of water beside it. When the rat eats his fill, he drinks. The plaster becomes as hard as stone in his stomach, and he dies. Of course, if we have to, we use arsenic.'' She turned and looked at him straight on. A mistake she regretted immediately. The man had the eyes of a hunter. ''That's for special rats.''

Clint arched his brows. ''Are you calling me a rat, Miss Whitfield?''

Kate didn't like the way the man seemed to intimidate her. ''Does it apply?'' she snapped at him.

''Someone rifled through my things in the hotel. Was it you?''

''Yep. Since you hadn't taken my advice to leave town, I decided to find out just who you were. Like I told you, we've been having a lot of problems with rustlers. I wanted to know if you were one of them.''

Kate spent the rest of the trip in tight-lipped silence, while Clint contemplated the pleasure it would give him to wring her slender neck.

It had turned dark outside when Alma knocked on Clint's bedroom door. ''Supper will be ready soon,'' she called from the other side.

''I'll be right down,'' he replied.

When Clint entered the parlor, the room was

ablaze with light, and Mattie and Lucas had already arrived.

"Clint," Mattie said as she took his arm, "I would like to properly introduce you to my son, Lucas. Lucas, say hello to your cousin, Clint Morgan."

The younger man gave a nod of acknowledgment, but didn't rise from his chair. Clint could see the haggard look on Lucas's face from yesterday's binge. Still, he was good-looking enough with his blond hair and blue eyes to turn any woman's head.

The last to enter the parlor was Sam, with Kate pushing his wheelchair. Clint's gaze remained on Kate. She looked stiff and uncomfortable in her simple, well-starched cotton dress that had long since gone out of fashion. Her thick blond hair had been pulled straight back into a chignon, which reminded Clint of an old maid. But he had to admit that the old maids he'd met hadn't had Kate's high cheekbones, perky nose, full lips, and flawless complexion turned golden by the sun.

Clint smiled inwardly. From the way Kate handled herself, he doubted she'd ever shared a man's bed. Too bad he wasn't in a position to take care of that little problem for her.

Clint was surprised when Alma walked in and announced supper was ready. He'd hoped a drink of whiskey, or something of a similar nature would be served prior to eating. Apparently Mattie didn't approve of spirits in her parlor.

As with the rest of the house, the dining room was ornate. An uncountable number of candles had been lit on the circular chandelier hanging over the table, causing the many crystals to sparkle. A built-in pine buffet and china cabinet were at the far end of the room, and a door to the butler's pantry stood open on one side. A beautifully carved table and chairs occupied the center of the room.

After placing Sam's wheelchair at the head of the table, Kate headed for her place. Clint followed and pulled the chair out for her. Though she regarded him suspiciously, she said nothing.

"Well, would you just look there," Lucas taunted. "Maybe dear sister has finally found a feller who's willing to pay her some attention."

"Lucas! Mind your manners!" Sam bit out in his raspy voice. "Now everyone bow their heads." Sam began grace. "Bless this food, Lord . . ."

To Clint, Sam's abrupt manner made the short prayer sound more like a command than a request.

Sam had informed Kate earlier about what Morgan did for a living, and she was feeling a bit red-faced. Although she wasn't sure what-all checking forts entailed, she had a strong suspicion that she'd jumped to the wrong conclusions. Accusing him of not knowing how to ride a horse or shoot a gun had been a bit farfetched. Common sense should have told her differently. After all, Cotton *had* ended up with a broken jaw last night when he'd connected with Morgan's fist. Now that she thought about it, there was also a ruggedness about him, an impression that he was a man who knew exactly what he was doing. It was his hard gray eyes that bothered her the most.

"Sam," Clint said as the bowls of food were being passed around the table, "Mattie has made me an offer."

"What kind of offer?" Sam grumbled.

"She asked me to stay on at the ranch for a while. Naturally, it depends on whether or not you're agreeable. It would be a nice rest before I have to head on to Maryland. Besides the pleasure of spending time with Mattie, I'd like to learn more about your ranch.''

Mattie's eyes became large pools of joy. If Clint was going to remain at the ranch, perhaps he would grant her wish to court Kate. ''Surely you can remain until October?'' Mattie asked. ''I realize you probably wouldn't want to be here when winter arrives.''

Clint looked at Sam, waiting for an answer.

''Stay as long as you like,'' Sam replied between bites of meat. ''Just don't get underfoot.''

Mattie quietly placed her fork on her plate and lifted her delicate chin. ''Since Clint will be staying here, Samuel, I believe he's due an apology from this family. You haven't been exactly hospitable, and Kate has gone entirely too far with the things she's said and done. Is this the way we treat our guests?''

Sam leaned back in his wheelchair. ''Now calm down, madam. Your nephew wasn't hurt. With Lucas's lies''—he peered at his son—''and not knowing who Clint was, Kate had every right to stand up for the family. Besides, with all that's been happening, we can't be too careful of strangers.''

Lucas concentrated on his food.

''She knows better now,'' Mattie persisted in her soft voice.

Sam grunted, but continued eating.

Clint wanted to hear more about the rustlers. ''Kate told me that someone has been stealing your cattle.''

''Nothing for you to worry about.'' Kate's smile didn't reach her eyes.

During the rest of the meal, Kate and Sam monopolized the conversation with talk about cattle and cowhands.

Clint's mind was still on the rustlers. It was impossible to keep a constant eye on a ranch of over a quarter of a million acres, and the Whitfields might be missing even more cattle than they realized. A man could spend days covering their land and never meet a soul.

Clint listened carefully as Sam and Kate discussed cattle business, storing in memory names he thought would be useful, such as the name of the foreman, and those of various others who worked on the ranch.

As soon as supper was finished, Clint excused himself and went to his room. His muscles and side still ached, and he was in need of a good night's sleep. Knowing the family wouldn't have been so talkative about the ranch if they were aware of his real occupation caused a grin. But that was something he could ill afford for them to find out. Even his mother wasn't privy to that information.

Chapter 3

C lint rose early the next morning, feeling considerably better. After securing the door, he
dressed in well-worn jeans, a blue shirt with the
cuffs rolled up, and boots. To wear finer clothes
was ridiculous, now that he'd be remaining at the
ranch. Satisfied no one would barge in, he sank
onto the large wingback chair by the cold fireplace
and proceeded to skim through the information
Sandoval, his contact in Washington, had sent
him in Topeka. He'd always made a habit of
keeping such information hidden just in case
someone like Kate found a need to search his belongings.

He'd already read the report several times during his train ride to Rawlins. He skipped the part
that told about Samuel Whitfield, his family, the
ranch location, and how long Whitfield had
owned the land. Next came a dossier on Gordon
Vale, the government cattle buyer, a man with a
flawless record. Placing the papers on his lap,
Clint wondered why he was even bothering to go
through them again.

No matter how many words and pages it took,
Clint could hone the problem down to a few para-
graphs. Sam Whitfield had a contract with the
government to sell steers to Gordon Vale for Indian reservations. After paying for the cattle, Vale

always watched the steers being loaded onto railroad cars. But the last two shipments of fat beef Vale had purchased from Whitfield and had seen loaded weren't the same cattle that were delivered to the Indian agent. The cattle that arrived were scrawny, a good many of them already dead. To make matters worse, it had recently been discovered that the Indian agent was selling some of the surviving cattle to local farmers, leaving the Indians with practically nothing. The Indians were slowly starving, and an uprising seemed imminent.

If Clint took the assignment, he was to check out the possibility that the railroad cars were being switched somewhere along the way, and discover if someone at the ranch was involved. Samuel Whitfield himself was under suspicion. He might very well have decided to double his money by not only collecting from the government but then turning around and reselling the good steers to another buyer. It was suggested that Clint remain at the ranch until the next purchase of beef, scheduled for the end of September. Then, if he was unable to find any leads or guilty parties on the ranch, he was to follow the railroad cars. But whatever it took, he was to put a stop to the cattle switching as soon as possible. He let out a grunt as he read the note on top of the papers.

Clint,
I know you said you're hanging up your gun but we could really use you on this one.

Thomas

Clint leaned his head against the back of the chair, closed his eyes, and weighed the pros and cons. For him, the glory of such work had long since faded into hard reality. Even so, flirting with death and relying on his own resources had become an addiction. At thirty, he knew he'd become too cold, too good, and too confident. It was those three things that had helped him make up his mind to retire while he was still alive, while there was still a chance for him to lead a normal life. He had only two options: return home to Maryland, or continue on with what he was doing and possibly die—a fate that wasn't uncommon for men in his profession. He'd already pushed his luck for too many years. It was that same blind luck that had kept him alive when he was a spy for the North during the War Between the States.

Thomas Sandoval had done everything in his power to convince Clint not to retire. This assignment was just another effort. What Sandoval didn't know was that while he was asking Clint to find out what was going on with the Whitfield cattle, Clint's mother's letters were begging him to visit her sister at the Whitfield ranch. If Clint didn't know better, he'd think the two were in cahoots. But Sandoval would have no way of knowing he was related to the Whitfields.

Clint's brow creased into a frown. Actually, he couldn't care less about the Whitfields. He didn't much like Sam, Lucas or Kate. If he was going to return home as planned, it was his mother he'd have problems with. If he left the ranch now, after such a short visit, she would be disappointed, but not to any degree he couldn't easily handle. If, however, Sam, Kate, Lucas or all three were involved in the cattle exchange, he would have to put them in jail . . . a situation his mother would never forgive him for. Cora Morgan had always led a sheltered life and would never believe any part of her family could be guilty of wrongdoing. And that included anyone who married into the family. If he ended up sticking one or more of the Whitfields in jail, he had no doubt that Cora would find out about it. On the other hand, the problem with the cattle had to be solved, and as a relative he was in the perfect position to handle the matter.

Finally, it was the Whitfields' cold reception that pushed Clint into deciding to take the assignment. And of course he still had a score to settle with the beautiful Miss Kate. Yes, he would remain at the ranch until Vale arrived. The old excitement at the possibility of danger surged through him like a hot bullet. No matter how much he'd tried telling himself for the last ten months that returning to Maryland was the right thing to do, he really wasn't ready to settle down to a quiet life.

He struck a match and held it to the papers. When the flame grew, he tossed them into the fireplace and watched them turn to ash. If it turned out that Kate was involved in the switching of cattle, he might decide to bed her no matter what the consequences. Women said a lot of things while experiencing irrepressible passion. Actually, he was hoping she really was guilty of cheating the government. He'd quite enjoy taking the snippy woman to jail. If not, he'd just leave. He didn't feel even the slightest twinge of guilt at knowing he would be using her. A gun wasn't the only way of getting even.

Clint thought about Mattie's asking him to woo Kate. An admittedly ridiculous request. However, if she thought there was a possibility of him courting her stepdaughter, Mattie would probably find every excuse possible for him to remain at the ranch and thereby remove any suspicion as to his real purpose for being there. Surely he had enough intestinal fortitude to keep his hands off Kate and thereby prevent further complications.

He'd have to send Sandoval a wire saying he'd take the assignment.

A good bright sunny day to be out and about, he thought as he shoved his hat on. While in town, he'd also purchase a gun to replace the one Miss Whitfield had taken.

As Clint walked about in search of a horse to ride to town, he discovered the ranch was quite self-sustaining. There was a large garden, a tannery for making saddles and other needed equipment, a blacksmith shed, four large barns, and a variety of corrals scattered about. He had just passed the smokehouse when he spotted Lucas standing by an empty corral, talking to three dirty, scruffy men who looked as if they'd be at home on a wanted poster. One looked to be about Lucas's age, but the other two must have been in their thirties. Clint headed in their direction. He'd covered half the distance before Lucas saw him.

"Well now," Lucas said, loud enough for Clint to hear, "look who we have here. Little cousin all dressed up to look like a cowhand." He looked at his friends. "Don't you boys think he should keep an eye on where he's stepping? I'd sure hate to see him get those shiny boots all messed up in a pile of horseshit."

The others laughed.

Clint found Lucas's comment about "little cousin" comical, especially since Lucas was at least a head shorter, but he made no comment. If there was one thing he'd learned over the years, it was to lay back, at least until he got to know the people he was dealing with.

"You may of caused me a bit of embarrassment the other day," Lucas drawled as Clint joined them, "but from the bruises on your face, I'd say you're the one who came out on the wrong end."

Clint smiled. "Your sister plays rough."

"She might play rough with you, but I can handle her."

Clint doubted that.

"After you took off last night, Sam said we're to treat you real nice. So, what can I do for you?"

"I have to go to town and I need a horse."

Lucas rubbed his chin. "Tell you what. To show you I got no hard feelings, I'll personally get you a horse. Even saddle him. Now you just wait right here."

Broad grins stretched across the other men's faces. The one with long brown hair and a face that looked more like it belonged on a skeleton than a living person spit tobacco juice on Clint's boot, then dropped his hand to his side, inches from his gun. His sunken, black, beady eyes gleamed with challenge.

Clint would have liked nothing more than to take him up on his dare, but thanks to Kate he wasn't armed. He was giving some serious consideration to picking the son of a bitch up and throwing him over the fence when the man suddenly relaxed his stance. A moment later Clint heard the chinging of Lucas's spurs as he returned, leading a horse.

"This one here'll give you a good ride," Lucas assured Clint as he brought a black horse to a halt. "Nice and gentle with an easy gait. In fact, since you got no horse of your own, I'll give him to you." He handed over the reins.

The stallion was a beautiful piece of horseflesh with good space between the eyes, clean withers and a deep chest. Ordinarily, Clint would have been eager to climb in the saddle, but Lucas's cocksure attitude and the knowing smirks of his companions only served to confirm what he already suspected. He was being set up. The animal had its ears laid back and pulled on the reins. Clint knew the minute he mounted he'd have a

bucking bronco beneath him. Obviously Lucas
had only given him the horse because the boy
was convinced he wouldn't want the black once
he'd been bucked off.

With his muscles still sore from Kate's reception, Clint wasn't anxious to mount the big horse.
Still, the time had come to show his cocky cousin
that he wasn't a bumbling greenhorn. Pulling his
hat down firmly on his head, he was about to
slide a boot into the stirrup when he heard the
crack of a whip and the reins were snatched from
his hand. The horse snorted and reared, but a
Mexican with a rather impressive mustache
grabbed the reins and quickly brought the animal
under control.

"What the hell is going on here?" Kate demanded as she rolled the whip back up.

"You almost hit me in the face with that goddamn thing!" Lucas yelled.

"You're lucky I didn't. Sam told you to make
Morgan welcome. He's going to be mad as hell
when he finds out you saddled Midnight for Morgan to ride. How do you think he'd react if he
had broken his neck!"

Lucas paled.

"Now get rid of your town trash and head out
to where you belong. You're not going to stay on
this ranch if you can't help work it."

Clint saw apprehension on the other men's
faces as they silently untied their horses,
mounted, and rode off.

"It ain't right for a damn woman to say things
like that in front of Brody and the others! You
seem to forget I'm not your little brother anymore." Lucas swung up onto the big buckskin.
"Just remember, Kate, one day you'll get the
wrong end of that whip." He gave his horse a
vicious kick in the ribs.

Kate watched grimly as Lucas rode off, then

turned to Clint, her face set in stone. "Why was he giving you a horse in the first place?"

"I wanted to ride to town, so Lucas brought me the black. As a matter of fact, he gave him to me." Clint had never liked explaining his actions. It galled him to find himself doing so to a female who probably thought she could even piss like a man.

"Well I'm taking him back. Pedro," Kate called to the Mexican, "unsaddle Midnight and release him in that far corral, well away from the mares. When you're finished, hitch up a buggy for Morgan."

"I've had my fill of buggies," Clint stated bluntly. "Is it that difficult to get me a decent horse?"

Kate gave him a withering look. "How well can you ride?"

"Whatever you give me, I'll ride. I don't like a horse that you have to beat to death to get him to move, but on the other hand, I don't like one that spends his time trying to throw me."

"Very well. Saddle Storm for him, Pedro. We want to be sure Mr. Morgan's stay is to his liking." Kate rested a hand on the butt of her gun. "I'll say this just one more time. If you want anything, ask me. And if I'm not around, you can sure as hell ask someone where I am. Didn't you have enough sense to realize Lucas is still cock-fighting mad over what you pulled?"

Clint's eyes narrowed. Did he really look that stupid? Kate's preventing him from mounting the black meant he'd have more time for his ribs and muscles to heal, and he was intrigued with having a woman do his fighting for him, but he couldn't let her challenge go unanswered.

"You're right, of course. Any fool would have known what Lucas was up to." It was as close as

he could come to letting Kate know he wasn't as
dumb as she might think.

"Yes . . . well, maybe you'll know better next
time." *He's far too glib*, Kate thought. "Here comes
Pedro with your horse. I've got other things to
do, so he'll ride to town with you."

"That won't be necessary," Clint assured her.
Just as he took the reins of a fine-looking Appaloosa gelding from Pedro, Clint saw Kate nod to
the Mexican. It looked as if Pedro would be traveling to town on Kate's order anyway. To what
extent would sweet Kate go to make sure her
father's word was carried out?

"You don't have to go all that way just because
of me, Pedro," Clint said amicably. "Then again,
if you really want to come along, I'd welcome the
company."

"I'm sure Pedro wants to go," Kate answered.
"He has a señorita in town."

The younger man nodded. "Jest give me time
to get my horse."

Clint swung up onto the saddle. As soon as
Pedro returned atop his cow pony, the two men
rode off, leaving Kate watching after them.

As they headed north, Clint turned to Pedro.
"I thought you might like to know I recognized
you as being Lucas's *compañero* in town the other
day."

Pedro gave Clint a sideways glance and spread
his hands in the air, expressing his lack of understanding as to what was being said.

Clint didn't believe him. "I take it Kate knows
nothing about your part in the antics?"

"*Señor, no le entiendo.*"

"Well let me make it a little clearer," Clint said
in flawless Spanish. "I have no intention of telling your boss, but I'm going to give you a word
of advice. If you want to keep your job, don't do

it again. The family might excuse what Lucas does, but you'd be wise to remember you're not a Whitfield."

Pedro smiled broadly. "That's the same conclusion I came to," he replied in perfect English.

Clint laughed.

When they arrived in town, Clint headed straight for the telegraph office.

"You gonna be long?" Pedro asked as he dismounted.

"Maybe an hour."

Pedro nodded and took off across the street toward the Hoof and Horn Saloon.

Just in case a copy of the wire he intended to send should end up in Kate's or Sam's hands, Clint selected his words carefully. Sandoval would know of his acceptance the moment he received it.

> Please be so kind as to inform my mother that my arrival has been delayed. I'm remaining in Whitfield for an undetermined length of time.
>
> Clint

He paid the telegraph agent, then headed for the gunsmith shop.

Kate guided White Cloud up the sloping side of the mesa. When they reached the top, she brought the stallion to a halt. Sounds of sharp whistles and "Yaws" drifted up from the rocky ravine below as the cowhands continued to push two hundred head of cattle toward Cripple Ridge. The herd moved slowly up the dry creek bed, raising dust and trampling down the occasional low green shrubs.

Kate couldn't see the ridge from her position. She didn't have to. The six well-armed men al-

ready hidden around the edge were part of the
trap she'd devised to catch the rustlers. If this
herd didn't attract them, she had no idea what
she'd do next. In a few months, practically every
cowhand on the ranch would be busy rounding
up four-year-old steers. By the time the job was
completed, over two thousand would be ready to
move to the railroad spur, then on to market. If
the thieves continued their ravaging at their present pace, the loss could be devastating and she'd
be hard put to meet that commitment next year.

Kate swung her leg around the saddle horn and
pushed her hat back. Sam had been right. At the
first melting snow, the rustlers had returned. She
had no idea how many cattle had been stolen so
far. She did know that because of the rustlers
there were seven good men buried in the ceme-
tery a half mile from the homestead—men who'd
died trying to stop the thieving.

As she'd done on previous occasions, Kate
wondered how the rustlers knew where and
when to strike. They even had a knack for covering their trail. It was mighty suspicious that they
only struck at places where just one or two men
were staying at the line shacks, and always shortly
after the men had relieved others, so there was
little chance of them being caught. They seemed
to know the ranch routine as well as she did.
She'd considered the possibility that some of her
men might be involved, but quickly dismissed the
idea. Most of them had been there for years, and
the new men had been hired after the rustling
had started.

Kate looked back down at the valley floor. The
hands had already moved the cattle out of her
view, past the base of the mesa she was on. But
she did see Lucas, trailing well behind the others.
He wasn't hard to pick out under any condition.

He never wore a hat and his blond hair shone in the sunlight.

His head bobbed, and Kate knew he was sleeping in the saddle. She was reminded of when Lucas was a baby and how on special nights she'd been allowed to hold him until he fell asleep. Unfortunately, as they grew older they always seemed to be at cross-purposes. Being the apple of her father's eye and too young to know better, she had taunted and teased Lucas unmercifully as they were growing up. Of course Sam should have stopped it. Instead he encouraged her. Now Kate wished she could undo the hurt and embarrassment she had caused her brother. Over the years, she'd tried to make up for it by giving him various responsibilities. He walked away from almost everything, causing more work for the cowhands. But she had a ranch to run, and could no longer afford to pamper him. Lucas's resentment ran deep. Maybe, in time, things would change.

She swung her leg down and stuck the toe of her boot in the stirrup. On top of everything, now she had Clint Morgan to contend with. Since he was Mattie's nephew, she guessed she'd have to be nice to him, but it wasn't going to be easy. She doubted she'd ever forgive him for making a fool of her in front of Mattie, and especially in front of her men. Before they'd even returned to the ranch, the men had already begun teasing her about letting a greenhorn pull her out of the saddle. Kate released a disgruntled sigh. Maybe she was letting this affect her too much, but dammit, she had worked hard over the years to get the men's respect and prove she was capable of being boss. It had been especially hard to get the old-timers to come to her when something went wrong instead of always going to Sam. Of course, there was another way of looking at it. Cotton, the man Morgan had socked, had fared even worse. Clint Morgan had proven to be more capable of taking care of himself than any of them had anticipated.

She watched Lucas and his horse disappear from view.

Why was Sam having her watch after Morgan? She resented it mightily, even if he was Mattie's nephew. She thought about Clint's gray eyes. There was a hardness about them, reminding her of some kind of a predator, maybe a snake, coiled and waiting to strike. Could Morgan be connected with the rustlers? she suddenly wondered as she gathered the reins in her gloved hand. Or did that thought come from thinking about his eyes or her strange need to prove she wasn't someone he could intimidate? Still, it did seem strange that he'd shown up all of a sudden. Just a little too coincidental as far as she was concerned, even after going through his things and reading his letters. She had to admit she was at the point of suspecting everyone, but who was to say this man hadn't pumped lead into the real Clint Morgan? Or, no matter who he was, how did anyone know he was honest? He could even be looking to see where he wanted his men to strike next. Kate decided that if he was up to anything, she'd find out. She had every intention of keeping someone by his side like flypaper. At least until she made her mind up one way or the other. Mattie seemed to accept him on blind faith, but Mattie was the type of person who believed everyone was good. Kate could only hope Mattie didn't get hurt if the truth about Morgan turned out to be bad.

Kate's attention was suddenly drawn to the overhanging cliff down the ravine. She scanned the area. There was a quick, blinding flash from the sun reflecting off something. A rifle barrel?

Kate hoped whoever it was didn't ride off until she could get there.

Kate yanked her hat down, nudging White Cloud over the steep side of the mesa. His hooves pounded the earth as he plunged downwards, jarring Kate and dislodging rocks and dirt. When they reached the bottom, Kate turned him in a westwardly direction as if she was riding away. If someone was watching the herd, she wanted to surprise him from behind.

Ten minutes later, Kate was on foot, revolver drawn. As she cautiously approached the stand of trees, she watched for any movement ahead. Suddenly she heard a horse galloping away. Damn, she'd missed him, and the trees had hid his identity. After checking to make sure there weren't any others hiding, Kate holstered her gun. She smiled when she saw fresh boot prints embedded in soft earth. Maybe the rustlers were finally going to take her bait. Still, it was a shame she hadn't caught the man. She would have made sure he told her who his partners were.

Kate headed back to where she'd left White Cloud. There was nothing to do now but return home and wait to see if her trap was going to work.

When Kate arrived back at the homestead, she saw the Appaloosa tied to the hitching post by the back door. She found Pedro with some other cowhands standing by a corral of cow ponies that had just been brought in from the range.

"Smoky," Kate called to a ranch hand. "Check his right front hoof." She turned White Cloud over to him. "He's limping, so he probably picked up a stone."

"Sure thing, boss."

Kate walked away and Pedro followed. As soon as they were out of hearing distance of the others,

Kate stopped and looked at the dark-skinned man. "Well?"

Pedro pulled a paper from inside his shirt and handed it to her. "He sent a telegram, bought a revolver and rifle, shopped for clothes, then was ready to come back."

"I wonder what he plans on doing with all that artillery?" Kate read the copy of the telegram, then stuffed it in her back pocket. "You did a good job, Pedro. What do you think of Morgan?"

"I don't know. He seems agreeable enough. He sure is a big man." Pedro frowned. "I did find out one thing. He speaks Spanish."

"Oh? The man is full of surprises. How did you find that out?"

"I did as you instructed. I pretended I didn't understand him, but he started talking to me in perfect Spanish. Made that pretending kind of useless."

Kate looked toward the Appaloosa swishing flies with his tail. "Unless I'm with Morgan, or until I tell you differently, I want you to follow him."

"Follow him? Hell, Miss Kate, I'm just a cow-hand, not some Pinkerton man."

"Wipe that disgusted look off your face, Pedro. I want him to know you're following him." Kate kicked a clot of dirt with the toe of her boot. "Besides, it won't be for long."

"Whatever you say, boss, but I don't like it."

"I take it Morgan is in the house."

Pedro grinned. "Yep. He's talking to Sam about you showing him some of the ranch this afternoon. That's something else he told me in Spanish."

"Well, Sam better have told him no!"

"If you do have to go, am I supposed to come along?"

"No, there's no need. Find Henry Blankenship

and see if he has anything for you to do. But tomorrow I want you watching Morgan if I'm not around. I'm going to the office right now to put an end to any more of Morgan's bright ideas."

Having already received Sam's agreement to have Kate show him some of the ranch, Clint sat relaxing in an old cowhide chair, gazing around at the musty-smelling office. The small room was crammed with ledgers and dusty Indian artifacts. A gun belt was looped over a set of longhorns hanging on one wall. Rifles were on racks, and a worn, beautifully tooled saddle sat atop a sawhorse. All memories of the past, Clint thought. Even the desk was as weathered as the man sitting behind it. Hearing Sam clear his throat, he returned attention to the old man.

"Son," Sam said, "I guess I owe you an apology for the way things have gone since you arrived. At least that's what Mattie says." He brushed back a tuft of gray hair. "We ain't usually so inhospitable."

Clint knew the old man was just spouting words. There wasn't so much as a glimmer of regret on his lined face. "I understand perfectly. We got off on the wrong foot, so to speak, and apparently I didn't arrive at the best of times. You mentioned last night that you were having trouble with rustlers?"

"The varmints have been stealing too many of my stock," Sam said gruffly. "First it was the Indians, which I'm sure we haven't seen the last of, then it was the railroad. Now rustlers."

"Were you against the Union Pacific going through?"

"You're damn right. One thing always leads to another. There were the railroad workers and Fort Steele was built to protect the damn workers, the railroad brought people, and towns like Medicine

Bow and Rawlins started sprouting up." Sam moved his wheelchair around so he could look out the window. "Even so, I was ready to take on the railroad and the whole damn army. It was Kate that talked me out of it and made me see how useful the railroad could be for shipping steers." He snorted. "I gotta admit it's worked out for the better. Still, I miss the way it was when a man could travel forever and never meet a soul. Now there's trains with engines that belch black smoke and scare cattle by blowing that blasted whistle."

"Have you any clues as to who the rustlers are?"

Sam turned his wheelchair around and studied Clint. "You seem to be awful damn curious about them fellers."

"Like I said last night, I'm interested in learning more about your ranch." Clint continued to press the subject. "If there's a chance of running into them while Kate's showing me around the ranch—"

"That ain't likely, considerin' we haven't even been able to catch 'em ourselves." Sam smirked. "But to set your mind at ease, I can tell you they only strike at night."

Clint was about to tell Sam that wasn't what he meant when someone knocked. Without a moment's pause, the door banged open and Kate barged in.

"Sam," Kate bit out, "what is this about me taking Morgan around the ranch today? You know I haven't got time for such tomfoolery!"

"No sense in you gettin' all fired up, girl. I've already told Clint you would."

With Kate standing in front of him, Clint had a good view of her backside. His gray eyes traveled down to her narrow waist, well-shaped derriere

and long legs. "Too busy baiting rats?" he asked
nonchalantly.

Kate balled her fists. "Keep your nose out of
this," she ordered over her shoulder.

Sam laughed. "You should be more gentle with
our guest, Kate." He looked at Clint. "Wait outside, boy. I want to have a private word with my
daughter. She'll join you shortly."

Clint rose from his chair and left.

"Why the hell are you doing this?" Kate asked
as soon as the door closed.

"Ain't no need for you to get yourself in a
dither, girl. It's not as if you'll be spending the
whole day showing him around. Mattie suggested it this morning, so just take him a ways
and bring him back. At least it will get Mattie off
my back for the way we've failed to welcome her
nephew."

Kate was furious, but she could tell by the stern
look on her father's face that he wasn't going to
budge. Morgan was more trouble than he was
worth. She thought about telling Sam someone
had been spying on the herd, but changed her
mind. She'd wait and see what happened.

Kate marched out of the house, determined to
make Morgan regret he'd ever stepped foot on
Whitfield land. She'd keep his butt busy. By the
time she got through, there wouldn't be a muscle
in his body that didn't ache.

Because White Cloud was at the blacksmith's,
Kate saddled a roan gelding. Even after doing
that, it was still another thirty minutes before
Clint finally made an appearance.

"What the hell took you so long?" Kate demanded.

Clint grinned. "Mattie stopped me to ask if you
were being more hospitable." The lie slipped out
without the least amount of effort. He'd deliberately remained in his room. Looking down from

his window, he'd enjoyed watching her pace back and forth. "But I'm sorry. A man should never keep a beautiful woman waiting."

"Hogwash!" Kate mounted the roan.

"And I'm sorry if I offended you by calling you beautiful," Clint said as he swung onto the Appaloosa. "Or maybe it's calling you a woman that has you riled."

Kate gritted her teeth and returned his easy smile. "You didn't offend me, Morgan. I've had compliments from better than you. I just don't trust sweet-talkin' men." She rode off at a fast clip.

Chapter 4

As Kate and Clint rode across the open range, Kate's anger vanished. She loved the valley and the high, jagged mountains that stretched across either side; it was all a part of her. She often cursed the hard winters, but if she could, she probably wouldn't change a thing.

"This sure is pretty country," Clint commented.

Kate nodded. "I can't show you much of the ranch considering what time it is, so I'll just take you south a ways."

"You don't know how much I appreciate it."

Kate made no comment. She'd been keeping a surreptitious eye on Clint. It was obvious that he was accustomed to being in the saddle. He rode with a relaxed air, and though the Appaloosa was frisky, Clint had no trouble keeping him under control. Kate had also noticed Clint's well-used gun belt. It made her wonder at his proficiency with the .45 nestled in the holster. She flashed back to two nights ago when she'd hog-tied him. Living on a ranch, there wasn't anything she hadn't seen, including some mighty fine male bodies. But when Clint stepped into the hotel doorway that night, his height, powerful shoulders and muscular arms had been clearly outlined. Then yesterday, when she'd seen him in daylight for the first time, his rugged good looks had come as a shock. His even white teeth were a pleasing contrast to his bronzed skin, and his full sculptured lips seemed to promise pleasures yet to be tasted—a combination she felt sure had attracted more than his share of women. Even she was obviously not immune.

Aggravated at the direction in which her thoughts were taking her, Kate called back to Clint, "We got a lot of rattlesnakes so you should keep your eyes peeled. On the other hand, maybe you'd fit right in with them."

Now what's she got up her craw? Clint wondered. He'd been busy putting to memory the lay of the land. From what he could see in the distance, there appeared to be a lot of draws and canyons branching off the valley floor. Steam rose into the thin air from various hot springs, and he used them as landmarks. Occasionally he saw maverick cattle that quickly skirted away into the thick bush, and once there was a small herd of elk. Kate turned east, and soon they crossed a shallower portion of the North Platte River, the horses' hooves splashing rivulets of water onto their riders' boots.

"Tell me, Morgan," Kate asked when they'd reached the other bank, "how come you speak Spanish so well?"

Clint brought his horse alongside hers. "Picked it up when I was in South Texas."

"It's my understanding you make a living by checking out forts."

"That's right."

They were momentarily separated as they took different paths around some cottonwoods.

"You seem to be pretty comfortable on a horse," Kate said when they were again side by side. "Can you break horses?"

"Why do you ask?"

"My men have rounded up a small herd of wild mustangs, and they'll be driving them into a corral on the south range. I thought you might like to help break them. As long as you're going to be staying here, why not do some work instead of pestering me all the time?"

"No thanks."

"No thanks? Does that mean you can or can't break horses?"

"What it means is that it's damn hard work, and I want no part of it. Remember, I'm just a visitor."

"You still haven't answered my question."

"Yes I have, it just wasn't the answer you were looking for."

Annoyed by Clint's evasiveness, Kate glanced at him out of the corner of her eye. He sat tall in the saddle, looking off to his left as though he were studying something. Following his gaze, she saw trees, bush, grass and water. Nothing unusual. Downriver was a small hot spring, its vapors quickly disappearing into the air, but that was nothing spectacular. There were other much larger ones about. "What do you know about cattle?" Kate asked, her gaze returning to the direction they were headed.

Clint reined Storm in, waiting until Kate turned to look back at him.

"Why did you stop?"

Clint rested his hand on the saddle horn. "Subtlety is definitely not one of your best qualities," he stated smoothly. "Since we left the house, about the only time you've spoken is to ask a question. So let's get this over and be done with it. No, I don't know a lot about cattle, and yes, I have broken a horse or two. I can't use a whip, but I'm rather accurate with a gun, and I'm not married. Now, is there anything I've left out?"

Kate was at a total loss for words.

"You act as if I'm one of the damn rustlers." Seeing the hostile look that leaped into her green eyes, Clint suddenly realized he'd actually hit upon the truth!

"I don't trust you, Morgan," she said uneasily. "You look more like a gunfighter than some man who goes around checking out forts. Just how fast are you with that gun?"

The irony of the situation tickled Clint's fancy, and his rich laughter rang out across the valley. Kate suspected him of being a cattle thief, and he suspected her of the same thing. "Next you'll be asking me for some sort of demonstration. I'm good enough to protect myself, and I think that's all that really matters."

"I don't recall you doing such a good job the other night," Kate retorted. "I'm giving you a warning here and now. If you do *anything* wrong or suspicious while you're on this ranch, I'll personally see you tied up again, but the rope could be around your neck and you could be hanging from a tree."

"Are you threatening me?"

Seeing the humor glistening in his gray eyes, she let a wicked grin lift the corners of her lips. "I'm not threatening, I'm stating a fact."

"I wouldn't try putting a whip or rope on me again if I were you."

Clint's humor had faded, and Kate was satisfied. Convinced she had won the little tug of wills, she rode ahead, again taking the lead. Morgan might be a big man, but she doubted he was a fool. He'd know she meant every word of that warning.

Clint judged they had traveled about a mile farther when he saw five men riding in their direction, with Lucas in the lead. As the men drew nearer, one of the cowhands broke away and headed toward Kate and Clint. The others rode on.

"Howdy, Miss Kate," the slender man said cheerfully.

"Jake," Kate acknowledged. "This is Clint Morgan, Mattie's nephew. Sam wanted me to take him on a short tour of the ranch."

Jake tipped his hat.

"Seen anything?" Kate asked.

"Nope," the cowhand replied, "but we're ready for them."

"Good. Well, you go on and catch up with the others."

Jake nodded, again tipped his hat to Clint, then rode off.

Clint wondered if the men were out searching for rustlers. He had a strong feeling Kate wasn't going to fill in the answer.

Clint wasn't sorry when Kate finally turned and headed back in the direction of the homestead. The scenery, though beautiful, had become fairly repetitious.

When they came to a quiet water cove, Clint allowed the Appaloosa to lower its head and drink. "I haven't seen many cattle," he commented. Kate, who was looking out across the valley, seemed to be miles away. "Somehow, I thought you had more."

"We have over seventy thousand head," Kate finally answered. "Too bad you didn't come a little earlier. You could have watched a roundup. We brand the calves and cut off the bulls' balls. You'd see how good cowpokes use their teeth to—"

"I get the picture," he stated dryly.

Kate bestowed a whimsical smile. "What's wrong? Can't take it? Or maybe you don't really want to know about ranching. Anyway, it's mavericks you've been seeing, and they're meaner than hell, so try to stay clear of them. If a black bear were to come down from the mountains and get into a fight with a maverick bull, I'd bet on the bull. This is open range, and cattle roam.'' She reached out and stroked her horse's neck.

Clint studied the beautiful woman comfortably seated atop her horse. The brim of her hat shaded her eyes but he could still see the long, thick lashes. Her full lips had a pouty quality to them, and strands of long, silver-blond hair had escaped from beneath her hat and hung down her back. There was a natural feminine grace about her despite her efforts to appear as tough as any man.

He'd discovered something very interesting during their little trip. He'd seen the attraction in her eyes when she had thought he wasn't looking. Maybe that's why she acted so unfriendly toward him. He made her nervous, and she didn't like it one damn bit. If he'd guessed right, that made her vulnerable, something he decided to store in his mind for future use. He wanted to keep her talking. "How many bulls are needed for a spread like this?"

"Seven per hundred cows."

Clint saw the pride in her expression. "What kind of price do you get for the steers?"

"Used to be if you could get steers to California, you could make three hundred dollars a head, but all that's changed. Nowadays it's thirty to forty dollars a head." She gave an exasperated sigh. "You couldn't stay here long enough to even begin to learn about cattle or ranching, and I can't picture you wanting to know things like how to clean a screwworm from a cow's sore, or how to reach in and pull a calf when a cow's having trouble giving birth. Furthermore you'd have to know how to live, sleep, and sometimes eat in the saddle, and I don't think your ass could handle it. So why don't you just sit back and learn what little you can without bothering me with a bunch of questions?''

Clint grinned. "You might be surprised just what my ass can handle."

Kate fidgeted in the saddle. She wasn't sure what he meant by that statement, and she wasn't about to ask. The man was just too damn attractive.

"Have you ever been to a big city?"

"Yes, Morgan," Kate said impatiently, "and I didn't like it. Why are you asking?"

"It just seems a shame for a woman like you to be stuck out in the middle of nowhere." Clint noticed her jaw tighten as it did whenever he paid her a compliment. "I guarantee you'd have a lot of men come calling. Do you ever think about getting married?"

"I've thought about it," she said honestly, "but when I do get married, it won't be to some city dude." She looked down the valley again, shadowed now along the eastern slopes as the sun neared the mountains. "I'm perfectly happy right where I am. This is where I was born and this is where I'll die. There is nothing as important to me as this land. It comes before everything."

"Sounds like something Sam would say."

"And he'd be right."

"What comes second?"

"My family."

"Doesn't sound like much of a life."

"I'm content," she said wistfully. She turned and smiled at him.

Her smile lit up her entire face, and Clint felt his groin start to tighten. He pulled his gaze away and looked down at the sandy ground. Suddenly his eyes focused on the dry tracks of an unshod pony. They were coming from the river, and the depth of the tracks told Clint the pony had a rider.

The Indian and his mount had passed by about six hours ago.

"Looks like you've had a visitor," he said, pointing downward.

Kate immediately dismounted. "An Indian," she whispered, more to herself than to Clint. "He rode through here this morning," she spoke up, "so there's no need for you to worry. Stay put. I'll be right back."

Leading her horse, Kate followed the tracks and quickly disappeared into a thick stand of cottonwoods.

Wondering if the lady had bit off more than she could chew, Clint slid from his horse and tethered him to a sapling. Silently, he followed.

When a large slough partially surrounded by boulders and trees came into view, Clint stopped. He watched Kate slowly circle one side of the pond, looking for additional tracks, but obviously not finding any. Clint had to admit it looked like man and horse had gone straight into the water until he spied a couple of broken branches leading away from the pond. The Indian had taken his horse across the rocks to keep from leaving any more tracks.

Not sure where the trespasser had disappeared to, Kate stepped on top of a boulder. The terrible stench told her at least one cow had gotten bogged down at the far end of the pond and died. Holding the roan's reins firmly in her hand, she peered into the murky water.

What does she expect to see, Clint wondered. A body? "Is everything all right?" he called.

Kate jumped, and a rabbit ran from its hiding place right in front of the roan's hoofs. Startled, the horse reared, pulling on the reins and spinning Kate around.

Speaking softly, Kate managed to calm the frightened horse, but as quickly as the roan had pulled away, it suddenly came forward. She was already precariously balanced, and the unexpected slack in the reins caused her to fall backwards. She landed spread-eagle in the water.

Sputtering, Kate tried to stand, but her boots sank into the soft mud and she fell back down. Even though she'd fallen into the shallower part, every inch of her was covered with mud and green slime. Frustrated, she worked herself into a sitting position and took stock of her situation. Seeing her hat floating on the water, she reached out, grabbed it, and jammed it back on her head.

"Damn you, you useless piece of horseflesh!" she yelled at the gelding, now standing peacefully.

Kate was so vexed at her situation, it took a few moments before she heard Clint's laughter. Seeing him standing near the water's edge looking clean and smug only served to infuriate her more. "Who the hell do you think you're laughing at?" she yelled. "Damn you, Morgan! It's because of you I'm in this fix. I told you to stay put!"

Clint couldn't remember when he'd enjoyed a more entertaining sight.

Hating the broad smile smeared across Clint's face, Kate again tried to stand. To her mortification, she slipped and fell. In a fit of anger, she slammed her fist into the water. That the man had the gall to stand there and laugh was more than she could handle. She was tempted to draw her gun and shoot him, but it probably wouldn't fire now. And she'd never be able to explain the man's death to Mattie. Besides, she had no desire for anyone to find out what had happened. "If it's not too much trouble, Morgan, why don't you help me out of here!"

"My pleasure. Don't go away." Clint was still chuckling as he disappeared into the trees.

"Bastard," Kate mumbled.

She had finally managed to get her footing when she heard Clint whistling. Looking up, she watched as he came back into view. He had a long branch and that smile was still plastered across his face. She decided not to let him know she could now pull herself out. Pleasurable anticipation crept up her spine as she hunched down.

Silently Kate watched Clint climb upon the same boulder she'd been standing on and extend the branch. She looked him straight in the eye and placed both hands firmly on the branch. With a quick, hard jerk, she pulled Clint off balance. He landed in the water as she was sloshing out. Steadying herself on the bank, Kate turned and looked down at him. "Now, Mr. Morgan, let's see how funny you think *that* is!"

With as much dignity as she could muster, Kate moved her muddy body to her horse and mounted.

"You're not going to leave me like this?" Clint yelled.

"You bet your sweet ass I am. You can follow the river back to the house," she said as she rode off.

When Kate took her place at the dinner table that evening, she wasn't at all surprised to find their guest's chair vacant. Sam began saying grace, but Kate didn't listen. She was too busy enjoying the fact that Mr. Morgan had chosen to remain in his room. *Probably nursing his aches and wounded pride*, she thought. *Maybe now he won't go around acting so smug!*

"Does anyone know where Clint is?" Mattie asked as soon as the amens were spoken.

Kate spooned turnips onto her plate.

"I stopped and knocked on his door on my way down to supper," Mattie persisted, "but there was no answer." She looked at her stepdaughter. "Do you know where he is, Kate?"

All eyes turned in Kate's direction.

"Damn!" Kate muttered. "Hasn't anyone seen him?"

Lucas laughed. "Did you get tired of being treated like a lady and shoot him?"

Mattie sucked in her breath.

Kate looked longingly at her food before shoving her chair back and standing. "I'll fetch him."

"You aimin' to tell us where he is?" Sam barked out.

"I said I'd find him. I didn't say I knew where he was!" Kate left the room, silently calling Morgan every foul name that came to mind. The man continued to be nothing but trouble.

After checking Clint's room and finding it empty, Kate took off to her own room to change clothes. "If I could drag myself out of that slough, so could he. He wasn't even in the deep part!" She unbuttoned her dress and let it fall to the floor.

By the time Kate left the house, nearly four hours had passed since she'd last seen Clint. She wasn't at all pleased at having to search for him in the dark, let alone missing her supper. At least White Cloud had a new shoe and was ready to ride.

Kate entered the barn, and checked to see if the Appaloosa was there. He wasn't. Knowing her fate was sealed, she grabbed a blanket, saddle, and bridle, and headed for White Cloud's stall. Her foul mood was turning darker by the minute.

As Kate saddled her horse, she wondered if she should take some of the hands with her, then decided against it.

Clint sat on the ground, leaning against a tree trunk. No matter what his discomfort, he was bound and determined to make Kate return for him. He was mad as hell that she'd ridden off, giving absolutely no consideration to his well-being. But what else could he expect from such a woman? It wasn't much in the way of paying her back, but for now it would placate a small part of his need for retribution. He knew that as soon as the family discovered he was missing, she'd have no choice but to return, and she wasn't going to be the least bit pleased about it. In fact, if he'd calculated correctly, she should be arriving any time. If she brought some men along to help with the search, his pleasure would be twofold. She would end up having to explain exactly what had happened.

He thought about how his afternoon had gone after Kate's departure. Because he'd been attacked by droves of mosquitoes, he'd left the bog as quickly as he could get his feet on firm ground. After making it back to the river, he'd stripped and rinsed everything off in the cold water, including himself. He'd then placed his clothes on the rocks to dry and proceeded to clean his revolver. But the waning sun had done little toward drying his clothes. Come nightfall, he'd been forced to put them back on, even though they were still damp, making his jeans especially uncomfortable. Then he'd settled down among the trees to await Kate's arrival. At least with his revolver in working condition, he didn't have to worry about predators. Besides, the horse would alert him to the presence of any wild animals that might venture near.

Clint heard the rhythmic cadence of a horse's hooves. He leaped to his feet and cupped a hand over the Appaloosa's muzzle to keep him from nickering.

With the moonlight gleaming a path across the water, it wasn't difficult for Clint to see the white stallion or its rider. Kate rode by, but Clint made no effort to make his whereabouts known. Once she was out of sight, he led his horse away from the trees. As soon as he knew she was out of hearing distance, he mounted and headed back to the house.

To Kate's aggravation, Clint's horse was nowhere to be found. Either Clint had taken off in the wrong direction or the Appaloosa had somehow got loose and wandered off on his own. Of course he'd head back to the barn, but it wouldn't have been difficult to miss him. Left with no other recourse but to see if Clint was still at the slough, she dismounted, tethered White Cloud to a tree limb, and took off in that direction.

Because of the denseness of the trees, it was like trying to walk blindfolded. Limbs slapped her in the face, she tripped and fell, and when she finally reached the pond, Clint was nowhere in sight. "Morgan!" she called.

No answer.

Kate was starting to worry. By the time she made it back to where she'd started, scratches and an uncountable number of mosquito bites covered her face.

After mounting, Kate sat for a moment trying to figure out what she should do next. There was really no choice. She'd have to go back and get some men to help with the search, something she should have done in the first place.

When Clint entered the house, Mattie was waiting for him. He wasn't in any mood to deal with yet another woman tonight.

"Thank the good Lord you're all right," Mattie said worriedly. Her face was drawn and she kept wringing her hands. "Did Kate find you?"

"No, I returned on my own." Seeing how

drawn her face was, and the way she kept wringing her hands, *almost* made Clint feel guilty, something he hadn't felt in a good many years. He shouldn't take his anger out on his aunt.

"Are you all right?"

Seeing the real concern in her blue eyes, Clint felt some of his anger fade away. "I'm fine," he replied in a gentler tone. He took her elbow and led her into the parlor. "Have a seat, Mattie. We have to talk."

Mattie obediently sat on a plush brocade chair; Clint remained standing.

"I assure you, I was never in any danger. I'm perfectly capable of taking care of myself, and I don't need anyone standing around worrying over me."

Mattie noticed traces of dried mud streaked through his hair and his damp, wrinkled clothes. "I understand," she said meekly.

Clint placed his hands on his hips and shifted his weight to his other foot. "It's nothing personal. I've been on my own too long to feel the need to supply answers."

Mattie concluded that her nephew could indeed take care of himself. With that revelation, she felt considerably better. "It's all right, dear. I'll try not to be a bother. Now you must go change clothes . . . Oh, I'm sorry. There I go mothering you again. Would I be out of place if I had your supper sent to your room?"

Clint grinned. "I'd appreciate it." It occurred to him that Mattie's kindly disposition made it awfully hard to get angry with her.

When Clint left the room, Mattie smiled. He is such a handsome, virile man, she thought. She clapped her hands together. He'll make Kate a perfect husband.

White Cloud was in a full gallop when Kate headed him toward the bunkhouse. Suddenly she yanked back on the reins, bringing the stallion to a sliding stop. One of the old ranch hands was leading Morgan's unsaddled horse to the barn. Kate headed White Cloud in his direction.

"Smoky!" Kate said as she pulled up beside him. "Did that horse just wander in?"

"No, Miss Kate. Mrs. Whitfield's nephew rode him in."

Kate leaped off her horse and tossed the reins to Smoky. "Bed him down," she ordered briskly.

By the time Kate entered the house through the kitchen door, she was seething.

"Bessy," she barked out at the cook, who was sitting at the kitchen table, "have you seen Clint Morgan?"

"No, Miss Kate, but Alma took his supper to his room a short while ago."

Kate marched through the kitchen, then took the stairs two at a time. When she reached Clint's door, she barged right in without knocking. "Where the hell have you been?" she demanded.

Clint sat on his bed with pillows propped behind him. A tray with empty dishes sat on the small round table next to the chair. "You should be more careful when you enter a man's room. At least I have my jeans on." He swung his legs over the side of the bed.

Kate tried to ignore his muscled body, and the short, curly black hair on his chest that disappeared into the waist of his pants. "Don't flatter yourself. Living on a ranch, there's not much I haven't seen." She trained her eyes determinedly on his face. "Now I asked a question and I want an answer!"

Clint stood and slowly closed the distance between them. His eyes never left Kate's. "I was at the river waiting for you. When I saw you ride by, I returned here."

"You did what?" she asked furiously.

Clint derived a considerable amount of pleasure at seeing her green eyes flash with indignation and her small hands ball into fists.

"Are you telling me you deliberately made me come looking for you?"

"That's exactly what I'm saying. Did you enjoy your ride?"

Clint saw the slap in the face coming and easily caught her wrist in midair. He twisted her arm behind her back, forcing her body against his. "Well, now," he said softly. "That's the first feminine reaction I've seen you make."

Kate stopped breathing as he slowly, deliberately molded his body to hers, crushing her breasts against his hard chest. A sudden, unexpected thrill leaped through her body, and she had to take a deep breath to fight off the unwanted sensation. "How dare you do this! Get your hands off me!" The fabric of her shirt was thin, and as she struggled to free herself, her breasts rubbed against his chest, causing her nipples to harden. "I'm going to beat the hell out of you!" she threatened, embarrassed at her body's unwanted reaction to his nearness.

Clint pulled her arm up a little farther.

The sharp pain in her shoulder ceased her struggling. "Turn me loose, you damn bastard!"

"I'm just making sure you don't try slapping me again." Seeing her glance at the door as if to judge what it would take to reach it, Clint grinned. "I have no intention of forcing you into my bed, if that's what you're worried about. Though you're a very beautiful woman, Miss Whitfield, you're not my type. I prefer a woman who wears dresses and isn't afraid of her own femininity. I have no use for a woman who acts like a man, swears like a man, and probably wishes she *were* a man."

He released her so fast Kate almost fell.

"Now we're even, as far as today goes. Is there anything else I can do for you, Miss Whitfield?" He arched a meaningful eyebrow.

"Not likely, Mr. Morgan," Kate said as she stomped from the room.

Still grinning, Clint returned to his bed. At least he had managed to instill the thought of being a woman in Kate's pretty head, which should make Mattie happy. Whether Kate chose to do anything about it was an entirely different matter. But with only her cotton shirt between them, he'd felt the ripple of excitement that had shaken her body. Maybe Kate Whitfield was more woman than she wanted to believe. Though she hadn't known it, a look, a word, or just about any sign of encouragement was all he would have needed to take her to his bed. *Keep your distance, Morgan*, Clint reminded himself. But he could still feel the pleasure of her body pressed against his. She'd never know how close she'd come to being kissed. He suddenly realized that keeping his hands off her wouldn't be easy. She was beautiful and tempting, and he had a healthy male appetite.

Kate headed back down the stairs, knowing Sam would be waiting for a report. One side of her wanted to go get her whip and return to Clint's room to teach him a lesson, but another side knew she didn't dare. Clint had ignited feelings she hadn't experienced in a long time, and she hated him all the more for it. And how dare he say she wasn't his type! He probably liked women who snuggled up to him like some cat wrapping itself around his legs and purring. Well, he was right, she wasn't his type. She wouldn't do that for any man, no matter how appealing he was.

Kate reached up and scratched a mosquito bite

as she went down the hall. And to think she had been worried that something had happened to the useless man! She'd have been better off if he had drowned. On top of that, she'd missed her supper—while Clint had obviously enjoyed his—her face was scratched and covered with mosquito bites, and all because she'd left him in the mud, which he'd justly deserved!

Sam was sitting behind his desk when Kate entered the office and plopped down on a chair.

"You certainly took your time," Sam barked out. He leaned back in his wheelchair and studied his daughter. "Well, you goin' to speak up? What happened to your face?"

In as few words as possible, Kate told her father what had happened at the slough, and that Clint had returned before she found him. She wasn't about to tell him what had happened after that.

Kate wasn't surprised when her father broke out laughing. Sam was a hard taskmaster, but beneath the bluster there had always been a keen sense of humor. However, what with cattle being stolen and men getting killed, he hadn't shown much of that side lately.

Sam quickly sobered. "Why are you lookin' so serious, girl?"

"I don't trust Morgan."

Sam's eyes narrowed. "Why not? Is there something you haven't told me?"

"How do we know he's the real Clint Morgan? Maybe this man killed him and has taken his place. He looks more like a gunfighter to me."

"Why? Because he changed out of his city clothes?"

Kate swung a leg over the arm of the chair, but suddenly aware of the vulnerability of that pose, she moved it back down. "I think he's involved in the cattle rustling."

Sam leaned forward. "That's a mighty strong accusation, girl."

"Well, there's one way to find out. What if we tell Clint about the steers on the ridge? If the rustlers try to make off with the herd, we'll know Morgan is behind it. When I was with him this afternoon, Jake and the others were riding back from getting the cattle settled. The trap is ready. I didn't tell you, but this morning I saw someone spying. Maybe it was one of Morgan's men."

"The rustling started before Clint arrived." Sam rubbed his chin, deep in thought. "However, your hunches are usually pretty good. We'll give it a try. If you're wrong, I don't want to hear another accusation against the boy. If Mattie finds out about this, she's gonna be mad as hell. Are you gonna tell Clint about the ridge?"

Kate fidgeted beneath her father's hard gaze. "I think it would be better coming from you. I hope we're not getting worked up over nothing."

"We? Seems to me this is all your idea."

After Sam's harsh words, Kate was starting to have second thoughts. "Maybe I'm wrong. Maybe the rustlers have even moved on. It's been a month since they last hit."

"No, they'll be back. They probably still have a healthy purse from the last strike, and they're just sittin' on their haunches until the right time. I can feel it in my bones."

"I'm doing my best to catch them, Sam."

"I know, girl."

Sam reached in his desk drawer and pulled out a letter. "I want to show you this. It's a reply to my ad in the Cheyenne paper. Since old Doc Sawyer died, I've been looking for someone to take his place."

Kate perused the letter. "It says this . . ." She glanced back down at the letter. "Dr. Putnam will arrive in six weeks. Are you planning to have him stay here?''

''Yep, until he gets settled in town.''

''Don't you think we already have enough company? Sam, we got—''

A knock on the door startled them both.

''Come in,'' Sam bellowed.

Lucas ambled into the room. ''I just rode in from town and thought you might like to know I heard some news about our rustlers,'' he stated proudly.

Sam let out a grunt. ''Since when did you give a damn about what goes on around this ranch?''

Kate watched Lucas's happy expression fade and become hard. It was the same hard look she'd seen on Sam's face many times.

''That ain't fair. I care about the ranch as much as anyone else in this family.''

''Except when it comes to the work,'' Sam accused.

''I've done jobs well and you know it. Maybe if I was given more authority, you'd find out just what I can accomplish. It just ain't right my answerin' to Kate all the time. I'm your only son. Kate should be made to take a position that's befittin' a woman. She should be raising children.''

Kate remembered when, on more than one occasion, she'd actually considered stepping down, but it wasn't in her nature. Besides, she agreed with Sam. If the land was placed in Lucas's incapable hands, it would probably go to hell. Still, knowing her brother, he might up and surprise them all. Unfortunately they couldn't take the gamble.

''Do you want to hear my news or not?'' Lucas barked out.

''Say your piece, boy.''

Lucas rested his hip against the desk. ''I was in town havin' a drink with Brody, and he told me there were some strangers at the saloon last night. They was huddled together, but Brody said he overheard one of them say the name Whitfield, then he heard *cattle* and the word *ridge*. We figured they was the rustlers. Naturally, I came right back to tell you about it."

Sam glanced at Kate, then back at his son. "Does anyone else know about this?"

"Nope, and I told Brody to keep it to himself. Sam, after what I just told you, I think I oughta be in on catchin' them varmints."

"Maybe if you'd concentrate more on work once in a while instead of—"

"Forget it! It's always the same thing. I don't know why I even bother trying."Lucas stormed out of the room.

Kate turned to her father. "You're too hard on him, Sam."

"Someone has to be. You and Mattie are always finding excuses for him and lettin' him waller in self-pity."

"That's not true."

"The hell it ain't. And if you haven't come to realize it yet, he uses me as an excuse to keep you and Mattie feeling sorry for him." He reached over and slammed the ledger closed. "I can understand him raisin' hell, gettin' drunk, and rollin' with whores, that's all part of growin' up. Though you might find it hard to believe now, I did more than my share of that when I was young. But it's time Lucas started learning to be a man and stand on his own two feet instead of wanting everything from the golden spoon."

"He just turned nineteen in January, Sam."

Sam's weathered face turned red. "More excuses! Soon he'll be twenty, then thirty. At nineteen you were practically running this ranch."

"Yes, and because I'm a woman, there's no excuse for me to get drunk, shoot up the town, and bed every man I meet. Why is Lucas any different? Maybe if I'd been a man, I would have turned out just like him.''

''Never. You're made of sterner stuff. Besides, you've got pride.''

''Pride? Is that what you call it?'' Kate leaned forward. ''From the time I was sixteen till I turned twenty, you made sure any man who got near me was run off the ranch or out of town! You weren't about to let a man fool around with Sam Whitfield's daughter.'' Kate stood, tense with anger. ''You talk from both sides of your mouth, Sam. You excuse Lucas for reasons I disagree with, then turn around and damn him for things I think you should be more tolerant about.''

Sam banged his fist down on the desk. ''We've had this fight too many times, and we both know the other's not going to change their thinking as far as Lucas is concerned!''

Kate straightened. ''I'm going to find Lucas and tell him he can join the ambush party. If he's willing to stay out in the cold, then I say let him. I'm not going to discourage him on this!'' She slammed the door behind her. She heard her father call her name, but she kept walking.

Kate searched everywhere for her brother, but finally quit when one of the cowhands informed her that Lucas had ridden to town. Feeling as if the weight of the world were on her shoulders, she headed back to the house. What was done was done, and there was nothing she could do to change it. Lucas probably wouldn't be back until morning, or maybe even the following day. Nothing had gone right today.

Concern about Lucas, plus the arguments with Morgan and Sam, had caused her head to pound. She turned toward the house, nodding at one of the cowhands riding to the bunkhouse.

As she walked, Kate thought about Clint's accusation that she wasn't his type, wasn't a *real* woman. How clearly she could remember back to when she was sixteen. She'd certainly thought of herself as a grown woman then, and had been experiencing all the desires that went along with it. Living on a ranch, seeing animals breeding, had strange effects on her. Jock Freedman had been bringing her little gifts, and was always stealing kisses, and when he wanted to make love to her, she was quite willing. Kate released a disgusted laugh at the memory. The experience had been both painful and disappointing. She thought about the time, years later, when she'd tried again, but that wasn't even worth remembering. She didn't consider bedding worth the effort. Afterward, when she'd overheard one of the men talking about loving a woman until she begged for mercy, she shrugged it off as just a lot of bragging. Still, she had wondered if that was possible. But if making love was nothing more than she'd experienced, why would a woman want to get married and put up with it every night?

She rubbed her temples. Why was she even thinking about these things? It had all been so long ago, and there were far more pressing problems. She opened the door and went into the house.

Chapter 5

At four-thirty the next morning, Kate headed toward the cook's shack for breakfast. Though the stars had disappeared, the sky was still black. Just thinking about eating with the hands made her smile. It had taken a lot of years to earn the men's respect, and she liked to take an occasional opportunity to be with them, to listen to their problems. With the exception of the new men who had been hired because of the rustlers, there wasn't a man on the ranch she hadn't known for years.

Kate entered the building at the same time the men began to straggle in. She sat in the center of one of the benches that ran the length of the long tables. The delicious aromas wafting through the room made her mouth water. The cook's helpers brought huge bowls of mush and gravy, large platters piled high with potatoes, eggs, steak, bacon, pork chops, sausage, apple pie, and biscuits to the tables.

Soon the room was a beehive of men's voices, and the clanking of silverware and plates could be heard everywhere. Coffee strong enough to stand an ax handle in it filled heavy earthenware mugs. When the coffee kettles were empty they were replaced with full ones.

Kate filled her plate. Between bites of food, she talked with the men seated around her.

"Miss Kate," Slim Collins called from the end of the table. "You gettin' sweet-eyed over that feller you been showin' around?"

Others at the table laughed and shook their heads.

"What would she see in the likes of him?" another man asked.

"He's mighty pretty," Slim countered, his broad grin showing a missing front tooth.

"Maybe *you're* taking a shine to him, Slim," a brawny cowpoke called out before bursting out laughing.

Kate was used to their ribald remarks. "I don't think any of you have to worry about dusting off your good clothes, or waiting for the preacher to arrive, if that's what you mean."

At five-thirty, the ranch hands began filing out to mount their horses and head for the range. Soon the only people left in the long room were Kate; the ranch foreman, Henry Blankenship; and the men cleaning up the tables.

"Henry," Kate said to the burly-chested man with the curly brown hair, "I saw some unshod pony tracks over at the slough near Humpback Canyon. Have you heard any reports of Indians?"

"Nope, but I'll pass the word around for the men to keep an eye open. It'd be about right if we had to add them to our problems."

"I was thinking the same thing." Kate rested her elbows on the wooden table. "You know, I would have thought that slough would be dried up by now. I want a fence put around it before any more cattle get bogged down in it. I suspect it's already happened to one or two because there's a god-awful stench around the place."

"I'll see it's taken care of, boss. Anything else?"

"Have some men check to see if there are any others that haven't dried up." Kate toyed with her spoon. "Time passes too fast, Henry. It's hard to believe that in a few months we'll be hiring extra hands to round up the steers."

Henry nodded. "Talk about time passing, next month I'll be fifty. That's even harder for me to believe."

Kate grinned, then told him what Lucas had said about the strangers in town.

"I sure hope they try to grab them cattle on Cripple Ridge. Then we can put an end to the damn bastards once and for all. Them was good men we've lost." He took a noisy sip of coffee. "You plannin' on staying close by?"

Kate nodded. "Those men can't stay in that canyon forever. We'll give it a week. If nothing happens, we'll have to give it up."

"I reckon I'd best be spreading the word to keep an eye out for Injuns too." He stood and climbed over the long bench. Seeing Kate still in deep thought, he reached out and placed a beefy hand on her shoulder. "Don't worry, boss. Eventually them varmints are going to make a slip, and we'll nab them."

"I know, Henry. It's the waiting and worrying that I hate."

By the time Kate left the cook's shack, the eastern sky was streaked with yellow and orange. She inhaled deeply, drawing pleasure from the sweet smell of the pine trees covering the hills. Morning had always been her favorite time of the day. She stopped and listened to the sounds that were so familiar to her. The blacksmith banging on the anvil; pigs squealing in the distance, wanting their mash; and cows bawling as they waited their turn to be milked.

Whitfield is a ranch anyone would be proud to work on, Kate thought as she continued on her way. Totally self-sustaining. Of course, with the long, bitterly cold Wyoming winters, it'd had to be. Otherwise it wouldn't have survived this long.

After saddling White Cloud, Kate rode off to town to visit the widow of one of the hands the rustlers had shot. Muriel Hawkins was going to St. Louis to live with her son and his family, and should be packed by now. Kate had money for her, and wanted to visit with the older woman before saying good-bye.

It was close to noon by the time Kate returned. As she neared the house, she saw Clint Morgan sitting relaxed under the apple tree, a drink in hand and a napkin and empty plate resting on the glider swing. It galled her that he could be so lazy, even more so that he'd obviously charmed the cook, Bessy, as well as Alma into serving him his meal outside. She started to ride past without saying a word, but decided she didn't want him to think the little scene in his room last night had scared her off. She brought her horse to a halt in front of him. "Is this how you've spent your day so far?"

"Why don't you ask Pedro? You've had him following me everywhere, so I'm sure he can give you a detailed account. I'd hate to see how you treat people who aren't related."

Kate tipped her hat to the back of her head and smiled sweetly. "But it's for your own safety. Most of my men haven't seen you, and Mattie would never forgive me if you got shot because someone thought you were a rustler. The men are real touchy about that right now."

White Cloud stretched his powerful neck and Kate yanked on the reins to keep him from nipping Clint.

"Is Pedro going to stay by my side during my entire visit?" Clint asked casually.

"Why? Is there something you want to do that you don't want me to know about? When I think it's safe, I'll call him off. Since you're just sitting around, you might want to mosey over to the empty corral behind the tannery around two this afternoon. I'm going to break Midnight. If I don't succeed, maybe you'd like to give it a try."

Clint laughed. "You don't give up, do you?"

"No, and maybe that's something you should remember." She turned White Cloud around and rode off.

At exactly two, Clint climbed onto the split rail fence next to Elmer Johnson, one of the hands he'd met that morning. The towheaded man was a farrier and had only worked for the Whitfields a short time. Clint figured they were about the same age. Eight other men had also gathered to watch Kate break Midnight. Clint nodded to a couple of them he recognized.

Two ranch hands stood inside the corral, ready to catch Midnight should Kate get thrown. One cowpoke was in the middle holding the black stallion by a lead rope. Kate stood off to one side putting on chaps. The big animal kept flicking his withers and rolling his eyes in Kate's direction, as if he knew exactly what was about to take place.

"Elmer," Clint said, "how come it doesn't bother the black to be saddled and bridled, yet he won't let anyone ride him?"

Elmer laughed. "You got me."

"Isn't he one of the ranch horses?" Clint watched as Midnight shifted his rear so as to get a better view of Kate.

"From what I've heard," Elmer drawled, "Miss Kate bought him from some drifter that passed through a couple of weeks ago. Supposedly, she checked the stallion over real good, except for one thing. She didn't ride him. He danced about in-

stead of ploddin' along, and she just figured he
was right spirited.''

Clint watched Kate pull on her leather gloves.

Elmer chuckled. ''It wasn't till the next day that
she found out the damn critter don't like havin'
someone climbing on his back.''

''Hasn't anyone else tried to ride him?''

''Nope. Miss Kate is bound and determined to
break him herself. I gotta say I don't blame her; I
ain't never seen a finer piece of horseflesh.''

Kate pulled her hat down and walked toward
the stallion. Clint had a feeling he was in for quite
a show.

Kate mounted, settled herself in the saddle,
then nodded. The minute Midnight was released,
the hard-muscled haunches gathered and he
bolted straight up, twisting and kicking. The men
cheered Kate, whistling and waving their hats in
encouragement. Dust rose into the air as Midnight snorted, bucked, and wrenched. Kate only
lasted halfway around the corral before she went
flying through the air, hitting the ground with a
hard thud.

As soon as the two cowpokes had caught the
stallion, Kate climbed back on. Clint was beginning to see a definite pattern to Midnight's bucking style. But what really held his attention was
Kate. Clint found the sight of her in her men's
clothing with her arm raised in the air and her
lithe body moving in unison with the horse most
erotic. He couldn't help wondering if she'd ride
a man as well.

By the fourth time Kate met the ground, the
men along the fence were mumbling their concern. The cowhands in the corral ran over to see
if Kate was all right, but she waved them away.
A streak of perspiration ran down the back of her
green shirt, and her face and clothes were covered with dirt. This time she was much slower

getting to her feet. She dusted herself off as best she could, then glared at Midnight, who was moving nervously in the far corner of the corral.

"Catch him," Kate ordered.

Clint had to admire Kate for her courage and riding ability, but the stallion was just too much horse for her to handle.

"She's goin' to get herself killed," Elmer whispered. "Even a man would be hard put to break that beast."

Clint had arrived at the same conclusion. He placed a hand on the top rail of the fence and leaped over. Kate was just fixing to put her boot back in the stirrup when he came up behind her. Before she had a chance to see him, he swept her up in his arms and took off toward the gate.

"What the hell are you doing?" Kate demanded, struggling against his firm hold. "Put me down! A few more times and I'd of broke him!"

Clint kept walking. "The hell you would have. Midnight's sides are hardly heaving. I'm doing what someone should have done twenty minutes ago, *my dear*."

Seeing the direction Clint was headed, one of the men released the leather hoop holding the gatepost and opened the gate for him.

Kate was so mad she could see red. "I'm warning you, Morgan, if you don't let me down this minute, you're gonna regret it!"

Clint carried her out of the corral.

"Did you hear what I said?" Kate doubled her fist and smacked him on the chest. "You good for nothing bastard!"

Clint stopped at the horse trough, leaned his head down, and planted a punishing kiss on her lips. When he drew his head back, the men broke out in cheers.

Knowing her men had witnessed the entire fiasco, Kate's face flamed. "You mark my word, Clint Morgan, you'll regret this," she hissed. "If I had my whip . . ."

"It seems to me that all you can do is make threats. I think you need a good cooling off." Clint grinned, then stretched out his arms and dropped her into the trough. As she disappeared beneath the water, he turned and walked away.

Kate came up spitting water and spitting mad. As she shoved her wet hair from her face, she yelled, "You haven't heard the last of this!"

Clint's steps never faltered.

When Clint rounded the corner of the tannery, he was surprised to find Pedro standing there. He stopped and stared at the young man, wondering if the Mexican was going to give him trouble over what had just happened. He certainly didn't expect to see a twinkle in the man's chocolate-brown eyes or a quick grin spread across the dark face.

"Now why haven't I thought about using that as a means to put an end to a woman's ranting?" Pedro placed a hand over his heart and looked up at the sky as if in thought. "And there are definitely times when they need to learn to shut up."

"That's true, but what would we do without them? You might like to know you can relax. I'm not planning on going anywhere." Clint looked toward the house just as Kate opened the back door and entered. She was carrying her boots, her soggy clothes were molded to her slender body, and she'd left a trail of wet footprints in the dirt. "If I change my mind, I'll let you know." Clint continued on to the house. As long as Pedro continued to dog his footsteps, there was little he could do about looking for clues as to who was behind the cattle swindle. At least not during the daytime.

As Clint entered his bedroom, he saw Kate sitting in the wingback chair by the fireplace. She hadn't changed her wet clothes, her thick, strag-gly hair was now draped over one shoulder, and the tops of her boots were still clasped in one hand. A puddle of water was already forming around the base of the chair.

Clint closed the door, then leaned against it.

Kate smiled sweetly and stood. "I've been waiting for you," she said, her voice husky.

Clint was reminded of a wildcat trying to purr.

"I think it only right that I should share my bath with you." Kate moseyed over to his bed-side, then poured the water from her boots onto the middle of his bed. "Wasn't that nice of me?" She fluttered her thick eyelashes at him. "Now, if you'll kindly move away from the door, I have to go to my bedroom and change clothes."

"Why bother?" Clint asked calmly. "Since you're feeling so friendly, the least I can do is reciprocate. You can change right here and I'll give you something of mine to put on."

"I've had enough of this, Morgan!"

"I think you should call me Clint."

"I'll call you what I damn well please! Now—"

"And I also think it's time you stopped curs-ing."

Kate glared at the big man filling the doorway. Though he hadn't moved an inch, she was sud-denly feeling queasy about being alone with him. "I've had all I'm going to take from you. Now move away from that door."

"For such a little person, you sure do a lot of threatening. But I guess I can do as you ask."

He moved away from the door, but to Kate's chagrin, he was headed directly toward her.

"Maybe I should be more hospitable and help you off with your wet things before you come down with a cold."

Kate started to back up, but stopped upon remembering the bed was right behind her. She'd been so angry with him at the way he'd treated her in front of the men that all she had thought about was retaliation. She hadn't taken into consideration the pitfalls of such a rash action. "You come one more step, and I'll scream so loud everyone in the house will be running."

Suddenly Clint took a dive at her. Before Kate could react, she was knocked onto the bed, in the exact spot where she'd dumped the water. To make matters worse, Clint was now on top of her, pressing her body down into the feather mattress. She tried to scream, but his mouth smothered her words. Knowing it was useless to struggle, she remained perfectly still, refusing to let his kiss have any effect on her. But this kiss was different than the one at the trough. His lips were soft, coaxing, devouring, causing her pulse to race and sending delicious, tingling sensations through her body. Her lips parted, and when his tongue entered the sanctity of her mouth, she shivered with delight and anticipation as to what would happen next. All thoughts of escape had disappeared.

Clint lifted his head, nibbled gently at her bottom lip. "The word is *please*," he said softly, his lips brushing hers as he spoke.

Confused, Kate opened her eyes. "What are you talking about?" she asked breathlessly.

"If you wanted me to move from the door, you could have said please instead of ordering me."

His words snapped Kate from her stupor. "I'll not say please to any man."

Clint heard her intake of breath as his hand cupped one full breast. "Then I guess you want to stay."

"Please," Kate blurted out.

"Please what? Please don't stop, or please let you go?"

"Please let me go."

Clint grinned down at her. "Please let me go, Clint," he reminded her.

Kate was tempted to bite him, but thought better of it. The way things were going, he'd probably bite her back. She had to get out of his room. Now! She couldn't let him know his kiss had stirred yearnings that had been suppressed for years, or that his hand had turned her flesh to fire. He's nothing but a damn rustler, she tried reminding herself. When would she learn not to come near this man unless she was properly armed? Swallowing her pride, she said in a strained voice, "Please, Clint, let me go."

"Now, that wasn't so hard, was it?" He rolled off her.

Kate jumped off the bed so fast she almost fell. As soon as she had the door open and knew she could get away safely, she squared her shoulders and looked back at her nemesis. He sat relaxed on the edge of the bed with a smile stretched across his devilishly handsome face. "You're no gentleman, you're a demon!" she accused. "Even a ranch hand knows how to treat a woman better than you do."

Clint's smile turned wicked. "I'm no demon, but I'm damn sure the devil's delight. So if I were you, sweetheart, I'd be very careful."

"I think there are a couple of things we need to get straight. First of all, I'm not afraid of you."

"Then you're a fool."

"And secondly, if I decide to let a man bed me, it will be on my terms. Not his." Kate went out the door, slamming it behind her. She marched down the hall, entered her own bedroom and stripped off her clothes, letting them fall to the floor in a wet heap.

If Sam hadn't laid down the law about everyone treating Morgan properly, she would have personally seen to it that the man was tarred and feathered for the way he'd treated her. She grabbed a towel from the washstand and began drying herself.

Please Clint, indeed! It's a wonder he didn't have me whine, "Please, Mr. Morgan." Well, if he thinks I'm some simpering fool who is going to crawl to him on my belly because of his good looks, he's in for a big surprise!

After pulling out a neatly folded blue cotton shirt from the chiffonier, Kate slipped it on. Jeans followed.

And if he thinks he can force me to start running scared, he's in for another shock! She grabbed a towel and sat on a chair. "Oh, how I wish I were a man," she muttered as she stared off into space. "I'd beat him to a pulp."

The next morning, the loud serenade of birds awoke Kate with a start. Seeing the sun was already up, she jerked the covers back and immediately sucked in her breath. Pain shot from her shoulders all the way to her fingertips. She lay still for a moment, then slowly turned onto her side. Every bone and muscle in her body ached. Without a doubt, being bucked around by that brute of a horse yesterday, and meeting the ground so many times, had taken its toll.

Painfully, Kate rose from her bed, determined to get dressed. She made it as far as the back of the chair, which she quickly grabbed for support. "There's no way in hell I'm going to be able to put my clothes on, let alone make it down the stairs," she mumbled. Stiff-legged, she snatched up a boot and wobbled to the corner of the room. Though her back didn't seem to want to bend, she finally managed to lean over and pound the heel of the boot several times on the floor.

Moments later, Addie May arrived. "Alma sent

me up," she said shyly. "Did you want something, Miss Kate?"

Kate recognized the young brunette as the new girl Mattie had hired. "I need you to send Alma up here right now, and tell her to bring the liniment." Kate groaned, wondering if she could make it back to the bed.

"Is anything wrong?" the girl asked worriedly.

"I'm not dying, if that's what you mean. Just go get the damn liniment!"

"I'll be right back."

"And say nothing about this to anyone but Alma."

"Yes, ma'am."

Kate spent the remainder of the day on her bed, covered with liniment and trying not to aggravate her sore muscles or bruises. She had broken horses before, albeit a few years ago and without Sam's knowledge. As soon as he'd found out what she was doing, he'd put a halt to it. But she'd never had a pounding like Midnight had given her. She wasn't about to admit it to a soul, but Clint had been right to put a halt to it. It was the way he'd accomplished it that made her so furious.

By supper time, Kate still had no desire to leave the confines of her bedroom. But thinking about Clint Morgan's devilish grin, she changed her mind. She wasn't about to let him gloat over her physical discomfort.

With Alma's help, Kate finally managed to get into a brightly flowered cotton dress with a high neckline and long sleeves. She'd refused to put the corset on, even though Alma insisted it wasn't decent for a woman to go about without one. But that was a statement she'd heard often. Not only from Alma, but from Mattie as well. How they thought she could ride a horse laced up in one of those contraptions was beyond all comprehension.

Kate finally wobbled out of her room. With one hand holding her skirts up to keep from tripping on the hem, and the other hand grasping the oak banister, she slowly descended the stairs, one step at a time. She was almost to the bottom when she heard Clint leave his room. A moment later, the soles of his shoes were tapping down the stairs behind her. Kate gritted her teeth and took the last three steps at what she hoped appeared to be a normal pace.

"Permit me to escort you to the dining room, my dear," Clint said as he took her by the arm.

Kate stopped and yanked her arm away, immediately regretting the sudden movement. She had to bite her lip to keep from wincing. "I hope you enjoyed sleeping in your wet bed last night, Mr. Morgan," she stated in a strained voice.

"Oh, I did." Clint grinned down at her. "It brought back fond memories of our time together and the kiss we shared."

"Shared?" Kate snapped at him. "You're deluding yourself!"

Clint took her arm and placed it in the crook of his elbow. "I think not. You were definitely kissing me back by the time I was done." He didn't fail to notice her stilted walk, nor the strong smell of liniment. Though he made no comment, he did slow their pace. He had to admit, she did have spunk.

"That's the most ridiculous thing I've ever heard. If you were any kind of a gentleman, you wouldn't even bring the subject up. You certainly have a high opinion of yourself. As far as I'm concerned, the kiss lacked everything," she stated flippantly. "Compared to other men I've kissed, you would definitely be at the bottom of the list."

Clint laughed. "Well then, I guess we'll just

have to give it another try before too long." Just before they entered the parlor, he added, "Alma was kind enough to see that my wet bed was changed."

"Too bad she didn't say something to me, or I would have prevented it from happening," Kate snapped as they entered the parlor.

"Who said nothing to you about what, dear?" Mattie asked from her place on the sofa.

"Alma was saying she'd had a fight with Bessy, the cook," Clint replied.

"Oh, think nothing of it, Clint," Mattie said. "Those two are always fighting. They wouldn't know what to do with themselves if they didn't."

It occurred to Kate that Clint seemed quite adept at coming up with quick answers.

Sam rolled his wheelchair in, and Lucas followed closely behind. A few minutes later, the family adjourned to the dining room. When Kate was seated at the table, she expelled a silent sigh at finally being able to relax her aching body. Leaving the table might prove to be an entirely different matter.

"Heard you tried to break Midnight yesterday," Lucas said as he sat next to Kate. "Then I heard . . . Goddamn, Kate! What's that god-awful smell? Liniment? Where you trying to break the horse or was he breaking you?" He started laughing.

Mattie gasped. "Kate. You didn't."

Kate glanced at Sam. The set expression on his face spoke volumes.

"Breakin' horses is what we got cowhands for," Sam bit out. "I told you a long time ago that I didn't want you trying that again."

"Well, Sam," Lucas continued when he'd caught his breath, "you can thank Clint for putting a stop to it. He was even kind enough to cool her down." Lucas laughed all the harder.

To Kate's mortification, Lucas wasn't about to stop there.

"Guess that kiss was the only way you could shut her up, Clint. Damn, I wish I'd been there to see it."

Mattie was absolutely delighted to hear that Clint had kissed her stepdaughter. Perhaps a romance was finally beginning to develop. She wasn't sure what Lucas meant about Clint cooling Kate off, but it didn't matter.

"How come you let her ride that black beast after I gave him to you, Clint?" Lucas persisted.

"I took him back," Kate snapped. "He wasn't yours to give away, Lucas."

Sam interrupted before a fight between the two could start. "If Lucas gave that horse to Clint, then that's who the stallion belongs to!"

Kate stared at her father in disbelief. "You can't do that!"

Sam banged his fist on the table, rattling the glasses and bouncing the silverware. "The hell I can't, girl. You already have a horse, and you got no business being around that damn black stallion. I don't want to hear another word about it. Clint," Sam bellowed in his raspy voice, "I want to see you in my office after supper. Now, everyone bow their heads. Bless this food, Lord . . ."

Kate could think of no better end for her half brother than to have his tongue cut out.

As soon as supper was completed, Clint pushed Sam into his office.

Sam spun his chair around and waited for Clint to close the door. "What's this about you kissin' Kate?" he demanded as Clint settled himself on one of the comfortable chairs.

"I'd think you'd want to thank me for saving her neck instead of getting upset over a harmless kiss."

"I appreciate what you did, but I just want to make sure you don't go gettin' any ideas. Kate is off-limits."

"Does that apply to all men, or just me?"

"Kate's got a ranch to take care of, and she ain't got the time to be dallying."

Clint pulled a cigar from his vest pocket and offered it to Sam. The older man shook his head, and Clint bit off the end. "Sounds to me like you're more concerned about not having someone to run your ranch than accepting the fact that Kate's a woman." He struck a match and lit his cigar.

"That's damn nonsense. Of course I know she's a woman!"

Smoke slowly trailed from Clint's mouth. "Then you've accepted the fact that as a woman, some day she's going to want to get married and raise a family."

"No good-for-nothin' cowpoke is going to come along and marry her and take over my ranch!" Sam blurted out.

Clint knew it wasn't wise to pursue this, but Sam's attitude was starting to make him mad. "Kate's old enough to make her own decisions, or you wouldn't have made her responsible for this ranch."

"I'll handle her," Sam replied, his voice getting louder. "You may be Mattie's nephew, but I'm telling you that I don't want you tryin' to take advantage of Kate!"

Clint leaned back in his chair and studied the old man. "Since you feel no qualms about speaking your piece, then I see no reason for not speaking mine. To begin with, I'm not one of your hired hands, and I don't like being ordered around. I also don't rape women, if that's what you're insinuating. You don't want to lose Kate because she's the best man you have on this ranch. Well,

I have news for you. Your daughter is ripe for the taking, and you'd be well advised to accept that. But just to set your mind at ease, I have no intention of running off with Kate. At the same time, I'm not going to sit and listen to any man preach to me about what I should or should not do. And that damn well includes you.''

Sam was turning red from the neck up. ''Who the hell do you think you're talkin' to?''

Clint leaned forward and stared Sam right in the eye. ''To a man who had the guts to turn this raw land into a profitable ranch,'' he said softly. ''A man who I believe is just about as bullheaded as I am. But you've let this ranch and being crippled blind you to life, Sam. The land will always be here, but the people won't, and that includes you and Kate.'' Clint stood to leave. To his surprise, Sam waved a hand at him.

''Sit down,'' Sam said in an almost gentle voice. ''I don't know why everyone thinks that when strong words are exchanged they gotta up and leave. In my day, you either talked it out or settled it with fists or a gun.''

Clint hesitated before reclaiming his seat, making it clear that the decision wasn't made because Sam had ordered him to do so. His lips spread into a lopsided grin. ''If we handled this with fists or a gun, I believe you'd be at a disadvantage.''

Sam pulled a .45 revolver from beneath the plaid blanket covering his useless legs, then placed it on his lap. ''I haven't become so old that I can't still protect myself.''

Realizing he'd underestimated the wizened old man, Clint broke out laughing. ''It looks like I'm the fool,'' he finally said.

Sam's face softened. He found himself liking his nephew, something he hadn't expected to happen. There was a hardness to Clint that was easily recognizable because it reminded Sam a lot of himself when he was young. The fact that Clint obviously backed down to no man made him like the boy even more. "You know, Clint," Sam said reflectively, "though it may not seem apparent, I care for my children. Yes, even Lucas. If I didn't care I wouldn't waste my time ridin' his ass. But he's weak, and that's somethin' a man like me has a hard time coming to grips with. So that leaves Kate. You're damn right I don't want to lose her, but can you honestly blame me? I suspect that if you were in my shoes, you'd feel the same way.

"And of course there's the problem with the rustlers, and wonderin' when and where they'll strike next." Sam watched for some clue of interest on Clint's face, but his expression remained the same. "We've got two hundred head of cattle grazing on Cripple Ridge, and because I don't have anyone guarding them, that concerns me, even if they are well hidden. It's too tempting for them rustlers." Sam knew Clint could find out where the ridge was located just by asking most any of the ranch hands. "Our biggest problem has been that the rustlers always seem to know where we're the most vulnerable. So if we seem a mite jumpy, you can understand why." Sam looped his thumbs under his suspenders. "Ain't gonna be any peace on this ranch till them damn men are caught."

Clint thought it strange Sam would leave a herd unguarded, but he chose not to question the old man's reasoning. Instead, he tried to figure out if there could be any connection between the stolen cattle and the switching of the reservation steers. But try as he might, he couldn't come up with any correlation. It had to be coincidental that both were happening at the same time. "Why don't you band together with the smaller ranchers over in the big valley?" he asked casually.

"Now that's the interesting part. We're the only ranch that's being hit. Besides, I take care of my own problems."

"It sounds to me like someone on the ranch is involved."

"We thought about that, but if it's true, catchin' 'em is an entirely different matter." Sam turned his wheelchair toward the door. "Well, it ain't nothin' for you to be worryin' about."

Clint watched Sam leave without another word. Apparently their meeting was over. "Were you serious about giving me the black stallion?"

"I said so, and I don't go back on my word," Sam replied over his shoulder.

As the old man disappeared down the hall, Clint frowned. Samuel Whitfield wouldn't have let him off so easily had the old man known about what had happened in his bedroom yesterday. At least one good thing had happened. He owned a horse. Now all he had to do was break it.

Chapter 6

Clint rested his arms on top of the fence and the toe of his boot on the bottom rail. Midnight trotted around the corral, tail arched, his satiny black neck bowed. Every bone and muscle spoke of fine breeding. Sam's gift had been a pleasant, unexpected surprise.

Clint grinned. Living with the Sioux had given him a distinct advantage over Kate in that he knew why Midnight could be saddled but acted like a bronco when mounted. It was an old Indian trick. A couple of braves would train a horse to accept a bridle and saddle. Then one brave would mount him and the other one would continually flay the horse's front legs with brush or twigs, teaching him that to have anyone on his back meant pain. They were very careful not to damage the horse in any way. Then, when the braves had the horse trained to refuse a rider, they would sell him to some unsuspecting soul. Of course they made sure the money was in their hands before allowing anyone to mount the beautiful animal. A few days later the Indians would return, willing to buy the horse back, but for a considerably lesser price. Usually the buyer was more than willing to get rid of the useless animal. They could do this over and over with the same horse.

"Afraid to mount him?"

"I'm letting him get used to me," Clint commented dryly, not bothering to turn as Kate joined him by the fence.

"He's not much use if you don't break him. I say you're afraid." Kate waited for a rebuttal, but none was forthcoming. Clint's silence irritated her. "Would you like me to have one of the men do it for you?" Still no reply. "Dammit, I want that horse back! I paid good money for him and I don't appreciate him being given to a man who doesn't have the guts to ride him!"

Clint dropped his foot to the ground and looked down at the woman by his side. Her stance was rigid, her green eyes flashing. "Nevertheless," he said in a quiet voice, "the horse is no longer yours, nor do I intend to part with him."

"You're going to be sorry you made me your enemy. My time will come to get even. I can be very patient."

Clint smiled. "So can I, sweet Kate."

Kate spun on her heels and marched off. Maybe the stallion would kill him and get him out of her hair. She pulled her hat off and slapped it against her leg. Sam should never have given Clint the horse in the first place.

Clint had put Midnight in his stall and was going back to the house to change for supper when he saw Lucas headed in his direction.

"Wait up!" Lucas called.

Clint slowed his pace.

Lucas was grinning from ear to ear as he fell in step with Clint. "Well, you got that damn killer beast all nice and gentled?"

"Nope."

"When you aimin' to do it? I'd like to watch."

"What you mean is you'd like to see me eat dirt."

Lucas chuckled. "You got that right."

"I'll try not to disappoint you. Being Sam's son, I'll bet you know just about everything that goes on at this ranch."

"Damn right I do. Some day this is all going to be mine. When that happens, I'll make sure the place is run properly."

Clint could clearly hear the bitterness in the boy's voice. "You don't think Sam and Kate are doing a good job?"

"There's ways of cutting costs and getting a larger profit, but neither one of them will listen to me."

"Well, I'm sure your time will come," Clint commented dryly. "Tell me, have most of the cowpokes worked on the ranch for a long time?"

"Yep, except for the new ones Kate hired because of the rustlers. But nobody's gonna catch those varmints unless the cattle are rounded up and constantly watched over."

"Have you pointed that out to Sam?"

"Hell, he never listens to me."

By the time they entered the house, Clint had made up his mind to get on friendlier terms with Lucas. The boy obviously liked to brag, and if Clint buttered up to him, Lucas might be able to give him some insight into what was happening with the government cattle.

Kate stood at her bedroom window, looking down. Though it was only dawn, Clint again had Midnight inside a corral, but this time roped tight to the fence. What she couldn't figure out was what Clint hoped to accomplish by fanning a saddle blanket at Midnight's front legs. Couldn't Clint see that it only served to spook the horse? Midnight's nostrils were flared and he had his ears laid back. Obviously Clint knew nothing about breaking horses. Either that or the man had gone loco. Yet he continued to slowly fan the blanket with what appeared to be infinite patience. He's a fool, Kate thought. I should let him find out for himself that he's wasting his time. He stopped fanning and began stroking the horse's quivering withers, settling the horse down. Watching his hands, Kate began to wonder how it would feel to have him caressing her in such a manner. Would he be as gentle and patient with a woman? An odd, unfamiliar ache began in the pit of her stomach, her legs became weak, and suddenly she was reliving the pleasurable memory of his wanting, demanding lips pressed against hers. She shook her head. She was the fool, not Clint.

Kate headed for the bedroom door. She had to put a stop to his antics before Midnight killed him. She wasn't going to be denied that pleasure by anyone, including a horse.

Clint kept up a barrage of soft words as he again fanned the blanket at the stallion's front legs. Midnight had to learn that there would be no pain and that nothing was going to happen to him. At the same time it allowed the big horse to get used to Clint's smell. Clint had been doing this for a good hour, but finally the stallion was beginning to settle down. Clint loosened the rope and slipped it off Midnight's neck, allowing the animal to trot to the other side of the corral. In a couple of hours Clint would come back and start the whole process over again. It was the only way to break Midnight without breaking his spirit.

"Get out of that corral before the horse tries to kill you!"

Clint looked up and saw Kate holding the gate open for him. Taking his time, he strolled out.

Kate immediately secured the gate. When she turned, she discovered Clint was still walking. "Stop right there!" she demanded. "I want to have a talk with you." To her aggravation, he continued on until he arrived at the water pump. She hurried forward. "I am responsible for everyone on this ranch." She watched him pump the handle, and when the water started coming out he leaned down and drank his fill.

"What's your problem now?" Clint asked nonchalantly before wiping his mouth off.

"Though it wouldn't bother me one bit, I don't want Mattie hurt by discovering her *beloved* nephew had been killed by a horse of mine."

His gaze traveled up the length of her, finally stopping at her flashing green eyes. For him, her anger was a challenge as to how long it would take to get her in his bed. *Keep your distance,* he reminded himself. The beginning of a smile tipped the corners of his mouth. "I hate to disappoint you, but nothing is going to happen to me. By tomorrow night, Midnight, who by the way, belongs to me, will be broken."

"Hah! And just how do you plan to do that? By fanning a blanket?"

"I'm flattered to know you've been watching. Maybe you'll learn something."

"I think you're the one that's in for a lesson. Care to make a wager?"

"What are we betting on?"

"You having Midnight broken by tomorrow night."

"Well now, I guess it depends on whether it's worth my time. Just what are you willing to wager?"

"Fifty bucks."

"Fifty bucks? That doesn't sound to me like you're very confident. Why don't we make the bet more worthwhile?"

"All right, a hundred."

"I'm not talking about money, Kate."

Kate's eyes became narrow slits. "Are you saying what I think you're saying?"

"How could I possibly know what you're thinking?"

"Forget the whole damn thing!"

"Strange, I never took you to be a coward. Like I said, you're not so sure of yourself after all."

Kate knew what he was getting at. He wanted her in his bed! Though she wouldn't allow it to happen, she couldn't deny a momentary excitement at the possibility. At the same time, she'd like nothing better than to see him eat crow. But there was something else niggling at the back of her mind. Clint was too sure of himself, and it was making her confidence waiver. "Money or nothing."

"Then it will be nothing." Clint chuckled. "Be glad. You would have lost. On the other hand, sometimes by losing, you end up winning." He reached out and gently ran a finger across her full lips. "Maybe another time."

Kate slapped his hand away and left, unwilling to let him see how the mere touch of his finger on her lips had so completely unnerved her.

Though Kate managed to keep her distance the rest of the day, she watched Clint closely. By late afternoon, the horse didn't spook when he fanned the blanket. Then he saddled the big stallion, and she was sure Clint was going to break him. Instead, he kept mounting and dismounting. Time and time again. Near supper time, he took Midnight back to the barn.

The next morning Kate again stood at her window watching Clint go through the whole thing again. Fanning the blanket and climbing up and down on the saddle. By mid-afternoon, she could no longer stay away. Clint had said he was going to break Midnight, and she wanted to be there when it happened.

By the time she reached the corral, Lucas, as well as other cowhands, had arrived. Apparently they had also been watching the entire process, and like her knew the time for reckoning was at hand. She climbed up on the split rail beside her half brother.

"So you want to see him fall on his face too," Lucas said in his usual cocky manner. "Maybe he'll break a bone or two."

"I don't think so."

"What do you mean, you don't think so? Ain't no one gonna break that killer horse, and most certainly not him."

Having watched Clint work with the horse for nearly two days, Kate had concluded that everything the man did was for a well-thought-out purpose. "I have a sneaky feeling Clint's going to ride him."

"Twenty bucks says you're wrong."

Kate watched Clint untie the rope from the fence and lead the horse to the center of the corral. The depth of his self-confidence unsettled her. Still . . . "You're on, but I want to see your money first."

Lucas pulled his money out and Kate nodded. She could hear other betting going on between the cowpokes.

Everyone became silent as Clint climbed into the saddle. Kate held her breath. The horse stood perfectly still, waiting for Clint to dismount as he'd done previously. But instead, Clint nudged the stallion with his heels, and all hell broke loose.

The mighty horse bucked, twisted, kicked, reared, and even tried to bang Clint against the corral fence several times. Having no success at throwing his rider, Midnight deliberately fell to the ground, but Clint jumped free. As Midnight scrambled to his feet, Clint leaped back into the saddle. Kate felt a grudging admiration blossom inside of her.

The contest between man and beast seemed to go on forever. Sweat glistened on Clint's temples and caused his shirt to cling to his strong body. Kate watched the muscles rippling across his back. Her admiration grew by leaps and bounds, even if he was a rustler. She was beginning to wonder if Midnight would ever give up, then she saw him starting to tire. A few minutes later the black stallion stood peacefully in the middle of the corral, his sides heaving. Everyone broke out cheering, including Kate. She held her hand out, and Lucas slapped the money in her palm.

Clint waved his hand, and one of the cowpokes jumped off the fence and opened the gate. Clint rode the stallion out of the corral.

"I ain't never seen anything like that," Lucas commented dryly.

"Neither have I," Kate said softly.

"How did you know Clint was goin' to do it?" Lucas asked suspiciously.

Kate jumped down. "Purely a lucky guess," she called over her shoulder.

As Clint rode away from the corral, he gave Midnight his head, allowing the big steed to stretch out at a full gallop for nearly a mile. The first thing that grabbed Clint's attention was the awesome silence. In his determination to conquer the mighty horse, he'd even forgotten it was still daylight. Clint laughed into the wind. You didn't have a chance in hell, my dear Kate, unless you had hobbled him. But had you done that, he would've ended up with a broken leg and you would've had to shoot him.

Clint finally brought the horse to a walk, then reached down and stroked the thick, damp neck.

He reined the stallion to the left and right several times, pleased at how quickly the horse was learning to react.

A few minutes later Clint heard another horse approaching at a full gallop, but he paid little heed. It had to be his shadow, Pedro. The man was never out of sight.

"Ooooeee," Pedro said with respect. "That was some riding."

Clint grinned. He was actually beginning to like the Mexican. "Something I don't care to repeat anytime soon." With Pedro riding by his side, Clint turned Midnight back toward the homestead. The horse had earned a good rubbing down and some oats.

He thought about Kate standing on the corral fence when he'd ridden off. That damn floppy hat she wore had been pulled down low, but he'd seen her cheering and her face lit up with excitement. It was a look he certainly hadn't expected. But then he was never quite sure what that woman was going to do next. He much preferred a fiery woman to a docile one, and Kate certainly fit that description. There was no doubt about it. The more he was around the beautiful blonde, the more he wanted her. September was a long way off, and he hadn't had a woman since leaving Topeka, something that was gnawing at him more and more due to all his idle time. Things would be a lot simpler if Kate lived on another ranch or even in town. Being part of the family created one giant brick wall. He could ill afford to bed her, then have her go running to Mattie or Sam. No, he'd have to figure out a way to make her come to him. He never could refuse a challenge, especially from a woman. He knew if he was smart, he'd forget all about her and concentrate on his assignment. But that was the big problem. There was nothing to do except hang around the cowhands and keep his ears open. Normally when he was in a situation like this, he was able to seek a little pleasure while waiting.

Clint decided that tonight he would check out that herd on Cripple Ridge Sam had told him about. It wasn't likely, but maybe in some way that herd was connected with the reservation cattle. That morning an old-timer by the name of Al had told him how to get there. If that produced nothing, he'd be back to twiddling his thumbs. Too bad Kate had to be so damn inhospitable. Bedding her would certainly help pass the time away.

By the time Clint had Midnight bedded down and was ready to return to the house for a bath, Lucas had already informed him about losing his bet with Kate. Clint chuckled. The woman never ceased to amaze him.

It was a good hour after everyone had gone to bed when Clint silently slipped out of the house and headed toward the barn. It didn't take long to saddle Midnight, and a few minutes later he had the horse headed toward Cripple Ridge. The stars were like a crown of diamonds sitting on black velvet, and the luminous moon helped to guide his way. Midnight's ebony color, and his own black clothes, made it easy to blend with the night.

When Clint arrived at the entrance to Cripple Ridge, he started to ride up the old wash bed, but at the last moment changed his mind. This was the direction the men had come from when Kate was showing him around, and the man named Jake had said everything was ready. Ready for what? Clint wondered. He decided to make a wide circle and take a look through the trees.

Clint judged it to be another twenty minutes before he was satisfied with his position. After tethering Midnight to a tree, he walked the remaining distance, then stopped dead in his tracks when he heard a noise up ahead. Silently he crept forward. There was enough moonlight for him to see the shadowy figure hunched down. Clint was only a few yards away when the man raised a rifle to his shoulder and pointed it at the cattle.

"I wouldn't do that," Clint warned.

The man jerked around, and Clint recognized the almost skeletal features of the very man who had spit tobacco juice on his boot the other day. A cold grin spread across Clint's face even though the man's rifle was now pointed at his chest.

"Are you planning on killing some cattle, bud?" Clint asked calmly, "or were you going to alert your partners that it's safe?"

"The name's Brody, *bud*. I could ask what the hell *you're* doing here, but it don't matter 'cause you won't be leaving here alive." The straggly headed man laughed. "You ain't very smart, *Mr. Morgan*. My pals are in town. We never had any intention of stealing this herd. We ain't about to ride in when there's six men hidden, just waiting for us."

"What are you talking about?"

"Hell, you don't know nothin'. It's a trap that bitch Whitfield set up to catch us."

Sam had told him the herd was unprotected. Obviously the trap was for him as well. Again lady luck had been on his shoulder when he'd decided not to ride up the draw. Had he gotten out alive, he'd have played hell trying to explain what he was doing there.

Enjoying the opportunity to brag to someone, Brody continued. "I been keepin' an eye on this herd from the time they moved 'em here. I just been lettin' those men stay out here a few nights afore I sent some bullets their way to let the bitch know she ain't puttin' nothin' over on us."

"Who else is involved in this rustling?" Clint asked, keeping his eyes fixed on Brody and waiting for him to make a move.

"Enough damn talk. Get ready to meet your maker."

Clint made a dive off to the side just as Brody fired the rifle. The sound alerted the hidden men, and a sudden bombardment of bullets rang in the air, none coming anywhere near the two men on top of the ridge. But the noise covered the shot Clint fired, dropping Brody in his tracks.

The moon was now down, and because of the trees and the rocks covering the ground, Clint had to move cautiously back to where he'd left Midnight. By the time he had the horse untied, he could hear the men approaching from below, and an occasional wild shot being fired. Clint wasn't worried. He'd be long gone before they arrived.

Midnight danced around nervously, and Clint had to grab the saddle horn to swing himself onto the saddle. He reached down and stroked the horse's neck. "You've done just fine," he crooned. "Let's go home."

Kate was awakened by someone nudging her shoulder.

"Miss Kate," Alma gasped, completely out of breath from running up the stairs, "you have to get dressed. There's men out by the back door that want to see you. They say they've caught a rustler!"

Kate leaped out of bed as Alma set the lantern she'd carried in on the nightstand.

"Have you told Sam?" Kate asked excitedly as she pulled off her gown and grabbed for her jeans, lying across the chair.

"Yes. Luther is getting him dressed."

Kate pulled her clothes on as fast as her nervous fingers would allow. Finally, her plan had worked. She rushed out of her room, but as she turned the corner in the hall, she suddenly wondered if by chance the man who had been caught was Clint Morgan. She decided to take a quick peek into his room to see if he was there.

When she opened the door, she hadn't expected to see light. Nor had she expected to find Clint sitting naked on the edge of his bed.

"Do come in," Clint said with a wide grin. "Is there something I can do for you?"

Kate gulped loudly. "I . . . I . . ."

Clint raised a dark eyebrow.

Thinking of nothing else to say, Kate blurted out, "I hadn't expected to see you getting up so early in the morning." Without another word, she slammed the door shut.

By the time Kate had grabbed a lantern and gone outside, Sam and Lucas were already waiting.

"I heard all the commotion and wanted to know what was going on," Lucas answered before Kate had a chance to ask.

One of the two cowhands on horseback brought a bald-faced nag forward. A body lay across the saddle, face down. When the horse had been brought to a halt, Kate held the lantern high, and Sam reached out and grabbed a handful of straggly hair. He lifted the dead man's head to see his face, then let it drop back down.

"Brody!" Lucas gasped.

"Now I know who it was I saw watching the cattle being moved to the ridge," Kate commented dryly.

"I've seen him before."

The deep voice made Kate jump. "What the hell are you doing out here, Morgan?" she asked the man standing directly behind her.

"Curious," Clint calmly replied.

"What happened?" Sam asked the two young cowhands who had delivered the body.

"He was in the trees, near the rim of the ridge, Mr. Whitfield," the man with curly red hair answered. "One of us got him with a bullet right to the heart, but we don't rightly know who. We was all shootin' at him."

Clint managed to maintain a stoic expression.

"How did you know he was there?" Kate inquired.

Buckeye reached up and scratched the back of his head. "I don't know that either. I just figured someone must have seen him and took a shot, then the rest of us began firing."

"So you don't know if anyone was with him?"

"No, Miss Kate, but it doesn't seem likely. We searched all over."

"We? You mean all six of you?"

"No, ma'am, four of us."

"So only two of you stayed with the cattle?"

"Yes, but they were doing just fine getting the herd settled back down. We figured if the other rustlers tried to move in, we could shoot them from above."

"Damn! That means that if any of the others were with him, there's not much chance in hell of following their tracks since you trampled all over the area." Kate looked at the other cowhand sitting quietly on his horse. "Do you have anything to add?"

The man looked at her sheepishly. "No, ma'am."

"You boys see that this varmint is buried." Sam reached up and brushed the gray hair from his eyes. "Then ride back to the ridge and tell the other four men to pass the word around that this man talked before dying, and that we now know who his accomplices are. Maybe they'll run scared and we can finally put a stop to this. Ain't no use in anyone staying out there now. After you've taken care of Brody, ride back to the ridge and tell the boys to come in." Sam looked at his son. "Take me back inside," he ordered. "Kate, I want to talk to both of you in the parlor."

Lucas immediately pushed his father into the house.

Kate was consumed with disappointment as she watched the two men ride off, taking the dead man with them. She'd thought sure the rustlers had taken the bait and they'd caught them all. Seeing the face of the dead man had thrown Kate's thoughts in an entirely different direction. Brody Kincade had been one of Lucas's friends.

Kate glanced up at the gray sky. "Almost dawn," she whispered. It suddenly occurred to her that Clint was still standing behind her. She turned and faced him. "What are you doing here? The meeting doesn't include you, so you can just hightail it back to your room, the kitchen, or somewhere. This is family business."

Clint smiled. "Next time you come to my room, you really should stay longer. I'm even beginning to think you might be my type after all."

Kate squared her shoulders, gave him a dirty look, and followed the others inside. Seeing Brody had brought forth some serious questions.

As soon as Kate disappeared through the doorway, Clint hurried around to the front of the house and silently stepped onto the wide porch. It had been a warm night and all the windows were open. He wanted to hear what was said when the family thought they were alone. He might even find out why Sam had told him the cattle at the ridge were unguarded.

The parlor was well lit when Kate joined her father and stepbrother. Alma came in right behind her bringing hot coffee. Kate inhaled the delicious aroma. All of a sudden she was feeling exhausted, and she hoped the coffee would snap her out of it. It was too late now to go back to bed. She gladly accepted the cup Alma handed her and took a seat on the sofa.

As soon as Alma left the room, Kate looked at her half brother, now standing by one of the front windows. "The dead man was one of your so-called friends, Lucas."

Sam's green eyes settled on his handsome, blond-headed son. "This time, I think your explanation had better be a damn good one."

"I had no way of knowing he was one of the rustlers," Lucas whined. "Sure, I've hung around with Brody, I've known him for years. But he never did anything that would make me think he was involved in the rustling." Lucas looked down at the cup of coffee he was holding. "He's the one that told me about overhearing the two strangers in town. I guess it's doubtful now that there were any strangers."

"And did you by chance tell Brody about the cattle bein' on Cripple Ridge?" Kate asked quietly before taking a drink.

"No!" He glanced at Sam's accusing eyes. "Well . . . I may have."

"What do you mean you may have?" Sam snarled.

"The night you said I couldn't help trap the rustlers, I rode to town and got drunk. Brody was with me. As mad as I was, I may have said something about it. I don't remember."

Sam's big hands balled into fists. "Well I'll tell you something you can damn sure remember! This Brody has undoubtedly told his partners about those cattle, and that it was a trap. He was probably there just to check out what you had said. Now that he's dead, the others will know the truth, which makes the plan useless!" Sam's face was turning red. "God knows what else you told the bastard. Your goddamn cockiness has gone too far this time, Lucas. You have to have been the one that's been feedin' the rustlers information. That's the only way to explain how they always knew where and when to hit. I can see the whole picture as if I was standin' by your side. Just to prove you're the man on this ranch and know everything that's goin' on, you bragged. And that braggin' has cost the lives of too many good men, and cost us too many cattle! And with your *friend* Brody being dead, we're not likely to find out who the others are."

Kate wanted to put an end to the verbal pounding Lucas was receiving, but in her heart she had to agree with everything Sam had said. Just knowing Lucas had done so much damage caused a hard knot in the pit of her stomach. Still, her heart went out to him. She knew he hadn't done it on purpose, and it was sad that he'd had to go to such measures to prove he was a man. She set her empty cup and saucer on the side table.

"None of this is going outside of this room," Sam continued in a harsh voice, "because I'd have no choice but to string you up if just for the men that have been killed. So you've got two choices. Either leave this ranch or start workin' on it. And by workin', I mean every goddamn job you can do to keep busy. If you're told to move cattle, watch cattle, or take care of sick calves, you do it without a word of complaint. Do I make myself clear?"

"Dammit, Sam," Lucas protested, "you're not being fair! It's not as if I personally killed those men."

"Boy, this is another time that you'd be well advised to keep your mouth shut! Now make a decision. Do you go or stay?"

Lucas rose to his feet and set his cup down with

a bang, the coffee sloshing over the side and onto the table. He started to walk out of the room.

"Lucas!" Sam demanded.

Lucas stopped and looked at his father. "This will rightfully be my ranch some day, and I'm not about to leave."

"Then you understand the terms?"

"Perfectly."

"Get some men and start driving those cattle off the ridge. Take them to where we take the cattle for the roundup. I'll be checking with the men later to be sure you did your share of the work."

Lucas went out the door without saying another word.

Sam turned to his daughter. "I suppose you think I'm being too hard on him?"

Kate looked lovingly at her father. "No, I think you've been extremely generous, considering the land and cattle has always come first and family second. And who knows? Maybe this is what has been needed for Lucas to finally see what it takes to be a real man."

Kate's obvious affection for him made Sam shift uncomfortably in his wheelchair. "Well, we'll see." Sam grunted. "Looks like you've been barking up the wrong tree about Clint. Brody's lived in this area since he was a boy, and I wouldn't be surprised if his cohorts have too. In fact, they're probably more of Lucas's so-called friends. But unfortunately, it's nothing we can prove. As far as I'm concerned, Clint is innocent. And for your information, Mattie says Clint is the spitting image of his father. He also remembers quite clearly certain members of the family long deceased. Which blows to hell your theory about him not being the real Clint Morgan. I don't think I need tell you that she wasn't the least bit happy to discover her nephew was under suspicion of being a rustler. So from now on, I don't want to hear anything more about your suspicions. He's not to be tailed any longer, and he's to receive the respect that should be given to a relative.''

Kate gritted her teeth. Admittedly she had been unfair, but the man still struck her as being dangerous. Or, was he dangerous only to her?

"I'm going to my office," Sam announced. "Now that we've found the source of our problems, maybe the rustling will cease."

Kate watched her father wheel himself out of the room. He looked tired and bent. This morning had been full of revelations. She hadn't realized how deeply Sam cared for Lucas.

Clint crept off the porch and went back upstairs by way of the back staircase in the kitchen. So he'd been right. Kate had thought he was one of the rustlers. He laughed softly. Not only that, she had even suspected him of having stolen Clint Morgan's identity. The woman certainly hadn't left any stones unturned. No wonder she'd had him followed. Unfortunately, nothing had been said about the reservation cattle. All he could do now was continue talking to the men on the ranch and hope one of them might drop a clue as to what was going on. He also wanted to check out the railroad spur and the area around it.

One good thing had come out of this, he thought as he entered his room. He wasn't going to be followed any longer. He shoved the latch closed. He pulled off his clothes and was reminded of how Kate had charged into his room, thinking he was getting dressed instead of going to bed. Had she arrived a few minutes earlier, she'd have found the room empty. He turned off the lantern and climbed into bed. After four or five hours of sleep, he'd be fit as a fiddle.

Chapter 7

*T*he haze cleared. Clint had finally captured the leader of a band of Mexican bandidos who were raping and terrorizing the southern end of the Arizona Territory. He was riding hard, with Jesus Ortega on the horse beside him, hands tied behind his back. Clint knew that only by keeping Ortega alive and by his side could he be assured that he, himself, could make it to safety. Should the gang catch up with him, they'd be more concerned about their leader's life than his.

Clint's beard itched from lice, and sweat ran from his temples, stinging his eyes. Still he pushed on, keeping the two horses side by side and holding on to the reins of the bandido's mount. Suddenly the Mexican reached over and snatched Clint's knife from its scabbard, then leaped sideways, knocking them both from their horses. Clint had no idea how Ortega had gotten loose from his bonds. They fought, matching blow for blow, but finally Clint managed to get to his gun, which had fallen on the ground, and kill the bandido. Feeling a painful throbbing and sticky dampness on his leg, Clint looked down and saw the deep gash across his thigh where Ortega had knifed him. He pulled off his shirt, ripped off a strip, and managed to tie the cloth around his leg to stop the bleeding. He knew he had to cauterize the open wound that went practically to the bone. Gritting his teeth, Clint pulled himself over to where Ortega had dropped his knife and used *it to pry off the ends of two bullets. His hands were shaking, but slowly he managed to pour the gunpowder down the center of the wound. He pulled a match from his pocket, struck it, then touched it to the powder.*

Clint jerked straight up in bed, his face covered with sweat. It took a few moments for him to pull himself together and realize where he was. Slowly he climbed off the bed and went to the washstand. Dipping a hand into the pitcher, he splashed his face, welcoming the feel of the cold water. His hands were still trembling. The nightmares came and went. By now he should be used to them. Would he always be cursed with the past?

It was nearing ten-thirty by the time Clint finally left his bedroom and went downstairs. Upon hearing Mattie in the parlor gently scolding a servant for improperly polishing the furniture, he veered off to the kitchen. He hadn't realized how hungry he was until he entered the large room. The delicious aroma of bread baking, combined with the smell of the dried spices that hung from the cupboards, made his stomach growl.

Seeing Clint, Bessy, the cook, immediately stepped down from the stool where she'd been sitting and slicing apples for pies. *Oh,* she thought as she stared at the tall, comely man, *if only I were younger. My, my, my.* "I was beginning to worry about you going without breakfast," she said as she smoothed the white apron covering her ample body. "Now you sit right down at the kitchen table, Mr. Morgan, and I'll have a big steak and a platter of eggs ready in no time, if that's all right."

Clint answered with a smile. "You certainly know how to make a man happy, Bessy. I can't ever remember having had better food than yours."

Bessy giggled with pleasure. *What's wrong with*

Miss Kate that she can't see what a charming devil Clint Morgan is and go after him? She went down into the larder to fetch meat and eggs.

Having eaten every bite of food Bessy had set in front of him, Clint thanked the cook and left the house. After a short visit with Elmer at the blacksmith shack, Clint took off in search of Kate. Now that he'd been proven innocent of any wrongdoing, maybe she'd be more receptive to his company. He needed to make peace with her. Kate was his best source of information about what was going on at the ranch. Lucas might claim he knew everything that went on, but Clint seriously doubted it. Maybe Kate would even become more docile and he'd find her less attractive. He laughed at that thought.

"You know where Kate is?" Clint called to a ranch hand riding by on a dun cow pony.

"Nope," the man replied as he continued on.

Clint asked several other men the same question, and all had the same answer. Deciding his only option was to ask Sam, Clint was about to turn back to the house when he saw a bull of a man headed in his direction. Clint had met Henry Blankenship the second day he was at the ranch.

"Howdy, Clint," the foreman said as he drew near. "You look like you're lost."

"I'm looking for Kate."

"She's down in that meadow on the other side of the house. But I wouldn't bother her if I was you." The foreman rubbed the back of his neck. "She's fire-spittin' mad about something, and when she's like that it's best to just leave her alone. It's probably 'cause them other rustlers are goin' to get away clean."

"At least the boys caught one."

"I'm like Kate. I'll be happier when they're all dead."

"How many men have the rustlers killed?"

Henry's wide face became hard. "Too damn many. Seven. We buried the last two about a week before you came. It ain't easy seeing men you know laid to rest ahead of their time. Two of them were good friends of mine and the Whitfields'."

Clint nodded solemnly.

"Well, I gotta be getting on. You goin' to take my advice about leavin' Miss Kate alone?"

"Probably not."

Henry chuckled. "Don't say I didn't warn you."

Kate took the small rocks she'd collected and placed them in a line along the top of an old, dilapidated fence, making sure they were only inches apart. Satisfied, she moved away and picked the whip up off the ground. A flip of her wrist uncoiled it. She raised her hand and sent the end of the whip forward. With each crack of the leather, the fence rail splintered. When she'd finished, the ten rocks were still in place.

"You missed."

Recognizing the low, baritone voice, Kate didn't bother turning toward her unwelcome guest. "You're wrong," she said as she coiled her whip.

Clint leaned against a tree and looked at the partially standing fence. "Are you telling me you aimed between them?" he asked, with considerable doubt.

"Check for yourself."

Clint looked at the fence, at Kate, then back at the fence. He couldn't resist finding out if she was telling the truth.

The nicks were clearly visible, and almost perfectly centered between the rocks. Clint saw other scars on down the rail, leaving no doubt that Kate had practiced here before. He shook his head, amazed at her skill. There wasn't a man he knew who could perform that feat any better, and very few who could do it as well. He turned to compliment Kate, but the words never left his lips. She was standing a short distance away, her whip now trailing on the ground behind her and her feet spread. He didn't like the look of wicked pleasure on her face or the glint in her large green eyes.

"This time I'm armed, Morgan," Kate declared in her throaty voice. "You should have listened when I warned you I'd get even for what you've done." Kate watched his hands drop to his sides, the right one only inches from his revolver. His gray eyes had turned to stones.

"If you think I'm going to stand here and let you use that damn thing on me again, you've got another thought coming."

Kate dismissed his cold matter-of-factness. She wasn't about to let him talk her out of getting even. She'd looked forward to it for too long. And Sam's snapping at her for believing Clint was one of the rustlers had been the last straw. Clint had caused one problem after another from the day he arrived. "Then you'd better draw your gun," she stated confidently. "Or maybe you don't dare because you know I can draw blood before you can clear leather."

Kate waited eagerly for Clint to go for his gun, but he didn't make a move. Apparently her verbal taunting hadn't been strong enough. Her anger grew as she remembered how he'd made her return for him at the slough, and the unnecessary worry she'd put herself through imagining that something had happened to him. Then there was the horse trough he'd dropped her in, and her humiliation at having the men witness it. Now he even had Sam on his side. And last, but certainly not least, were the kisses. He was a devil and he was trying to put some kind of spell on her. No man had ever forced her into compromising positions, and she was going to put an end to his heavy-handedness once and for all. "You talk big, but when it comes to facing someone armed, you're nothing but a damn coward."

"As I recall," Clint stated, his voice threaded with anger, "you made that same statement about breaking Midnight. You're the one who arranged my beating when I came to town; you're the one who searched through my things without permission or an apology; then you left me stranded at that slough with nothing to protect myself. Darlin', I've done nothing to you that you haven't asked for."

Clint knew Kate was going to use the whip when her nostrils flared. But his draw was faster, and he cleanly shot the whip in half before the frayed end had a chance to reach him.

Kate stood with her mouth open, unaware the leather handle had slipped from her grasp. Never had she seen such a display of speed and marksmanship, which infuriated her all the more. His hand had moved so fast she hadn't really seen it. She'd been so sure she had the upper hand. Was there no way to get even with the man? "Well, are you going to just stand there and point that gun at me? I warn you, if you shoot, every man on the ranch will be after you."

Clint holstered his revolver. "I have no intention of shooting, but I'm sure giving some serious thought to taking you over my knee and spanking the hell out of you."

"You wouldn't dare!"

Clint's eyes narrowed. "Wouldn't I?"

His cold grin told Kate there was nothing he'd enjoy more. She backed away, and was weighing the possibility of outrunning him when a man yelled from up near the house, "Heard a shot! Is everything all right down there?"

The cowpoke was hidden by the line of trees that circled the meadow, but he was within hearing distance and Kate felt considerably safer. She looped her thumbs around her suspenders, then, grinning knowingly at Clint, turned in the direction of the caller.

Before Kate could call out, Clint stepped up behind her. Reaching around, he clamped his hand over her mouth while his other arm circled her waist. She tried to struggle, but quickly discovered the effort was painful when he tightened his hold.

"Everything's fine," Clint called back. "Just having some target practice."

"Okay."

Kate sank her teeth into Clint's hand, and followed that with a hard sock in the ribs with her elbow, but he still didn't turn her loose.

"Dammit, Kate," Clint barked out at her, "I came down here to have a talk with you. But if you keep this up, your behind is going to receive a thrashing like you've never known!"

Kate had never thought of herself as a coward, but she wasn't foolish enough not to recognize a genuine threat when she heard one. In her entire life nobody had ever laid a hand on her, and the thought of it happening now was thoroughly demoralizing. She became still. Not even a finger twitched.

"That's more like it," Clint growled. He slowly removed his sore hand from her mouth, waiting to see if she was going to scream out. When she didn't, he took his arm from around her waist, placed his hands on her shoulders and spun her around so she was facing him. "I don't know what it is about me that keeps eating at you, lady, but like it or not, I plan on staying till the end of

September, at which time, you'll be happy to know, you'll never have to set eyes on me again."

"Good!"

"In the meantime, if you'll stay off my tail—"

"Your tail?" Kate gave him a scathing glare. "You're the one that keeps dogging me!"

"Speaking of dogging, where is Pedro?" he asked sarcastically.

"I called him off."

"How magnanimous of you. And just why did you have him following me in the first place?" He wanted to hear what excuse she'd come up with.

Determined not to be intimidated by the man's size, Kate stepped back and straightened to her full height. She was still lucky if her head reached the top of his shoulder. "I don't have to answer to you for anything, Clint Morgan." She poked him on his shoulder with her finger to get her point across. "You don't live here."

He reached out and poked her back. "Then I guess Sam can answer my questions."

Kate balled her fists, fighting the urge to slug him. "Very well, the reason I had Pedro following you is because a man who ties his holster down doesn't do his talking with his mouth. I don't trust gunfighters."

"Did it ever occur to you that my work takes me across all kinds of territory, not to mention that I have to avoid hostile Indians? I'd be a fool not to know how to protect myself."

He had a valid point, but Kate wasn't about to give an inch. She looked up into his eyes, fringed with long black lashes, then immediately looked away. His eyes seemed to have some kind of magical power, and it made her uncomfortable. "So what is the purpose of all this? If it's because you just wanted me to stand here and listen to you, well, I have. Now, I'm leaving!"

Clint cast his eyes toward the sky. What would the woman come up with next? "I came down here to suggest a truce. I hadn't planned on getting into a tug-of-war, or on being threatened with a whip by a woman who doesn't have enough sense to know when to leave well enough alone! The way things have gone since I arrived, I suggest we stay out of each other's way before one of us does the other in."

Kate was furious at him for giving her yet another warning! Just who the hell did he think he was?

Watching Kate's fingers wiggling close to the butt of her revolver, Clint knew exactly what was running through her mind. "It'll hurt like hell."

"What will hurt like hell?" she demanded.

"Your hand when I shoot that gun out of it." Without thinking, he reached over and brushed away the tendrils of silver-blond hair that had fallen over her eyes.

Kate jumped back, putting more distance between them. What he'd just done seemed so personal . . . even tender, certainly not something she had expected.

"So, do we have a truce?" Clint asked softly.

"Fine, as long as you stay out of my way."

Kate marched off, and Clint made no effort to stop her. Kate's beauty and curvaceous body were starting to wear on him, even though she was the most cantankerous woman he'd ever known. He decided to ride up into the foothills and see if he could locate an old line shack one of the hands had told him about. It might prove to be a good vantage point should he find a need for one. Then tomorrow morning, he'd go to Rawlins and check out the railroad switchyard. He needed to know where and how the Whitfield cattle cars were transferred. Leaving would also serve to keep Kate out of his hair for the time being.

* * *

As soon as Kate got to where White Cloud was tethered, she mounted and rode off. Until she could simmer down, she needed to put as much distance as possible between her and Clint Morgan. How dare the man act so bossy and overbearing? Maybe she should have another talk with Sam. No, he'd already said he didn't want to hear her spouting any more bad things about Morgan. And talking to Mattie would only upset the woman. Clint had the right solution. They needed to stay out of each other's way.

After checking to be sure a proper fence had been strung around the slough, Kate started to head White Cloud south, then at the last minute turned him west. She had thought to watch the cattle being moved from Cripple Ridge, but changed her mind when she realized that Lucas would only think she was spying on him. How she hoped their problems with rustlers had finally come to an end and everything could return to normal. Her only regret was that they hadn't caught the other men involved and made them pay for all they'd done.

After a while, Kate realized she was letting White Cloud wander aimlessly. But she couldn't think of anything she wanted to do. She was feeling listless, yet at the same time fidgety.

She was completely lost in thought when she looked up and realized that her horse was approaching one of her favorite places on the ranch, a wonderful hot spring that was nestled in the foothills and well hidden with bush and trees. Farther up the hill was an old line shack that hadn't been used for years. She had never told anyone about the pool because when she was younger, she'd thought it was enchanted. But she had gone there to bathe many times in the privacy of the sheltering trees. Some of the boulders that supported the sides had paintings on them. They were similar to the ones she'd found on the walls and ceilings of caves in the area. She urged White Cloud to a faster pace.

By the time Kate had White Cloud tethered, she was anxiously looking forward to a nice, warm bath. She quickly made her way through the maze of tall shrubs and cottonwoods, wondering why she'd waited so long to return.

Kate quickly undressed, then reached up and pulled the hairpins out of her hair, allowing the thick mane to fall down her back. She raised her arms and stretched, drawing pleasure from the feel of the hot sun against her naked body. Feeling better than she'd felt in days, she stepped down into the edge of the pool, then inched her way into the water. Though it wasn't intolerably hot, it always prickled her skin, and it took a few minutes for her to become accustomed to the heat.

Remaining near the edge, Kate sat on one of the lower rocks, which allowed the water to reach her neck. Finally submerged, she became totally relaxed. She closed her eyes, allowing the soreness that still lingered in her muscles to fade away. She was at peace with the world. Then the uninvited face of Clint Morgan invaded her thoughts. Her eyes flew open, and she quickly glanced around. She was alone, yet he had seemed so close.

"Damn!" She expelled a disgusted grunt. Not only did he seem to turn up practically everywhere she went, now she couldn't even get rid of him when she closed her eyes! And if what he said about remaining until the end of September was true, it would be impossible for them to stay out of each other's way. She couldn't stay gone all the time. Oh, he'd probably like that, but she wasn't about to allow him to inconvenience her. Why should she be the one to leave when this was her home? He already had her doing things that weren't normal for her. Being belligerent or hateful wasn't normal. Nor was wanting to take a whip to him, or wanting to settle a score for the things he'd pulled. She'd always gotten along well with the men on the ranch. But on the other hand, she'd never encountered anyone quite like Clint Morgan. At this point, she wasn't even sure what normal was! And how, after all that had happened, could she be physically attracted to the man?

She splashed her face with water, trying not to dwell on that startling revelation. She didn't *want* to dwell on it. She didn't even want to think about it. Why, it was preposterous . . . Oh, God. It was true! How could she have been so stupid when it had been staring her in the face from the very beginning? She fell back against one of the rounded rocks, aghast. Was it possible to dislike someone and yet desire him? How had she allowed such a thing to happen? Maybe he was telling the truth when he said he was the devil's delight. She'd been right. He had put a spell on her.

Kate closed her eyes and placed her hands on her temples, wanting to stop the thoughts that were racing through her head. She took several deep breaths and slowly opened her eyes. She couldn't ignore the truth. She could try fighting it, but it wouldn't change a thing. Clint was not only strikingly masculine, there was a self-assuredness about him that blatantly stated he was quite competent when it came to making love to a woman. He didn't even have to verbalize it. And she knew, as sure as she knew her own name, it was that self-assuredness that had piqued her interest and been her downfall. Like it or not, she now found herself wondering what it would be like to have him make love to her.

And now that she could plainly see what had obviously been in the back of her mind for some time, it explained a lot of other things, like why she kept butting heads with him. She had been trying to find some weakness that would make her feel superior. Something to use as a barrier. She still couldn't get over how fast Clint had drawn his gun, or how he'd shot the whip in half without even taking an apparent aim. Thank heavens her hand had been away from her body! That had been one of the wars she'd lost, and she didn't care to think about the others.

Kate looked up at the sun. With it glaring down, plus the hot water, the heat had become overpowering. She dunked her head under the water, washing the damp hair back that was clinging to her face, then climbed out onto a large rock. As she twisted her hair to wring the water out, she wished there was someone she could talk to. It was all so complicated.

As soon as she was dry and dressed, Kate headed back to the homestead, her thoughts still on Clint. It seemed that because she now realized what had been motivating her actions, she couldn't get her mind off the tall, muscular man. She thought about the pleasure his kisses had given her, and the thrill that surged through her body when he'd placed his hand on her breast. And the more she thought about it, the more she wanted him.

At supper that night, Kate couldn't seem to take her eyes off Clint. It was as if she were seeing him for the first time. Her scrutiny included his full, chiseled lips that easily spread into a smile, his strong jawline, and the thick black hair combed back smoothly except at the back where it met his collar and turned upward. Even though he wore clothes, she had no trouble visualizing the naked, hard-muscled body she'd seen by accident just the night before.

By the time Kate reached her bedroom, she was in such a dither that sleep was impossible. Never had she felt this way about a man, which was frightening. She was used to being the one in control of a situation, not some man.

Kate tossed and turned on her bed all night, but by dawn she'd arrived at a decision. Seeing Clint day after day would continue to feed her imagination, so she was going to be done with it and ask him to make love to her. She wasn't at all pleased about asking him for anything, but she'd tried to think of other ways to approach the problem and hadn't come up with a single solution. It wasn't as if she'd had practice at this particular predicament. She'd never asked a man to make love to her. She had no idea how women approached such things, and she didn't know how to flirt. She'd always been open and straightforward. Subtleties were foreign to her. The way she saw it, she really didn't have a choice. She'd learned a long time ago that the best way to solve a problem was to get rid of it. Kate was sure that once again, the reality of the act of making love, even with someone as handsome as Clint, would get rid of this silly gnawing and she'd finally be able to concentrate on more important things. Pleased with her decision, Kate's eyes grew heavy, and she fell asleep.

Kate slept later than she had in years. Yet by the time she'd dressed, she felt as if she hadn't slept for a week. She still intended to ask Clint to make love to her, but in the light of day, she found she was dreading it. There was only one thing to do. Say it and get it over with.

Her first stop was Clint's bedroom. Hearing no reply to her knock, she opened the door. The room was empty. She took off in search of Mattie. Maybe she'd know where Clint was.

Kate found her stepmother in the sewing room. It wasn't a large room, but the windows offered plenty of sunlight and fresh air in the summer. A tall sewing table stood in one corner, with embroidery hoops lying on top. A sewing basket sat on the floor by one of the comfortable chairs. Mattie was busily stretching material over the sharp nails that surrounded the outer portion of the quilting frame standing in the middle of the room.

Since Mattie hadn't seen her come in, Kate took the opportunity to study the woman. She had never realized Mattie was so small. Mattie was one of the few truly sweet people God had placed on this earth. And though she could never bring herself to say how she felt, Kate loved her stepmother dearly. But over the last few years, Mattie seemed to continually harp about the way Kate dressed, and how she should act more like a lady. Kate had felt a decided strain in her relationship with her stepmother that was partially due to her. Kate knew it was nothing more than stubbornness on her part, and suddenly she felt guilty about it. After all, Mattie was only doing what she thought right.

"Mattie, do you know where Clint is?" Kate asked.

Mattie looked up. "Kate, I didn't hear you come in. Clint left early this morning. He said something about riding to Rawlins, and that he might not be back for a couple of days. Why do you ask?"

"I have to go into Whitfield and thought he might want to go along." She didn't like having to lie to Mattie.

"Are you feeling all right, dear?"

"Yes. Why do you ask?"

"Well, you're so late in rising, and you have

dark circles under your eyes as if you haven't had much sleep. You really should take better care of yourself, Kate.''

Kate gently ran her finger along the sharp nails that circled the large quilting frame and held the material in place, then jerked her hand away when one of them pricked her. ''Really, I'm fine. Why would Clint want to go to Rawlins?''

''I haven't the foggiest idea, and I didn't ask. Kate, I talked to Lucas this morning, and he said he was being sent to one of the line shacks, and that Sam was bound and determined to make him work till he dropped. Now don't smirk. It's not becoming on a lady.'' Mattie suddenly smiled. ''Come sit down and talk to me. We seldom have visits anymore.''

Mattie sat gracefully on a chair and motioned for Kate to take the one beside her. ''You know, Kate, I'm not so foolish an old woman that I don't know you and Sam keep things from me. I realize you think it's for my own good, but for once I'd like to know the truth about what's going on. I'm not as fragile as everyone seems to think. Lucas and Sam had another argument yesterday morning after that dead man was brought to the house, and I want to know what the argument was about.''

Kate pulled her hat off and ran her free hand around the crown. ''Mattie, maybe Sam's been right about Lucas.''

''How can you say that?'' Mattie gasped.

Kate started to cross her legs, then thought better of it, knowing Mattie would not approve. ''I don't mean necessarily in the past, I'm talking about now. Maybe it's you and I that have kept Lucas from growing up. We pamper him. We listen to his complaints and problems and try to do whatever we can to make things easier for him, even if it's just to lend an understanding ear. Sam says we are constantly making excuses for his lack of responsibility. He also says that Lucas deliberately plays on our sympathy, and that he's never been asked to do anything that isn't expected of every other man that works on this ranch. And I'm beginning to think Sam's right."

"I see." Mattie picked up a pillowcase she'd been working on, then pulled out the embroidery needle that was stuck in the material. "Does all this have to do with what happened yesterday morning?"

"Perhaps." There were more wrinkles on Mattie's face than Kate remembered. Maybe we have been too protective of Mattie, too, she thought. She proceeded to tell Mattie about the conversation that had taken place among Sam, Lucas and herself.

Mattie placed the pillowcase on her lap and considered what Kate had told her. "I can tell you believe Lucas was the one who slipped and told Brody about the cattle. Such a terrible thing. You're probably right, of course, though I'm sorry to have to say so." Mattie sighed. "When will it ever end?"

Kate patted Mattie's slender hand. "Hopefully it is ended. I do know one thing. After all that's happened, I'm sure Lucas has learned to keep his mouth shut."

Mattie smiled faintly. "Unfortunately, bitter lessons are the easiest ones to learn." She stood and went to the window. She looked out at the men busily moving about, some walking, some on horses and others standing; all attending to their work. "You're right of course, the time has come to make Lucas stand on his own two feet. Why couldn't he be more like Clint? He's such a fine, strong man."

"He'll be leaving in a few months," Kate said as she joined Mattie by the window.

"He told you that?"

"He said he was leaving the end of September."

"Such a short time."

Not short enough, Kate thought. "Let me help you stretch that material across the frame."

"Don't you have other things you should be doing?" Mattie didn't try to hide her pleasure at Kate's offer.

"Not immediately. Besides, it's too difficult for one person. You should have someone up here helping you."

Kate not only helped Mattie stretch the material, she also helped spread the cotton. Kate was surprised at how much she enjoyed the work. It made the afternoon pass quickly by.

But by supper that night, Clint still hadn't returned, nor was he there the next morning. Kate wanted to kick herself for not keeping Pedro by his side. At least she would have eventually found out what Clint was up to. He'd probably remained in Rawlins because he found some saloon girl to his liking.

Chapter 8

Having returned late from his three-day trip to Rawlins, Clint decided to spend the night at the line shack he'd located after his fight with Kate four days ago. It was in surprisingly good shape with a sturdy corral. Even the straw mattress was in better condition than some he'd slept on over the years.

After putting Midnight in the corral, Clint made his way through the thick growth of trees. The only sounds were the occasional churning of the old windmill at the side of the shack and the hooting of an owl. He stood on a flat boulder, looking down at the large house of the homestead below. Due to the lateness of the hour, there were no lights shining through the windows. Should he deem it necessary, this line shack was a perfect hiding place and would allow him to keep an eye on what was going on below. Especially since the old shack wasn't used anymore. It would also give him a place to change into his night riding clothes without drawing suspicion should someone at the house see him dressed in black.

After sleeping until noon the next day, Clint was well rested. Glancing around the dust-covered one-room shack, he decided to give it a good cleaning. When that was completed, he went outside to clear away the dead growth and weeds that almost blocked the entrance. It was nearing dusk by the time he decided to return to the house. His body was sticky from perspiration, but the day's labor had come as a relief. Sitting around, or wandering about the ranch talking to cowpokes, had been beginning to wear on his nerves.

His clean clothes already stashed in his saddle-bags, Clint mounted Midnight and headed down the bushy side of the mountain in the direction of the hot water pool to bathe. When he'd first located the line shack, he'd looked down at the scene below and saw the natural pool. He thought at the time that he would definitely take advantage of this natural hot spring as soon as he could.

Suddenly his stomach growled quite loudly, reminding him he hadn't eaten since yesterday afternoon. He nudged Midnight to a faster pace. He wasn't about to miss supper after going to the trouble to bathe.

The moment Kate entered the dining room, her gaze fastened on Clint. Well, it was about time he came back! And, as always when he came down to supper, he wore clean clothes and was freshly shaven. Kate had thought that after not seeing him for four days his appeal would have diminished. She should have known better.

Kate patiently watched as Clint seated Mattie at the table, then waited for him to come around and pull her chair out. But to her aggravation, he took his place beside Mattie. Kate was forced to seat herself.

As soon as grace was said, Sam peered at his nephew. "What kept you so long in Rawlins, boy?" the grizzled man asked in a gruff but friendly manner.

Clint placed the linen napkin in his lap and

grinned. "Sam, you know that's a question I can't answer in front of the ladies."

Sam smiled knowingly.

Clint didn't miss the flush that came to Kate's cheeks. "Anything happen while I was gone?"

"No, thank heavens," Mattie spoke up, wanting to move on to a different subject. "I pray we've seen the end of this rustling business." She took a deep breath. "Samuel, why isn't Lucas joining us for supper tonight? Surely you haven't sent him to some line shack for the next couple of months."

"No, madam, I haven't. Your son chose to spend the evening in town playing cards. At least that's what he told Henry."

Kate paid scant attention to Mattie's comment. She was too busy fighting the disgusting pang of jealousy that had balled up into a hard knot in the middle of her chest. Naturally Clint had visited the whorehouses in Rawlins, but the least he could have done was not mention it! Here she'd been waiting to tell him he could have her, and all this time he'd been off making love to another woman! No—probably not a woman, women! Well, she wasn't going to be one of them.

That was a lie. She wanted him more than she could fathom ever wanting any man, and the days when he'd been gone had seemed to pass with the speed of a tortoise. The least he could have done was let the family know he'd be having supper with them. She *might* have dressed a bit differently.

During supper, Clint glanced at Kate off and on, watching various expressions play across her smooth features. A raised eyebrow, a brief smirk, a half smile. She obviously had something on her mind but remained silent. She wore a simple gray dress that did nothing to compliment her beauty, and as usual, her hair was pulled tightly back into a chignon, which was only relieved by her full brows and large eyes. He knew she'd expected him to pull her chair out, but out of sheer orneriness he'd chosen not to. If she'd had the courtesy to at least say hello, he would probably have reacted differently. She was an enigma, and he was even more convinced that to bed her would be equivalent to playing with fire—the problem was, he *liked* playing with fire. The thought of feeling Kate naked beneath him seemed well worth getting singed. He tried reminding himself to keep his mind on his assignment and shove all else to the back of his head. But that really wasn't what was gnawing at him; it was his male pride he was having trouble with.

He'd never known a woman who hadn't found at least something attractive about him. That is, until he met Kate. Admittedly he hadn't been his most charming around her, but she'd never given him much of a chance to act the gentleman. Kate looked up, catching him staring at her, and he smiled. To his dismay, she smiled back. There was a look in those beautiful green eyes he'd never seen there before. Were it coming from anyone other than Kate, he'd have called it passion.

When supper was over, Clint went with Sam to his office to enjoy a drink, a cigar, and some conversation. Clint managed to get away before too long, and went out on the wide front porch to sit and enjoy the cool night air. He hadn't been there five minutes when Kate joined him.

"This is a pleasant surprise," he said quietly, not bothering to stand.

Kate braced her back against the porch post and faced him. He looked relaxed, but he was sitting in the night shadows and she couldn't get a good look at his face. "I wanted to talk to you."

"Oh? What could you possibly want to talk to

me about? Whips, guns, cattle, or maybe sloughs?''

Kate's hands started shaking. ''I think we should bed together.'' She waited for him to make some kind of reply, but there was only dead silence. ''Well? It isn't as if you haven't shown interest.''

Clint could never remember being quite so dumbfounded. Ever since he'd arrived, she'd remained untouchable. Now, out of the clear blue, she wanted to sleep with him? Although he was more than willing to accommodate her, he was having a hard time believing it wasn't some kind of a trick. Despite the look he'd seen in her eyes at supper, there wasn't even a hint of passion in her words now. She might as well have asked if he wanted a cup of coffee. Was she serious, or just trying to get him to say yes so she could have a big laugh? ''I like Sam,'' he said slowly, cautiously, ''and I'm not sure it would be right to take his daughter's maidenhood.''

''Well then, you have nothing to be concerned about,'' she stated matter-of-factly. ''I'm not a virgin.''

Clint was startled by her bold statement. At first he didn't believe her, but there was enough light coming from the house for him to see her small chin raised in proud defiance, while her lovely face showed no emotion whatsoever. Not that it really made any difference. He much preferred an experienced woman. He tilted the chair back on its rear legs, still suspicious. ''Why are you so interested all of a sudden?''

''I find you attractive, so why mince words?'' Kate was finding the conversation more difficult than she had anticipated. She didn't like having to state what it was about him that attracted her, and though she'd managed not to show it, it hadn't been easy to admit to her lack of purity.

Why did he keep asking questions instead of just agreeing? "You have certainly given me the impression that you have similar feelings." She turned and plucked a tree rose to hide her nervousness, then raised it to her nose to inhale the flower's sweet odor.

Clint was becoming more than a little piqued over her attitude. He set the chair back down with a bang. "What happened to our agreement to stay out of each other's way?" he asked, needing time to think about what the hell was going on.

"Why are you beating around the bush? Either you're interested or you're not. So what's it going to be?"

Under normal circumstances, he would have taken her up on her offer without a moment's hesitation—if one could call it an offer at all. Actually it sounded more like a business transaction. Because there was not even a hint of feeling in her offer, he wondered if he'd end up with an ice maiden sharing his bed? Maybe she wasn't a virgin, but he'd wager his life's income she'd never experienced true sexual satisfaction. She didn't know how to flirt or to gaze at him with that special look that told a man the woman was willing. Yet she had to be feeling some kind of desire for him or she'd never have made the offer in the first place. But dammit, he didn't like her cold proposition one damn bit. Maybe it had to do with her always trying to act like a man and issuing orders. "I don't think so," he finally said.

There was a moment's pause before Kate asked, "Why?"

Clint stood and walked over to her, his anger continuing to grow. Taking her face in his big hands, he slowly ran his thumb across her desirable lips. "You're very beautiful." He leaned down and gently pressed his lips to hers, letting them linger for a long moment before pulling away. "But I don't like a woman who thinks she's a man." He stepped away, but not fast enough to avoid the hard slap to his jaw.

"How dare you tell me whores are better than I am," Kate accused before returning to the house.

It took a moment before Clint realized what she was talking about. He had been kidding at dinner, but maybe he *should* have paid the ladies of the evening in Rawlins a visit as Kate envisioned. Celibacy was just not in his nature.

Clint returned to the chair he'd been sitting on. He had no business fooling with trouble, and Miss Whitfield had been trouble ever since he arrived at the ranch. Morality certainly had nothing to do with it. In his line of work he'd long since learned that morality was nothing more than a word. From the first day he'd arrived, he and Kate had been in a battle of wills. Kate was bound and determined to prove she had the upper hand, and he was just as determined to prove her wrong. Her asking him to bed her was just a continuance of the same thing, and he still didn't like it one damn bit.

Kate could hardly see straight by the time she slammed her bedroom door shut. How dare the man turn her down! She'd been so sure. . . . Maybe he prefers *men*, she thought viciously as she yanked off her dress, causing the small pearl buttons to pop off and fall to the floor. But she didn't really believe that. Not when she could still feel the warmth of his lips pressed against hers.

After removing her two petticoats she turned off the oil lamp and plopped down on the large four-poster bed. She was so humiliated. How could she look Clint in the face again, knowing he was laughing at her weakness? Never, never

would she make such a fool of herself again, and
certainly not over some worthless man!

As the days passed, Kate did everything in her
power to avoid Clint. She ate most of her meals
at the cook shack, stayed out on the range,
worked around the ranch, or remained in her
room. When she did see him, he was talking to
cowpokes or riding out toward town. He acted as
if nothing had happened, which should have
made her happy. Instead it made her angrier with
each passing day. She couldn't stop thinking
about him refusing her favors, couldn't forget that
he preferred whores and that on more than one
occasion he'd called her a she-man! She was obsessed with getting even. She wanted him to feel
even smaller than he'd made her feel.

Kate met with Henry every morning for a report
on what was happening around the ranch, and
often Sam and even Lucas would join them. With
Lucas by her side, she checked the tannery, the
smokehouse, the storage bins, and anything else
that needed looking into during this lax time of
the year. But she still managed to plan.

Two weeks later, Kate knew exactly how she
was going to make Clint regret he had turned
down her offer. Since he didn't consider her much
of a woman, she was going to prove him wrong.
She'd become so feminine and desirable he
wouldn't be able to sit because of his swollen desire for her. A trip to Rawlins with Mattie would
take care of the clothes, and then a visit with her
old friend, Star Hupple, would put the finishing
touches to her plan. One way or another, she'd
have Clint chasing after her like a cur dog with
his tongue dragging the ground. Then, when his
passion was high and he could hardly wait to bed
her, she'd laugh and tell him *she* was no longer

interested. She could hardly wait to see *his* reaction.

The full moon was already rising by the time Clint arrived at the horse barn for his nightly ride, hoping against hope to find anything that might offer some information toward solving the switching of the reservation cattle. Only by traveling at night could he avoid being seen, and he certainly couldn't afford to make Kate suspicious of him again. He smiled. Since their talk on the porch a couple of weeks ago, she had been avoiding him like the plague, and doing a damn good job of it.

Kate was bone tired as she headed for home. She hadn't planned on returning so late. She'd spent the afternoon watching a couple of hands removing the fence around the nearly dried-up slough, and just when she was ready to head back, a mountain lion had been spotted. She and one of the hands had ridden after him, but weren't able to get a clear shot. When it turned dark, they gave up the chase. At least she had the satisfaction of knowing they'd run the big cat away. But Kate knew she wasn't sorry he'd escaped. She'd never liked the idea of shooting one of those big cats.

Because of her late start, she was now looking at still another five miles before she could finally eat and go to bed. Feeling chilled from the brisk breeze that had kicked up, she reached behind the saddle and untied the leather saddle straps holding her jacket. At least there's a full moon to help me see where I'm going, Kate thought as she pulled her jacket on.

White Cloud snorted and began dancing to the side. As they crested one of the sloping hills, Kate grinned upon seeing what was making him skittish. Just ahead she could make out a double-striped skunk with its young following behind in single file. Like White Cloud, Kate was perfectly willing to give the family all the space it needed. She reined White Cloud to the left just as a shot rang out. Kate heard the thud of another bullet hitting the ground as she sank her heels in the stallion's sides.

White Cloud raced forward; Kate hugged his powerful neck. Another shot rang out, the bullet whining past her ear. She had no idea which direction the shots were coming from, and she was well aware that the white stallion made for an easy target in the moonlight. If she could only make it to the dark stand of trees ahead, she might be safe. "Come on, boy," she urged her horse. "You can do it."

The land flattened out. Another shot. Kate felt White Cloud stumble, but he remained on his feet and quickly regained his full stride. The trees were getting closer . . . closer.

It seemed to take forever before White Cloud finally galloped into the merciful shelter of the bushy thicket of pine trees. Their height and widespread limbs blocked out what light the moon had to offer, and Kate slowed the stallion. As they moved deeper into the trees, she could hardly make out what was in front of her. Deciding she was momentarily safe, she brought White Cloud to a halt, snatched her rifle from the scabbard, and leaped to the ground. "Sorry, boy," she whispered before giving him a hard whack on the rump. As the horse galloped away, Kate quickly scooted beneath a tree, dragging the rifle with her. Hopefully, whoever had been doing the shooting would continue following White Cloud. If not, she was armed.

Having heard the shots, Clint was already headed in that direction. He pulled up on the reins when he saw Kate ride into the trees. Smart girl, he thought.

A moment later White Cloud raced out the far end of the trees and Clint was finally able to catch sight of the man doing the shooting. He was mounted, and in hard pursuit of the stallion. They were both headed directly toward Clint, but his black clothes and black horse kept the other rider from seeing him. From where Clint waited, he could clearly see that Kate was not on the stallion's back. He lifted his rifle and took aim. A wild turkey suddenly blew up in the air, causing White Cloud to turn sharply to the right. The man fired again. White Cloud's front legs buckled and he plummeted to the ground. Clint pulled the trigger a minute too late to save the horse, but he hit the man, knocking him out of the saddle. Clint waited, rifle still aimed, but the man didn't move. Clint nudged Midnight forward.

After checking to be sure the man was dead, Clint walked over to White Cloud. The big horse was down, his sides heaving, his breathing wheezy and heavy. He raised his powerful head, then let it drop back to the ground. Clint reached for his revolver. He couldn't let the horse suffer anymore.

Kate remained dead still, hardly daring to breathe. It seemed an eternity since she'd heard the last shots being fired. They'd been farther away, and it appeared she had managed to elude her hunter. On the other hand, he could be searching for her. If he found out she wasn't riding White Cloud, he'd know she was in the trees, and armed. Would he be coming after her?

Kate waited . . . listening. She had no intention of moving until daylight. Slowly, carefully, she pulled the revolver from her holster, wondering why she hadn't done so sooner. As she rested it on her lap she was surprised that her hands were shaking. Why would someone want to kill her? Unless she caught the culprit, she'd probably never know. One of the rustlers? She was guessing.

"You're safe now. Go home."

Kate froze. Though the words were little more than a whisper, they sounded close. Carefully she raised her revolver. Was the gunman playing with her? For what purpose? He probably wasn't sure where she was hiding and was hoping she'd answer. She didn't move a muscle.

"Go home, Kate," the voice again whispered. "There's a horse waiting for you. Go home."

A shiver started at the base of Kate's spine and worked its way up. The voice seemed to be moving from tree to tree. Kate snapped her head to the left, just in time to see a dark figure silently disappear behind a tree. It was too late to get a shot at him. Next time he spoke, she'd shoot, and think later. She pointed her revolver straight ahead and waited. Realizing her breath was coming in gasps, she clamped her lips shut. It only served to make breathing more difficult. Her gaze darted from one shadow to another, searching for any possible movement. Then, to her relief, she heard a horse galloping away.

Kate remained with her back glued to the tree, not sure what she should do. What if there was more than one person? How could anyone walk so silently among trees in the dead of night? Was she hallucinating? Was the shadowy ghost telling her the truth, or was it a trap? Kate shook her head. What was she thinking? There were no such things as ghosts! She was just letting her mind run away with itself. It had to have been a real man. Now the question was; did he want to help her or kill her?

Carefully Kate inched from beneath the tree,

then listened. Nothing. She stood, her cramped muscles causing her to wince. It occurred to her that the man had known exactly where she was. It was a big stand of trees, yet he'd been able to make sure she'd heard him. And that also meant he could have shot her at any time. But he hadn't. Nevertheless, she refused to leave the shelter of the trees. She'd change hiding places and wait until morning as she'd originally planned. In choosing another place to hide, Kate made sure she had plenty of room to stretch her legs.

It wasn't until she was settled again that Kate realized the man had said "a horse" was waiting, not *her* horse. Her heart leaped into her throat. She prayed nothing had happened to White Cloud.

It was her tenth birthday. Sam was gleaming all over when he'd taken her to the back of the house and told her to cover her eyes. "Can you see?" he'd asked. "No," she'd replied anxiously, her hands making everything dark. He took her arm and led her to the side of the house. "Okay," he said, bringing her to a stop, "you can look now." A cowhand stood in front of her holding the end of a rope. The other end was circled around the neck of the most beautiful white colt her young eyes had ever seen. "It's yours," Sam had said. She had giggled excitedly. "He's so beautiful. Just like a white cloud!"

Kate couldn't remember ever having had a more wonderful birthday. She'd never owned a horse of her own until then. She and the colt grew up together. She'd talked to White Cloud constantly, telling him her troubles and woes, convinced he understood every word she said. He was her friend.

A tear trickled down Kate's cheek. She hoped her horse was safe.

As soon as it was light, Kate cautiously walked

out into the clearing, her rifle in readiness. After having been cloistered by the trees, the valley seemed open and huge, and she felt vulnerable. Shrugging her shoulders in an attempt to ward off the ominous feeling that seemed to be riding on her back, she looked in every direction, but there was no one in sight. So far, the man had been right. She took off walking, fearing he had also told the truth about other things.

Kate spotted the buzzards first, then the white mound up ahead. Her pace slowed, but she forced herself to continue on. When she drew near, she began screaming and shooting to chase the buzzards away. Several just hopped off to the side, remaining close enough to be the first to reclaim the meal. By the time she reached White Cloud's side, tears were streaming down her face. Bile rose in her throat at seeing his tongue hanging out the side of his mouth. He'd been shot in the side and flank, then again between the eyes. Someone had been kind enough to put the big horse out of his misery. Flies were greedily buzzing around and she wanted to kill them, just like she wanted to kill the buzzards to keep them from feasting.

Unable to look anymore, she lifted her head and took off walking, not bothering to wipe away the tears that continued to flow. She didn't look back.

A short distance away stood another horse, saddled and tied to a bush. Nearby a man's body lay sprawled on the ground. He too had already been mangled by carnivorous beasts, and Kate couldn't bear to look long enough to see if she recognized him.

Kate mounted the piebald horse with a Whitfield brand and continued on, shutting down her emotions. She didn't want to think about White Cloud or anything else that had happened. Maybe later when her feelings weren't so raw.

Clint remained hidden by the trees until Kate was well out of sight. Last night he'd ridden off, but when Kate didn't come out of hiding, he'd silently circled back. He felt her pain, and had to steel himself to keep from letting it affect him. He'd already done all he could to help her, and he didn't want her asking questions as to why he was in the area. He had to admit the lady knew how to take care of herself. Though she was a continual thorn in his backside, his respect for Kate continued to grow.

Tired, her body nothing but dead weight, Kate rode to the men who were stacking hay in the barn.

"Lucas," Kate called as she dismounted.

Lucas tossed the pitchfork and ran over to Kate's side. Her face was streaked with dirt and tears, her shirt ripped at the shoulder. "What happened?" he asked worriedly. "Where's White Cloud?"

"He's dead. Do you know who rides this horse?" Kate handed the reins over.

"No."

"Well, see that someone cools him down. Find Henry and tell him there's a dead man about five miles south. Have him look for White Cloud, and he'll find the man. I'm going to the house." Lucas nodded and Kate was grateful that for once he accepted her order without an argument.

Kate entered the house through the back door and went up the stairs leading from the kitchen. She didn't want to see Sam and spend the next hour or so explaining what had happened. All she wanted was sleep.

It was late afternoon by the time Kate had awakened and dressed. Alma was walking down the hall when Kate left her room.

"Your pa is waiting to see you."

Kate sighed. "All right, Alma, I'll go to his office."

"He's not there. He's in the parlor."

"Very well."

The first thing Kate noticed when she entered the parlor was the reek of cigar smoke, something Mattie would never allow under normal circumstances.

"I take it you're all right?" Sam barked out in his gravelly voice.

Kate was surprised to see Lucas and Clint there. The men were seated about, each holding a glass of whiskey and a cigar. From the solemn looks on their faces, Kate knew they had been discussing her. "May I ask what this gathering is all about?"

"We're trying to figure out why you shot that man. Now, would it be too much trouble to tell me what happened?"

Kate looked at her father. "I don't know what happened," Kate stated simply. "All I know is that someone was shooting at me. Later I found a dead cowpoke I didn't recognize."

"Found?" Lucas dropped the half-smoked cigar into the spittoon sitting on the floor by his chair. "You mean you didn't kill him?"

"No, I didn't." Kate dreaded the next question.

"Who did?" Sam roared.

"I don't know," Kate said as she sat down. "I was on my way back to the ranch when shots were fired. I made it to a stand of trees, jumped off of White—" Her throat constricted.

"We gotta ask you questions, girl," Sam said kindly. "It's the only way we can get to the bottom of this."

"I know. What I don't know is why Lucas is here, and I certainly don't think this is any of Clint's business."

"Now don't go getting riled. Lucas and Clint are family."

Kate didn't bother looking in Clint's direction. More and more she was resenting the influence he seemed to be having on her father. But Sam wanted him there, and she could tell by that set look on his craggy face that he wasn't going to have Clint leave. "I sent White Cloud on," she continued. "I was hoping that the man doing the shooting would follow him. After that, I heard some more shots, then nothing. I didn't see anything because I was in the trees."

Sam slapped his hand on the arm of his wheelchair. "Damned if this doesn't beat all. Who the hell would want you dead? Maybe one of those goddamn rustlers." He rubbed his chin in thought. "And who shot the man? No one at the ranch seems to know anything about it." He looked back at Kate. "The dead man has been identified. He's one of the new men Henry hired. Said the man claimed he'd come up from Texas." He shook his head. "None of this makes any sense."

Lucas took a long drink of whiskey. "Considering what happened, Kate, I'd suggest you stay around the house for a while."

"Why? So you can take over?"

Lucas curled his lip. "I understand that bit about some mysterious Injun riding around the ranch came from you also. Something else you conjured up in your head?"

Kate rose to her feet and looked menacingly at her brother. "And just what do you mean by that, Lucas?"

"First it's Injuns, and now you're saying some ghost came out of nowhere and killed the bad man? Sounds pretty farfetched to me. I think there's somethin' you're not telling us."

Mattie came into the room, and Alma trailed

right behind carrying a silver tray with coffee and china cups.

"Since there's obviously nothing wrong with Kate," Lucas said to his father, "I'll pick the new doc up at the railroad station like you ordered. And I'll watch for any ghosts, Kate." He was laughing as he left the parlor.

"Doctor?" Kate asked.

"Dr. Oliver Putnam," Sam replied. "I received a telegram this morning that he'll be arriving this afternoon."

"Just what I need."

Clint had sat quietly watching and listening. He was surprised that Sam hadn't asked more questions. He could personally think of at least a dozen, but he already knew most of the answers. He accepted a cup of coffee from Alma, handing her his empty glass in return. After what Lucas had said, he could understand why Kate hadn't mentioned that someone told her she was safe. But there was also a different sort of angriness about her that was hard to pinpoint. Her full lips had a pinched quality to them. Was it because of Lucas, White Cloud, or both? He spoke up. "I'm curious. When did all this take place?"

Kate ignored him.

"Well?" Sam asked.

"Around nine last night."

Clint took a hard look at Kate, suddenly noticing the way her slender hands remained tightly clasped, the stiffness in her back, the tiny, occasional twitch of her right eyebrow. Could it be Kate who was switching the cattle after all? "And you were five miles from the house? What had you been doing?"

"Sam, I'm not going to sit here and have Clint asking me questions. I'll talk to you when we can be alone."

With each tick of the clock, Clint's curiosity

grew. Was she hiding something? "I admit it's none of my business, but I'm inclined to agree with Lucas. After what happened, it seems to me you ought to stay close to the house."

Kate finally looked at him. "There are certain things I need to take care of," she said sharply. "Perhaps you'd like to go to town for me and pick up some more plaster of paris."

Clint grinned. It would seem they had come full circle. She was back to calling him a rat again.

Sam cleared his throat. "I don't want you riding away from the homestead for a while, Kate, not until we get this matter settled as to who's after you."

Kate's anger flared. How could Sam take Lucas's and Clint's side against her? "That could take forever. And what if we never find out?"

"Your father is absolutely right, dear," Mattie chimed in.

Kate had forgotten Mattie was even in the room. Kate stood, her fists clenched. "Don't do this, Sam. When you were my age would you have let someone taking a shot at you prevent you from going about your business?"

Sam looked fondly at his daughter. "No, don't reckon I would."

"Well, I'm not either. It isn't fair to make me stay here just because I'm a woman."

Sam nodded his agreement.

"Don't worry, Sam," Kate said in a kinder tone of voice. "I'll watch my behind."

Prior to going in to supper that night, Sam introduced everyone to Oliver Putnam.

Lucas liked the doctor because he dressed in city clothes and apparently had little knowledge of the West. Therefore he wasn't intimidating like Clint.

Mattie thought that, even at thirty-two, he

looked much too young to be a doctor. But she liked his friendly, easygoing manner. He wasn't the least bit uncomfortable around the family.

Kate considered him quite good-looking, with his brown curly hair and straight nose. She even drew pleasure at the way his brown eyes had appraised her. There was no doubt that he was pleased at what he saw.

Clint didn't like him one damn bit. He had seen the way the doctor's eyes had lit up when he was introduced to Kate. Putnam was obviously shocked at seeing Kate dressed in men's clothing, but he recovered quickly. Nor did Clint like the way Kate had returned the good doctor's smile.

During supper, Clint remained silent while everyone else asked Oliver questions about his past and what Boston was like. Dr. Putnam seemed quite happy at being the center of attention.

Chapter 9

M attie sat quietly on the porch, enjoying the warm day but feeling like a useless old woman. She was still heartsick over what had happened to Kate two days ago, but no one paid attention to what she felt or thought. Early this morning, Lucas had driven Oliver to town to show him old Dr. Sawyer's office and see if it was satisfactory for Oliver's new practice.

Poor Lucas should never have informed outsiders about the cattle, or family problems. A shiver ran through her from just thinking that, had things turned out differently, at this very moment she could be sitting on this porch, Kate shot, and Lucas hung.

Mattie's thoughts softened, remembering how she had enjoyed the day with Kate working on the quilt. Dear Kate. Since Clint's return from Rawlins, Mattie had hardly seen her, and when she did, the girl always seemed angry about something.

Mattie clicked her tongue. Clint was avoiding her also. She new it was because he didn't want to talk about Kate. Or maybe he just didn't like being reminded that the girl paid him little or no attention. No, she doubted that he'd be suffering from hurt pride, because he didn't seem to like Kate any more than Kate liked him. It was all so aggravating, and it was crazy now to hope they would get together. She was old enough to know people couldn't be forced into loving each other, especially two souls as strong willed as Clint and Kate. But oh, what a handsome couple they would have made, and their children would have been so beautiful. Well, she thought tiredly, it just wasn't meant to be. Maybe Kate would marry Oliver Putnam. He was certainly a fine prospect, and Kate seemed to like him. It wasn't how Mattie had wanted things to turn out, but there was little she could do about it. Still, Clint would have made Kate a far better husband.

"Mattie, would you care for some company?"

Mattie looked up at Kate, standing only a few feet away. "Of course, my dear," she answered, pleased to have someone to talk to.

"I've decided to purchase some new dresses, and I thought you might like to help me select them."

Shocked, Mattie dropped her lace handkerchief onto the porch floor. To hide her reaction, she leaned over and picked it up, wondering what on earth Kate was up to now. Was Oliver's arrival the reason behind such a drastic decision?

Kate felt ridiculous at having brought up the subject, especially after years of absolutely refusing to dress in the latest fashions, or even caring about what other women wore. She shifted her weight to her left foot and rested a hand on the butt of her gun. "You've been after me for years to dress and act more ladylike, so I thought, what with everyone thinking I'm going to get killed if I ride out on the range, maybe we could spend a week in Rawlins and get me properly outfitted."

"Yes," Mattie replied, still in shock. "I think that would be a splendid idea."

"How about we plan on leaving in two days?

It's a long ride by buggy, so we'd have to start early.''

''That would be wonderful,'' said Mattie excitedly. ''It seems like an eternity since I've been on a trip. You'll be sure there are men traveling with us?''

''Yes. I wouldn't ask you to do anything dangerous.'' Kate shifted to her right foot. ''Aren't you going to ask why I'm doing this?''

Mattie grinned. ''No, it would be a wasted question. You never have told me anything until you were ready.''

Kate returned Mattie's smile. Her stepmother always had a way of making her feel relaxed, and sometimes even pleasurably childish again. ''I'd rather no one knew what we're up to. It'll be a surprise.''

''I think that's a grand idea. I'll just say I need to pick up a few things.''

As soon as Kate had left, Mattie suddenly felt years younger. She clapped her hands together and smothered a giggle. By golly, she felt sure Clint had something to do with this. He hadn't forgotten her request to make Kate into a lady.

After talking to Mattie, Kate decided to ride into Whitfield. She didn't tell anyone where she was going because after what had happened, Sam might insist someone ride along with her.

Just in case anyone *was* lurking about who might want her dead, Kate traveled among the trees as often as possible, keeping her eyes open for any signs of trouble. Seeing a stand of pine trees brought to mind the man who had saved her life. She'd thought he would have made himself known by now. For the life of her, she couldn't understand why he wanted to keep his identity a secret. He must be one of the new hands on the ranch. Whoever he was, he was obviously a man who knew how to take care of himself, and she'd looked forward to meeting him, if for no other reason than to express her thanks.

Kate stood up in the stirrups to take a better look around. Seeing nothing, she settled back into the saddle. A thought suddenly occurred to her. The two men might have been riding together. Actually, they could have been two of the rustlers. The dead man may have taken a job at the ranch just to get information about the herd that was fixing to be assembled. And what if the second rider hadn't gone along with killing a woman, they'd gotten into a fight, and the second man ended up shooting the first one? It all made sense, and explained exactly why the other man hadn't come forth. And if she'd put everything together correctly, her life was probably no longer in danger. Kate felt considerably better, but she still kept a close eye out for trouble. She'd tell Sam her theory when she returned to the ranch.

As Kate rode down the main street of Whitfield, she saw the usual group of old men sitting on chairs in front of the mercantile store, smoking their pipes and basking in the sun. Max Freiker was sweeping out the barbershop, and Kate returned his wave.

Kate brought her horse to a halt at the Hupple boardinghouse, situated on the outskirts of town. Instead of dismounting, she sat staring at the big two-story house. She still wanted to get even with Clint, and admittedly there were a few minor problems, the biggest one being how to go about it. She'd decided to talk it over with Star Hupple, but Kate could already feel doubts building. Though settled and older now, Star had been one of the first prostitutes in the area years ago. When the idea of seeking Star's help had first entered Kate's head she hadn't given it much thought. Now she grimaced, realizing she might not have thought this through as well as she should have. Even though she and Star had been friends a long time, Kate didn't know how she was going to broach the subject of why she was here. Was she going to say, "Howdy, Star, I came to find out how I can get a man to climb into my britches?" Not likely. Besides, no one in town would ever suspect her of even having such thoughts, including Star.

Deciding this whole thing was a bad idea, Kate was about to turn her horse around when she heard, "Kate! Are you going to just sit there, or are you coming in?"

Kate hesitated. Star stood in the doorway, holding the screen open. Kate judged the older woman to be somewhere in her late forties or early fifties by now, but there wasn't a line on her face. Star still used henna, making her hair a brassy red, but it was smoothly brushed back, with a ribbon tied around it. Her calico dress was well starched and proper, and her face mirrored her pleasure at having Kate pay her a visit. Kate smiled. Maybe Star was a little coarse, but her heart was as big as her ample waist. "Are you busy?" Kate called as she slid from the saddle.

"Never too busy to visit with a good friend."

Kate opened the wooden gate and followed the stone path. As she entered the house, Star wrapped a beefy arm around her shoulders.

"I've got a lemon pie that should be just right for cuttin'. So you sit right here in the parlor and I'll fetch you a piece."

"I can go into the kitchen," Kate offered.

"Why, I wouldn't hear of it. Nice folks like you should be entertained in the parlor."

Star hurried off to the kitchen, and Kate sat on one of the wooden chairs. The high-stuffed brocade sofa and chair were too uncomfortable. She glanced around the immaculately kept room, doubting that a speck of dust could be found anywhere. The large rug was worn, but still of good use, and the hardwood floors were polished to a luster. She knew the rest of the house was just as clean. In all the years she'd known Star, the house had never looked any different. Kate had often wondered if Sam had purchased the boardinghouse for Star, because as she grew older, Kate had come to realize that prostitutes earned very little money. But she'd never asked. It really wasn't any of her business.

Kate's mind drifted back in time to before Sam married Mattie. Star had spent a lot of time at the ranch, and Kate had thought she was going to be her new mother. Being older now, she knew that Sam would never have married a prostitute, even one as nice and kind as Star. In later years, Star married Cornelius Hupple, who died five years ago after being bitten by a mad dog.

Kate was reminded of the first time she'd met Mattie. Sam had been gone for a month to purchase cattle. When he returned, he'd brought Mattie with him, introducing her as his new wife and Kate's stepmother. At first Kate had resented Mattie's presence. She had wanted her father to marry the fun-loving Star, who at the time was slender and the prettiest woman Kate had ever known. But Mattie was even prettier, and soon her kind, gentle, soft-spoken manner had drawn Kate's love. Kate and Star had remained friends over the years, but with the ranch taking up most of her time now, she no longer visited Star as much as she used to.

"Here you go, honey," Star said as she entered the room. "Maybe this will put some meat on your bones. You're always too thin to my way of thinkin'."

The delicious-looking slice of pie covered practically the entire saucer, and Kate quickly cut herself a bite. As she ate, she watched Star shifting about on the high-stuffed chair until she was comfortable. The sight made Kate think of two boulders balanced atop each other.

"I heard you lost White Cloud," Star said sadly. "I'm so sorry. I know how much that horse meant to you."

Kate nodded and set the unfinished pie on the narrow table next to the wall. She still didn't want to talk about the horse.

"How are Mrs. Whitfield and Sam doing?"

"Oh, they're fine." Kate cleared her throat. Because of her reason for coming here, her embarrassment was growing by leaps and bounds. But after having come this far, and knowing she needed Star's help, she had to go ahead and spit out what was on her mind. "I have a favor to ask, Star."

"Of course, honey. What is it?"

Kate took a deep breath. "I want you to teach me how to seduce a man."

Star smiled knowingly. "Though none of your family would probably agree with me, you're certainly old enough to have them kind of feelings, but maybe you need to give it a little thought before you go jumping into the water."

"I only want the two of us to know about this," Kate added. "There's a man who thinks I'm not good enough for him, and I want to change his mind."

"How could anyone think that? You're not only beautiful, you're a mighty wealthy woman. The man has to be either snow-blind or addle-brained!"

"He says he likes his women more feminine."

Star shook her head. "He's feeding you a crock of . . . sorghum. He probably just wants to make you feel insecure so when he tries to get you in his bed, you'll go willingly."

Kate squirmed, not sure how to put into words what she wanted to say.

"I've seen Mrs. Whitfield's nephew in town." Star saw the anger that leaped into Kate's green eyes. "In fact, I saw him the first day he arrived in town and caused Lucas to get bucked off his horse. I know you won't agree with me, but it made me feel right good to see someone put your brother in his place. Of course I didn't know who the stranger was at the time. I tell you, there's a man that would make any woman wonder. I'm not so old that thoughts didn't enter my mind."

"Don't waste your thoughts on him, Star. He's not worth it."

"And he's the reason you're here. Am I right?"

"I want to pay him back for the insult he gave me," Kate said through clenched teeth.

"Because he said you aren't feminine enough for him? Why let that bother you?"

"You don't understand. Are you going to help me or not?"

"Just what is it you want me to do?"

"I want him to find me irresistible, and I'm not sure how to—"

"You're not making any sense. You act like you don't like him yet you want to be irresistible? I don't understand. Do you want him to fall in love with you, share your bed, or both?"

Kate leaned forward, resting her elbows on her legs. "I want him to want me in his bed so bad that he can't eat, sleep or drink for thinking about it. I want the pleasure of hearing him beg me, then telling him I wouldn't go to bed with him even if it meant I'd die tomorrow. I want him to know the humiliation—"

"Kate, did you ask him to take you to his bed?"

"Yes, dammit!" Kate jumped to her feet. "And he turned me down, saying I wasn't woman enough for him. Yet he certainly didn't have any problem going to Rawlins for a couple of days and sleeping with . . ."

"It doesn't bother me to hear the word *whore*, Kate."

"Well, anyway, I'm going to prove him wrong. I'm going to Rawlins and buy clothes, and I'm going to be the most feminine woman he's ever met. Then I'm going to tease and taunt until he can't walk straight for the bulge in his pants. That's the part I want you to teach me. Star, you have to do this. It's important to me."

"When are you going to Rawlins?"

"Monday."

After several grunts, Star pulled herself off the chair. "Then you come see me when you get back, and I'll give you my answer. Besides, you might change your mind by then."

"Why can't you give me an answer now?"

Star placed her arm around Kate's waist and escorted her to the door. "Because, honey, I need time to think about this. I don't want to do anything you or I will regret, and I don't want Sam getting mad at me." She opened the screen door.

"I won't tell him. If you won't teach me, Star, I'll pay someone to do it. One way or another, I'm going to make Clint Morgan regret what he did." Or didn't do, she thought.

Star smiled kindly. "I'll be waiting until you get back," she repeated.

Star remained in the doorway until Kate rode off. Slowly she walked back into the parlor, poured herself a glass of whiskey, and sat down. Having known so many men over the years, it was clear that something was all wrong. No man in his right mind would refuse a beautiful woman like Kate. She also knew that Kate's reaction didn't make sense. The girl had every right to resent the insult, but why didn't she just turn away and be done with him? Why was she so bound and determined to get even? Star let out a snort, well aware of the other men Kate had turned her nose up at. Yet Kate was still naive enough not to take into consideration the possible repercussions of what she was planning. There were a good many men around that would think nothing of forcing themselves on her if she pulled such a stunt on them. But because of what she'd heard in town about Clint Morgan, and considering how he seemed to be deliberately manipulating Kate, Star had a feeling that Morgan wasn't that type of man. And if Kate got all gussied up and lady-like, wouldn't she be doing exactly what Morgan wanted?

Star took a sip of her drink. Though no one knew it, she'd always thought of Kate as a daughter. The happiest times in her life had been when she, Kate, and Sam were together. She'd loved her husband, Cornelius, in her own way, but nothing like she'd loved Sam Whitfield. She still loved him. However, Sam hadn't married Mattie just because of her beauty. He'd fallen hopelessly in love with the lady. But even after he'd married, Sam still came by to see that Star was getting along all right. He'd even become friends with Cornelius. A soft sigh escaped her lips, just thinking how long it had been since she'd seen Sam. Not since his accident. She'd wanted so bad to go to the ranch and nurse him back to health, but she couldn't, nor would she have been welcomed. But she had kept in touch with Kate, and through her and others she heard how Sam was doing.

Star smiled. Few other people knew as much about Kate as she did. Cowhands tended to talk and brag a lot when they bedded a prostitute. And though smart ladies of the night didn't carry tales, they did talk among themselves. Since Star had continued to keep in contact with Violet, one

of the older women working as a card dealer at
the Hoof and Horn Saloon here in Whitfield, she
was well aware that Kate could no longer claim
to be a virgin. So it wasn't as if the girl was experiencing the first signs of desire. It was Violet
who had delivered the message to Clint Morgan
the first night he was in town. Having seen the
man naked in his room, Violet had gushed with
the news that Mr. Morgan was not only handsome and had a beautifully muscled body, he was
extremely well endowed. So Star could assume
the man didn't have a problem in that way. Also,
Kate wouldn't have asked him to her bed if he
hadn't made her think he was interested. Another thing to consider was that over the years
Sam had done everything in his power to keep
men away from his daughter. Star had never
agreed with that decision, even if it really wasn't
any of her business.

Star finished off her drink. A most complex situation, she thought as she stood. She picked up
the saucer with Kate's half-eaten pie and headed
for the kitchen. She needed to start a big pot of
stew for her boarders' supper.

Kate didn't go straight home. Instead, she sat
in the hotel lobby, looking out the window,
watching the women pass by. She studied the
way they walked and their hair, hats, faces and
dress. One way or another, she was going to teach
Clint Morgan a lesson he'd never forget!

Five days later, Kate stood in the dressmaker's
shop, wishing she were home, and thoroughly
regretting her decision to come to Rawlins to purchase "a couple of" dresses. She was already accusing herself of being every kind of a fool to have
allowed herself to go through all this just to get
even with Clint Morgan! And now that Mattie had

the opportunity to fulfill her longtime desire, she wasn't about to let Kate leave without a complete wardrobe.

After all the measuring and selecting of materials, at last a couple of the dresses were ready for fittings. Kate didn't like having to undress in front of four ogling women—the two chubby helpers; the beak-nosed seamstress, Mrs. Chalmers; and Mattie. Nevertheless, since it didn't seem to bother them, why should it bother her? Kate became overjoyed at seeing the stockings with bold red and blue stripes, held up with lovely lacy garters, and gladly put them on. The next minute she felt ridiculous when the two assistants insisted on helping her don the voluminous lace-trimmed pantalettes and chemise. Surprisingly, she found the material to be soft and quite pleasing against her skin. They were nothing like the stiff underclothes she kept tucked in her bedroom drawers. She smiled shyly at Mattie, who was comfortably seated on a chair, watching the whole procedure.

Upon seeing the corset, Kate finally balked. "Oh no, Mattie. I refuse to wear that!"

"Nonsense, child. A proper lady is never without one." Mattie waved her hand at the seamstress. "Go ahead, Mrs. Chalmers."

Kate bit her bottom lip to keep from spouting obscenities as the corset was placed around her waist and laced in the back. "I can't breathe!" Kate yelled at the woman doing the lacing. She tried to jerk away, but had to admit the seamstress was strong. Mrs. Chalmers held on to the strings, and finally managed to tie them.

"A lady always has her corset as tight as is bearable," Mrs. Chalmers admonished in disgust.

Kate glared at the woman. Then, when she saw what was being brought out next, her mouth dropped open. It had to be the most ridiculous contraption Kate had ever seen. It was a collapsible half-circle steel affair made of lightweight hoops attached by flexible tapes. Not knowing what they were going to do with it, Kate stood still and waited. Surely they didn't plan on putting this on her also.

"I selected one of the larger crinoline cages, Mrs. Whitfield," the seamstress explained to Mattie as it was being tied around Kate's waist. "If you prefer smaller ones, we have those too, but this model of bustle is the most popular with the ladies about town."

It hung from the waist to about Kate's ankles, and she could just picture it flopping as she walked. Petticoats followed. The first was a heavy, embroidered flannel, and it was followed by five ruffled ones made from muslin. The seamstress bragged about the bottom of the skirts being four yards around, but Kate wasn't impressed.

Kate couldn't understand why women put up with wearing so many clothes day after day. As heavy as they were, it was surprising women could even walk. Just thinking about the routine she was being put through should be enough to make any woman shudder. She'd thought her cotton dresses and two petticoats were too much, but they were nothing compared to what the dressmaker and Mattie were having her put on. Kate now understood why women needed help dressing.

As one article followed another, Kate wondered how a man could possibly make love to a woman dressed like this. Picturing in her mind what the man would have to go through just to undress a woman, Kate broke out laughing.

Mattie gave her a questioning look, but Kate wasn't about to explain.

However, the dress made it all worthwhile.

Made of royal blue satin, it gave color to her cheeks and made her hair look almost pure silver. It had a high neck and long sleeves, and from the waist up it molded her body to perfection. The skirt contained yards of material that draped gently to the floor. Kate continued to stare in the mirror, finding it difficult to believe the image was hers. She looked beautiful!

Next was an evening dress, and though the brilliant green satin material was beautiful, the décolletage was so low it left nothing to the imagination. "I refuse to have my breasts exposed for public view!" Kate stated emphatically. "Good Lord! If I leaned over they'd fall out!"

"That's ridiculous," Mrs. Chalmers stated impatiently. "It's very conservative. Most of the dresses I make are much lower."

"Not in the town of Whitfield," Kate snapped back at her. Kate knew the seamstress was already put out with her, but the feeling was mutual.

"Kate is right. It simply will not do. Perhaps you can insert some lace," Mattie suggested.

"Margaret," Mrs. Chalmers called, not bothering to hide her disgust, "fetch me some lace!"

By the time Kate and Mattie were ready to return home, Kate had no idea what she was going to do with so many clothes. After all, she still had a ranch to run.

As Clint guided Midnight toward town, he wondered how much longer it would be before Kate and Mattie returned. He wasn't the least bit pleased that he'd had virtually no opportunity to tell Kate he'd changed his mind about bedding her. And even though he'd enjoyed his long talks with Sam, and listening to tales of the old days, somehow the house didn't seem right without the women around. Even Lucas joined them on occasions, even though Sam seemed less inclined to talk when the boy was there. Sam also talked a great deal about the ranch, and was now quick to answer any of Clint's questions. But as had been his fate so far, Clint kept hitting that proverbial brick wall. From all indications, the reservation steers had to have been switched *after* leaving the ranch, so he was relegated to sitting on his haunches and waiting until September to get the problem solved.

Then there was Oliver. He also sat in on a lot of the conversations, enthralled at every tale Sam spun. The problem was, the good doctor seemed in no hurry to set up his practice. His excuse was that he wanted to have a rest before going back to work. Clint was more inclined to believe the baby-faced man remained at the ranch because he had his eye on Kate and was waiting for her to return.

Clint nudged Midnight into a lope. He was on a mission for Sam. Clint shook his head. He still couldn't believe Sam had trusted him enough to send him on this errand. How could the old man be so certain he wouldn't run to Mattie as soon as she returned and tell her what Sam had told him about a woman named Star? Thinking about Star and Sam made Clint chuckle. Sam wasn't nearly as hard-nosed as he'd have people think. Oddly enough, the more Clint was around Sam, the more he found himself respecting the man. Sam was straightforward and didn't pull any punches.

After his short visit, Clint planned to stop by the telegram office. He was going to ask Thomas Sandoval to check Putnam. Clint wanted to be sure the man was indeed a doctor.

Star recognized Clint the moment she saw him standing on the other side of the screen. "My, you're even more handsome close up, Mr. Morgan," she cooed as her eyes brazenly checked him out from head to toe. "Please come in." Though she was quite taken with the man, Star was also trying to figure out why he was at her doorstep. The Whitfields couldn't possibly have found out why Kate had paid her a visit.

"How did you know my name?" Clint asked as he entered the house.

"Word gets around fast in such a small town. Besides, I saw what you did to Lucas that first day you were in town. Won't you have a seat?"

"I can't stay but a minute."

"What a shame. And here I was, hoping you wanted to pay me a *special* visit, Mr. Morgan."

Seeing the twinkle in her hazel eyes, Clint smiled broadly. "Had I known you were such a fetching woman, I probably would have. Please, call me Clint."

"You're here now," Star teased. She ran a finger across his strong jaw. "We could always go upstairs."

Still smiling, Clint raised a dark eyebrow. "That we could. And believe me, it's most tempting."

Star laughed, thoroughly enjoying their bantering. She was delighted at the gracious ease he projected. He didn't seem to be the least bit uncomfortable with the situation. Of course they both knew nothing would come of their flirting. "Besides being so damn good-looking, you're obviously a man who knows exactly how to handle his women. Now, why don't you tell me why you're here?"

Clint chuckled. "Sam wanted me to see if you are in need of anything." He watched Star's face soften and could see the caring in her large eyes.

"Sam's a good man," Star whispered. She cleared her throat. "You tell him I'm just fine. Is he doing all right?"

Clint nodded and stepped back out on the small porch. "I know you probably wouldn't feel comfortable contacting Sam directly, but if you do need anything, I'm easy to get in touch with."

"Thank you for coming by, Clint."

He leaned down and kissed her cheek. "Believe me, it's been my pleasure."

Star went into the parlor and collapsed on a chair while blotting tears. Sam still thought enough of her to see to her well-being. She thought about the tall man who had delivered the message, and smiled. She'd flirted outrageously with him to see how he'd react. Kate definitely had a bigger problem on her hands than the girl knew. Clint could probably outfox Kate coming and going, because Kate had never learned to be devious where men were concerned.

Star knew Kate needed to live her own life, and if the girl wanted to get even with Clint Morgan, she had the right to do so. Unfortunately, it was unlikely that Clint would get hurt—but Kate could. Nevertheless, Star knew she would do what the girl wanted. She wished she could be a ghost and see the fireworks when they started exploding, and there was no doubt in her mind that eventually that was exactly what was going to happen.

By the time the women returned home and Clint had once again feasted his eyes on the beautiful Kate, he knew the battle of wills was over. Suddenly, he no longer gave a damn about the repercussions. Since when had he been so foolish as to turn down a woman's gift freely given? He'd already put it off too damn long. Tomorrow he'd inform Kate that he was ready to accept her proposition.

* * *

"So," Star said, "you want to get this Morgan man to the point where he can no longer resist you. Like a dog chasing a bitch in heat."

"Something like that," Kate replied with a considerable amount of wariness. Where Star had seemed cautious last week, she now seemed to be licking her chops.

"All right, I've decided to teach you what you want to know. I'll tell you right now, I'm no authority on ladylike ways, but I can teach you how to entice a man."

Star scrambled off the sofa, pursed her red lips, and looked Kate over from head to toe. "I don't know what's the matter with this man. Even those jeans and shirt leave no doubt that you're a woman."

"He likes women who wear dresses," Kate said angrily. "He calls *me* a she-man!"

Star walked a complete circle around the pretty young woman. "The first thing I'd suggest is that you do something with that hair. It's as straight as a fence post, and you keep it all pulled back, making you look like you've been scalped. You need to put it in curlers so it'll curl real pretty around your face. I've got some I'll let you use. I also have rouge that'll give your cheeks and lips color."

Kate wasn't about to put any paint on her face, but she said nothing.

"The eyes are the key to flirting with a man. I was once told a proper woman never looks a man straight in the eye. She keeps her eyes downcast."

Kate couldn't remember Mattie ever telling her that, but she'd ignored a lot of things Mattie had said over the years.

"So you have to be clever about how to give him the message that you might be interested. I'll act like you're the man, and you watch my eyes so you can see what I mean.'' Star turned side-ways. She looked down, then slowly raised her eyelids and looked at Kate out of the corners of her eyes, smiled slightly then lowered her eyes again. ''Now, you try it.''

Kate was worn out when she left Star's house two hours later. Never had she suspected there could be so many ways to draw a man's interest, and she doubted that she'd remember half of them.

As per Star's instructions, for the next couple of nights Kate stood in front of the mirror practic-ing what she'd been taught. She fluttered her eyelashes, tilted her head at various angles in or-der to judge what she considered appealing, and slowly raised her eyelids for just the right effect. Using a bedpost to serve as a man, she also turned so as to *accidently* brush against it, or so her hand would just happen to wind up where she figured the man's crotch should be. She wasn't at all sure she could actually do the latter, but this was what Star had shown her, and she'd practice it until she felt she had it down to perfection. Getting even with Clint Morgan had become an obses-sion, and she'd do whatever it took to achieve her goal.

By the end of the week, Kate was feeling con-fident and ready to work her wiles on the devil himself.

Chapter 10

Clint stuffed the telegram from Sandoval in his pocket and left the telegraph office. That damn greenhorn Doc Putnam really was everything he'd claimed to be.

As Clint headed Midnight back toward the ranch, his foul mood continued to deteriorate. Ever since Kate's return, Putnam had stuck by her side like a leech, hanging on Kate's every word. So Clint had waited until he could get Kate alone. But Kate was still avoiding him, just as she had prior to going to Rawlins. Well this time it wasn't going to work. He made up his mind that the next time she took off from the ranch, he'd follow her. He was tired of playing hide-and-seek. Realizing how his attitude had changed, he cursed himself. He was acting like some stallion who smelled a mare in heat and was ready to leap the fence to get to her, and he didn't like it one damn bit! He'd never had to chase any woman.

It was noon when Kate entered her room and secured the lock on the door. She had work to do.

After bathing in a tub of hot water and washing her hair, Kate fetched the bandanna holding the curlers from the armoire and placed them on the washstand. Star had said that making curls was a very simple process. Take a damp strand of hair, place the curler at the end, and roll upwards.

Doing her hair proved to be more difficult than Kate had thought. She kept getting the hair tangled, and it tried her patience to the limit when she finally managed to get the second curler rolled up only to have the first one fall down.

When she had finally finished, Kate was afraid to move her head for fear everything would come tumbling down. Carefully, she inched her way to the bed. Star had said a nap was always necessary in order for a woman to look fresh.

Kate attempted to lie down. She quickly discovered that to rest her head on curlers was not only painful but impossible. However, still determined to do everything right, she sat up and stuffed pillows behind her back. Having to remain in a sitting position, and at the same time make sure her head didn't bang against the headboard, sorely tempted Kate to just give up the entire project. It was too much trouble. But all she had to do was think of Clint's smug smile and her determination immediately returned. Eventually, her eyelids grew heavy, and she drifted off to sleep.

Kate awoke with a headache. During her nap, her head had fallen onto the pillows, causing the curlers to dig into her scalp. Some of the curlers had worked their way loose, but fortunately most were still in place. Kate refused to allow the headache to affect her suddenly excited mood. Tonight she would have her *coming out* party . . . supper . . . though she and Mattie were the only ones who knew it.

A few moments later there was a light tap on the door, and a maid entered. Kate knew that Mattie would also be joining them shortly to supervise Kate's toilette.

* * *

Kate sat on a stool in front of the mirror, watching the curlers being removed from her hair. She was already convinced her plans for the evening were doomed. With each clinking sound of another curler being dropped into a bowl, her green eyes grew rounder. And by the time the task was finished she was in shock. She looked in the mirror at Mattie, hoping for some sort of reassurance, but the older woman just stood there clicking her tongue and shaking her head.

Finally noticing the horrified look on Kate's face, Mattie tried giving her a reassuring smile. "I'm sure it will look much better once Addie May gets it brushed." For the life of her, she couldn't figure out what could have possessed Kate to roll her hair in curlers. Why hadn't she waited and just used a curling iron where it was needed? But the girl was obviously nervous, and she didn't want to upset her any more by asking. Kate had never used anything on her hair before and probably just didn't know better.

The vigorous brushing only seemed to make matters worse. Strands of hair began to cling to the brush, then fly up and out. Kate was reminded of pictures she'd seen of lions with huge manes sticking out all around, the only difference here being that Kate's hair curled at the ends. "Addie May," she addressed the maid, "try puling it into some sort of a bun with your hands."

Addie May tried, but never having dressed another woman's hair before, the effort was futile.

"Stop," Kate ordered, seeing her hair becoming tangled again. "I'll go down with it looking like this. Just pull it back and tie a ribbon around it."

Mattie placed a finger to her lips. "Maybe if . . ."

Kate looked at her stepmother. "Mattie, there is no maybe. We both know that short of dunking my head in a barrel of water, there's no hope of doing anything with this mess. I'd even be willing to do that if there was enough time for it to dry." Kate knew there was another alternative. She could stay in her room. But she refused to let anything keep her from going downstairs. Not after all the preparations she'd gone through!

Addie May chose a pink ribbon that matched the pink lace roses sewn about the waist and skirt of the lovely white dress. It wasn't her place to say anything, but she thought Miss Kate looked absolutely beautiful, hair and all.

Kate discovered her next problem when she tried leaving her room. She had never thought of the doorway as being narrow, but it took several minutes for Mattie and Addie May to push and manipulate her bustle so she was able to make it into the hall.

"I'm sure that if we go to Whitfield," Mattie said, a bit out of breath, "we can find a bustle at Meg Ryan's shop that won't stick out so far."

"It's a little late to be thinking about that," Kate replied impatiently, tempted to remind Mattie that she had been the one who chose the size of the cage.

Kate cursed under her breath when, halfway down the stairs, the heel of her shoe got caught in her skirt hem. Had she not had a firm grasp on the banister, she would have toppled all the way to the bottom.

But when Kate entered the large dining room, she held herself proud, refusing to give any indication of what all she'd gone through that day. And it was worth every bit of discomfort when she saw the look of consternation on Clint Morgan's face. And was that admiration she saw in his eyes? Maybe even a touch of pleasure? It's doubtful, she thought as she tried gliding gracefully into the room. That would be asking too much.

Before she reached her seat at the table, Oliver had already pulled the chair out for her. She felt uncomfortable having to sit on the edge of the seat, but her bustle left her little choice.

"How ravishing you look," Oliver gushed. He pushed the chair back in for her.

Clint assisted Mattie.

Seeing how Clint's eyes had turned to stone, Kate felt quite smug. Her plan was already working. Things might even progress faster than she'd anticipated.

Sam pushed himself into the room and up to the end of the table. "What in hell's name have you done to yourself?" he asked the minute he saw his daughter. "You look like a damn harlot!"

Kate didn't flinch a muscle. His words were no more than she had expected. "I—"

"Samuel Whitfield!" Mattie gasped. "How dare you say such a thing to your daughter?"

"I personally think Kate's attire makes for an attractive addition to the supper table," Clint commented dryly. He unfolded his napkin and placed it on his lap. "I'm sure you must feel quite proud at having such a lovely daughter."

Sam studied Kate. "Damn. You might be right at that. She *is* right pretty all decked up like that. But I suggest, girl, you do something with your hair, and don't go wearing them clothes out on the range. You'd scare any horse you tried to mount, and I'd probably have to fire every hand on the ranch to keep them away from you. Now everyone bow their head."

In his own way, her father had given her a compliment, and Kate found herself having to struggle not to laugh with joy. He had even acknowledged she was a woman! Her momentary pleasure quickly fled when she realized it was Clint who had actually influenced Sam to change his mind. Since when did Sam start listening to a stranger? Well, maybe not a stranger, but darn close to it. She started to make a tart comment to Clint, but suddenly remembered it wasn't proper to look men straight in the eye. So how do you talk to someone? she suddenly wondered.

"At my home, we always dress for supper," Oliver commented congenially as soon as grace was over.

"There's a lot of difference in living on a ranch and living in a town," Lucas snapped back. He was already tiring of the man.

"Oh, well of course. I didn't mean anything by the comment."

"Pay no mind to Lucas," Sam grumbled, casting Lucas a withering look. "Care for some potatoes, Doc?" He held out the bowl.

Clint looked across the table at Kate. Practically from the time she'd sat down, she'd continually stared at her plate. Was she feeling ill?

As the meal progressed, Clint found it more and more difficult to keep his eyes off Kate. He'd always been aware of her beauty, but tonight she was breathtaking. It was quite apparent that Mattie wasn't the only one who had bought something in Rawlins. Though Kate's silver-blond hair seemed to have a mind of its own and twisted in every possible direction, it served to highlight her high cheekbones, her small nose that turned up just a fraction at the end, her eyes, and made her lips appear even fuller. The white dress made her sun-kissed skin look almost copper-colored. His desire for her was making him more than a little uncomfortable, something that would be obvious to everyone if he didn't settle himself down before supper was finished. However, since she'd never dressed this way before, was it for his benefit or Putnam's?

In order to get his mind off the vixen, Clint turned to Mattie to say something, but forgot what it was when he saw the warmth in her eyes and the smile on her lips. "Thank you," she mouthed.

What the hell for? Clint wondered.

Oliver said, "Sam, what do you do with all the cattle you own?"

"We sell steers and horses to the forts, and also for Indian reservations. Besides that, we ship cattle back east. Though I'm still not pleased about the railroad, it does allow us a larger market."

Clint had expected Kate to join in the conversation, but she remained silent. As the two men continued discussing cattle, Clint looked toward Kate. To his surprise, she slowly raised her eyelids, then fluttered her long lashes at a ridiculously fast pace. At first he wasn't sure what she was doing, but when she added a sly grin, he realized she was actually trying to flirt with him. She also probably thought she was being coy. It was the most absurd thing he'd ever seen, and he had to clamp his mouth shut to keep from laughing out loud. Finally, he managed to paste a sober look on his face. "Kate," he said, with deliberate concern, "do you have something in your eyes?"

Kate was startled by the question. "Why would you ask that?" Realizing she was looking straight at him, she immediately glanced down at the plate of food she'd hardly touched.

"Because you keep batting your lashes and seem to have trouble looking up. Perhaps I should see if I can—"

"No! That won't be necessary." Kate looked him straight in the eye, and held his gaze to prove her point.

Clint smiled. "Good, I was starting to worry."

Kate wanted to throw something at him. Had all her practicing been to no avail, or was the man simply incapable of being aroused?

"It certainly wouldn't hurt to have Clint look," Mattie chided. "You don't want to take a chance of getting pinkeye."

"I'm fine," Kate insisted when Clint began to rise from his chair. "Look at my eyes! Do they look red?"

"I'll have a look," Oliver said.

"That won't be necessary." Clint was already out of his chair before Oliver could rise. It only took a few long strides for Clint to reach Kate's side. "Just let me look," he said softly.

Knowing she was fighting a losing battle, Kate threw her head back, and she was suddenly looking up into a pair of warm gray eyes with flecks of blue. She stopped breathing when Clint leaned over to take a closer look, his lips only inches from hers. Then he straightened back up and smiled. "I don't see anything wrong," she heard him say. "Her eyes look just fine."

"If you should have any more trouble," Oliver offered, "let me know. I have a solution you can use to rinse them out."

Kate could only nod her acknowledgment. When Clint returned to his seat, she didn't feel nearly as warm as when he'd been beside her. The room came back into focus, and it occurred to her that others were also seated around the table. She felt embarrassed. Had Mattie or Sam noticed her foolish reaction to Clint's nearness? She took a surreptitious glance around the table. Mattie's expression hadn't changed. Sam, Oliver and Lucas were busy finishing off their slices of spice cake, and Clint . . . . Seeing his knowing half grin made her ire rise. Was he just playing with her? She wanted to cross her eyes at him, but why give the satisfaction of getting that sort of reaction from her? After all, that wasn't what she'd set out to do tonight! Instead, seeing no one else paying attention to her, she leaned back in her chair as far as her bustle would permit, thrusting her breasts forward. She deliberately let her gaze travel from the top of his head down to where the table hid the rest of his body. Something else Star had shown her. If he could look at her in such a manner, there was no reason why she couldn't do the same to him. Her gaze slowly returned to his face, and she could see humor in his eyes. He's probably thinking how irresistible he is, Kate thought. What a shock he's going to have when he invites me to his bed and I turn him down.

When supper was over, Clint took hold of the handles on the back of Sam's wheelchair.

As Kate passed by, she made a point of brushing her breasts across Clint's arm. Acting as though she hadn't noticed, she followed Mattie out of the room.

"Oliver, we're going out to enjoy a cigar," Sam stated in his gravelly voice. "Care to join us?"

"No, I'll wait with the ladies in the parlor."

Sam nodded. "Lucas?"

"I'm goin' to play poker with the boys in the bunkhouse."

Now that he thought about it, Clint realized Lucas had said hardly a thing during supper. "Care if I join you later?"

"Hell, no. You'll have a better time than staying in the house."

"How would you know?" Sam snapped.

Clint pushed Sam's chair out onto the porch. It was a warm night, but there was a soft, welcome breeze. Clint handed Sam a cigar, then struck a match and held it out to him before lighting his own cigar.

Sam broke the silence. "I'm worried about Kate."

Clint walked to the edge of the porch and looked out across the moonlit valley. "Why is that?'' he asked, not really wanting to get into a discussion.

"She's taken a fancy to some man."

"Oh? How do you know that?"

"Why the hell else do you think she's gettin' all gussied up? Think it's Oliver?"

Clint sent a smoke ring floating into the air. "Maybe she's just decided she wants to be a woman for a change. If she is interested in someone, how would I know? We don't exactly get along."

"You don't know her as well as I do. She's up to something. I can feel it in my gut."

Clint was grateful when Sam lapsed into silence. "I'm going to take a stroll, Sam," Clint said as he stepped off the porch. "I'll be back shortly."

"Take your time, boy. I'm not eager to go back in and work on some damn puzzle the women brought back from Rawlins."

Clint chuckled as he took off. He wasn't laughing just at what Sam had said, but also at himself. He'd been a damn fool not to take Kate when she'd made the offer. Since when had he become so self-righteous? When he'd leaned down to check her eyes, her hair had smelled clean and sweet, and he'd been strongly tempted to place a kiss on the soft, creamy bend of her neck. But making a wiser choice, he'd returned to his seat. At least one thing had been settled tonight. She was still interested. In fact, after she had swept her breasts across his arm, he was beginning to suspect all her dressing up had been for his benefit. Still, as unpredictable as Kate was, he couldn't be sure.

Kate continued her campaign to get even with Clint for rejecting her. She had remembered Star saying that it was too bad there wasn't another man around whom Kate could use to tempt Clint even more. Well, there was now, and she had every intention of using him to her advantage.

Kate remained around the homestead area, taking Oliver with her wherever she went. Each night she wore a different gown, each one more daring than the last, and flirted with Clint at every possible opportunity—but from a deliberate distance. She wanted to be sure that when she allowed him to have a moment alone with her, his desire would take precedence over everything else. Then, when she refused to have anything to do with him, he'd find out how it felt to have the shoe on the other foot!

Kate was amazed at how adept Addie May had become at styling her hair. To Kate's delight, the clever woman had come up with a new way to arrange it, and instead of curlers, Addie May used a curling iron. Kate didn't know what happened to the curlers, nor did she care. Though she tried telling herself that all the extra attention was time wasted, deep down she was enjoying acting like a lady. And with Mattie's instructions, she was even learning to move more comfortably with her new clothes and to watch her language. Unfortunately, she wasn't having fun with her campaign to make Clint jealous. Kate found Oliver's character, looks, and demeanor lacking in everything. The man was a complete bore. His puppy-dog attitude made her want to retch. She did feel guilty at using him for her own benefit, but she was still determined to get even with Clint.

However, she wasn't sure all her efforts were working and her aggravation at Clint grew stronger with each passing night. Other than on the first evening, he seemed to take her for granted, and the insufferable man no longer complimented her or paid attention to how she looked or what she wore. Even so, she'd noticed that he now wore nice trousers, lace-fronted shirts, and various vests to supper. If he wore a blue brocade vest, his eyes looked pale blue. A green vest? His eyes looked like they had green specks. Of course it was ridiculous, but each night was like seeing him for the first time.

A week later, Kate sat in the middle of her bed with nothing on but her pantalettes and chemise. She was waiting for Addie May to come help her dress, but at the same time she was contemplating her lack of success with Clint Morgan. Nothing had turned out the way she'd expected. He didn't seem a bit closer to compromising her. Either that or he was a mighty fine actor. Admittedly he hadn't had an opportunity to express how he felt what with her keeping him at a distance. Still, he could show some kind of expression instead of looking stoic all the time. On the opposite end of the fence, Oliver was constantly plying her with compliments and had tried to kiss her on more than one occasion. Now, to her chagrin, he was talking to Sam about remaining as the ranch doctor. True, he had taken care of a few broken bones and cuts, but they'd never needed a doctor on the ranch, and they didn't need one now. It wasn't that far to town.

She laid back on the pillows and released a heavy sigh. She wouldn't have thought she'd ever lose interest in getting even with Clint, but that was exactly what was happening. It had been her hurt pride at being rejected that had made her go to all these extremes, and it was pride that was telling her to quit. She'd been a fool to think she could attract a man who no longer even showed interest. And how was she supposed to refuse his offer to make love to her if he didn't ask? Sam had been right. She *was* acting like a harlot. And there were other problems. Even as angry as she'd been at Clint for refusing to take her to his bed, her desire hadn't waned. If anything, it had grown stronger, if that was possible. She thought of the nights she laid in bed, her need almost unbearable. The more he ignored her, the more she wanted him. He had put the devil's spell on her. Her gaze fell on the dirty corduroy pants still lying on the floor where she'd left them, the plaid shirt nearby, the gun belt slung over the chair post, and the sweat-stained hat on the seat. Slowly she rose to a sitting position. There was more than one way to draw attention.

Clint was the first to arrive in the parlor prior to supper, curious to see what Kate would be wearing tonight. Last night she'd worn a cream-colored affair with a neckline so low that Mattie and Sam had been shocked. From what Mattie had said, there had apparently once been lace to hide the swell of the breasts; Kate had removed it. Seeing Oliver ogling Kate had made it very tempting to sock the good doctor right in the nose. Clint went over to the console and poured himself a straight shot of whiskey. Who was the real Kate Whitfield? The one who ran the ranch, or the woman who for the last week had flirted outrageously with both him and Oliver? The woman was a damn chameleon. He'd become angrier with each passing day, wondering if Kate had decided to let Putnam take his place in her bed. Not that he was jealous. That was ridiculous. However, he did feel that since he'd received the first offer he should be the one to test the kettle.

Everyone had already entered the dining room when Kate made her appearance. Clint hadn't been prepared to see her in pants and a shirt, both of which could use a good washing. Even her boots needed cleaning. At least her hair was smoothed back and twisted into a long thick braid. Kate was still beautiful, even dressed as a man.

She went directly to her chair, pulled it out, then swung a leg over the seat before plopping down.

Seeing looks of shock on everyone's faces, especially Oliver's, Clint broke out laughing. When Sam said, "Well, girl, looks like you've finally come to your senses," Clint laughed all the harder. And when he saw Kate's eyes shooting daggers at him, he laughed so hard his sides hurt.

Because he was unable to explain what he found so funny, and because everyone was looking at him as if he needed to be taken to the madhouse, Clint rose from his chair and left the room. He wasn't just laughing at the others, he was mostly laughing at himself. He found tremendous humor in the realization that for the last couple of weeks the man Thomas Sandoval had often referred to as being a feelingless, cold-blooded hunter had actually let a slip of a woman turn him damn near into a sex-starved schoolboy! No one, including himself, would ever have believed it.

Clint was still laughing when he walked out onto the wide porch. He had just managed to get his laughter under control when a fist struck him in the back. He swerved around, ready to knock the hell out of whoever had thrown the punch, when he saw Kate, her hands on her hips.

"Just what do you find so funny?" Kate demanded.

Clint grinned. "It would take too long to explain, and I think our supper is getting cold."

"It can wait," Kate replied tartly.

"I think that is exactly the problem. We've waited too long."

"You're talking in circles."

"On the contrary, I'm making perfect sense. Why don't you meet me by the windmill around noon tomorrow? We'll talk about it then."

Kate felt slighted when he went back inside. But what else should she expect from a man who never answered questions? Well, he'd wait until doomsday before she met him anywhere. Gritting her teeth, she entered the house, slamming the door behind her.

The next morning, Clint slept later than usual, and after breakfast he rode Midnight up to the old line shack to deposit some clothes.

By the time Clint had returned and left Midnight in the corral, it was nearing noon. He was fed up with fighting his physical need and intended asking Kate point-blank if her offer was still open. If she said no, he might very well take her into the mountains and claim his prize anyway. She'd offered, and now, by God, he was going to take.

By twelve-thirty, Clint knew Kate wasn't going to keep their appointment. He left the windmill and took off toward the house. This time she wasn't going to avoid him.

Not finding Sam in his office, Clint went in search of Mattie. He finally located her in her sewing room.

"Good morning, Clint," Mattie said to her nephew.

"I'm looking for Kate. Do you know where she is?"

"Yes. She took . . ." Mattie stopped to thread some yellow floss through the eye of the embroidery needle. "She took Oliver on a tour of the ranch. He's such a nice man, don't you agree?" She continued embroidering flowers on a small pillowcase. "I'm making a pillow for Soodie Updike's baby that's due any day. Maybe you could drive me to town in a couple of days to take it to her."

"Of course." Clint looked down at the perfectly matched squares of the nearly finished quilt. The wooden frame took up a large portion of the small sewing room, and he felt cramped for space. "You know you can buy pillows already made," he commented offhandedly. His jaw set, he moved to the window to look out.

"Yes, but it's not the same when they're meant as a gift. Besides, it fills my time. With the children grown, I seem to have so much time on my hands, and I'm too old to go riding anymore. Besides, it isn't safe."

"How long do you think Kate will be gone?"

"She took a picnic basket, so I imagine they'll be gone all day."

"Isn't anyone concerned that her life could be in danger?"

"Both Sam and Kate are convinced that the man who shot at her was one of the rustlers. Thank the good Lord, they feel we've seen the last of those terrible men."

Clint turned and looked at his aunt. She seemed almost lost in the big chair she was sitting on. "Where is Lucas?"

"Sam sent him and some men out to check on a bear that one of the hands reported had killed a cow."

So much for spending time with Lucas, Clint thought.

"I know the boy wasn't right in what he did, Clint, but I'm confident it won't happen again. I'm sure that's why we haven't had any more trouble with the rustlers."

There was a tired sadness in her expression, and Clint actually found himself feeling sorry for his aunt. He looked back out the window. What was happening to him? Since when did he start giving a damn about anyone? Yet piece by piece, he was allowing himself to get involved. He was starting to care about Mattie and, oddly enough, Sam as well. He found himself becoming more and more worried about them, but damn if he could figure out why. His intuition told him they were in danger. "Kate isn't going to get her picnic."

"Oh? Why is that?"

The right corner of his lips curved into a wicked grin. "Because clouds are building, and I think we're in for a storm."

Mattie set her embroidery down and joined Clint at the window. "Why you're right," she said excitedly. "I know it's terribly wicked of me, but I have always enjoyed a good thunderstorm. The ranch hands hate them because the lightning and thunder spook the cattle."

Clint stiffened. *And cattle stampede when they're spooked*, he thought. "I'll talk to you later, Mattie."

Mattie couldn't understand why Clint hurried out of the room. "Oh well," she muttered as she returned to her chair, "I guess I just don't understand young people anymore."

Clint again searched the house looking for Sam, but came up empty-handed. He finally located the older man by the barn, talking to Henry Blankenship.

"The boys found Kate's Indian," Sam informed Clint when he joined them. "He was old, and was probably just wandering until he died. The men buried him on the spot."

"And no one has seen any others in the area," Henry commented, "so that's another problem it looks like we don't have to worry about."

Clint pulled his hat down to block the strong rays of the sun. "Sam, didn't you tell me that those two hundred cattle Kate had put on the ridge to trap the rustlers have been moved?"

"Yep. We're keepin' them together so that in a couple of months, when it comes time to start roundin' up them two thousand steers for shipment, we'll already have some in that herd.

'Course they'll have to be culled out. When the men were movin' them they said they picked up a couple a hundred or so more."

"How many cowpokes do you have watching them?"

"Five," Henry answered.

"And it's my understanding that the cattle are in open range."

Hearing concern threaded in Clint's words, Sam moved his wheelchair around to take a better look at the big man. "What's on your mind, boy?"

"I'm thinking the rustlers have been awfully quiet. Four hundred head of cattle out in the open is certainly a tempting prize. There's a thunderstorm building, and a storm would give rustlers a perfect opportunity. You know the herd's going to be nervous, and it wouldn't take anything to stampede them. Then all the rustlers would have to do is ride in and drive them away."

Henry snickered. "I think you're worryin' about something that ain't gonna happen. They think we're on to them."

Clint looked at the clouds moving over the mountaintops, then back at Sam. "You have to think like a rustler in order to catch one. If I was one of that bunch," he drawled, "and no one had come looking for me by now, I'd think it was all a big bluff. Say I got away with four hundred cattle. At forty, or let's say thirty dollars a head, split by maybe six men, that's two thousand dollars in my pocket. That's a lot of money, and I'd sure want to go after them."

Sam grunted. "He makes sense, Henry."

"But what if Morgan's wrong?"

"And what if he's right?" Sam barked out at his foreman.

"We ain't got no men, Sam. I got 'em out on jobs or they're at the line shacks, and we won't be hirin' extra men till we get ready for the roundup."

"Well, there's you and me, Henry," Clint said with a grin, "and we can warn the others so they'll be on guard." In one way, Clint hoped he was wrong. On the other hand, he was looking forward to finally putting some action back into his life.

Kate welcomed the opportunity to get away. It was time to start thinking about something other than Clint Morgan. Just remembering all the trouble she'd gone to in order to make herself desirable—and then to have him not pay any attention—still made her spitting mad. Today she was going to suggest Oliver move into town. She didn't need him either.

Spotting the clouds only served to aggravate Kate all the more. Not only would she and Oliver have to turn back, but again she'd been absorbed with thoughts of the useless Clint Morgan and hadn't even seen the storm coming!

"I'm sorry, Oliver, but we're not going to have our picnic."

"Why? You have no idea how I've looked forward to spending a day alone with you."

Kate pointed to the clouds.

"Surely a little rain isn't going to hurt anything."

"A little rain?" Kate asked impatiently. "Oliver, that's a full-blown thunderstorm. We need to get back to the house as soon as possible."

When they returned to the homestead, Kate saw about six men also headed in to escape the storm. When their horses were put away, Kate and Oliver went to the house.

A few minutes later she came running back out. Sam had told her what Clint said, and like Sam, she thought it made more sense than anything else she'd heard.

The cowhands who had ridden in were enjoying cups of coffee when Kate barged into the cook shack.

"Come on," she called from just inside the door, "we have to ride."

"What's going on?" Pedro asked.

"I'll explain on the way."

Kate left, and as one the men rose from the bench and followed.

It was a long, hard ride. By the time Kate caught sight of the herd, she could hear an occasional drop of rain thudding against her hat. She looked at the low, gray layer of clouds quickly covering the sky, and heard the distant rumble of thunder. There was no doubt in her mind that when the storm broke, it was going to be a bad one.

As they drew nearer and saw the cowhands working the cattle into a large circle, Kate motioned for her men to spread out and help. Instead of following, Kate suddenly brought her horse to a halt, staring at the strange scene ahead. The outer limits of the circle were darkened by the clouds. But in the center of the herd the sun shone, and rays of light beamed down on the animals' brown hides. It even made their faces look whiter, and the grass seemed almost blue-green in color. In all her years of ranching, Kate couldn't remember having seen such a strange sight.

"Oliver must be disappointed not to get his picnic."

The cold baritone voice snapped Kate back to reality. "Sam told me I'd find you here." Kate noted the oilskin poncho tied with saddle straps behind the cantle of his saddle, and the wet spots on his gray Stetson.

"The men you brought will help. Of course this might turn out to be a wild-goose chase."

"Yep." Kate nudged her horse forward. She wasn't about to give him the satisfaction of knowing she thought his theory was a sound one.

Clint turned Midnight around and pulled along beside her.

Kate studied the area as they rode closer to the herd. It was open land, and there wasn't any place to hide or set a trap should the rustlers attack.

"If they come, looks like we're going to have to fight them in the open," Kate commented.

"If they come, darlin', we're not only going to have to fight them in the open, we're going to have a stampede on our hands, plus a storm to contend with. The cowhands were telling me that while they've been watching the herd, they've picked up even more cattle. They figure there's about five hundred head standing out there. Maybe you should go back home."

Kate yanked her horse to a halt. "These are my cattle, Morgan, and—"

"Oh? We're back to Morgan again?"

"I have every intention of staying—and fighting if necessary. I might also remind you that this is still my ranch and you're a visitor. So why don't *you* ride back to the house? And while I'm at it, just how did you get so all-fired smart about what rustlers might do?"

Clint chuckled. "You sure do have a suspicious nature. Sam told me that you actually thought I was in on the rustling."

"I suspect anyone and everyone." She wondered what else Sam had told him. "The truth is you're nothing but a stranger who's come into our midst, even if you're related to Mattie. So why shouldn't I be suspicious?"

"I've heard women are often attracted to men they don't trust. You've certainly proved that theory over the last couple of weeks."

Kate felt fury pour through her like melting steel. She reached for her whip, but Clint was too close. Before she could even get it uncoiled, he snatched it from her hand. "I should have killed you that first night in town. I've taken all the insults I'm going to take from you! One way or another, you're going to regret ever having met me. But right now, I have cattle to take care of. Who knows? If bullets are fired, maybe one will end up in your back." Even as angry as she was, she knew she could never shoot a man in the back, but she liked having him think so.

"You know, your problem is that you need a man to show you how to put all that fire to good use. Maybe you've been right all along. I guess I have no choice but to bed you."

"Are you asking?"

"I don't ask. I take."

"Well, you're not going to take me," Kate seethed, "and if you're asking, the answer is no." Finally, she'd had the opportunity to refuse him. But that wasn't right either. He'd actually put it in such a way that it seemed he was doing her a favor! She had a sudden urge to do something stupidly feminine like reaching over and pulling his hair out. Then, to add to her upset, he dropped the whip on the ground and rode off. Despite her anger, Kate felt an unwanted spark of excitement kindle deep within her. Since meeting Clint, she'd jumped from one side of the fence to the other about going to bed with him. One minute she didn't want him touching her, and the next she longed for him. Now a new feeling was taking over, or maybe it had been there all along. She was afraid of him. Not that she thought he would physically harm her. Quite the contrary. She was afraid that he would ignite something within her she'd never experienced before.

"Don't be a ninny, Kate Whitfield," she muttered as she rode forward, "he's no different than any other man. You're just letting your imagination run away with you." Still, her mouth had become dry and she would have sworn her heart was beating faster.

Seeing a couple of steers break away, Kate headed after them. They spun off in a different direction, but Kate's mount was a good cow pony. With little direction, he darted to the right, then left, preventing the steers from going anywhere. Soon they rejoined the growing circle of cattle. Several times she spotted Clint guiding Midnight in the direction of steers that needed to be brought in. Kate found it odd that he handled the job so capably, especially since he'd said he knew little about cattle. The kind of ability he was showing wasn't learned overnight.

Kate forgot all about Clint as she and the others formed a wide circle around the five hundred head of cattle. Now all they could do was wait and see what happened.

Chapter 11

K ate shifted her weight on the saddle and tried to peer into the pitch-black night. Hard, stinging rain seemed to be coming from every direction. Even with her hat pulled down, her face and hair were drenched, and her body was covered with goose bumps from the icy water running down the inside of her oilskin. Still, she remained on her horse and at her lookout post. She watched the lightning flash in the distance and heard the thunder rumble, but so far the main part of the storm had kept its distance. Henry, and later Clint, had tried to get her to stay beneath one of the cottonwood trees that dotted the huge valley, but both times she'd refused. She knew they wanted her to move because she was a woman, but she was also the boss of this spread and refused to ask anything of her men that she herself wouldn't do. She wasn't any more miserable than they were.

Knowing that trying to watch for rustlers in all this dark rain was futile, Kate looped the reins over the saddle horn and wiggled her stiff fingers, trying to get circulation back into her numb hands. Her buckskin gloves were soaked and had long since failed to keep her hands warm. She returned her hand to the rifle resting across her legs and over the front of the saddle. It was covered with the bottom of her oilskin, but at the rate the rain was falling, she wasn't sure how long she'd be able to keep it dry. Again she hunched down and lowered her head, trying to avoid what rain she could, and listened to the thunder. All she could do was wait, and hope that the storm would soon pass. Not only were she and the cowhands miserable, the cattle were getting restless and starting to bawl.

Kate hadn't realized she'd dozed off until an earsplitting crack of thunder directly overhead woke her. She jerked straight up, managing to catch her rifle before it slid to the ground. She kept a tight hold on the reins as her mount nervously danced about. A bolt of lightning hit the ground not fifty yards away. The deafening clap of thunder caused her horse to rear, but her boots were firmly planted in the stirrups, and she kept from sliding off the slippery saddle. She'd just gotten her horse back under control when the next lightning struck. The cattle were bawling in earnest now. Convinced that if the rustlers did come she'd never see them, she was tempted to ride forward to help the men trying to settle the herd back down. She had to remind herself that her job was to act as an outer guard, which meant staying put.

The lightning was merciless, and the rain continued to pound down. Something suddenly caught her eye, and she moved her gaze more to the right. Several bolts of lightning lit the sky at the same time, and she could clearly see the six riders coming from the south, their horses at a full gallop. She jerked her rifle up, aimed, and began pulling the trigger.

Kate heard more shots being fired and men yelling. The rustlers were now out of her sight, but she held her position in case they circled and came in her direction. Though it was still raining, the intensity of the storm had finally slackened.

Then Kate heard the sound that all cowhands dreaded—the rumble of hooves pounding the ground. Fear climbed up her backbone. The cattle were stampeding and headed in her direction. She jerked her horse around, sank her heels in his ribs, and leaned low to get as much speed from the animal as possible.

Suddenly Clint was riding beside her, yelling something that she couldn't hear. He kept pointing to the right, but she urged her horse straight ahead. He reached out and grabbed the reins close to her horse's bit, forcing the gelding to turn in the direction he'd been pointing.

Kate's fear grew when she saw the shadowy figure of what looked like a large cottonwood looming not ten yards ahead of them. She was convinced Clint would run them both right into it when he finally brought their horses to a sliding halt.

"What are you doing?" Kate yelled, trying desperately not to let fear take over. The thunder of hooves was so loud she wasn't even sure he could hear her.

"We can't outrun them," Clint hollered as he leaped from Midnight's back. "Your horse is too slow!" He reached up and pulled her from the saddle.

Kate struggled fiercely. The pounding sound was now so close she was beginning to panic. "Have you gone mad?" she screamed as she watched both horses take off running.

"Dammit, grab a branch! Our only chance is to climb the tree!"

He lifted her up, and in desperation she grabbed hold of a sturdy limb. It was wet and slippery, but her gloves allowed her to hold on.

With Clint pushing on her rear, she finally managed to pull herself up.

"Keep climbing!"

Having no light to see by, Kate had to inch her way upwards. Then the clouds started to part, and she could see an unending line of frantic cattle heading straight for the tree, their hooves making the ground shake. Her gaze shifted below to Clint. She tried to yell out a warning, but the noise drowned out her words. Her throat tightened as she watched him jump up and grab the same branch she'd used. He'd just swung up on it when the first steer ran by, its long, sharp horns missing him by inches. He climbed up the tree as if he were part wildcat.

"Kate! Grab hold of the trunk and hold on for dear life!" Clint shouted.

Kate felt the bark scratch her cheek as she threw her arms around the trunk. She wanted to close her eyes, but couldn't. Below, cattle were thundering by on either side, their horns flashing like silver. The tree was continually hit, causing it to shake and lean, and she had to fight the terror that was eating at her.

It seemed an eternity before the tree stopped swaying, though Kate knew what had happened could be counted in minutes. Everything became deathly silent. Tentatively, she looked up. She could actually see a few stars!

"It's over," Clint said softly.

Kate hadn't even been aware that Clint was on the other side of the trunk, directly in front of her. Cautiously she released her arms, still maintaining her balance. The branch she was standing on began to shake and she grabbed a limb in front to steady herself. She wasn't sure how she'd managed to get into such a precarious position. With everything happening so fast, she could barely remember climbing the tree. She looked at the ground below, seeing no possible way of climbing back down.

"Now how the hell do you expect me to get down?" she barked at Clint. Her nerves were still on edge, and she was starting to quiver. "If it hadn't been for you, we wouldn't be up here!"

"If it hadn't been for me, lady, you'd be dead. At least it would have put an end to your damn yowling."

"I was doing just fine before you rode up and turned my horse!"

"Shut up, Kate."

"Shut up? I'll shut up as soon as you get me down from here, and not before. Of all the dumb, stupid, things to do—"

Clint's anger was at the breaking point. He reached out, grabbed her around the waist, and lifted her to the branch he was standing on.

"What are you doing?" Kate shrieked. "You're going to get us both killed." Try as she might, she couldn't get her feet firmly planted on anything.

"I just saved your life, Kate Whitfield," Clint said angrily, "and by God, whether you like it or not, I expect a thank-you!"

"A thank-you? It'll be a cold—" Kate heard the branch crack. Before she could grab hold of anything, she was falling through air. She landed with a hard thud.

Dizzy, Kate shook her head. When the ground stopped reeling before her eyes, she moved her arms and legs, making sure nothing was broken. Glancing around, she saw Clint pulling himself off the ground. Her fury knew no bounds.

Clint was about to ask Kate if she was all right when he saw her headed in his direction, water sloshing beneath her feet. From the way she moved toward him Clint could tell she was mad as hell.

As soon as Kate was close enough, she swung her arm in a wide arc, but Clint dodged the blow. Again she swung, and again she missed. "Put your fists up and fight like a man!" she challenged.

"The time has come for us to settle our differences, Kate Whitfield." Clint pulled off his oilskin poncho.

"I agree. In fact, it's past due." Seeing he wasn't going to fight, Kate reached for her gun. The holster was empty. She had no idea where or when the revolver had fallen out. "It would be just like you to shoot an unarmed woman." Bravely she stood waiting, ready to meet her fate. But instead of going for his gun, he unbuckled his gun belt and let it fall on his poncho. His leather vest followed.

Suddenly realizing what was on his mind, Kate took several steps backwards.

"I'm going to give you exactly what you've been asking for, lady." Clint pulled his shirt off.

"Oh no you're not." Even as furious as she was, Kate hadn't failed to notice his muscles flexing as each article of clothing was removed. "Don't you dare lay a finger on me," she ordered. "I wasn't good enough for you before. Well, I have news for you. You're not good enough for me now! Just because we're stranded, and you suddenly have the urge, doesn't mean I'm going to change my mind one damn bit."

Clint slowly moved forward. He had every intention of claiming what she'd been dangling in his face for so long.

"Just what do you think you're going to prove?" Kate made a dart to the side.

"It's the best way I know of shutting you up."

Kate reached down, grabbed a handful of mud and flung it at him, but he continued stalking her. She could even see the undeniable glint in his eyes. Carefully she moved backwards, watching closely for him to make any sort of move toward her.

"You're the one who asked me to your bed, Kate, and you've taunted me every possible way you could think of. The time for reckoning has arrived."

His voice was as soft as a kitten's fur, but her senses were acute. She could smell the rain in the air, and even the wet grass beneath her feet. He stopped and stared at her, making her even more leery. His thick hair was mussed, and he looked so damnably handsome, even with mud on his face. Kate sucked in her breath. No! She wasn't going to let this happen! Not after all the things he'd said and done. "Go back to your whores in Rawlins," she hissed.

"You're the one who said that, not I." He took a step forward, and she took a step backwards. "You've done everything possible to prove to me you're a woman. But clothes alone don't make a woman, Kate. I'm going to show you just how much of a woman you really are."

Kate tried not to listen, but his silky soft voice was having an unwanted effect on her. A shiver worked its way up her spine, a shiver that had nothing to do with her wet clothes and the chilled night air. She didn't dare try to define the excitement that rushed her blood through her veins as Clint moved closer.

"You've wanted me all along. Now I want you. So why are you fighting me?"

Kate wasn't sure what she wanted anymore. Her body was saying one thing and her mind another. She wanted him to pay for all the humili-ation he'd put her through. But somehow it no longer seemed as important. Damn him! As if it were an omen, clouds covered the moon and everything turned dark. "The men will be back any moment looking for us."

"Oh, no. They're going to be too busy rounding up the cattle. It's going to take some time before they even realize we're missing. We're not likely to see them till dawn." Clint took another step forward and, when he saw Kate hesitate, reached out and yanked her to him, pinioning her arms behind her.

Kate tried struggling, but the effort was useless. She thrashed her head back and forth, but his lips found hers. His kiss was hot, hard, searing—then coaxing. He kissed her jaw, then nibbled her ear. His tongue trailed down her neck, and he sucked gently at the curve. Unexpected, wild feelings ripped through Kate, the likes of which she'd never known. The smell of his body, the feel of his strong arms holding her, added to her building desire. Even the returning rumble of thunder overhead seemed to add fire to the moment. His lips reclaimed hers, and she opened her mouth, allowing the erotic invasion of his tongue. His lips still on hers, he swung her up in his arms. Kate clung to him, her face and breasts pressed against his warm, naked chest, the short hairs caressing her face and increasing the fire. She didn't know where he was taking her and she didn't care. Her need for him was ringing in her ears. That he was finally going to make love to her was all she could think about.

Kate didn't lift her eyelids until Clint came to a halt. Seeing he was standing by a deep stream, her eyes widened and the ardor she'd felt fled. Was he going to drop her in the water again? She was about to give him a piece of her mind when he set her on her feet. She watched him strip, then step into the stream. Chest deep, he submerged himself, then came back up. Rivulets of water went in every direction as he shook his head. He turned and held his arms out to her.

"Care to join me?"

The glint in his eyes combined with his ornery grin was all Kate needed. Without a second thought, she yanked off her boots and entered the stream, not bothering to undress. Surprisingly, the water wasn't cold.

Clint was much taller, and when Kate drew up in front of him, the water almost reached her shoulders. Her heart was pounding with anticipation. He gently rinsed her face before cupping it with his hands. Light kisses touched her eyes, her nose, each side of her mouth, before he claimed her lips. Kate's legs were turning to jam, and she wasn't sure she could remain standing. Slowly he slid her suspenders down and began unbuttoning her shirt. As he removed it, his mouth trailed down her neck, gently sucking, drinking the water that had lingered. He nibbled her bare shoulders, causing her to quiver. She drew in her breath as he undid her jeans and his hand slid inside, coming to rest on the furry mound between her legs. When his finger moved inside, she gasped at the waves of pleasure that swept through her entire being. As he manipulated his finger, she automatically spread her legs, not wanting him to stop.

"You have no idea how I've waited for this moment," Clint whispered in her hair, his voice husky. Hearing her soft moans of pleasure was all the response he needed. He reclaimed her lips, devouring the sweet taste of her mouth, feeling her tongue intertwine with his. His need for sexual release was overpowering, but he continued to take his time, demanding Kate to soar in the sky with him.

Kate was so racked with a consuming fire and the throbbing between her legs that she wasn't even sure when her pants had been removed or when Clint laid her on the thick grassy bank. But then he was beside her suckling the soft mound of her breast, his hands burning every inch of her flesh until she thought she would scream for want of him.

Clint moved between her legs, thrusting deeply within her, groaning at the tightness that surrounded him. He'd held himself in check for too long. Finally he was taking what he'd waited for. But to his surprise, Kate continued to lie perfectly still, even though her passion was high. "Put your legs around my waist and move your hips, Kate," he whispered in her ear.

"Why?"

Her breathing was heavy, and for a moment Clint didn't understand what she'd said. He pulled back, then again thrust himself inside her, pleased at hearing her guttural moan. He suddenly realized just how lacking her experience was. "Because it will make it more pleasurable for both of us." Whether she complied or not, he knew there was no way in hell he could stop now.

There was an explosion building inside of Kate that she was afraid would go away if she moved. Her breathing raspy, she tentatively moved her hips. Discovering the pleasure of moving him about inside her, she became more aggressive.

Clint could feel Kate's tension rising as she neared the crest of molten passion. She began to writhe beneath him, and as his movements increased, so did hers. She became a woman possessed, thinking only of her burning need, unaware how pleasurable that need made it for him. Now she was all instinct and raw desire. She clung to him, digging her nails into his shoulders. She kissed his neck and chest, then she lay back, her tongue circling her full lips. When he kissed her, her tongue eagerly darted in and out of his mouth.

Everything seemed to burst inside Kate, and wave after wonderful wave cascaded on the other. Somewhere in the back of her mind, she heard herself scream, but it seemed so far away. She felt Clint shudder, then he was lying on top of her, keeping her blissfully warm.

Clint gently ran his thumb across Kate's swollen lips. "You're beautiful. I was a fool to turn you down when you asked me to your bed."

Kate smiled nervously. "I swore to get even."

"And that you did. I don't think I've ever wanted a woman as much as I've wanted you."

"Well now you've had me. It will have to stop here."

Clint rolled onto his side, pulling her into the protection of his arms. "You know as well as I do that we won't be able to remain apart, not after what we've shared."

"You're wrong," Kate muttered against his chest.

Clint smiled. "We gave each other unforgettable pleasure, something neither of us will be able to turn our backs on. It won't stop here. Now get some sleep, Kate, it'll be morning soon."

"Kate, get up. I see riders in the distance."

Kate opened her eyes and saw Clint standing over her, fully dressed. The stark reality of what had happened was like being kicked by a horse. At least at some time he'd covered her with her oilskin. She had never allowed a man to see her naked in the daylight and she wasn't about to start now. She raised up on one elbow, trying to clear the cobwebs from her head. The sun was shining in her eyes and there wasn't a cloud in the sky.

Clint gave her an ornery grin. "There are riders coming."

"Where are my clothes?" Kate snapped at him. Her gaze darted from place to place.

Clint was surprised. After what they had shared, he'd expected her to be more docile—or at least friendlier. Her attitude aggravated him. Obviously she hadn't changed a bit. "Are you going to thank me now for saving your life, or are you still going to insist you could have made it on your own?"

Kate clamped her jaw shut.

"The men are getting closer."

Kate glared at him, then he extended his arm, her clothes clutched in one big hand.

"I'm waiting."

"Thank you for saving my life," she said with a mock sweetness.

"That'll do for starters." He tossed her clothes to her. "They're still wet, but I don't think you want those men to see you the way you are now."

Kate cringed at the thought of having to dress in front of him. She tried putting her clothes on beneath her oilskin, but it kept sliding off. Admitting she had no other choice, she stood, turned her back, and finished dressing. Though she hadn't looked at Clint, she could feel his eyes burning holes into her back. When the job was completed, she looked out over the land. Heartsick, she stared at the dead cattle strewn about.

When the five men rode up, both Kate and Clint were surprised to see Lucas leading the group.

"We were worried like hell that something had happened to you," Lucas said as he brought his horse to a halt. He suddenly broke out laughing. "You two look like hell. What did you do? Waller in the mud?"

I'd like to rub mud on that damn smile of yours, Kate thought. "You'd probably look the same if you'd gone through what we have," she snapped at him. "Were the rustlers caught? Did they get any of our steers?"

"No to both your questions."

At least some good news had come out of this, Kate thought as she picked her coat up off the ground. "When did you get back, Lucas?"

"Last night, big sister. And just so you'll be kept informed as to what's going on, Sam said it was too late for me to be of any help here. Me and the men came looking for you as soon as we found out you were missing. Now climb up. It's a long ride back, and Mattie and Sam are worried sick."

Kate could tell Lucas was enjoying giving orders, but then maybe he was finally coming into his own.

Lucas kicked his foot free from the stirrup, and she used it to climb up behind him. There were no extra horses, so they would have to ride double. Clint mounted behind one of the cowhands.

The long ride home allowed Kate time to think, and she badly needed to come to grips with Clint's ability to make her body come alive. She knew it would only be fool's play to try to convince herself that it was just something she could ignore. Never in her wildest dreams had she thought coupling could drive her to such wild, uncontrollable pleasure. Her body was becoming warm just thinking about it. She glanced over at Clint, but he was busy talking to Billy Lee, the cowhand he was riding double with. Her mind flashed to the two other men she'd allowed to bed her so many years ago. Because of them, she'd thought herself incapable of deriving satisfaction from any man. Now she could see just how inept those men had been. At the time she'd thought it only right when they told her to lie still, and if she had started to feel anything, they were al-

ready finished and ready to get dressed. If she
knew where they were now, she'd be tempted to
shoot both of them!

Kate saw the herd stretched out about a half
mile away. Because her thoughts had been centered on herself, it occurred to her, she hadn't
asked two very important questions. She leaned
forward. "Lucas, did we lose any men?"

"Nope."

"Do you know how many steers we lost?"

"The boys figure only about fifty."

As they passed the outskirts of the herd, a couple of cowhands raised their hats in recognition.
Kate reached for her hat, then remembered she
didn't have one. She'd also lost that somewhere.
With no other option, she waved her hand.

Kate tried concentrating on the open valley they
were traveling across, the mountains, the trees,
but her attention faded, and she drifted back to
what was uppermost on her mind. Such as, what
was she going to do now? She'd thought she
knew how this would all end, except it hadn't
turned out the way she'd expected. It was sort of
hanging in the wind as if waiting to see what
would take place next. She'd thought once they'd
bedded, she'd be rid of her desire. And even
though she'd been loathe to admit it, he *had* saved
her life. Her horse would never have outrun the
stampede. He'd also been right about the rustlers
attacking, another thing she should be grateful
for.

She pushed her hair back from her face and
held it in place with her hand. Now that it had
dried, it seemed to be blowing everywhere. Kate
sighed, stealing another glance at Clint. He looked
so tall and strong. Had he gotten any sleep last
night? If he hadn't, no one could tell by looking
at him. No, she thought, there were no answers.
For now, what would happen next between them

would continue to hang in the wind a little longer. But there were a few things she'd come to accept. She wasn't sorry. And though it didn't seem possible, she no longer felt animosity toward Clint. From the beginning she'd hated him, or at least thought she did. But maybe all along she'd actually been fighting an attraction that she didn't want to accept. And just maybe, even though she'd wanted him to make love to her, she'd been afraid of the outcome. And she should have been, because he'd awakened a desire that scared the hell out of her. It was even scarier that she didn't want this first time to be the last time.

When they arrived at the homestead, Mattie came rushing out the front door, tears running down her cheeks. Kate slid off the rump of Lucas's horse and hurried onto the porch to assure the older woman she was fine. A moment later, the manservant pushed Sam out. Kate knew she was loved, but she'd never taken into consideration just how deep that love was. Her heart went out to Sam and Mattie at realizing how long they'd had to sit and wait before finding out she was safe and well. This was her family, and nothing except the land was more important. She went into the house with them, busily explaining everything that had happened. Well, almost everything.

The cowhands had already ridden off, but Clint remained standing in front of the porch. He'd seen the smile and nod Sam had given him, and he was sure Sam knew he had saved Kate's life. At seeing the love and concern the family shared, an almost-forgotten feeling of being wanted welled up inside him. Then he heard a voice behind him.

"I wonder if they'd of worried if it had been me out there?"

It was a callous statement, and Clint looked

around at the young man standing behind him. "Family reacts differently when it comes to a woman then they do a man, Lucas."

"Now ain't that the truth."

"Do you know if Midnight has returned?"

"Yep. One of the hands bedded him down in his stall."

Clint decided this would be a good opportunity to try again to befriend Lucas. Perhaps being with the boy might even soften Kate up a tad. "Do you think those rustlers are going to make another attempt on the herd?"

"I doubt it. There's too many men guarding them now, and they'll be watchin' for trouble."

"Did you locate that bear you were searching for yesterday?"

"Naw. Looks like I'm going to have to take some of the boys and go back out tomorrow looking again."

"How about I ride with you?"

Lucas cast a suspicious look at the big man. "Suit yourself. We'll be leaving first thing in the morning. It'll probably end up bein' a useless trip what with the rain destroying the tracks. I'll bet the critter has long since gone back up in the mountains by now."

"I'll be ready." Clint stepped onto the porch and entered the house. As he passed the parlor, he heard Kate's husky voice, but he couldn't hear what she was saying. One thing was for sure, she wasn't telling Mattie and Sam everything.

Clint didn't see Kate the rest of the day, nor did she show up for supper. But Mattie was quick to offer a reason.

"Sam," Mattie said as she took her place at the dinner table, "Kate just came in a little while ago, and she looked so tired I suggested supper be sent to her room so she could get a good night's rest."

Oliver cleared his throat. "I offered my professional help, but she turned me down."

"I've never heard her complain before." Sam leaned back in his chair, deep in thought. "There's something funny goin' on. I feel it in my bones."

"She almost got killed last night!" Mattie reminded him. She reached over and touched Clint's arm. "We can't thank you enough. Bless the Lord that you were there to save her."

"Mattie's right, boy. If I can ever return the favor, just let me know."

Clint smiled. "Believe me, it was my pleasure."

The next morning Clint left with Lucas and a couple of hands to search for the rogue bear. Once away from the homestead, Lucas seemed to be in no hurry.

"Kick those damn horses in the ass and get on up to where that bear was located," Lucas ordered the two older cowpokes in a coarse voice. "We'll catch up with you."

They nudged their horses into a gallop and rode off.

"Shouldn't we stick with them?" Clint asked.

"Hell no. The bastards are paid to work on this ranch, no matter what the job."

The rest of the trip was spent with Lucas expounding on how he'd ridden every whore within a hundred miles as well as some uppity women in town. "They can't keep their hands off of me," Lucas bragged.

Clint smiled, even though he knew Lucas was trying to impress him. Clint was reminded of when he was a young boy and had his first sexual experience. It had been so wonderful that he immediately decided that for the rest of his life he was going to do nothing but bed every woman in the world. Admittedly he'd been younger than Lucas, but like Lucas, for a while he'd given it a damn good try. Clint chuckled. It hadn't taken long for his father to point out that life wasn't just comprised of sex.

When it was decided there were no signs of a bear, Lucas sent the men back, then insisted Clint go to town with him for a drink. Clint trailed along, asking seemingly unimportant questions off and on about the cattle, and still coming up with no answers.

"I have a couple of things I want to do," Clint said as they entered Whitfield. "I'll meet you at the saloon shortly."

Lucas nodded and moved his big buckskin horse toward the end of town.

Knowing there was only one stone left that he hadn't turned over, Clint had decided to send Sandoval another telegram, this time requesting a new, thorough check on the government cattle buyer, Gordon Vale. Again he worded the wire carefully, informing Sandoval to send the reply to Rawlins and to have them keep it until he was able to pick it up. Clint didn't expect a reply for a couple of weeks.

By the time Clint made it to the small saloon on the outskirts of town, Lucas was already well into his liquor. As the drinks continued, Lucas became cockier, then surly. When Lucas tried to pick a fight with one of the other customers, Clint used his fist to knock the boy out and put a stop to it. Clint carried the limp body out of the saloon. Lucas was already coming to by the time Clint hoisted the boy onto his buckskin.

It was late afternoon when Clint and the sullen boy neared the homestead.

"Why the hell did you have to sock me?" Lucas snapped angrily as they put their horses away.

Clint grinned. "Look at it this way, Lucas. That

was a bear of a man and you were about to break a bottle over his head. He'd have been a lot harder on you than I was."

"Maybe, but I could have handled him."

"The hell you could have."

They left the barn and made their way to the house.

Lucas couldn't leave it at that. "You underestimate me, Clint."

"Oh? Well, maybe so."

Kate had spent the day in a fog, trying to come to grips with the overwhelming passion that Clint had awakened in her. Last night had been plagued with unfulfilled desires. She'd been obsessed with a need to have him make love to her again. Her hands had roamed her body, pretending they were his hands. It had taken every bit of willpower she could muster not to join him in his bedroom. It was all so overpowering, and she wasn't sure how to handle it. She desperately wanted to feel that pleasurable driving madness again, but then what? Would the desire ever go away or would it remain constantly there?

Later that morning, Kate was informed by one of the cowhands that a large herd of wild mustangs had been spotted only about a two-day ride away. She was on her way to find Henry Blankenship and tell him to send some men out to round up the mustangs when she suddenly came to a halt near the smokehouse. She would take a couple of men and handle the matter herself. There wasn't really anything to do around the ranch that Henry or Sam couldn't handle until time came to round up the steers for shipping. After driving the rustlers off the night of the thunderstorm, she was convinced they would lay low for some time. Hopefully, permanently. But more importantly, she needed to get away from Clint. She needed time to think.

She shoved her floppy hat back and glanced around the nearly empty area. Maybe the longer she put off letting Clint make love to her, the more she'd learn to control her bodily needs. Then she and Clint could occasionally taste the fruit of passion, but it wouldn't get out of hand. It sounded like a good, practical idea. Yes, that's exactly what she would do, but first, she needed to get away for a while to get her emotions under control.

Kate had supper that night in the cook shack with Henry, to go over any last minute problems that might come up while she was away. With everything in readiness for her trip, Kate had one last matter to take care of. Telling Sam.

When Kate entered her father's office, she discovered Sam had company. It had been almost two days since she and Clint had made love, yet just seeing his handsome face and the unhidden desire in his eyes made her knees tremble and her pulse beat faster. She quickly averted her eyes, refusing to let him have such an effect on her. It didn't work. Flashes of what they shared streaked through her head.

"What's on your mind, girl?" Sam asked.

Kate cleared her throat in an effort to make her voice sound steady. "A large herd of mustangs has been spotted. I'm going after them. I've already informed Henry that I'm taking Cotton and Billy Lee with me."

Clint took a draw on his cigar, then let a smoke ring trail into the air. "When do you plan on leaving?"

"First thing in the morning," she said over her shoulder, her eyes still on her father. "We'll get forty to sixty dollars for each mustang the army buys."

Sam nodded.

Kate quickly left the room before Sam could come up with some reason to keep her there. This is absurd, she thought as she headed up the narrow staircase. I can't even be in the same room with Clint without getting palpitations! Taking off for a while will be good for me, she tried assuring herself.

Sam looked at Clint and released a grunt. "I wish I knew what was wrong with that girl."

"What makes you think something's wrong?" Clint asked. He took another puff on his cigar.

"She's been pushing herself like the devil's after her, and she ain't been actin' right since before she started all that dressin' up for supper."

"Isn't anything wrong with a woman wanting to dress properly, Sam. You also have to take into consideration that she's been shot at and then almost got killed during that stampede." Clint stood and headed for the doorway. "Tell you what," he said as he turned back around, "if you're so concerned about Kate, why don't I just go with her. I can keep an eye on her plus help catch the mustangs. If there's one thing I do know about, it's horses. Besides, it'll give me something to do other than just sitting around."

"I'd be beholden. Kate can take care of herself, but with all that's been goin' on, I think you tagging along might be a good idea. I'll send Addie May up to tell her."

"That won't be necessary. Kate will find out in the morning. While we're gone, maybe you should make sure Oliver moves to town and gets his practice going."

"You think that's who has been making Kate act so strange?" Sam bellowed.

"It would certainly seem that way. I'll see you when I get back, Sam."

Clint was smiling as he left the house to prepare for his excursion with Kate. So much for Oliver, he thought. He chuckled softly. Things couldn't have turned out better even if he'd planned them. He was at a dead end in his investigation, and other than making love to Kate, the couple of months until roundup were looking mighty boring. As he had in Sam's office, Clint again wondered if Kate was doing this to escape him. Well, if that was what she had in mind, it wasn't going to work. He'd unleashed a fiery woman full of wanton desires, and he'd be damned if he'd let her crawl back into her little hole of maidenly security. By God, until he left the ranch she was his, and he was going to make damn sure she knew it.

Chapter 12

Kate watched the pale gray light up the distant mountain peaks as she, Billy Lee, and Cotton rode away from the homestead leading two packhorses loaded with supplies and equipment. The jacket she wore kept her warm, and the crisp air would hopefully clear her head. Even after breakfast and two cups of coffee, she still didn't feel wide awake. Again, sleep had not come easy last night.

Kate glanced over at the two men riding alongside. Both had worked on the ranch for practically five years and Kate felt comfortable around them. They were burly men, jovial, and their hair hung past their collars, but that's where the resemblance stopped. Billy Lee's face was scarred with pox marks, and his nose was hawk-shaped. His hair was carrot red, and Kate felt sure that his features would make people who didn't know him think he was mean. Cotton, on the other hand, reminded her of a big, cuddly animal. His hair and full beard were brown, his face round, and his cheeks rosy.

These were two of the men Kate had ridden into town with that first night Clint Morgan arrived and caused Lucas to be thrown from his horse. Kate knew that even though Billy Lee and Cotton had fought with Morgan that night, they had become somewhat friendly since Morgan had come to stay at the ranch. Kate wondered how friendly. Curious as to what their opinion now was of Clint, she decided to bring his name up in their conversation.

"How is your jaw?" Kate asked Cotton.

"It's comin' along just fine, Miss Kate." Cotton grinned. "I tell you, I've been in a lot of fights in my time, but I gotta give Morgan credit. He planted a fist on me the likes of which I ain't never known."

"You sound like you're not mad at him." Kate drew her horse closer so he wouldn't have to talk so loud.

"Why should I be mad? I shouldn't have leaned over him like I did and gave him a clear shot. I've talked to Morgan on more than one occasion, and I gotta say I like the man. I'll bet he was madder than a hornet though that night we left him hogtied, but I've never brought the subject up."

Billy Lee laughed. "Hell, Cotton, you just don't want to find out if he can hit you that hard again."

They had ridden about four miles when Billy Lee heard a horse coming up from behind. Turning in the saddle, he saw Clint Morgan riding in their direction, leading a packhorse. "I think we're gonna have company," Billy Lee called to Kate.

Kate and Cotton looked back at the same time. Kate groaned and Cotton whistled softly between his teeth. "Speak of the devil," he commented.

Kate brought her horse to a halt and motioned the men to go on.

"Where do you think you're headed?" Kate demanded when Clint rode up. *I need this time alone!* Already her heart was starting to flutter, and she hated her weakness.

"With you, darlin', and you can't say there's

not enough provisions, because I've brought more than my share.''

''Well you can just turn around and go back. I don't want you along.''

''You're lying, Kate Whitfield, you're just not willing to admit it. But it doesn't matter. Sam ordered me to go with you, and we can't disobey Sam, can we?''

Kate shoved her hat back while staring in the direction he'd come from. ''You're the one who's lying,'' she accused.

''I'm perfectly willing for us to ride back and let him tell you.''

Kate knew that to do so would cause too long a delay. She wouldn't put it past Clint to have waited to catch up until he was sure she wouldn't go back. How else would he have known which trail they took? ''All right, you can come along. But I warn you, you're not going to sit around and watch everyone do all the work.''

''I don't intend to.''

''I thought you didn't like breaking horses.''

''I don't, but as you well know, that doesn't mean I can't.''

''I'm not going to give you a share of the take like Cotton and Billy Lee will be getting.''

''Darlin', are we going to sit here squabbling, or are we going to catch up with the others?''

Kate knew her fate was sealed. She'd tried to get away from him, but maybe some things just weren't meant to be. ''I expect you to pull your share of the load,'' she reiterated.

Clint laughed. ''I wouldn't have it any other way.''

For two days they traveled across country, the altitude getting higher and the southern end of the jagged mountains growing nearer. They stopped only to eat or sleep. Kate was happy at being out in the open range, and at the same time disappointed that her sleeping bag always seemed to end up on one side of the campfire and Clint's on the other. Being constantly with Clint, looking at him, studying his every move was driving her insane with desire. But to her growing aggravation, he showed no interest whatsoever. There wasn't even a gleam in his eyes, or a knowing smile.

Kate was surprised at how well the three men got along. At times they talked about cattle, land, and horses. Other times they laughed over experiences in their past. Kate wondered if the tales Clint told about funny incidents with Indians were really true or if he was just making them up. Cotton teased Clint about being left hog-tied, and Clint reciprocated with jovial references to Cotton's broken jaw. Kate couldn't believe that either man could find humor in what had happened, but soon even she and Billy Lee were laughing with them. She was being treated as one of the boys, yet given womanly considerations, for which she was grateful. Prior to the trip, she'd thought of Clint only as an antagonist, or a man who had shown her the delights of sex. Now she was seeing a different side of his personality, and she found herself liking him more and more.

On the third morning they reached the area where the mustangs had last been spotted. They all spread out, searching for tracks. It was Clint who discovered them. He whistled, and the others rode over and joined him.

"They must have seen the men and took out of here, because these tracks are a good four days old. From the looks of it, they're still headed south," he said, pointing at the tracks farther down, "and there's close to fifty head."

The others nodded.

Through the rest of the morning and on into the early afternoon, the small group followed the horse tracks into small meadows, across streams, and up into the foothills covered with thick, green brush and trees. At times Kate could see down to the valley they'd left. It had narrowed to almost a slit, and the Rocky Mountains were closing in. The terrain became steep, forcing them to travel in single file. At times they had to dismount and lead their horses because of the soft dirt and loose rock.

Kate didn't know when or how it had happened, but at some point Clint had become their leader. Billy Lee and Cotton seemed perfectly willing to follow. She had to admit Clint knew what he was doing, and was far better at tracking than she or the others. Still, she wasn't particularly happy that she had been relegated to bringing up the rear. If the horses kicked up dust, she was the one to get the full brunt of it. It wasn't a position she was used to and she didn't like it one damn bit.

Kate found the scenery spectacular, with more and more towering slabs of red rock coming into view. However, the sun was pitiless, and she could feel perspiration between her breasts. She was sure that she, like the men, probably had a damp streak running down the back of her lavender shirt.

When they crossed a trickling stream, Kate stopped and dismounted. Quickly she untied the red bandanna from around her neck, doused it in the cool water, and rinsed her face. It was almost as heavenly as . . . No. There was no comparison, but she did feel considerably better. After wringing out her bandanna, she tied it around her forehead to help buffer the heat. Galled at not being able to relax for a few moments, she mounted up and took out after the men, who were already disappearing from view. They hadn't even missed her! What if she'd fallen off the mountainside? Would they return a week later?

Though his concentration was centered on the tracks he'd been following, Clint was well aware of the difficulty Kate was having. He'd even known when she stopped for water and was about to pull up and wait when she'd caught back up with them. She'd chosen to come on this drive, and he refused to pamper her. He did admire her for not complaining or demanding to be treated like some frail queen, but her need to feel she was on the same level as any man still made him angry. At the same time, he wanted to possess her. When he'd made love to her that night, she'd been more woman than he'd dreamed possible. He wanted to watch her body come alive again. Dammit, he wanted her to be a woman and proud of it!

Kate couldn't believe that Clint never seemed to tire. Even Cotton and Billy Lee were showing signs of fatigue from the altitude as well as the arduous climb. Kate was convinced that if they had to walk their horses again up the rocks, she'd just sit and wait until someone came back with news that the herd had been located. But still she continued on. When Clint did finally circle back to ask if she wanted to rest, she replied with a sharp no. She wasn't about to cry mercy. Besides, the horse droppings they now passed were fresh, and she knew they had to be getting close to their destination.

It was mid-afternoon when Clint finally raised his hand, bringing them all to a halt. Kate watched him dismount, say something to Billy Lee and Cotton, then make his way back to her.

"I'm going ahead on foot," he informed her, his voice hushed. "I think the mustangs are on the other side of that cliff." He pointed ahead.

Kate nodded, watching Clint move away, making nary a sound. His silent movements triggered something in the back of her mind, but she couldn't put her finger on it. As he topped the rise, all she could see was a shadow of a big man against the bright sunlight. Her mind immediately flashed back to the man in the woods who had saved her life. She suddenly realized that though she'd only seen his shadow disappearing behind a tree, he'd also been big . . . and so silent she hadn't even known he was about. No, she told herself, it couldn't have been Clint. The heat is just playing tricks on my mind. There was no reason for him to be so far from the house, especially at that time of night.

It was a good thirty minutes before Clint returned. Everyone dismounted and gathered around him. He squatted, picked up a dry twig from the ground, and began drawing lines in the soft dirt.

"It looks like there's a canyon right here," Clint said, pointing with the twig, "with a small stream. The mustangs are over here. From what I could see, the canyon didn't look like more than a slit in the mountain, so it could very well be boxed in. Now, the meadow where the horses are grazing has red rock cliffs on this side. The other side is a thick wall of pines, making a perfect covering for us. If that canyon is closed off, tomorrow morning we can position ourselves in an arc. Kate, you'll be here," he scratched an X on the ground to mark the spot, "Billy Lee at this point, Cotton here, and I'll take the far end. When I get into position, I'll fire a shot. We all ride forward and drive the mustangs into the canyon. Kate, do you have any suggestions to add?"

Kate was taken aback by the question. *Now he asks my opinion!* she thought angrily. But he had thoroughly covered everything. "No."

"I'm fixing to circle up and check out that canyon. I suggest we camp here, and tonight we take turns keeping an eye on the herd, just in case they decide to take off." He grinned. "Looks like we can all look forward to jerky and hardtack tonight."

Billy Lee and Cotton chuckled. Kate said nothing.

A few minutes later, Clint left. Kate helped strip off saddles and packs, hobble the animals, and roll out sleeping bags. Because Clint had chosen to sleep on the other side of Cotton and Billy Lee on previous nights, she made sure that's where his gear was put this time.

Though Clint had said that the mustangs were still a good distance below, they all tried to be as quiet as possible. It had been a good three years since Kate had been on a wild horse roundup, and even though they had a lot of hard work ahead of them, she was excited.

Kate took a short nap. When she awoke, Clint still hadn't returned. "I'm going to take a look at the mustangs," she announced to Billy Lee and Cotton, who were sitting on the ground, quietly discussing something.

"They're a mighty pretty sight," Cotton called after her. "We already checked them out."

Kate walked in the same direction Clint had taken earlier. The last few yards she crawled on her hands and knees, the smell of the dirt-covered rocks invading her nostrils. Crawling out on a huge flat rock surface, she lay down on her stomach, the heat of the mammoth rock penetrating through her clothes. Her vantage point was perfect, and she gazed in awe at the scenery below. The surrounding cliffs abounded with sheer slabs of reddish, rust-colored rock rising straight up from the valley floor, and spiraling columns of a like color standing as huge sentinels, reminding

Kate of gigantic chess pieces. They looked as if they had been there since the beginning of time.

The large, grassy meadow was much farther down than Kate had imagined. She estimated there were at least sixty mustangs spread out, nipping the grass, their sleek coats shining in the sunlight. They were of varying colors and sizes, some big, some small. Some were probably army horses that had gotten away by one means or another, others strays from ranches or Indians, and there were probably geldings and young stallions as well as mares. Because the army only purchased large mares, the mustangs would have to be culled once they were trapped in the canyon. Even so, the ones they kept were going to make for a healthy profit, even after Billy Lee and Cotton received their cut.

Realizing a small stone was digging into her shoulder, she shifted about until she was comfortable, then returned her attention to the wild horses. She watched a couple of yearlings trotting around, playing what looked like a good old-fashioned game of tag. Her gaze traveled, coming to rest on a bay stallion trying to mount a mare. Normally she wouldn't have thought anything about it, but for some reason she became transfixed, unable to look away. When the mare wouldn't cooperate, the stallion nipped at her neck, forcing her into obedience. Kate's hand squeezed into fists, her own need growing as strong as the stallion's. When he mounted the mare, Kate sucked in her breath.

"You'll be getting a fine-looking bunch of horses."

Kate had no idea where Clint had come from, but he was here, and that was all that mattered. She rolled onto her back.

Clint hadn't expected to see the amorous look on Kate's dirt-streaked face. She lay there, silently waiting, fire dancing in her green eyes as she stared up at him. He had no earthly idea why she desired him, but he certainly wasn't going to turn his back on her. After all, wasn't this why he'd tagged along?

The thought of Billy Lee and Cotton being close by flashed through Clint's mind, but he was already moving his shirt. The trees above offered total seclusion, and they were a quarter of the way down the mountainside. He unbuckled his pants, then reached down to remove his boots, his eyes never leaving hers. His britches had already grown tight for want of her.

Transfixed, Kate stood and began unbuttoning her shirt. Somehow, Clint's seeing her naked in the light no longer bothered her. In fact she gloried in it. Her breathing was already shallow and her throat had become tight with expectation. She watched the sunlight caress the hard planes of his face and bathe his broad shoulders. Her hands stopped when Clint pulled off his pants and she could see the evidence of his desire. Just knowing he wanted her as much as she wanted him gave her a sense of feminine confidence she'd never experienced before. Wild, untamed desires shot through her like lightning bolts.

When she removed her shirt, Clint's eyes feasted on her creamy white shoulders, the swell of her full breasts, the dark nipples, already hardened, begging to be kissed. She slid her pants past her flat stomach, over rounded hips, and down long legs, perfectly molded because of her active life. Though his desire was strong, he reached out and removed the pins from her hair, then buried his hands in the thick glossy mane that tumbled down her back. "You should never keep your hair bound atop your head. It's much too lovely." Unable to wait another moment to taste her ripe, parted lips, he leaned down and claimed his kiss. "Has anyone ever told you you have a body that would drive a man mad with desire?" he asked softly against her lips.

His praises were like music to Kate's ears. Knowing he thought of her as desirable made her heart sing its own tune. "No," she whispered, not even sure she'd said the word out loud.

Clint cupped a full breast in one hand, brushing his thumb across the swollen bud. "I've wanted you from the first day I laid eyes on you."

"I . . . I didn't know. Clint, please make love to me. I don't think I can wait a moment longer."

Seeing the glazed look in her eyes, he laid down with her on the rock, every fiber in his body demanding satisfaction. Still he held off. His tongue, lips, and hands roamed her body, tasting her, feeling her.

"Clint . . ." Kate gasped as her hands trailed across the tight muscles in his shoulders, loving the feel of him. Her head was swimming, and every cell in her body was screaming for satisfaction. "I can't . . ." She sucked in her breath as he nibbled the inside of her thighs. "Oh God," she moaned, "I don't think I can stand it another moment."

Clint thrust deep within her tight, moist pond of pleasure. "Make love to me, Kate," Clint whispered, his voice raw with desire.

Like a woman possessed, Kate's body took on a life of its own. As he moved in and out of her, her hands slid to his haunches, encouraging him, wanting him, demanding he not stop. She found herself wanting to please him as much as he was pleasing her. She raised up enough to kiss his chest, his arms, his lips, before falling back down and writhing with pleasure. "It feels so wonderful," she whispered unknowingly. His lips came down on hers just as she was consumed with the wondrous spasms of climatic pleasure.

Kate lay languid, her head resting on Clint's arm. In a way, she felt humble. She wanted to thank him for giving her such ecstasy, to tell him what a marvelous lover he was, but the words stuck in her throat. He'd probably been told that by many women. "Did I please you?" she finally asked, needing to know the answer.

Clint chuckled and trailed a finger over the curve of her breast and down to her navel. "Oh yes, my darlin'. If we keep this up, I may never want to leave."

Kate raised up and smiled down at him. "If we keep this up, I'm not going to be able to walk."

Clint chuckled. "I would be more than happy to test that theory, sweetheart, but unfortunately it won't be right away. We have to get dressed. Billy Lee and Cotton are probably wondering where we are, and I've worked up a hell of an appetite for beef jerky and hardtack." He gently pulled his arm from beneath her head and started dressing.

Kate studied his every movement. For some time she'd enjoyed watching just about everything he did, whether it was riding a horse, talking, laughing, or even eating. She rather liked the stubble that now covered his chin and jaw, and the beginning of a mustache. As fast as his facial hair grew, he'd probably have a beard by the time they returned to the ranch. "Clint, you have a scar on your leg, and what looks like an old bullet wound below your shoulder blade. How did you come by them?"

"From the war." Clint could clearly remember both wounds, and others, but as for the war, he'd managed to come out unscathed. All his wounds had come from outlaws.

Kate wanted to ask questions about how he'd been hurt, but it was apparent he didn't care to talk about it. Suddenly she wanted to know everything about him. Where he stayed when he wasn't going from fort to fort, what he liked to eat—

"I'll go on ahead," Clint said as he finished buckling his gun belt back on. "I'll say we've been watching the herd, and I came on back because you felt the need for a little privacy behind a bush."

A frown creased Kate's forehead. It bothered her that Clint always had an answer for everything. "Very well," she said quietly. But her serious mood quickly vanished, and by the time she arrived back at their temporary camp, she was in the best of spirits.

"Well, what do you think?" Cotton asked.

It took a moment for Kate to realize he was referring to the horses. She flashed him a brilliant smile. "I think those mustangs are going to make us a pretty little penny." Sam had always paid the men a share of what money was received from wild mustangs. She knew Billy Lee and Cotton were already looking forward to some extra change in their pockets.

Early the next morning, the mounted foursome moved their horses slowly down the rugged mountainside, leaving the packhorses and supplies behind. When they reached the bottom, they made a wide circle so as not to alert the herd. Kate took her position among the trees bordering the meadow, then dismounted to be sure the bandanna was still tied firmly around her horse's muzzle to keep him from whinnying to the mustangs. Satisfied, she climbed back on the saddle. Seeing trees in her way, she repositioned her mount to where she'd have a straight shot to the meadow. She drew her revolver and waited for Clint's gunshot. The trees were too dense and the men were too spread apart for her to even catch a glimpse of one of them. She was anxious to ride forward, which she knew made it seem like the others were taking forever to get situated. She swatted at one fly, then another, suddenly wondering where they were all coming from. Looking down, she discovered she had her horse straddled over a large heap of horse dung. She started to move him away when the shot rang out.

"Yaw," Kate yelled, causing her horse to leap forward into a full gallop.

As soon as Kate cleared the trees, she could see the mustangs up ahead. They were already on the run, the bay stallion leading the way. Seeing they were swinging in her direction, Kate fired bullets into the air, successfully turning them in the opposite direction. Her horse leaped over low bushes and across a small stream, never breaking stride.

Kate could now hear the other men yelling and shooting, but she kept her eyes straight ahead, devouring the excitement that raced through her blood.

The mustangs made several more swerves in an effort to escape, but each time they were blocked by one of the other riders. Finally the herd turned as one and ran three abreast into the canyon. Kate could see Clint and Cotton ahead, already moving in to block off the narrow entrance.

Wondering where Billy Lee was, Kate slowed her horse and turned in the saddle to see if he was behind her. She saw his sorrel running forward, but Billy Lee wasn't on the saddle. Knowing the mustangs couldn't escape now, she turned her mount and headed back in the direction Billy Lee would have been coming from.

Kate found the cowhand in the clearing, a short distance from the trees. He was sitting on the ground with a dazed look in his brown eyes. His thick, bushy red eyebrows were pulled together in a *V*.

"Well that's a hell of a way to be catching mustangs," Kate teased. "What happened?"

"Gopher hole." He climbed to his feet. "My horse took off. Figured I'd just sit here till someone came to fetch me."

"Is something wrong? You winced when you stood."

"Must have twisted my ankle."

Kate swung a leg over the saddle, then slid off. "Which ankle?" she asked as she removed the bandanna from the horse's muzzle.

"The right one."

"Sit back down and I'll take a look."

"It ain't nothin', but I'd be obliged if you'd give me a ride instead of makin' me walk."

"Well if it ain't nothin'," Kate mocked, "then I see no problem with taking a look."

Mumbling, Billy Lee sat back down. "I suppose you're goin' to tell me the boot has to come off."

Kate lifted her arched eyebrows. "Can you think of any other way of doing it?" Turning her back to him, she straddled his leg and planted her feet. She felt his left foot being positioned on her buttocks to help her pull the boot off.

As soon as Kate had his sock removed, she gently rotated his foot, making sure the ankle wasn't broken. Satisfied, she straightened up, looking down at the pox-marked face. "You lucked out."

"I told you so." He started pulling his sock back on.

"Nevertheless, I think you should soak it in that mountain stream."

"Hell, Miss Kate, I don't want to do that!"

"Don't argue with me, Billy Lee. The cold water will help keep the swelling down."

"All right, but come tomorrow, I aim to be working with the rest of you."

"I'm sure you will." Kate swung up on the saddle and Billy Lee mounted behind her.

"Where did you learn all that doctorin' stuff, Miss Kate?" Billy Lee asked as Kate turned her horse in the direction of the canyon.

"From Mattie. She's doctored just about every kind of a hurt a man can have. Of course when Doc Sawyer moved to town, a lot of things changed. I hope Oliver Putnam is as good as the old doc was." A smile spread across Kate's face, remembering when Mattie first came to the ranch. Because she was small, and in Sam's estimation frail, Sam had balked at her taking care of breaks and wounds. But Mattie had been persistent. When Sam realized just how good she was at it, he finally gave in.

Once Kate had Billy Lee's foot soaking in the water, she grabbed her rifle and moved inside the canyon to stand guard over the mustangs while Clint and Cotton went to get the packhorses and gear that had been left behind.

Kate spotted a gradual slope on one of the huge red rocks standing near the entrance. About ten feet up was what looked like a level spot. Realizing to get higher would allow her a better view, she slowly began making her way up. Her feet slid several times, but she managed to grab the side of one of the pockets that were scattered across the porous stone. Finally she reached the ledge she was seeking, only to discover it wasn't as deep as she'd thought. Though there was enough room for her to sit, she couldn't lounge. She carefully turned and quickly plopped down, preventing her feet from sliding out from under her.

Kate took her first good look at the small U-shaped canyon, with red rock boulders in the center, precariously balanced atop one another. The floor of the canyon was heavily covered with green brush, especially along the edges of the stream that seemed to sprout up from under the ground and trickled out. Several skimpy young pine trees struggled to grow near the center boulders.

From her perch, Kate couldn't see all the horses, but she could certainly see the stallion. As she watched, she decided she was going to claim him for herself, but this time she'd be smart enough to let one of the hands break him. She'd name him . . . Cinnamon, because that's what his coat reminded her of. There were scars on his hind legs where he'd obviously been in fights to keep his herd. And it was a fine herd. However, at present, Cinnamon wasn't at all happy. Kate watched him try running up the side, only to come right back down and try again at a bushy spot near the back, searching for a means of escape from his confines. He stopped, raised his head, and sniffed at the air.

Kate laughed softly as he swerved about on his hind legs and began stirring up the mares. "So," she muttered, "because you're not happy, you're going to make sure the ladies aren't either."

Suddenly the stallion took off at a dead run, straight toward the entrance, his mares right behind him. She snatched her rifle from her lap, but not having time to aim, she had to shoot at the ground well ahead of him. He was moving even faster now. Knowing of only one fast way down, Kate tossed her rifle, then slid down the rock on her rear. By the time her feet touched ground, the stallion was going out the canyon entrance. She pulled her revolver and shot into the air, finally bringing the rest of the herd to a halt. She had no idea how many mustangs had taken off with the bay stallion. Kate fired a couple of more shots and the mustangs trotted to the back of the canyon.

"What the hell happened?" Billy Lee yelled. "I thought them damn critters were goin' to run right over me!"

Kate saw him hobbling toward her, trying to keep his bare foot off the ground as much as possible.

"That stallion's smarter than I gave him credit for," Kate answered. She holstered her gun, then leaned over and picked up her rifle. She released a groan upon hearing Cotton and Clint ride up.

"How did the mustangs get loose?" Clint asked, not bothering to dismount.

Kate reached around and dusted off the back of her britches.

He didn't like the way she was deliberately ignoring him. "Are you going to answer my question?"

Kate gave him a withering look. She didn't like the commanding tone of his voice, and she certainly didn't like accounting to him for anything, especially mustangs that now belonged to her. "They got away, and that's all you need to know. If you don't like it, you can always ride back to the ranch. Billy Lee, go get your boot on, then I want you to guard the entrance. Now that the stallion is gone I doubt you'll have any trouble keeping the mares inside." She looked up at Cotton, quietly sitting on his horse. "Get my horse. You and I are going after that stallion."

Cotton glanced at Clint before riding off.

"You're not going to catch him," Clint commented, watching Billy Lee hobble away.

The one thing Kate couldn't tolerate was to have someone try to usurp her authority, she'd had enough of Clint's acting like he was the great authority. She'd worked too damn hard and long to get where she was today, and like it or not,

Cotton and Billy Lee worked for her, not Clint! "You may know about breaking horses, but that's a lot different than handling mustangs. How many times have you been on a roundup?" She didn't give him a chance to answer. "From the time you joined us, you've taken over. Did you ever wonder why I brought Billy Lee and Cotton? Because they have rounded up more mustangs than you've probably seen in your entire life. And though it's been a while, I've been on a few roundups myself. So you can just step aside now and let us take care of what needs to be done!"

Clint looked down at the woman, her thumbs looped inside her gun belt, her stance rigid. "Very well. Why don't you take Billy Lee with you and I'll watch over the mares?"

"Because Mr. Morgan, I don't want to lose the rest of the mares," she spit out at him. "That stallion might take it into his head to return, and Billy Lee will know what to do."

Her snippity attitude was making Clint's temper rise. "Well I couldn't do any worse than you did, *Miss Whitfield!*"

Kate was already angry at herself for letting the stallion get away with some of the mares. She didn't like one damn bit having it rubbed in her face. "We'll see just how quick you are at throwing stones when I return with the other horses, and then when you have to help break them."

Cotton returned with her horse, and a moment later the two rode off in the direction the stallion had taken.

Before I leave the ranch, Kate Whitfield, Clint thought angrily, *you're going to learn that the sun doesn't rise and set on your ass! You're not going to catch those mustangs because the stallion is too smart, and you don't know a damn thing about tracking unless the tracks are staring you in the face!* He rode

back to the canyon entrance and saw Billy Lee
returning with both boots on.

"Miss Kate sure can get herself in a dither,"
Billy Lee commented a bit sheepishly. "Think
they'll catch the stallion?"

It was obvious Billy Lee was feeling more than
a little uncomfortable after what Kate had said.
"Nope." Clint climbed off his horse and settled
on a rock next to the cowpoke.

"Want a chew?" Billy Lee held out the small
tin of tobacco, but Clint shook his head. "I reckon
Miss Kate's just upset cause them mustangs got
away. She don't normally act that way."

"Unless she thinks someone is undermining
her authority," Clint commented. "Sounds like
she plans on breaking the horses here."

Billy Lee broke off a chunk of tobacco and stuck
it inside his cheek. "Yep, but I got a feeling
you've already thought of another way of doing
it."

"Where would you build the corral?"

"It would be my suggestion to do it in the
meadow. What's on your mind?"

"It would take a lot less wood to put a barrier
across that narrow entrance than it would to build
a corral. Then all we'd have to do is rope break
them, take them back to the ranch on a line, then
finish breaking them there."

"Damn if it wouldn't! Never done it that way,
but it sure makes sense. A lot of times them army
men at the forts want to break the horses themselves. If that's the case, it would make it a lot
easier on us. Have you talked to Miss Kate about
it?"

Clint released a robust laugh. "No, she's not
likely to listen to anything I suggest. However,
she might listen to you and Cotton. You talk it
over with him. I'm going back to camp and catch
some sleep. I'll take the first watch tonight."

Cotton started to say, "Sure thing, boss," but stopped himself just in time.

Leading Midnight, Clint walked back to camp, his thoughts centered on mustangs. On more than one occasion he'd had a horse shot out from under him, or chased away, and on two occasions he'd only managed to survive by catching a mustang and breaking it. From the time he was a child, horses had been a part of his life. Before the war, his father kept a fine line of Thoroughbreds that he'd brought over from England. Up until he'd gone to work for the government, Clint had been totally involved in the breeding and training of the fine animals. His six months living with the Sioux had added to his knowledge. In his estimation, there were no better horsemen to be found. Kate might know a lot more about running a ranch than he did, but when it came to horses she couldn't hold a candle to him. It was because of his knowledge of horses that he was convinced the stallion would return. All Kate would have had to do was set a trap and wait. But she'd been too angry to listen, and now she'd made him angry. He'd be damned if he was going to help her capture the stallion. Not that he expected her to ask for his opinion, because she was bound and determined to remind him she was the boss. Bedding Kate was sweet pleasure, but not worth putting up with her temper. All he wanted to do was get back to the ranch as soon as possible. That was why he'd told Billy Lee about rope training the mustangs, a trick he'd learned from the Indians.

He and Cotton had just brought the packhorses down when they'd heard the gunshots, so the gear hadn't been unloaded and the camp set up. The packhorses were still tied to the tree where they'd been left. Seeing no other recourse, Clint unsaddled Midnight, hobbled him, then proceeded to unload the gear. When the packhorses were unloaded, he hobbled them also, so they could graze. Then he stretched a rope between two trees to tether the horses at night. He untied his sleeping bag from behind his saddle and rolled it out on the ground. A few minutes later, he was sound asleep.

Night had fallen when Kate and Cotton returned. Clint had already set up camp; he had a fire going, and beans and flat cakes were cooked and ready for supper. Having already eaten, Clint was just fixing to go relieve Billy Lee so the cowhand could enjoy his meal.

Because neither Cotton nor Kate seemed inclined to offer any information as to what had happened, Clint said, "Food's ready. I'm taking first guard." He grabbed a blanket, his rifle and his duster.

"I'll relieve you at one in the morning," Cotton called out as Clint faded into the night.

Kate filled her tin plate with beans from the big kettle hanging from the cooking hook over the fire, grabbed some flat cakes, and settled on her sleeping bag to eat. Her sleeping bag was on one side of the campfire and Clint's on the other, as usual, which was just fine with her. She wasn't the least pleased that Clint had been right. They hadn't caught the stallion. In fact, they hadn't seen hide nor hair of the mustangs. It was as if they'd vanished into thin air. To add to her anger, Cotton had mentioned several times that he wished they'd brought Clint along. Brought Clint along indeed! He wasn't even supposed to be there at all.

"Where's the mustangs?" Billy Lee asked as he appeared in the firelight. He immediately began spooning beans onto a plate.

Kate closed her ears to what they were saying. She didn't want to hear it. She took another bite of the flat cake, wondering where Clint had learned to cook. Even the beans were tasty. Was there anything the man didn't do well?

Realizing the time was drawing near for Cotton to relieve him, Clint stood and stretched his legs while clasping the blanket tightly around his body. The night air was as cold as an old maid schoolteacher, and he was glad he'd had enough forethought to bring the blanket. He was thinking about how good it was going to feel to stretch out in his sleeping bag when he heard the mares shifting restlessly. He let the blanket slip to the ground, then quietly moved to the right until he was directly in line with the narrow entrance to the canyon.

The mares were nickering, then Clint heard what he'd been waiting for: the pounding of hooves. His finger curled around the trigger of his rifle. The hoofbeats came to a sudden halt. In his mind, Clint could picture the stallion sniffing the air. Then all kinds of yelling echoed around the red rock walls as Kate and the others tried turning the stallion away. The hoofbeats picked up again and Clint knew the stallion was headed straight for him. He raised the barrel of the rifle, aimed it at the sky, and pulled the trigger just as the stallion came into view. The bay reared onto his hind legs, his black mane flying, his front legs flashing in the air, striking at Clint and screaming his anger. Clint could hear the mares starting to run forward behind him, and he pulled the trigger again . . . then again. The stallion came back down snorting, then spun around and galloped away. Clint turned and again fired into the air, forcing the mustangs back into the canyon.

Cotton was the first one to reach Clint. He stopped, gasping for breath. "Are . . . are you all right?" he managed to say.

Billy Lee came running close behind, shortly followed by Kate, their breathing equally heavy.

"I'm fine," Clint said calmly.

Kate finally managed a deep breath. "I thought for sure we'd lost the mares."

"Now, darlin', you know I'd never let that happen," Clint said loud enough for everyone to hear.

Kate flushed. "Since everything is under control, I'm going back to camp and get some sleep," she announced stiffly.

"I'll go with you," Billy Lee said as he fell into step with Kate. "I gotta give Clint credit. He's one cool bastard. I'd have gotten the hell out of the way if I had a stallion in front of me and a bunch of wild horses comin' at me from the rear. I got no desire to be run down. If I'm dead I ain't gonna be able to collect the money anyway."

"How do you know what he did, Billy Lee? You didn't see it."

"The hell I didn't! I saw the stallion trying to hit Clint, and could hear them mustangs were at a full gallop and headed right in Clint's direction. Hell, he wasn't about to move. The man must have ice in his veins."

Not when he makes love, Kate thought.

Finally able to breathe normally, Cotton asked Clint, "You think that devil is goin' to return?"

Clint raised his arms and stretched. "Yep. He's not at all happy about us taking his mares."

"I was just comin' to relieve you when I saw him run past. I'll feel a lot better when we get them mares corralled. We gonna start doin' that tomorrow?"

"Why don't you ask Kate?"

"Hell, I don't know. Guess Billy Lee and me just figured you was runnin' everything."

"When you get a chance, Billy Lee will tell you

about a suggestion I have. If you move straight ahead, you'll find a blanket on the ground. You're going to need it.''

By the time Clint returned to camp, Billy Lee was already snoring. He wasn't sure if Kate had gone to sleep, and he wasn't going to find out. He was getting damn tired of her sharp words, and before they returned to the ranch, he had every intention of letting her know exactly how he felt.

Chapter 13

After Billy Lee had relieved him as guard, Cotton joined Clint and Kate by the campfire. Because the morning air still had a hard nip to it, they all had their heavy coats on. Cotton poured himself a cup of coffee and sat on the ground. He took a tentative sip, letting the hot brew warm his insides.

"The only thing I don't like about being this high in the mountains is how cold the nights and mornings are," he complained. "Seems to take forever for the sun to warm a man up, then it's hotter than hell." He set his cup down and held his hands close to the fire.

"Cotton, last night I dreamt the rustlers made another raid." Kate shifted her position to get away from the smoke that was drifting into her eyes. "I should be at the ranch instead of here. I'd give anything if I could lay my hands on those hombres."

Cotton nodded his agreement. "Ain't no use worryin', Miss Kate. You bein' there probably wouldn't make a bit of difference."

"Will the stolen cattle have any effect on the shipment to Chicago?" Clint asked.

"Probably not." Kate looked back at Cotton. "You know, if they keep this up, there might not be anything to brand next year."

"That would mean losing the government contract, wouldn't it?"

Kate arched a smooth eyebrow and returned her gaze to Clint. She didn't appreciate him continually butting into her conversation with Cotton. "Believe me," she said snootily, "we've got that *well* taken care of."

The way she said it, Clint suddenly began reassessing Kate's innocence. Was it possible she could be involved in switching the cattle? He pulled his hat off and ran his fingers through his hair. A smile tickled the corners of his mouth as he remembered how suspicious Kate had been of him when he'd first come to the ranch. Now he was starting to act just like her. No, in all honesty, he didn't think she was guilty. She wasn't that devious a person, but more importantly, she'd never do anything to jeopardize the ranch or her family.

"Miss Kate," Cotton said as he picked his cup back up, "me and Billy Lee were talkin' this mornin' when he took over guard, and we came up with what we think is a mighty good idea."

"Oh?"

"We was thinkin' that it'd be a lot easier to block off the opening to the canyon and just rope break the mavericks." Cotton stroked his bushy beard. "Then, we could string 'em, head back to the ranch, and break 'em there. Be a hell of a lot easier."

Kate saw Cotton glance over at Clint, who looked more relaxed than any of them. Immediately, she knew where the idea had come from.

" 'Sides, it'd take a lot less wood choppin'," Cotton added.

It would also get us back to the ranch sooner, Kate thought as she took another drink. She'd already decided that she simply could not get along with Clint. The only thing they shared was lust for one another. And dammit, he was always right! He had taken over the tracking; he had insinuated she didn't know what she was doing when the horses escaped as well as when she went after the stallion; then he'd called her darling in front of her men! Yes, he'd introduced her to the joys of physical satisfaction, but now it was finished. She looked up and saw Cotton staring at her. Oh. She hadn't answered his question. "Since it's your idea, I see no reason not to go along with it. If it were Morgan's, I'd turn it down in a minute. Tell me, Clint, what do you think of the plan?"

"It beats having to break broncos."

"I should have known!"

"Has the ride here and chasing mustangs been too much work for you, Kate?" Clint reached over and refilled his cup with steaming black coffee.

"Of course not. Why do you ask?"

"Yesterday and now this morning, you seem to be in a tiff and itching for an argument."

Cotton kept his eyes on the fire, watching it greedily eat the wood.

"I'm not in a tiff," Kate retaliated.

Cotton climbed to his feet. "Sleeping on the ground always makes me stiff. Think I'll stroll over and tell Billy Lee what we're gonna do. He'll be glad to hear it."

"Are you always in such a snippy mood when you get up of a morning?" Clint asked before Cotton was even out of sight.

Kate started to rise.

"Oh, no." He clamped a big hand on her shoulder. "You're staying right here, and we're going to have this out."

"Let go of me! One of the men might see you—"

"They're going to see a lot more if you don't

get down off that high horse. Personally, I don't give a damn what they see."

"Well I do."

Clint didn't release his hold until she'd settled herself back down. "Why? Worried Sam might find out? You're a grown woman. When are you going to start standing up for what you want instead of dedicating your life to others?"

Kate put a clamp on her rising temper. "That's my business, not yours. I've told you I won't allow anything or anyone to come between me and my family, Clint Morgan. And that includes messing around with you."

"When you get up on your pedestal, you remind me of a hellfire and damnation preacher. Now what the hell are you so mad about?"

"I don't like you undermining my authority!"

"What makes you think I'm doing that?"

"Who took over from the time we left the ranch?"

Clint grabbed some limbs and tossed them one by one onto the campfire. "When the Apache raid a wagon, they let the man who's raided the most wagons be their leader. And when they war with other tribes, the leader is the one with the most experience. Therefore, it's not always the same man who's in charge, and no one takes offense at who's leading what."

"What's that supposed to mean?" Kate snapped at him.

"It means that you may know a lot about ranching, but you, Cotton, and Billy Lee don't know shit about tracking. And furthermore, you're not worth a damn when it comes to planning an attack unless it's pointed out to you. That alone should tell you why Cotton and Billy Lee were more than happy to let me take over."

"Maybe you would have found out just how good I can plan if I was ever given the opportunity. There isn't a man on the ranch that doesn't know I can do any job as well as he can!"

"What does that have to do with this?" He tossed his coffee onto the grass. "But now that you've brought it up, saying you can do any job a man can is a damn lie," he threw back at her. "When you learn to accept that, you'll find running the ranch a lot easier. You're not strong enough, and everyone but you knows it. You're harder on yourself than anyone else could possibly be. You can't go all day throwing cattle for branding; you can't work day after day pounding an anvil; and you don't even have the guts to admit that a horse as big as Midnight was too much for you to handle."

Kate curled her lip and again tried to get up, only to have Clint jerk her back down.

"Damn if you're not the most impossible woman I've ever met. I'm warning you, Kate, if you don't stop trying to leave, I'm going to throw you on the ground, climb on top of you, and when I see one of the men coming I'll plant one hell of a kiss on those sassy lips of yours! You just try telling me you're strong enough to prevent it!"

Seething, Kate proceeded to adjust her coat back around in its proper position. "Are you finished?"

"When I'm finished, I'll say so! Other than when I satisfy your need, you've been on my back from the first day we met. You've accused me of just about anything that comes to your mind, from rustling cattle to sleeping with whores, which by the way isn't any of your damn business. Now we can either try to be halfway decent to each other, or we can go to a full-scale war. You think about which it's going to be."

Kate knew that Clint was having difficulty controlling his temper, but so was she. "I don't ever want you touching me again."

"You're a damn liar," Clint said bitingly as he got to his feet. "I'll know what your decision is from the way you act, lady." He walked away.

Kate snatched up her cup and rinsed it out. Why couldn't the man just leave the ranch and get out of her hair? She heard Cotton returning and wondered if he and Billy Lee had overheard her conversation with Clint. She suddenly realized that neither of them had bothered to keep their voices down.

Kate turned to see if Cotton was talking to Clint, only to discover Clint had left the camp.

By the time Clint had walked off his temper and returned to camp, the fire had been extinguished. Cotton stood looking at him, waiting to be told what to do next.

"How do you want to close up that canyon, Clint?" Cotton asked.

Clint watched Kate start to walk away. "Kate," he called. "Cotton wants to know how we should close the canyon. I'm sure you already have it all planned out."

Kate came to a stop and slowly turned. "You cut trees and start piling them at the entrance."

"That might keep the mares in, but it's also going to keep us out."

"Strip them and make logs!"

Clint reached up and scratched the back of his head, tipping his hat forward. "Well, now, that seems like an awful lot of extra work, but if that's the way you want it done, that's sure the way we'll do it. Are you going to select the trees?"

"No," Kate said through clenched teeth. She'd be damned if she'd let his baiting get to her? "I'm sure all of you are capable of knowing which trees to cut."

"That sounds fine to me. You will help cut them, won't you?" He raised his eyebrows.

Kate was well aware that he was out to prove his point about her not being able to do everything a man could. She gave him her sweetest smile. "You're damn right."

Clint pointed to one of the axes lying on the ground, then walked away.

"You want me to carry that for you, Miss Kate?" Cotton offered.

"No!" Kate snapped at him.

The ax wasn't light. Nevertheless Kate carted it off to the stand of trees near the canyon opening. Cotton and Clint immediately set to work. Trees they'd selected were tall with thick trunks. Kate located a similar one, then positioned herself so she could watch Clint and hopefully get an idea as to what she was supposed to do. She'd never chopped down a tree in her life. Kate pulled the gloves from her back pocket and slipped them on, watching Clint's muscles ripple beneath the soft cotton shirt as he swung the ax, burying it deep in the tree trunk. He worked it loose, then followed with another powerful swing. The thuds of the striking axes echoed off the surrounding cliffs.

Kate was ready to prove a few things to Mr. Morgan. She swung the ax. To her aggravation, instead of the sharp blade going into the trunk, it bounced off, flew through the air, and landed behind her. She looked up to see if Clint had noticed, but his back was still turned.

Kate retrieved the ax, planted her feet, and swung with all her might. The ax cut into the tree, jarring her whole body, but she felt a sense of accomplishment. She'd show Clint a thing or two. The ax hadn't sunk very deep, but at least it was a start. She tried pulling the blade free, only to discover it took even more effort than sinking it in had. Finally managing to work it free, she took another hard swing. Again it sank into the tree, but it was a good foot above the first cut. The third strike landed between the first and second ones. Still Kate refused to give up.

When Kate heard Clint yell "Timber!" she couldn't believe he was already finished. She heard the loud splintering sound of the trunk breaking, then watched the tree start to lean, then fall, breaking off limbs of nearby trees until it hit the ground with a crash. Kate returned to her own tree, but a few minutes later she heard Cotton call "Timber!" Again there was a crash, and Clint was already working on his second tree. Kate looked at her own handiwork. She *was* starting to show a little progress, however there were now blisters between her fingers. Her arms felt like heavy sacks of flour, and her body was covered with perspiration.

"Cotton," Kate heard Clint call, "why don't you go hitch a harness to one of the packhorses so we can start moving these trees to the opening? If we can get it pretty well blocked off, Billy Lee can come help."

Kate saw Cotton take off to where the horses were tethered to the line rope. Even with Clint issuing orders, it didn't bother Kate in the least. What did she know about what needed to be done? She took another swing at her tree.

Several times, Clint glanced over at Kate, each time shaking his head. At the rate she was going, it would be a year before she was half finished with one tree. Still he said nothing, waiting to see how long it would take her to give up.

A few minutes later Kate saw Cotton returning, walking alongside the horse and holding the reins. A long rope had been attached to the harness. He secured the other end of the rope to one of the fallen trees. Still standing off to the side, he flicked the reins and guided the horse toward the mouth of the canyon. Kate was reminded of a big broom as the feathery limbs of the tall pine swept across the ground. By the time Cotton had delivered the third tree, a thick cloud of dust was rising into the air and floating back to her, causing her to sneeze and her eyes to water.

Kate continued working on her tree, even though Clint had already chopped down two. Clint had moved to where she could no longer see him. Her gaze traveled from her tree to Cotton, who was making another delivery to the mouth of the canyon. The ax dropped from her hand, and she took off after him. Surely she could be of more use moving the trees, allowing Cotton to continue chopping. It's not that I'm giving up, she assured herself, I'm just not quite as fast as the men.

Clint started on his third tree, sinking the ax deep into the thick trunk, then stepped back. The work was demanding, the sun glaring, but at least he was doing something constructive. The strenuous work also served to dispel a portion of the anger he was still feeling. He wasn't sure which angered him the most: Kate's damn stubbornness or the possibility that she was involved in the crooked cattle switching. He wiped the sweat from his brow, then looked at Billy Lee, comfortably situated atop one of the red rocks. That was where Kate should be, he thought as his anger surfaced again. If she'd plop her ass down and let the three men work, it would all be done in half the time, with less work for everyone. He reached down, grabbed up his canteen, and took a long drink of water. His gaze shifted to Cotton . . . and Kate? What the hell was she doing now? When she reached up and took the reins, he had his answer. He could tell by the way Cotton was walking alongside her and moving his hands that he was giving Kate instructions. Clint grinned. So she gave up! He set the canteen back on the ground, wondering how long she would last at her latest endeavor.

Clint was definitely feeling the strain on his muscles when he decided to take a rest. He was about to tell Cotton to do the same when he caught sight of Kate guiding the horse back for another tree. With Cotton and him both cutting trees, he had no idea how many trips she'd made. As he stood watching her, he noticed her movements were wobbly. She raised her head to check her direction. Seeing how red her face was, he took off in her direction. *Damn*, he thought. *Doesn't the woman ever know when to quit? Well I've had all the bullheadedness I'm going to take.* "Billy Lee!" he hollered. "Get over here!"

Billy Lee jumped down from the rock and reached Kate at the same time Clint did. Clint grabbed the hackamore, bringing the horse to a standstill.

"Just what do you think you're doing?" Kate demanded.

"Billy Lee," Clint said gruffly, "go chop trees, and tell Cotton to come here and get the horse."

Billy Lee handed Clint his rifle and left.

"Cotton isn't moving the trees, I am!"

"Not anymore. You're going to go sit under that tree by the entrance and guard those horses, because if you don't, I'm personally going to turn every damn one of them loose."

Kate gasped. "You can't do that."

"The hell I can't. You declared war the minute you picked up that ax. By trying to prove you can work as hard as a man, you doubled the load for us. It's taking twice as long as it would had three *men* been doing the job."

"You can't give me orders!"

When Cotton appeared from among the trees, Clint grabbed Kate's wrist and started walking toward the canyon. Kate tried pulling back a couple of times, only to be jerked forward.

They were almost to the tree Clint wanted her to sit under when a loud whinny echoed around the cliffs, followed by another. Looking up, Clint saw the stallion standing on an overhanging rock. He raised the rifle and took aim.

Convinced the stallion was about to be shot, Kate threw all her weight against Clint to knock him off balance, but it was like hitting a boulder. He shoved her away, then to her horror, he fired two quick shots, each striking just below where the stallion stood. The horse reared as the third shot hit, this time even closer. The bay turned and ran away.

"What are you doing!" Kate yelled. "You could have killed him!"

Clint looked at her, his expression cold and ungiving. "When I fire a gun, I don't miss. If I wanted him dead, it would have been accomplished with the first bullet." Again he grabbed her wrist and continued on. "Am I going to have to put you down, or are you going to sit on your own?" he asked as he reached the tree.

Kate sat in the shade. "I don't have to put up with this. No man has ever given me orders and it's not going to start with you! As soon as I get up from here, I'm saddling my horse and heading back to the ranch."

"You leave and the mares go free. I don't think Cotton and Billy Lee are going to take kindly to losing what money they'd hoped to make off this venture just because you didn't get your way. If they decide to give me a bad time about it, I may just have to end up killing them." He watched Kate's eyes getting bigger by the second. "From now on, I'm taking over. I've had enough of your temper tantrums. If you were a man, you'd probably be dead by now. I suggest you don't give me any more trouble. Now give me your bandanna.''

''Why?''

''Dammit, take off your bandanna,'' he ordered.

Her hands shaking, Kate untied the bandanna from around her neck and handed it to him. Not until he walked over and soaked it in the small mountain stream did she know what he was up to. He returned and tossed it in her lap, but remained standing by her stretched-out legs. Picking the bandanna up, she mopped her face, welcoming the cool water against her hot cheeks and forehead.

''Take your hat off.'' Without giving her time to do so, he reached down and knocked it off. ''Put the bandanna on top of your head until you cool down.''

Kate was reminded of something Mattie used to always say. ''Keep your head cool and your feet warm.'' She spread the bandanna out and placed it on her head.

''Now sit right here until I tell you to move.''

Kate didn't realize she'd been holding her breath until Clint had left. She was furious. Other than Sam teaching her things as she was growing up, all her life she'd been able to do as she pleased. Now Sam seldom told her what to do, and she was too old to be taking orders from Clint Morgan! And never . . . never! . . . had she been manhandled this way. She'd be damned if she was going to kowtow to any man! But at the same time, she knew Clint was equally furious, maybe even more so, and his anger was far more deadly. Hadn't she made a point of not pushing that anger over the edge? Well now she'd seen the result, and it scared the hell out of her. Would he really kill Cotton and Billy Lee? If the look on his face was any indication, the answer was yes. She could never remember feeling so small. And to add to her sudden misery, he'd been absolutely right about her foolishness causing more time and work.

Thirty minutes later, Cotton delivered another tree. Before untying the rope, he walked over and handed Kate a canteen. "Clint said you might be thirsty. He told me to give this to you," he said cheerfully.

"Thank you." Kate started to warn Cotton that his and Billy Lee's lives were in danger, but thought better of it. They wouldn't believe her because neither man had heard what Clint said. She contemplated going for her whip, which was still lying on her bedroll back at camp. Remembering what had happened the last time she'd thought to use it, the idea was quickly discarded. Besides, Clint could get to her before she could make it to camp. She had her revolver, but he had one too. Even as angry as she was, she could never shoot him in the back, and he was too fast a draw for her. There were no options left. She'd just have to be very careful not to make Clint angry again, at least until they were all safely home. Then she'd be on her own turf.

By early afternoon, the men had the barrier in place. Kate sat with her back against the tree trunk, watching them tie in place the gate that they'd made from large, stripped pine branches and rope. She had to admit, everything had progressed a lot faster with all three men working.

The job completed, the men stepped back, admiring their handiwork. When Clint motioned for Kate to join them, she slowly rose, eager to see how many horses were still in the canyon.

Watching Kate move toward him, Clint smiled. Her steps were slow, and not nearly as springy as they'd been this morning, and she definitely did not move with the fluid grace that came so naturally to her. Apparently she wasn't even aware of the bandanna still on her head until it fell off. When she leaned down and picked it up, he could see pine needles clinging to the back of her tight britches and full shirt. She straightened up, placed her hands on her sides and stretched her shoulders back. Satisfied, she continued on. She looked a mess, albeit a very beautiful mess.

"It's all finished, Miss Kate," Billy Lee said proudly when she joined them. "Ain't nobody gonna have to stand guard tonight."

"You left your hat under the tree, Kate," Clint commented.

"I'll go get it for you," Cotton offered.

"Kate, I thought you might want to go in and start rope breaking the mustangs," Clint said casually. "You said you wanted to get back to the ranch as quickly as possible."

Kate glared at him. He couldn't be serious! Cotton returned with her hat and she gave him a faint smile as a thank-you. "Since you're in charge," she said bitterly, "it's your decision. However, considering how hard you men have worked today, don't you think you deserve a rest?" *I couldn't climb on the back of a horse if it meant my life.*

"Perhaps you're right," Clint said magnanimously.

"Hell, Clint, I'm not even sure I can get on a horse."

"I'll go along with that," Billy Lee added, "and I didn't work as long as you fellers. I'm all for startin' tomorrow if that's all right with you, Clint."

Clint nodded. He was also looking forward to a rest, but he wasn't about to admit it in front of Kate. "In that case, I say we go to that pool down the way and wash up.'' He gave the two men a roguish smile. ''I'll be damned if I'm going to spend another night having to smell you two.''

''You ain't smellin' so rightly sweet yourself,'' Cotton said jokingly. His smile disappeared. ''But I'm lot likin' the idea of having to wash up in cold water.''

Kate glanced at Billy Lee. He had a sickly look to his face, clearly showing he wasn't interested either. Like Clint, he was already showing signs of a beard and mustache. But where Clint's was black, Billy Lee's was even a brighter red than the hair on his head, and not nearly as thick.

''Believe me,'' Clint insisted, ''you'll feel a lot better. So go get some clean clothes and let's get it over with.''

Kate thought . . . hoped . . . the men would balk, but to her aggravation, they turned and walked to the camp. ''Aren't you going to order me to bathe?'' she asked, her voice dripping with sarcasm. She was sorry the minute the words escaped her lips. Clint's gray eyes had turned to stone.

''That's an excellent suggestion,'' he replied. ''You can head upstream while we head down, unless you would rather I bathe with you.''

Kate bit her lip to keep from swearing, a habit she'd been trying very hard to break. Like Billy Lee and Cotton, bathing in cold water wasn't at all to her liking, and certainly not with Clint. ''I'll take care of it myself.''

''Very well.'' He reached out and took her hand in his.

Kate tried jerking it away, but his hold was firm. ''What are you doing?'' she asked suspiciously.

''I'm going to walk the lady back to camp. That is, unless you'd rather I carry you.''

Kate took a quick glance to be sure Cotton and Billy Lee were far enough away not to hear. ''Why are you saying all these things?'' she asked in a hushed voice. ''The men might hear.''

Clint's laughter rang through the air. ''Well, we'll just see what happens.'' Her hand still held firmly in his, they walked toward camp.

''What will Cotton and Billy Lee think?''

To Kate's relief, Clint released her hand before the men saw them.

''You will be a good girl and go take a bath, won't you?'' Clint asked as they walked the last few feet to their sleeping bags.

''Yes,'' Kate quickly assured him.

Billy Lee and Cotton each grabbed a handful of mane and swung up onto the bare backs of their horses.

''I'll catch up with you in a minute,'' Clint called as the men moved their mounts forward at a walk.

Billy Lee's wide, knowing grin spread from ear to ear as he leaned over and said to Cotton, ''I think maybe those two are becoming smitten with one another.''

''Hell, I already knew that.''

''What do you mean you knew?'' Billy Lee demanded.

Cotton scooted back so he wasn't so high on the horse's withers. ''You can see it as plain as the nose on your face when they look at each other.''

''Well I didn't see it.''

''That's 'cause you ain't been lookin'. Here comes Clint. Don't say anything to him about it.''

After she grabbed a clean shirt, jeans, and a bar of soap from her saddlebags, Kate wondered if there was some way she could get out of bathing. Heaven knows I could certainly use it, she mused, but just the thought of washing in that icy water already had her shivering. On the other hand, considering the way Clint was acting, it would be just like him to insist on checking her body to be sure she was clean!

Deciding to just go ahead and get it over with, she took off walking in the opposite direction the men had gone. When she arrived at the stream, she continued following it for some distance, knowing good and well she was only delaying the inevitable. She excused her delay by telling herself she was only walking the stiffness out of her bones. She began thinking how heavy that ax had been and how hard she'd worked at cutting that tree down, and remembered that when she left there wasn't more than a few chips out of the trunk. She giggled, then broke out with a hearty laugh. The more she thought about the tree, and how ridiculous she'd acted throughout the day, the harder she laughed, until finally she had to plop down on the ground and hold her stomach. Even Clint's anger struck her as funny. Just as she'd start getting herself back under control, she'd think of something else that had happened between the two of them in the past, and she'd break out laughing again.

By the time Kate calmed down, and even though her stomach, ribs and everything else in her body ached, she was in the best of moods. She drew her knees up and locked her arms around them, feeling better than she had in months. On the other side of the stream were a bevy of blue wildflowers growing close to the ground. She looked at the tall, sturdy pines scattered throughout the valley, then her gaze traveled upwards to the high, rugged peaks in the distance, knowing they looked closer than they really were. She inhaled deeply, drawing in the sweet smell of the pines and the thin, clean, crisp air. This was the land she loved, and when she took the time to study and admire its beauty, it never failed to make her feel better and put her thinking in proper perspective.

She'd been wrong, starting from the very first day she'd met Clint. And today she'd acted like a spoiled child, letting her temper run her mouth. She certainly hadn't acted like an adult who carried the responsibility of running a ranch. She thought of Clint's words that morning, about not having to act like a man to be boss, and though she'd been angry at the time, she now realized what he said made a lot of sense. Of course she was a woman, and of course the hands knew it. So why had she worked so hard to be like them? Ever since she could remember, she'd worked harder at being one of the men than at being a female. Why? Because she wanted to be like her father, which he encouraged? Or was it because she'd always felt that in order to be boss she had to prove she was as good and as tough as the men under her? But what difference did it really make? She *was* the boss, and she had all the men working to do what she ordered, whether she was male or female. If they weren't pleased with that arrangement, they could always seek jobs on other ranches. She even understood now why Clint had often referred to her as a she-man, and possibly what Mattie had tried telling her over the years. She didn't have to compete. It was as simple as that. Oh, she'd continue carrying her share of the load and doing what was required, but suddenly she no longer felt she needed to prove anything. She thought about what it felt like seeing herself all dressed up like a proper lady and decided that thanks to Clint she liked being a woman, though she wasn't about to tell him so. She smiled, feeling better about herself than she had in years.

Crows cawing loudly overhead suddenly made Kate realize it was getting late, and if she didn't get busy with her bath, Clint would come looking for her. Seeing a shallow pool on up ahead, she decided to bathe there. The water was going to be colder than a winter storm!

Clint stood at the edge of the camp, watching the yellow sun dip behind the high peaks, and wondered where the hell Kate was. She should have been back an hour ago. He'd tried telling himself she was deliberately staying gone to spite him and that he should ignore her, but even so, worry had already started replacing his own good advice. He rubbed his chin, feeling the coarse hairs, already long enough to be considered a closely trimmed beard. He'd be damned if he was going to give Kate the satisfaction of having him search for her.

He turned, ready to tell Billy Lee to go find Kate, when a movement in the trees caught his attention. Then Kate strolled into view, humming some unfamiliar tune. She appeared to have nary a care in the world, looking as fresh as the morning dew. Her dirty clothes were draped over her arm, and her hair was no longer in a tight bun atop her head. Surprisingly, she appeared to be in a happy mood. As she strolled past him without a word of acknowledgment, he turned and watched her go to her sleeping bag. With her back to him, he could see that her hair was hanging down her back, tied at the nape with a string of rawhide.

"Cotton," Kate called, "what are you cooking that smells so good?"

"Rabbit stew," Cotton said proudly, "compliments of Clint. He shot the little buggers."

"How long until we eat? After that cold bath I'm starved."

"Won't be much longer, Miss Kate," Cotton answered.

Realizing he was still staring at Kate, Clint

headed for the canyon to recheck the barrier that had been constructed. What could possibly have brought on this change of attitude? he wondered as he walked. What had happened to the fear he'd injected by saying he might have to kill Billy Lee and Cotton? Of course it had been a bluff, but it sure had shut her up. Now, out of the clear blue sky, she appeared happy about something. He chuckled softly. Kate Whitfield never ceased to amaze him—a quality he was beginning to find appealing as hell.

Chapter 14

The next morning, Cotton waited at the make-shift gate as Kate, Clint, and Billy Lee rode into the canyon. When the mustangs came into view, Kate's concerns vanished. She roughly estimated there were at least fifty horses nervously moving about. Now it was a matter of picking out which ones to keep and which ones to let go.

"Let's get to it," Billy Lee called.

Working as one, the three began culling the herd. Because the army was only interested in purchasing large mares, one by one the unsuitable horses were sent back out of the canyon with a yell to Cotton to let them pass. Kate was constantly speeding her horse up, then slowing it down, then kicking it forward again. There was grit in her mouth and eyes from the mustangs racing hither and fro, clouding the air with dust, but the exhilaration was worth every minute of discomfort. When they were finished, Kate counted twenty-seven big, sturdy mares.

Clint rode up beside her. Kate smiled at the way his black mustache and short beard now had a grayish cast due to clinging dust. "You look like you've been doing a little work," she teased. Seeing his lips spread into a devilish grin, her smile broadened.

"You don't look so good yourself. I'd say that

when we're through tonight, we're going to have to take another cold bath."

Kate tipped her hat back. "Maybe you can wash my back for me."

Clint's mouth twitched with amusement. "Now that you mention it, maybe I can."

Billy Lee pulled up in front of them. "I tell you, we got us one hell of a bunch of horses!"

Clint laughed. "You might not feel so excited once they're back at the ranch and you have to saddle break them."

"Yep, but when I get my share of the money, I'll feel good all over again. I'll get nearly as much money as I make in a year workin' as a cowhand, and I'm aimin' to buy me one of them fancy tooled saddles and a brand-new pair of boots."

"I say we get us something to eat before we start the hard work," Kate suggested. "What do you think, Clint?"

Clint arched a dark eyebrow, surprised she'd asked for his opinion. There wasn't so much as a hint of sarcasm. "Sounds good to me," he replied, already looking forward to washing her back.

As the men discussed the mares, Kate was feeling quite proud of herself. She'd accomplished exactly what she'd set out to do. Clint had absolutely no idea why she was being friendly, especially after their fight yesterday, and she was loving every minute of it. For once his face wasn't stoic, and she knew she had him confused. On her way back from the stream, she'd come to realize that after getting over the shock of his threats to release the mustangs and kill Billy Lee and Cotton, she really wasn't afraid of Clint. She had been when he first came to the ranch, and there was no doubt in her mind that he could be dangerous if someone tried to cross him. But shoot Cotton and Billy Lee? Never. And with the passing of her fear came the realization that she felt safe when he was around. However, he might have let the mustangs go just to get even with her.

After grabbing a bite to eat, the foursome returned to the canyon to start rope breaking the mares. Cotton and Billy Lee paired off, as did Kate and Clint. It was agreed that Clint would take the front and Kate the back. As soon as they had picked out the first mare, they slowly moved their horses toward it, Kate's and Clint's running nooses already raised and circling above their heads. The horse took off running, but Clint kept his horse in tight and sent his lariat flying, easily circling the horse's neck. He quickly wound the other end of the rope around his saddle horn. Kate roped both of the mare's hind feet below the hocks, and the mare hit the ground, fighting, kicking, snorting, trying to get back up. But Kate and Clint kept their ropes taut. They looked at each other, and Clint winked. Kate's full lips spread into a wide smile. Now it was a matter of waiting until the mare calmed down.

And so the day went, each horse requiring time and patience.

That night after supper, Kate and Clint left camp under the pretext of checking the mares. When they were far enough away from camp, the couple washed off in the mountain stream. Clint made a point of scrubbing Kate's back, but because the water was chillingly cold, his hands didn't linger long. Not bothering to dress, they took their time making glorious love on the valley floor, in the silence of night, the sweet aroma of wildflowers adding to their delight.

As they started back to camp, Kate was surprised and delighted when Clint took her hand in his. Though he'd held her hand before, this time it seemed so personal . . . so possessive.

"Tell me, Kate," Clint said in a hushed voice, "how come you asked my opinion this afternoon?"

"I don't know what you're talking about," she replied innocently.

"Let me put it differently. How come you're not angry or fighting me any longer?"

"Oh. That. Well, I thought about what you said the Indians do, and I realized it made sense."

"It's hard to believe something like that would bring on such a transformation."

"Would you rather we continued fighting?"

Clint chuckled. "No, but just because a cat purrs doesn't mean it won't scratch your eyes out if things don't go its way." He heard Kate laugh . . . a soft laugh that reminded him of bells.

"I have but one regret."

"What's that?" Clint asked.

"I wanted the stallion. I'd already given him a name."

As they neared camp, Clint released her hand, and Kate was already missing the warmth.

"You go to bed," he said softly. "I really am going to check the mares." He kissed her tenderly, then left.

Before Kate was even near her sleeping bag, she could hear Billy Lee and Cotton snoring, sounding like distant thunder, totally off key. Thinking what a wonderful day it had been, she smiled as she climbed into the sleeping bag. Worn out like Cotton and Billy Lee, she immediately fell asleep.

Clint was nearing the entrance to the canyon when a thudding sound attracted his attention. He moved silently forward. The moonlight afforded enough light for him to see the dark outline of the stallion trotting back and forth in front of the trees barricading the entrance. Clint stopped and watched. The mares were already coming to the tall gate, and the stallion kept nickering at them. He tried pawing at the wood with his hoof, but having no success he turned and kicked at it with his hind legs.

Clint couldn't believe what he was actually contemplating. I have to be out of my mind, he thought as he silently made his way back to camp. But the next thing he knew he was already throwing a saddle over one of the geldings. Kate would get her stallion, but he couldn't use Midnight to accomplish the task. The two stallions would end up in a fight. Clint silently rode out of camp.

Clint moved the gelding in the opposite direction, coming around between the trees as they'd done when the mustangs were first captured. He was halfway into the meadow, pushing his horse at a hard gallop when the bay swerved around. But the wild stallion had only one way to escape and that was in the direction Clint was coming from. The stallion veered off to the side. Clint cut him off, his lariat already swinging above his head. The bay stopped, then tried a different direction, but Clint was closing in. When the bay made a straight dash forward, Clint sent the lariat sailing through the air and wrapped the end of the rope around the saddle horn. Clint braced himself, then there was a hard jerk as the bay reached the end of the rope, flipping him around. He charged toward Clint, but Clint easily maneuvered the gelding away. Again the bay hit the end of the rope. Bit by bit, Clint moved the stallion closer to the trees. When he neared the first one, he galloped his mount around it, circling the rope around the trunk. Leaping from the saddle, he used the tree to take the pressure as the bay pulled, kicked, and reared. Slowly Clint took up the slack in the rope, drawing the bay closer and closer to the tree, leaving the stallion less and less room to fight. Finally Clint tied the rope off. There was no way for the stallion to escape. Clint found himself feeling sorry for the big fellow. He'd ruled like a king. Not a bad way to live.

After getting the gelding unsaddled and tethered, Clint walked over to Kate's sleeping bag and stood looking down at her. In a way, he was surprised to find her sound asleep—she'd worked just as hard as the rest of them today, but capturing the bay had to have made a lot of noise. She had positioned herself close to the campfire. From the light of the small flame, he could see she was resting peacefully, her beautiful face relaxed, her long lashes resting against her cheeks. The thick mane of silver-blond hair fanned the saddle that she used for a pillow. He was tempted to lie down beside her, to feel her body close to his.

You losing your self-control, Morgan? Clint chided himself.

He tossed some wood on the fire, then went to his sleeping bag on the other side of camp. After lying down, he stared wide-eyed at the stars. From the first night out, he'd had trouble going to sleep knowing that Kate was only a few steps away.

Several times during the night, Clint checked the bay to be sure he was all right. On his last trip, the stallion stood peacefully, no longer fighting the rope.

Before breakfast the next morning, Clint walked over to Kate, who was filling her cup with coffee. He picked up a tin cup and let her fill it for him. "You men will excuse us while we take a stroll, won't you?" Clint asked Cotton and Billy Lee, who had both chipped in to cook breakfast.

Cotton grinned. "Since when did you need our permission?"

Kate glanced nervously at Clint. Why did he want to go for a walk? He took her elbow, his touch sending tiny shocks of lightning up her arm.

"Where are we going?" Kate asked as they left camp. "Surely you don't want to . . ." Suddenly the idea of making love didn't sound like such a bad idea after all.

They walked slowly for some distance, being careful not to slosh the coffee from their cups. Kate was beginning to wonder what exactly Clint did have on his mind. Finally he brought her to a halt, and since they hadn't spoken, and because they'd be seen if they made love there, she was totally perplexed. "Did you want to talk to me about something?" she asked.

"You said you had already picked out a name for that bay stallion," Clint commented. "What was it?"

"Cinnamon."

Clint took a drink of his coffee, then raised his hand. When she looked in the direction he was pointing, she dropped her cup and her hand flew to her mouth. Seeing the excitement on her face, then watching her laughing with joy was all the reward Clint needed. Then she threw her arms around his neck, and he had to hold his arm out to keep from spilling coffee all over him. He wrapped an arm around her, then lifted her up until her face was even with his.

"Thank you, Clint," she said softly before kissing him thoroughly.

Though he was loath to do so, he set her back down on her feet. "Whatever will Billy Lee and Cotton think?" he teased.

Excitement still dancing in her eyes, Kate looked back at the stallion. "When . . . How . . ."

"You said you wanted the stallion; now he's yours. I promised to break a horse on this trip, so I guess I have no choice but to break him for you."

Kate giggled, feeling like a young child. "It can be done when we get back to the ranch."

"No, I'll do it, but you have to promise me something."

"What?"

"Promise you'll have him gelded as soon as we return to the ranch. If you don't, he'll never be of any use to you."

"I promise," she quickly assured him.

When Billy Lee and Cotton heard the news about the stallion, they were almost as excited as Kate.

After they'd eaten their breakfast, they all returned to the meadow. Clint had decided to go ahead and break the wild stallion without delay.

Billy Lee held the rope and pulled down on the bay's ear while Cotton and Clint proceeded to get the stallion saddled. Kate, standing off to the side, worried that someone was going to get hurt from the stallion's hooves, but then broke out laughing when on the first two tries the bucking animal sent the saddle flying to the ground. Finally they got the saddle on, and the cinch pulled tight. Clint climbed into the saddle, shifted his weight to get settled down, then nodded to Billy Lee to turn the horse loose. Admiration shone in Kate's green eyes as she watched Clint ride the bronco. As hard as the bay tried, he couldn't buck Clint off. In a surprisingly short time, Clint had him trotting around like he'd never known a wild day in his life. He had certainly told the truth when he said he knew horses.

For the next week, the foursome worked hard at getting the mares broken to the rope so they wouldn't balk when traveling back to the ranch on long tie-lines. And every day Clint rode Cinnamon, working him and refusing to let Kate ride him until the stallion was gelded. He knew insisting that Cinnamon be gelded made no sense.

Kate was no greenhorn. She'd been riding all her life and certainly had had no trouble with White Cloud. But for some totally unfathomable reason, he felt that she'd be safer on a cut horse.

On four separate nights, Kate and Clint found an excuse to get off by themselves so they could make love beneath the stars. Clint managed to ask questions about the roundup and the shipment of the steers, but Kate offered no information of value. He still didn't know what she'd meant about the government shipment being "under control."

Clint, Kate, Cotton and Billy Lee stood near the red rock boulder in the center of the canyon watching the mares wander about clipping what little grass was left. The mares no longer spooked when someone came near them.

"I gotta say," Cotton expounded, "we done a damn good job."

"Yep," Billy Lee agreed, "and I think we ought to celebrate. I got a bottle in my saddlebags. Miss Kate, would you mind us havin' a little nip?"

Kate released a hearty laugh. "Not at all. You boys deserve it."

"You gonna join us, Clint?" Billy Lee asked.

"You get the bottle out, and I'll be right behind you."

Kate was sure she'd never seen the boys walk so fast as they headed for the big gate.

"Well, Kate, you've got your mustangs and your stallion. Tomorrow we'll be heading back to the ranch."

As they took their time walking, Kate glanced at the tall, sheer red rocks, feeling a sadness at having to leave tomorrow. It was such a beautiful place. Chances were she'd never see it again. It was too far south for just a ride, and she couldn't picture herself making the trip alone. There would be no reason to return. Of course, being with Clint had made it special.

Deep in thought, Clint unconsciously placed his arm around Kate's shoulders. Since a week ago, when Kate had returned from the stream, she'd kept her hair hanging down her back, tied at the nape with rawhide. He was well aware it was for his benefit, and he appreciated the gesture. However, the look in Kate's eyes was beginning to bother him. The passion was still there, but now there was also a warm look of love, something he hadn't wanted to happen. He cared a great deal for Kate, but marriage was an entirely different matter. Though she probably hadn't given it any thought at this point, he knew that would eventually follow. "By the time we get back, it won't be much longer until the cattle roundup," he gently reminded her. "I have to say that staying at the ranch has been a most enjoyable learning experience."

"It's been a learning experience for me too." Kate tried making a joke of it, but she wasn't in a joking mood. "You taught me to enjoy being a woman, and for that I thank you." She kicked a small rock and watched it sail into the air. A lump formed in her throat when she tried to convince herself that it didn't matter that he'd soon be leaving. She felt like a child who had discovered candy, and like a child who had the candy taken away from her, she was heartsick.

The morning sky was still gray, the air cold, when the foursome left the small valley. Billy Lee, Cotton, and Clint held lead lines of mares with Cinnamon tied to the rear. Kate handled the packhorses.

The morning after their return, Clint left the house to see how the mustangs were getting along.

"Wait up!"

Clint turned to see Lucas hurrying toward him. Clint assumed Lucas had been watching from the kitchen window.

"I seen them mares you brought in last night and that fine-lookin' stallion. Earlier this morning, I heard Kate give the order to have him cut. Was that your idea?"

Clint moved on and Lucas fell in beside him. "She has no business riding a stallion that's probably spent his life out on the open range."

"I completely agree."

One of the cowpokes rode in front of them. "Get out of the way, you son of a bitch!" Lucas hollered.

"You know, Lucas, one of these days someone is going to kick the hell out of you."

Lucas rested his hand on the butt of his gun and laughed. "Not likely. He'd know he'd lose his job. Besides, I'd kill any man that laid a hand on me. There's one thing you gotta understand about cowpokes, Clint. They ain't gunmen. I doubt that there's a man on this ranch I can't outdraw."

"You're also a cocky bastard."

"I got every right to be," Lucas replied goodnaturedly. "I been thinkin' about how much the army is gonna pay for them mustangs. I could sure use that kind of money. Maybe some day soon you and I should go round up some more. Oh, but I forgot. You'll be leaving soon, won't you?"

"Yep."

"Well, who knows. Some day you might want to return. By then, I should be running this ranch. Well, I have to be gettin' on. Kate wants Jose and me to check the line shacks to be sure the rustlers haven't made an appearance again. I think it's a waste of time, but she doesn't listen to me. That'll all change before too much longer." Lucas branched off toward the barn. "See you later," he called over his shoulder."

Clint wondered if Kate had been like that at nineteen.

Clint spent the afternoon with Mattie. He drove her to town in the buggy so she could deliver the pillow she'd made to the woman whose baby had already arrived, then followed her in and out of the various shops, carrying her purchases. Mattie wanted to hear all about the trip, the mustangs, and how they were caught and handled, and Clint was more than happy to oblige her. He was sure Kate was giving the same report to Sam. Clint had become quite fond of his aunt, and actually enjoyed being with her. They even stopped and paid Oliver Putnam a visit. The doctor had moved to town and started his practice while Clint and Kate were rounding up the horses.

Late that night, Clint sat in the wingback chair in his room, trying to concentrate on the book he'd procured from the small library downstairs. After reading the same page three times, he closed the book with a snap and placed it on the round table beside the chair. He was tempted to go for a long ride, but changed his mind and began taking his clothes off.

By the time he climbed into bed, he thought he could go to sleep, but he lay there wide-eyed. He wasn't sure whether it was having a bed to finally sleep in that was making him so restless, or if it was knowing Kate was just a short distance down the hall. It really wasn't a question, because his body had already made the choice for him.

He reached over to turn the lantern off when his bedroom door creaked open. As if Kate had read his mind, she slipped quietly into his room.

"Are you angry with me?" Kate asked, not quite sure she was doing the right thing.

"No way in hell." He pulled the sheet back for her.

"I didn't know you slept without any clothes."

"There's a lot of things you don't know about me, darlin'. Now are you going to just stand there, or am I going to have to get up and drag you to my bed?"

Kate attempted a haughty look. "That won't be necessary, kind sir." She dropped her robe, showing him she had nothing on beneath it. "I'm perfectly capable of walking such a short distance and taking my pleasure."

"Then get yourself over here, woman, because I don't know how much longer I can wait."

Kate giggled, enjoying the effect she was having on him. His gray eyes were covering every inch of her body. "Are you sure you wouldn't rather have a drink of water first?"

Clint broke out laughing. "Why not?" he answered, deciding to play her game.

"That's not what you're supposed to say," she teased.

"And pray tell, just what am I supposed to say?" He laid back down on the pillows, making himself comfortable. "I could give you a merry chase, but we might be heard, or we'd look pretty damn ridiculous if someone caught us running down the hall stark naked. However, the thought of doing that seems to have some appeal to me."

"You wouldn't."

"You should know by now that given the right incentive, there's very little I wouldn't do." He started to rise from the bed.

"Stop. You win." She went to him.

The following morning, Clint left for Rawlins. The night before he'd told Kate he wanted to check out the train schedules for his trip to Maryland. He assured her he'd be back early the following day.

When Clint arrived at the telegraph office, his wire was waiting for him. He stepped outside the telegraph office and quickly read the information from Thomas Sandoval.

Looks like you may have found your culprit. After thorough questioning of the Indian agent involved, he finally admitted that Vale had approached him with a scheme about making extra money on the reservation cattle. The agent knew none of the particulars, but did know the beef received would not be the beef purchased. Vale would give him a small amount of money, claiming it was the agent's cut. However, Vale was smart in that he never told the agent the actual amount made. Vale also told the agent that if he said a word about it he'd be put in prison for being a part of the entire scheme. I'm not bringing Vale in. I'll let you catch him with his pants down.

Clint released a grunt. Obviously Sandoval didn't have enough to hang Vale. Clint crumpled the telegram. Sandoval was expecting him to get the evidence on Vale.

The days passed quickly, but to Kate's delight, Clint usually rode with her if she left the ranch. If they didn't make love during the day, they shared their bliss in her bedroom at night—or his. She kept telling herself that as close as they'd become, surely he'd at least delay his departure.

It was nearing dawn when Clint left Kate's bedroom, quietly closing the door behind him. Kate heard him leave but had pretended to be asleep, though she hadn't the foggiest notion why. Knowing she would have to get up shortly, she made no effort to go back to sleep. She slid her hand along the white sheet to where Clint had been lying, feeling the warmth that still lingered. She could even smell that faint, pleasurable scent that was his alone.

Realizing she was playing with time, Kate tossed the covers back and climbed out of bed. The hardwood floor felt cold beneath her feet, the cool air in the room chilled her naked body. Quickly she snatched up the white cotton gown lying across the chair, pulled it over her head, and jumped back in bed. She jerked the covers up and snuggled under them. Now she was safe, just in case Addie May should come in to see if she needed anything.

It occurred to Kate to light the lantern, but the dark room seemed to make thinking easier. And she did need to think. She couldn't even conceive what it would be like not having Clint make love to her. What would she do when he left and she was overcome with desire? Go looking for the first available cowhand? Just the thought of it made her cringe. Furthermore, she was getting tired of having to sneak around so no one would know what was going on between them. On the other hand, there was certainly no future with Clint. Though he spoke sweet words, he never spoke of love or indicated he wanted to stay longer at the ranch. On more than one occasion he'd talked about how he was looking forward to seeing his family. At different times she'd caught him watching her and thought she saw love in his eyes. But it always disappeared, and she wondered if it was something she'd created in her imagination because that's what she wanted to see. She was sure he loved her in his own way, but that was a lot different than being in love. She released a deep, painful sigh. Why was she doing this to herself? Why couldn't she just accept that he would leave and it would all be over?

There was a knock on her door, then Addie May came in carrying a lantern.

"Miss Kate? Are you awake?"

"Yes, Addie May, I'm awake."

Addie May set the lantern on the small round table, then disappeared, only to return a moment later with a tray. "I just knew you'd be wantin' some coffee."

Kate suddenly remembered telling Addie May to wake her early, because she wanted to send a rider to the fort to find out about selling the mustangs. If Clint hadn't left when he did, Addie May would have caught them together. She was becoming too careless. At last something was going right. From all indications, the rustlers hadn't returned.

Chapter 15

❧

S am sat in his office looking out the window at Kate and Clint standing near the windmill. They were laughing about something. Kate reached up and lifted Clint's hat, then brushed the front of his black hair under it. To Sam, it seemed an odd thing for Kate to do. Then Kate turned, and Sam could clearly see her face. She had a look that Sam didn't like one damn bit. His big hands gripped the wheels of his chair so tightly his knuckles turned white. Sometimes the hardest thing for a man to see is sitting right under his nose, Sam thought angrily. He'd thought all along that it was Oliver Putnam Kate was attracted to. That was why he'd made sure the man was settled in town before Kate returned with the mustangs. Why had it never occurred to him that Clint was the reason Kate had been acting so differently the past few months? Clint Morgan was a sly one. Soon Henry would be arriving in his office for his usual report. He'd ask the foreman if there was anything going on between Kate and Clint that he should know about.

By the time Henry had left his office, Sam was in a fit of anger. With the exception of himself, apparently everyone on the ranch was waiting to hear an announcement that Kate and Clint were going to get married! He'd given Henry hell for

not telling him what was going on, then he'd told
the foreman to have Kate come to his office immediately. He'd be damned if he'd let Clint haul
Kate off to Maryland. He was going to put an end
to it right now.

"Henry said you wanted to see me," Kate said
cheerfully when she entered her father's office.

"Sit down, girl."

Even though she wore men's clothing, Kate sat
properly. She looked at her father, waiting for him
to speak.

Sam rubbed his chin, searching for the right
words. "Now Kate," he said softly, "I want you
to know I understand that you must have needs."

"What are you talking about?"

Sam cleared his throat and tried again. "I'm talking about a need for a man. You been actin' mighty
peculiar what with all that dressin' up you did a
while back, going around hummin' . . . well, that
sort of thing. Even I can see how you'd be attracted
to a man like Clint."

Kate stiffened. Did Sam know about her and
Clint?

"I'm not the only one that's noticed there's
something goin' on between you two. What I'm
trying to say is, I don't want you havin' anything
more to do with him."

Kate chose her next words carefully. "That's
going to be difficult since he's staying in this
house."

"I don't see why." Sam leaned forward and
rested his elbows on his desk. "Now you listen
to me, Kate. Whatever's goin' on between the two
of you, I want it stopped. Now."

"I can't do that, Sam."

Sam's keen eyes studied his daughter. "Am I
allowed to ask why?"

Kate lowered her head. "I think I'm falling in
love with him," she said softly.

"Hogwash! Clint hasn't been here long enough for you to know how you feel about him. I'm well aware he's the type that women think they're in love with, but *think* is a big word. You're just infatuated."

"You met Mattie and married her in less time than I've known Clint," Kate reminded him.

"I'd been married, I was older, and I'd damn sure seen a lot more of life than you have. He's leaving soon. Has he asked you to go with him? Has he asked you to marry him? What do you plan on doing? You plannin' on taking off to Maryland with him? You think you'd be happy living among a bunch of snooty people and stayin' in a house day after day? And what about the ranch and your family? Am I supposed to turn all of this over to Lucas, who expects everyone to do his work for him?"

"Lucas has changed."

"If you think that, you're only foolin' yourself. If Lucas changes, it's goin' to be a long time down the road! He's playing' games. I just paid off some trollop who claimed he'd beat her, and made sure she left town. I've gotten him out of trouble more than once, and until he's willing to face up to his wrongdoings, I don't trust him any further than I would a wildcat."

"Sam, I have a right to lead my own life."

Sam slapped a weathered hand on the desk. "Bullshit! Your life is right here on this ranch! You haven't answered my question. Has Clint asked you to marry him? Has he even said he loves you?"

"No."

"Then be done with him. It's time you started remembering your loyalties are to this ranch and to your family. Not to some man passin' through that strikes a fetchin' pose."

Kate glanced around the room full of memorabilia. Being with Clint had made her realize that there had been an empty void in her life, just like this room. She didn't want to spend the rest of her life thinking about what might have been. "I have to give it a try, Sam."

"I won't allow it, Kate!" Sam's voice boomed through the room.

Kate's anger rose. "You can't fire Clint, and you can't send him out of the territory. That's why you had me come in here, isn't it? It had nothing to do with what I might want, only what *you* want. Well, it won't work this time, Sam." Kate watched her father's weathered face turning red. "I am going to do everything in my power to make Clint love me. If I lose, that will be *my* headache, not yours. You had your loves, and by God, I'm going to have mine!"

"You don't give a damn about this ranch or your family!" Realizing he was yelling, Sam lowered his voice. "Either you give this foolishness up or we no longer have anything more to talk about!"

Kate jumped to her feet. "You're a fine one to talk about not giving a damn about family! Since you had your accident you've pushed Mattie away, and now you're doing the same to me. The only thing you care about is this ranch and having me to run it for you! I'm not giving Clint up, Sam, so you're right. We have nothing else to talk about. And don't think I don't know why you haven't tried talking to Clint. He'd tell you to go to hell! He's one man you haven't been able to push around!"

Sam watched his daughter storm out of the room. Grabbing the big wheels of his chair, he pushed himself from behind the desk and out of the office. "Alma!" he bellowed as he went down the hall. "Alma!"

Alma heard him all the way in the kitchen. Sam

was practically to the doorway when she came rushing out. Seeing his face twisted with anger, she came to an abrupt halt.

"Where is Mattie?" Sam demanded.

"I'm right here," Mattie said calmly, walking out of the kitchen behind Alma.

"I want to talk to you in the parlor, madam!" Sam pushed himself in that direction. "Close the doors behind you," he instructed when they had entered the room.

"The way you're yelling, everyone in the house can hear you." Nevertheless, she slid the doors shut. "Now what's the matter?" she asked as she turned and faced her husband.

"Why haven't you put a stop to all this flutterin' Kate's doing? And don't tell me you don't know what I'm talking about!"

"What would you have me do?"

"Make that nephew of yours leave!"

"I can't do that, Sam." She clamped her hands together in front of her. "You see, I have prayed nightly that they would fall in love."

"Goddammit! Has everyone in this household lost all sense? You have never wanted for a thing. And why? Because of my money that comes from this ranch! That's why. Yet you're going to stand there and accept the possibility of Kate leaving?"

"Lucas can take Kate's place if that's what it comes to. Besides, Henry is a perfectly good foreman."

"Lucas doesn't have the brains or the balls to run this place. The only thing he can do is raise hell. I'm surprised he's even able to wipe himself."

Mattie's chin quivered. "You're not being fair."

"Fair? Take a good look at your son, madam. If I turned this ranch over to him, he'd sell everything he could get his hands on and we'd be lucky if we had five hundred head of cattle within three

years! And how long do you think he'd keep
Henry around? No, madam, it is you that's been
looking through blind eyes. Now I'll ask you one
more time. Are you going to get Clint the hell out
of here?''

''No, Sam, I'm not. Kate has a right to any happiness she can find.'' Mattie began wringing her
hands. ''Perhaps Clint will choose to marry Kate
and remain here.''

''Perhaps? He's been downright open about
goin' back to Baltimore. On more than one occasion he's talked about looking forward to enjoying the peace and quiet. That doesn't sound to
me like a man who plans on sticking around. But
so be it. If Kate leaves, the outcome will be on
your shoulders, madam. I suggest that from now
on you pray Clint doesn't have the same feelings
about Kate that she has about him.''

He wheeled himself back to the doors, and
Mattie opened them for him.

Am I wrong? Mattie asked herself. She thought
about how happy and relaxed Clint seemed lately.
But Clint always kept a stoic face, and it was impossible to determine what he was thinking. He
was a very private man. She went to the high-
backed chair by the window and sat down. No
matter which way she looked at it, she could not
picture Clint being happy living in a city. He was
too alive, and he had told her that he liked the
openness of the land and working with the stock.
No matter what Clint had told Sam, something
inside told her that Clint would never return to
Maryland to live. She leaned back in the chair and
closed her eyes. She'd just have to pray harder.

''Mmm, Kate, what you do to me,'' Clint said
as he rolled onto his back, crumpling the dry grass
beneath him.

Kate rested her head on his shoulder and

looked up at the sun. "You're the one who doesn't know when to quit," she teased.

Clint laughed. "I haven't heard you asking me to stop."

"I'm no fool. I know when I've got a good thing going." She turned onto her side and gazed at his handsome profile. She'd told Sam she thought she was falling in love, but that wasn't quite true. She was already hopelessly in love. She wanted their lives to be like in the storybooks Mattie had read to her when she was a child. They always ended with, "and they lived happily ever after." What would his children look like? It was something she'd given a lot of thought to lately. She was surprised she wasn't already pregnant. She knew she could use the slippery elm root Star had told her about, but she wouldn't. If Clint left without her, she would have something precious to remember him by. She wanted to be the mother of his children.

"Sam called me in his office this morning," she said quietly.

"And . . ."

"He knows about us."

"Everything?"

Kate sat up and reached for her clothes. "Not really. He's guessing."

Clint enjoyed watching her dress. "He was bound to find out sooner or later. What did he say?"

"He was furious. He demanded I have nothing more to do with you." She stood and pulled her pants on.

"And what did you tell him?"

"That I would live my own life exactly as I pleased."

Clint was curious as to what else had been said, but he didn't pursue it. After all, it wasn't as if he and Kate were in love. Soon he'd be leaving and they'd forget all about each other. "Good for you. It's about time you started standing up for what you want. You know, you have to be the most beautiful woman I've ever known, and although I like seeing you in dresses, I think I like you best in britches and a shirt."

Kate swerved around and looked down at him. He hadn't even started to get dressed. "That's a fine thing to say! You're the one who said I needed to learn how to dress and act like a woman. What's changed your mind?"

Clint grinned. "You don't wear one of those damn corsets, a cage, underskirts, and so forth when you're dressed like this. I like seeing those lovely breasts bounce when you're mad and tromp off somewhere."

"They don't," she gasped.

"Besides, do you have any idea how much trouble it is for a man to make love to a woman wearing all those contraptions?"

Kate laughed, remembering she'd thought the same thing when she'd bought the clothes in Rawlins. "There's nothing wrong with a man having to work for what he wants," she said lightly.

"Or maybe it's because the first time I had a good look at you, you were dressed like you are now. Mattie said at the time you looked like a man, and I remember wondering how she could ever think that."

Kate sat beside him and crossed her legs as he slipped on his pants. "Clint, I've never told you this, but now I want you to know I'm sorry about what happened when you arrived in Whitfield. I really did think I was doing the right thing."

He laid back down, propping himself up with an elbow. "Did I hurt you when I pulled you off your horse?"

"I have to admit, I suffered some bruises."

"Where?" He ran his hand down her arm. "Here?" He traced her lips with this thumb. "Here?" Then he trailed his fingers down her long neck and across her breasts. "Or here?"

"My bottom," she replied, feeling her need for him rising again.

"Too bad you're dressed. I'd kiss it." He released the top button of her shirt and moved his hand inside. His fingers toyed with her already rigid nipple.

Midnight nickered nervously. Removing his hand from inside Kate's shirt, Clint turned and glanced at the horses standing a few feet away. They were in an open field, but both were ground trained, so their reins hung loose. Ball-eyed, Kate's horse started moving off to the side, putting more and more distance between them. Then Clint heard a loud snort and a hoof scraping the ground. A big maverick bull wasn't more than ten feet away. "Don't move," he whispered to Kate.

Still in a daze of desire, Kate wasn't sure what he was talking about, but she could hear a clear warning in his voice. Unthinking, she opened her eyes and said, "Is something wrong?"

The words sent the bull charging, head down. Clint managed to knock both himself and Kate out of the way just as the mighty animal ran past them, making a swipe with his long, sharp horns. He spun back around, snorting, and scraping with his hoof.

Clint slowly rose to a crouched position keeping his eyes in direct contact with the bull's.

Shaking with fear, Kate glanced over at their gun belts. They were too far away to reach. She remained still, hoping the bull would turn and leave. But her hopes vanished when the fourteen hundred pounds of fury rushed forward again. Before she could scramble out of the way, Clint leaped onto the bull's head. He grabbed hold of the horns, his arm muscles bulging as he tried twisting the bull's neck. But he couldn't get the right leverage, and the bull sent him flying in the air.

Seeing her chance, Kate made a dive for the gun belts. She snatched the revolver from the holster and rose to her knees, but before she could lift the gun and fire the bull was upon her. A searing pain ripped across her side as she tried twisting away. She fell back and her head hit a rock. Everything went black.

As he climbed to his feet, Clint saw the bull standing beside Kate's limp figure. From the way her body was twisted, he knew the bull had gouged her. A cold deadliness engulfed him. He made a running leap onto Midnight's back, then knee reined the horse around. The bull came thundering toward them, but Clint had already pulled his rifle from the scabbard. He unloaded the bullets into the bull's head.

Clint galloped Midnight to where Kate was lying and slid from the saddle before the horse had even come to a halt. Kate hadn't moved. He was overcome with fear that she might be dead. Dropping to one knee, he placed shaking fingers on her neck to check for a pulse. "Thank God," he murmured. "She's alive." Gently he straightened her legs, then rolled her carefully onto her back so he could examine the damage. A long gash went from near her navel to her side. He pulled the torn remnants of her shirt away to get a better look. The wound was bleeding badly, but from what he could tell, nothing vital had been damaged. He didn't want to place her in a sitting position because it would only aggravate the wound, but he had no blankets to cover her with and he couldn't leave her alone to go to the ranch for a wagon. He had no choice but to bandage her the best he could and carry her back to the house.

His mind made up, Clint ripped the sleeves from Kate's shirt, formed a long pad, then placed it across the wound. Satisfied, he grabbed his shirt and started tearing it into strips and knotting the ends together.

The task completed, he carefully wrapped the strips of cloth around Kate's waist, wondering why she hadn't regained consciousness. Seeing blood on the rock beside her, he examined the back of her head and found a large bump. Removing the bandanna from his neck, he used it to wrap her head.

When there was nothing else he could do, Clint pulled on his boots, cursing himself for not having seen the bull sooner. Beside himself with worry, he hurriedly grabbed up the gun belts and slung them over the saddle horn. Ready, he leaned down and gently lifted Kate up in his arms.

Fortunately, Midnight remained steady. As if sensing the seriousness of the problem, he stood perfectly still as Clint stuck a boot in the stirrup. Holding Kate tightly in his arms, Clint put his full weight on the stirrup and swung his right leg over the saddle. He settled Kate against his chest. "All right, boy," he said as he took hold of the reins, "let's get Kate home."

Clint glanced down at the floor, wondering if he'd worn a path with his pacing. He shrugged. Of course he hadn't. He tried sitting, but as before, after a few minutes he was on his feet again. How much longer would it be before Oliver or Mattie came down with news about Kate? he wondered, running his fingers through his thick hair. He thought about Sam sitting alone in his office, also waiting for a report. He'd have joined the old man, but Sam had made it clear with just a look that Clint wasn't wanted.

How long had it been since Kate was gashed by the bull? Clint started pacing again. He felt like mashing someone's face to get rid of his pent-up anger at what had happened to Kate, but he couldn't even do that. In his mind, he relived what had happened a lifetime ago.

He'd kept Midnight at a hard gallop, wanting to get Kate home as quickly as possible. When he'd finally entered the house, he let out a loud yell for Mattie, then, taking the steps two at a time, he'd carried Kate to her room and placed her on her bed. When Mattie came rushing in and he knew Kate was in the best possible hands, he'd told Mattie he was going to get a shirt, then go for Oliver. He now felt guilty about leaving the room without a word of explanation. He hadn't wanted to take the time when he could already be on his way to town. Poor Mattie must have been horrified.

It had seemed to take forever before he'd returned with the doctor. When they entered the house, Sam was waiting in the foyer.

"Thank God you're here, Oliver," Sam said. "Kate's bedroom is upstairs and to the right, past the corner." That was when Sam had given Clint a look of pure hatred. "I want to be alone," he had stated before wheeling himself to his office.

Clint went to the window and looked out into the black of night. His eyes focused on his reflection in the glass. He looked as bad as he felt. Alma had tried to get him to eat something, but he couldn't, not while Kate lay upstairs in God knew what kind of condition.

Hearing the swishing of skirts, he spun around and watched Mattie enter the parlor.

"I'm sorry to have taken so long to let you know about Kate, but I've been with Sam," Mattie said, a bit out of breath from rushing. "He's been taken to his bedroom. I guess I don't need to tell you that Sam was sick with worry since it was a bull that had caused him to be crippled." Realizing she'd been remiss in telling Clint about Kate, she quickly said, "Kate's going to be all right, Clint. The doctor has examined her, her wound is stitched, and now he's sitting by her bed. Fortunately the gash isn't deep. And Kate's conscious."

Clint could never remember feeling such relief.

"Kate muttered something about grabbing a gun, but she's still disoriented and Oliver wants her to remain quiet. He's given her laudanum to make her rest," Mattie said kindly. "Please, have a seat, Clint."

Clint couldn't believe that a woman who looked so frail could have so much inner strength. She had his highest respect.

"I owe you an apology for leaving without an explanation," Clint stated simply as he sat across from his aunt.

"You owe me no apology, my dear. You did exactly the right thing. Now, I would like you to tell me what happened."

Clint described everything, starting out by saying he and Kate had been sitting on the ground talking.

Mattie was still wondering why Kate hadn't had her boots on, but she didn't mention it. "You are both so fortunate that this is all that happened. Few stitches were needed, and if I know Kate, she'll be sore, but up and around in a few days. It's late, and you need to get some rest. Tomorrow you might want to visit Kate in her room. I'm sure she'd like to see you."

"You are quite a woman, Mattie Whitfield."

Mattie smiled. "And I think you are quite a man, Clint Morgan. I owe you a great deal."

"What could you possibly owe me? Seems to me, my being here has caused more trouble than good."

"Oh, but you're wrong. Kate is every bit the woman I'd hoped she'd become, and you've made Sam do some serious thinking about his daughter. Oh, don't get me wrong. At present he is absolutely furious at you for taking his daughter from him. But can you blame him? He's worried about what will happen to the ranch should she take a notion to leave. However, that isn't all of it. You see, though Sam may not always show his affections, he loves Kate dearly. They argued this morning, and Kate told Sam she was falling in love with you." Mattie watched for any signs of surprise on Clint's face, but there were none. "In years to come, when you settle down to raise a family, you'll understand what it is like to feel you are losing your daughter's love to another man."

"But that's not true."

"No, but sometimes it takes a little while before the father comes to realize the love isn't being taken away, it's simply being shared. And it makes it especially difficult when someone like you, whom Sam has grown very fond of, is the very man who's stealing that love. Maybe now you can understand why Sam feels so bitter toward you. For some reason, I believe that if you were in Sam's shoes, you'd feel the same way. In many ways, you and Sam are much alike. I'm not sure he will ever be able to forgive you." Mattie wasn't really sure that was true, but she was trying to tweak Clint's inner sense of challenge.

"Well, I'll be leaving soon, so he'll have his daughter back," Clint said defensively. If Mattie felt any shock at the statement, it didn't show on her face.

"Before I got off track, I was talking about what

you have done for Sam. When the next man steps into Kate's life, and she wants to marry, Sam will have come to grips with himself and be more receptive to the man.''

Clint cocked an eyebrow. "Marry? You think she will marry?''

"Of course she will. Now that she truly feels like a woman, you mark my word, she's going to start thinking about having children.'' Mattie saw the muscles in Clint's jaw flex. "I'll write Cora and tell her when it happens, and she can inform you. Now I really must go to Kate, and you need to get your sleep.''

They left the parlor, and Clint took Mattie's elbow to escort her up the stairs. He went into his room, feeling like he was in a daze. He didn't like hearing that Kate would marry someone else. He plopped down on the bed. He didn't like hearing it one damn bit! Hell, Kate was his! Still, it wasn't as if he loved her. He had been so sick with worry about her dying that he was just feeling a little possessive.

Though dog-tired, Clint's concern over Kate kept him awake. He thought about his life over the past ten years. He suddenly realized it had been a lonely existence, but he'd never minded. He wasn't sure how it had happened, but now he was embroiled in a family that months back he couldn't have cared less about. As soon as the reservation cattle were loaded, he'd have to leave. Oddly enough, that was something he wasn't looking forward to. Through the years there had been people he cared about and protected, some going on with their lives, some dying. It was the innocent ones he'd seen die that had made him so hard. He had no sympathy for the murderers and users. He suddenly realized he couldn't remember the last time he'd had a nightmare. He laughed bitterly. *You're getting soft, Morgan.*

* * *

When Mattie entered the bedroom, Oliver moved away from Kate's bedside and joined the older woman. "She's resting quietly," he said in a hushed voice. "Kate's going to be just fine, Mattie. You did a good job of stitching her up. You should have been a doctor."

"Why, thank you, Oliver. I couldn't begin to count the injuries I've had to take care of on this ranch over the years. I could see the wound needed to be stitched right away, and I knew it would take a while for you to get here. Besides, I only had to take a few. But if she had been awake, I'm not sure I could have even done that."

Oliver patted her shoulder and started out the door. "I'll be back in the morning."

Mattie sat in the chair by the bed, then reached over and patted Kate's stilled hands. "Don't you worry, Kate dear, everything is going to turn out just fine," she whispered.

Though Clint was up early the next morning and anxious to see how Kate was faring, he knew he couldn't very well go barging into her bedroom. He had no option but to wait for Mattie's permission. He wandered around the house, finally ending up in the library, where he pulled a book from the bookshelf. Settled on a comfortable leather chair, he tried reading. After the first two pages, he gave up. What the hell's the matter with you? he chastised himself. Last night Mattie said Kate was all right, so why are you acting like some expectant father?

Even after having a talk with himself, Clint couldn't leave the house. He still felt a deep concern for Kate, and dammit, he wanted to see for himself that she was all right. He finally decided to go sit in the kitchen. At least he'd have Bessy to talk to.

Clint hadn't been in the kitchen more than fifteen minutes when Mattie finally came drifting in.

"There you are, Clint," she said brightly. "I've been searching the house for you. Kate's sore, but she's wide awake, and hungry as a bear. I'll take her breakfast up as soon as Bessy can fix it. In the meantime, Kate's waiting for you."

Clint's lips were already spreading into a wide grin as he left the kitchen.

"Do you think those two will *ever* get together, Mrs. Whitfield?" Bessy asked as she started cracking eggs.

"Indeed I do, Bessy. Has Clint eaten this morning?"

"No, ma'am. I haven't been able to get him to take a bite of food."

"Well, I'm sure he'll eat now, so cook enough for two."

It seemed strange to knock on Kate's door before entering, nevertheless, Clint did exactly that.

"Come in," Kate called from the other side.

Clint was glad he'd knocked when he saw Addie May sitting beside the bed. She immediately rose and left the room, and Clint claimed the chair. "How is it possible for a woman to go through what you have and still look so beautiful?"

Kate tried not to smile. It hurt her head. "That's exactly the words I needed to hear this morning," Kate replied.

Clint could clearly see the love in her eyes, and it made him uncomfortable. He'd be walking out of her life soon, and he wasn't looking forward to seeing that love turn to hurt.

"Mattie told me you were all right. What happened to the bull?"

"I killed him."

"Oh." Kate was at a loss for words. When Clint had first come in, she could tell he was happy to see her. Now she sensed him withdrawing. "Is anything wrong?"

"Now what could possibly be wrong?"

Kate wondered the same thing.

"As soon as the doctor says it's all right, I'll carry you outside and you can sit for a while in the sun."

"I'd like that. You can carry me out now if you like," she said mischievously.

Suddenly feeling relaxed, Clint smiled. "Oh, no."

"Does this mean we're going to have to stop our wicked ways for a spell?" Kate whispered.

Clint burst out laughing, and even though it hurt terribly, Kate laughed with him.

For the next week, Clint carried Kate outside every day and sat with her beneath the apple tree, even though she insisted she could walk on her own. They talked about anything that came to mind, and at other times they shared a comfortable silence. Kate had never known such happiness. And much to his amazement, neither had Clint.

By the second week Kate was moving around as if nothing had happened. The doctor had removed the stitches and, other than being a bit sore, she was feeling her normal self. She even started doing some riding, but only for short distances. Clint was always by her side, worrying the entire time. She felt pampered, and she was loving every minute of it, even though Clint never so much as kissed her. There was no doubt in her mind that Clint truly loved her.

But as the days passed, Kate's desire grew. One night she finally decided to take matters into her own hands.

Kate pulled her robe around her naked body and, convinced everyone was asleep, slipped out of her room and went to Clint's. She tried to open the door quietly, but as usual, it creaked. She did manage to close it without any noise. The room was silent as she carefully made her way to Clint's bed.

"Why are you here, Kate?"

The coldly spoken words made her hesitate. "I wanted you to hold me," she whispered.

Clint knew he should send her away, but he couldn't. "Come here, Kate."

Kate dropped her robe and crawled into bed beside him.

Clint could smell her fresh scent even before he carefully took her into his arms. He buried his face in her glorious hair. "You know we can't do anything," he murmured as he nibbled her ear. "God you feel good in my arms."

"Clint, I'm all right."

"I might hurt you."

Her hand slid down his body until she touched his already rigid manhood. "I guess we'll just have to be careful," she whispered.

Clint wasn't sure. But when she rolled on top of him and started kissing his neck, shoulders, and lips, he knew he had to have her. It had been too long since they'd made love, and his resistance was weak. He groaned softly. "My dearest Kate, I'll never be able to get enough of you." He claimed her sweet lips, knowing he'd spoken the truth.

Clint tried to be as gentle as possible. When he brought them both to the pinnacle of their desire, his lips covered Kate's to keep her from crying out.

Kate fell asleep in his arms, but Clint remained awake, knowing he was a lost man. He could no longer fight it. He was irrevocably in love. He gently caressed her cheek, then brushed the glossy hair from her face. He'd be damned if another man was going to have her. He wanted Kate by his side for the rest of his life.

Near dawn, Clint leaned down and kissed Kate awake. "You have to leave."

"Do we have enough time for—"

"No," he said gently.

Kate could hear the humor in his voice. She kissed his lips and climbed out of bed. "Then I guess we'll just have to continue this at another time."

"Go on back to your room, girl. I'll see you later."

Kate laughed softly, then opened the door and peeked out. Seeing no one in the hallway, she closed the door behind her.

Clint locked his hands beneath his head and grinned. He'd known he was in love when he saw Kate lying so still on the ground and the bull standing over her. But still he'd fought it, telling himself that he could ride away from her and never look back. He just hadn't wanted to admit that an unpredictable slip of a woman had actually captured his heart. Now that he'd finally come around to accepting his fate, he felt damn good about it.

Chapter 16

Clint sauntered out of the telegraph office, feeling more relaxed than he had in years. He was convinced none of the Whitfields were involved in the switching of the reservation cattle. He'd just sent Sandoval a wire stating as much and that he would see to it that their mutual friend Vale was taken care of.

A boy squatting in front of the next store over suddenly jumped to his feet. "Mr. Morgan?" he asked when he reached Clint's side.

Clint looked down at the blond youngster. He was barefoot, his britches were far too short, and there were freckles spattered across the bridge of his nose. "What can I do for you?" Clint asked with a grin.

"I got a message for you." The boy reached up and handed Clint a folded piece of paper.

Wondering who could possibly be sending him a note, Clint dug in his pocket for a coin.

"That ain't necessary, Mr. Morgan. I've already been paid."

Clint flipped the coin to him. "Well now you can say you've done a good day's work."

A broad smile spread across the boy's face before he took off running toward the candy shop.

Clint unfolded the paper and read the note.

Clint, I need to talk to you. Please come by the boardinghouse.

                                                    Star

The only thing she could possibly want would be to get in touch with Sam, Clint thought. He refolded the paper and stuffed it into his vest pocket. Before, when they were still speaking to one another, Sam had told Clint all about his relationship with Star, and had assured Clint that they were now nothing more than good friends. Nevertheless, Sam had no desire to have Mattie know anything about their past relationship.

Clint stepped down from the walk and was about to untie Midnight's reins when he noticed two women across the street wearing colorful day dresses. They were about to enter the general store when the brunette suddenly turned and, looking directly at him, offered a shy but ingratiating smile. Clint smiled back and tipped his hat before she disappeared into the store. She was a cute little thing, and he knew that had this happened a couple of months ago, he would probably have crossed the street and tried to strike up a conversation. Now he wasn't even tempted. Loving Kate had removed all desire to roam.

He chuckled as he untied the reins, unable to believe he was actually contemplating marriage. Yet, tonight he was going to tell Kate the truth about his working for the government. She probably wouldn't be pleased to know he'd come here to spy, but he wasn't worried about cooling her off. After she'd calmed down, he'd tell her he loved her, and that he'd return as soon as he'd finished his assignment. Hopefully she'd be willing to go to Baltimore to live. After the way Sam had been acting, he had no desire to live with the man's anger. Though in all honesty, he had fallen in love with the ranch as well as with Kate. He much preferred the open space, and returning to the city no longer had any appeal. Now that he thought about it, returning to Baltimore *never* had any appeal.

Clint shoved his foot in the stirrup and swung himself up into the saddle. There was no doubt in his mind that Kate loved him, but getting Sam to approve of the marriage would be an entirely different matter. He headed the stallion in the direction of the boardinghouse. Kate certainly wasn't the type he'd envisioned marrying whenever he'd thought about settling down, but then he'd never thought he'd fall in love either. He chuckled. One thing about it, if Kate agreed to marry him, their life together wouldn't be dull.

It seemed to Clint that what Star had to say must be important, because when he rode up to the boardinghouse she was already holding the screen door open. She had on a bright pink dress that clashed with her brassy hair, and the many ruffles circling her low neckline and skirt only served to make her already stout figure look even larger. But though she tended to be a bit bright in her dress, he liked her open, friendly manner. He tipped his hat and dismounted.

"Can I get you a piece of cake?" Star asked when they had entered the parlor.

Clint took a seat on the brown overstuffed chair, and was immediately sorry. The thing was uncomfortable as hell. "No, thanks. I have to leave shortly."

"Then how about a drink? I could certainly use one."

"I'll take you up on that. What was it you wanted to talk about?"

Star poured whiskey into two glasses, then handed Clint one. "Now that you're here, I'm beginning to wonder if I'm doing the right thing."

Clint laughed. "Why don't you just spit it out and we'll go from there?"

"Well, you see, I have a problem. I care for Sam, but that son of his is just about as bad as they come."

"Lucas?" Clint wasn't particularly fond of the boy either, but he felt her words were a bit strong.

"I don't know of Sam having any other sons," she said back at him. "It's no secret that I've known a few men in my life, and I consider myself a pretty good judge of character. I believe you're a man who can take care of himself, and I also think you're a fair man. So I'm going to let you decide what to do with what I tell you."

Star took a healthy drink of the strong whiskey and didn't bat an eyelash. "I don't know if you're aware of it, but about five miles due north there's a saloon called the Graveyard. It's Lucas's favorite hangout, and is frequented by most of the questionable characters in the area. Those men pretty much keep to themselves, and they don't come into Whitfield 'cause they know Sam'll have them run out. They're more apt to go to Rawlins. The Graveyard is in the hills up Rattlesnake Trail." She took another drink and sat down. "One of the girls that worked over there is now at the Hoof and Horn Saloon, and she's been doing some talking. Seems Lucas likes to beat his women, drink a lot, and brag about the men he's killed, though apparently no one pays him any mind. 'Course everyone knows Lucas is a braggart and a hell-raiser." She finished off her drink. "Want another?" she asked, seeing Clint's glass was also empty.

Clint shook his head. He was far more interested in her story.

"But Ellie, that's the gal that moved, said something that didn't make sense. She talked about Lucas always throwin' around money. Now

I knew that couldn't be right when I heard the story, 'cause Sam don't dish money out to Lucas. Not that kind of money. So my question is, where did that little bastard come by it? On the other hand, maybe the girl ain't tellin' the truth.''

Clint was wondering the same thing. ''Why don't you tell me how to get to the Graveyard Saloon, and I'll check it out?'' He stood and handed Star his empty glass. ''But I doubt Lucas will be there because he and Pedro are up at a line shack.''

''He was there last night.''

Clint frowned. ''Did the girl say that?''

''Ellie went back this morning to see some girl named Hazel. Ellie was goin' to try and talk her into movin' over to the Hoof and Horn. But accordin' to Ellie, Hazel had a broken arm. Lucas broke it two nights ago.''

''I'll go have a talk with Ellie.''

Clint was amazed at how fast the big woman could move. Before he could walk out of the parlor, Star already had the doorway blocked. ''What I told you can't go any further. It stops here.''

''Oh?''

''There's only one other person besides you and me that knows what Ellie said. That's already two too many. Clint, I don't know what Sam's told you about me, but it's because of him I own this boardinghouse. Sam's been a good friend and I want to return the favor. He's gotten that boy out of trouble more than once, but maybe if he really knows the direction Lucas is headed, he can put a stop to it.''

Clint reached out and patted Star's plump arm. ''I'll check into it, and I won't say a thing to anyone. But remember one thing, Star. If Lucas is man enough to carry a gun, he's man enough to suffer the consequences.''

As Clint rode out of town, he wasn't in nearly

as good a mood as when he'd arrived. He'd known a lot of men who derived pleasure from beating women. He'd never liked a one of them. Usually they were cowards, and weren't about to fight an able-bodied man. But before he said anything to Sam about Lucas, he'd find out for himself if Ellie had told the truth or if the girl had a grudge and was trying to get even. If she was telling the truth, he also wanted to know why Lucas wasn't out checking line shacks. He wasn't concerned about Lucas having money. Because the girl didn't have much of her own, it probably just looked like a lot. After everyone has gone to sleep tonight, he thought, I'll ride out to the Graveyard Saloon to take a look. He hadn't even considered asking Star who had passed on the information to her. She wouldn't have told him anyway.

That night, Clint went to Kate's bedroom shortly after supper. He chuckled when he found her lying on her bed as naked as the day she was born. He quickly stripped, then joined her.

"How did you know I'd be here?" he asked as he pulled her into his arms.

"By the twinkle in your eyes all during supper." She nuzzled his neck and caressed his chest.

"You're getting awful sure of yourself, lady."

"Ah-huh."

"And you've developed an insatiable appetite," he said lovingly before claiming her soft lips.

Kate drew her head back, laughing softly. "It's your fault. You shouldn't have taught me how enjoyable being a wicked woman can be. But if you don't like me to be so willing, I can always change."

He pulled her on top of him. "Don't you dare." Would he ever tire of this woman he now claimed as his? No, not in a hundred years. "Put me inside you, darlin'."

Kate looked at him quizzically.

"Straddle me."

Kate raised up on her knees, her long hair falling down on his chest. After a little adjusting she sat down on him. She gasped at the maddening sensation of feeling his hardness penetrate deep within her. She saw his jaw tighten, heard his moan of pleasure, and felt his hands grip her buttocks, slowly rotating them.

"How I love being inside you," he said in a raspy voice, "feeling how tight you are and how wet you get."

His words were like music to Kate's ears. She ran her hands across the hair of his chest, delighting in the feel of it. Then her fingers played with his nipples, and ever so slowly, she began raising her hips up and down, taking control, driving them both to the crest. Her movements became faster, using him, needing him, wanting him. A sheen of perspiration glistened over her body and Clint used it to slide his hands up and down her sides and over her breasts.

As Kate threw her head back, striving to reach her climax, Clint raised up and suckled each perfect breast, tasting her, loving her, knowing that short of death, nothing would ever take her away from him. He gently rolled her onto her back, wanting to take her to the heights she so desperately wanted.

"I love you," Kate whispered in a haze, not knowing she had spoken aloud. A moment later, wonderful bombs of every color burst in her head.

As soon as Kate had fallen asleep, Clint slipped out of bed and quickly dressed. He opened the door, then silently closed it behind him. Though Clint knew he would have gone to Kate's bedroom tonight anyway, he also knew he had used her. It didn't make him feel the least bit proud of himself. But he had to be sure she wouldn't come to his room later.

Clint heard the noise coming from the Graveyard Saloon even before he rode up. The place was nothing more than a large log cabin with a second floor. As he rode past the line of horses tied to the long hitching rail, Clint checked each animal. Lucas's big buckskin wasn't hard to spot, nor was the pinto belonging to Pedro that stood beside it. Apparently, Pedro had been all talk about staying away from Lucas, Clint thought as he dismounted.

Clint stepped onto the small porch, then looked through the window to the familiar scene inside. This type of saloon tended to a sameness repeated throughout the West. The men's clothes were well worn and mostly dirty, their gun belts low-slung. Their demeanor was such that the average man would know to leave them alone. Clint grunted. At least half of them were probably wanted by the law in one or more of the states and territories. Most were loud and drunk, or on their way to getting there. Midway across the room was a small platform with a chair on it, where a bull of a man sat with a shotgun resting across his massive thighs to make sure everything was kept under control. On back from him were stairs leading to the second floor. Up there would be the rooms where the saloon girls entertained their paying customers. A large pot belly stove sat in the center of the room to keep the place warm during winter. At the far end was a small stage. Tables and chairs filled the open area. The bar stretched the length of the left side, and it was at the bar that Clint's gaze finally landed on Pedro. Lucas was nowhere in sight.

With Pedro's back turned to the door, Clint took

the opportunity to enter. He headed straight for the empty table he'd spotted against the far wall. He pulled his hat down as he took a chair, then squinted his eyes. The place reeked of stale whiskey, sweat, and smoke.

The piano player, shoved off in a corner, struck a couple of chords. Clint watched three women step onto the stage. They all had wide, painted smiles which did nothing for their generally unattractive features. One brunette was fat; the mousy blonde was skinny. The other brunette was at least a little more acceptable, except a sling circled one arm. Even her makeup didn't hide the dark circle under her left eye. The women started singing off key.

"Well hello, handsome. What can I do for you?"

Clint looked up at the small blonde standing by his table. As with the other girls in the place, her purple dress hid little of what she had to offer. She leaned over, planting a full breast in his face and placing her arm around his shoulder.

"I ain't never seen you here before. My name's Rose. What's yours?"

Clint gave her a friendly grin. "Sorry, honey. I'm just stopping long enough to grab a drink. Maybe next time."

"You gotta be thirsty. You wait right here and I'll bring us a bottle of whiskey." Rose took off toward the bar.

The women on the stage were now dancing and swinging their dresses high enough for the men to see they had nothing on underneath. When the song was finished, the men whistled and cheered with enthusiasm. As the women made their exit, Clint saw Lucas coming down the stairs. He was wearing a black hat cocked on the back of his head. He tipped up the bottle of whiskey he was holding and took a long drink. Clint pulled his hat down farther to prevent being recognized.

"Ooooee," Lucas hollered down. "Did I give Boots a time she'll never forget. That whore never had it stuck in her so good."

Some of the men in the saloon looked up, but most paid no attention. Clint found it interesting that Pedro and a couple of men beside him laughed appreciatively. Lucas reached the bottom of the stairs, staggered over to the bar, then shoved his way in beside Pedro.

"Here you go," Rose announced as she placed a bottle and two glasses on the table. She pulled out a chair, shoved it next to Clint, then sat down beside him. "I can't believe you'd want to drink alone."

"You're absolutely right." Clint poured a drink for both of them, still keeping an eye on Lucas. "How's Hazel doing?"

"You know about Hazel?"

"A friend of mine was telling me how Lucas beat the hell out of her."

The blonde's face hardened. "You a friend of Lucas?"

"Nope. Met him a few times though. Can't say I was impressed."

Rose took a drink, then leaned forward, resting her breasts on the table. "That bastard. I even have bruises where he's beat me up, but never like he did to Hazel. She thought her arm was broke, but it wasn't. It might as well of been for the pain she's gone through. Lucas seems to get meaner with every passin' day."

Clint poured her another drink. "So why go upstairs with him?"

"Are you kidding? Duke would fire any of us in a minute if we refused. Lucas spends a lot of money here."

Clint watched Lucas pile money on the bar,

then he, Pedro, and two other men went over and sat at one of the corner tables. "Maybe Lucas has a problem," Clint muttered as the four men huddled with their heads together.

"He has a problem all right. He's plumb crazy."

Clint had heard and seen enough. He reached into his pocket and pulled out some money, then with a broad grin, stuffed it in between Rose's ample breasts. "I'll look you up next time I come through." He rose from his chair, tipped his hat and left.

As Clint headed Midnight back to the ranch, his senses were keenly honed. It was something he couldn't explain, but it always happened when he was getting close to catching an outlaw or solving a hidden treachery. But whatever the reason, this time it was centered on Lucas. Clint had never cared much for the boy, even though the rest of the Whitfield family meant a great deal to him now. After what he'd just found out, his feelings toward Lucas had plummeted considerably. Sam's son was not only untrustworthy, he was also sneaky and mean. An owl hooted, causing Midnight to shy off to the side. Clint reached down to give the horse a reassuring pat on the neck.

So now what are you going to do, Morgan? Clint asked himself as he nudged Midnight into an easy lope. He thought about why he'd held off from declaring his love to Kate tonight. After talking to Star, suspicions had already begun to form in his head. Was Lucas behind the cattle rustling after all? That would certainly explain where the money came from. "Damn," he exclaimed. He had fallen into a trap that was fatal to all government men. He cared about the people this would involve. With his next breath, he cursed Lucas for being the thorn that could destroy what he and

Kate had going for them. She'd remained firm against Sam, but as she'd said on many occasions, first the ranch, then her family. He knew that if circumstances were reversed, she'd fight just as hard for him. Hadn't she already stood up to Sam because of him? But finding out exactly who he was, and how he'd deceived everyone, would quickly change everything. Especially if he had to stick Lucas in prison. She'd feel used, and justifiably so. He was definitely between a rock and a hard place. There wasn't a damn thing he could do about it except turn his back, or go straight to Sam with the information he'd learned tonight. Or he could take Lucas aside and give him a warning. But that idea twisted his stomach. If he did that and Lucas *was* in with the rustlers, the other culprits would make a clean getaway. He thought about how competently Lucas had handled the death of Brody with lies. And of course there was the little matter of Lucas and Pedro not being out checking line shacks like they were told.

By the time Clint had put Midnight away and reentered the house, he knew he had only one choice. In the morning, he'd try talking to Sam, but it wasn't going to be easy. It ticked him off that his fondness for Mattie and Sam, plus his love for Kate, had made him vulnerable. He should be the one to handle this, but he was going to give the family a chance. Maybe he was jumping to conclusions, and Lucas wasn't involved in the rustling. But he knew he was only trying to fool himself with excuses. His gut told him he was right. It made a lot of pieces of the puzzle fit, and if Lucas was guilty, so was Pedro. ''Damn!'' he muttered as he entered his room.

The next morning, Clint made straight for Sam's office. He found Sam sitting behind his desk, looking off into space.

"What the hell do you want?" Sam barked out. "If you're aimin' to talk about Kate, you can just take your ass back out of here!"

Clint sat on one of the chairs and stared at the weathered man. "You'll be happy to know I'll be leaving as soon as the cattle are loaded."

"What are you plannin' to do about Kate?"

"Like it or not, Sam, whatever happens between us is none of your damn business. But that's not what I came here to talk about. Have you seen Lucas lately?"

"No, not that it's any of your business. The boy's out doin' his job. He should be riding back in a couple of days to help round up steers. In case you aren't aware of it, this is September. Cowpokes will be riding in from all over. Some that's worked for us in the past, some that ain't. We've had men come from as far away as California. Everyone knows when it's gettin' near shipping time, and that we pay top dollar. Those that don't know soon find out." Sam released an exasperated grunt. "Making sure the cattle are loaded properly is the one thing Lucas does well."

Clint's eyes became the color of tombstones. "I thought Henry took care of that."

"To a degree, but Lucas is actually in charge."

"Does Lucas also handle the loading of the reservation shipment?"

Sam slammed a fist on the desk. "Why all the goddamn questions? You'll be leaving, and the sooner the better. But by God, if I have to shoot you, you're not taking Kate with you. I haven't made any secret how I feel. I don't think you give a damn about Kate, but I can't say that doesn't make me happy. You got anything else you want to say?"

"Nope." Clint pushed himself up out of the chair. "You've already got that bull head of yours made up, so there's nothing I can say that would change your mind. You're making a mistake, Sam. You should make peace with her now, before the damage is irreparable. She would." He left the room.

Clint's thoughts were racing as he left the house in search of Kate. Was it possible that Lucas was also involved in switching the reservation cattle? The possibility threatened all kinds of ramifications, but first he needed to talk to Kate and find out exactly how Lucas was involved in the cattle loading.

Clint found Kate in front of one of the corrals, saddling a horse.

"Good morning," Kate said cheerfully. "Did Mattie give you my message?" She leaned down to tighten the saddle girth.

"I haven't seen her. What was the message?" he asked as he stroked the horse's withers.

"I'm riding out to take a look at the herd. The cowhands are culling out the steers. Before long, two thousand steers will be ready for shipment." She straightened and looked at him fondly. "I thought you might want to come along."

As always, Clint was captivated by her marvelous green eyes. This was the woman who had made him whole and caring, and whether she knew it or not, he was completely under her spell. God how he loved this woman. "Wait here, and I'll saddle Midnight."

It wasn't until they were well on their way that Clint decided to broach the subject of Lucas. They were riding side by side when Clint said, "Kate, tell me the process of loading the cattle."

Kate pulled her hat down to shade her eyes from the sun. "Well, we drive the cattle the short distance to the railroad spur, divide them up and put them in holding pens. Then it's just a matter of loading them into the railroad cars. The Union Pacific sends down an engine to cart them off. It takes three trips, then the cars are switched in Rawlins. From that point they're sent to the proper destination."

"So about seven hundred go out each trip. It must keep all the men busy switching and loading."

"It does at first, but in the last shipment that goes out, there's only four hundred steers. Those are loaded last because we have to wait until the government inspector checks them over. They're for the Indian reservations."

"Sam told me Lucas was in charge of the loading."

Kate laughed. "Not really, I couldn't afford to take the chance of him making a mess of everything. I let him handle the loading of the government steers because there isn't much involved with that few cattle."

"And you're there the entire time?"

"If I did that, he wouldn't think he was in charge. No, I collect the money from Gordon Vale, that's the buyer, then leave. Lucas came up with the idea about two years ago, and I decided to see if he could be relied on to handle it. I have to say, he's done a good job. Maybe now that he's finally working and showing some responsibility, I'll start giving him other jobs." Kate glanced up at the sun. "I guess you'll be leaving soon."

Clint nodded.

"I'm going to miss you." It wasn't easy to make her voice sound normal and keep her chin from quivering. "But we've had some good times together."

Again Clint nodded his head.

Kate knew she had to face the inevitable, but God how it hurt. She'd prayed practically every night that Clint would ask her to leave with him. It was because he didn't seem to want anything lasting from her that she'd hesitated declaring her love. So many times she'd started to tell him, but she couldn't bear the thought of him laughing, or worse yet, feeling sorry for her. And what if he should quit making love to her because he didn't want to be tied down?

As they rode on in silence, Clint tried to assimilate the information he'd been given. He didn't like what was filtering through his mind. If he was anywhere close to being right, then there was no future for a life with Kate. His need for Kate was suddenly so overpowering that he moved his horse closer to hers, then with one swoop of his arm lifted her off her saddle.

Kate's arms went around his neck. Her legs dangled down the side of Clint's horse, but she wasn't the least concerned about falling. Clint's strong arms would keep her safe. Then his lips were on hers, his kiss expressing his raw desire. She could already feel the pulsing throb between her legs. He brought Midnight to a halt, then gently lowered her to the ground.

Within moments, they were lying on the grass naked, entwined in each other's arms. Each of them feeling a desperate need for the other—Clint because he knew this could be the last time he'd ever be able to hold her in his arms and make love to her, and Kate suffering from the realization that he'd soon be leaving for Maryland.

They gave and received, and soon Kate was sure she would die a most glorious death. She reached up and lovingly caressed the sides of Clint's face before indescribable pleasure swept through her entire being.

"Oh, Clint," Kate said when she could finally speak, "I never knew being bedded could be so wonderful until you came into my life." She reached up and smoothed back the tuft of black hair from his eyes.

"Just think what all you've missed," Clint said softly, trying to make light of it. He hated himself for what he was going to have to do. She would never know that in the throes of her ecstasy she had again whispered "I love you," or how much it meant to him.

"We'd better be getting on," Clint said as he reached out for his clothes.

"We can stay longer," Kate replied hopefully.

Clint tossed her clothes to her. "You're the one who always says there's work to be done. Now get dressed like a good girl."

Kate was taken aback by the hard tone that had crept into his voice. Normally, he would have welcomed the opportunity to spend the afternoon making love, so why had he suddenly changed?

Soon they were dressed, and again headed in the direction of the small herd. It bothered Kate that Clint said very little on the way. Normally he was quite talkative. He said even less on the way back to the homestead. When he did speak, it was about trees, grass, or whatever, but there were no endearments spoken or any of his usual teasing. His attitude was that of a man who had shared a moment of mutual bliss but, now that he was satisfied, would just as soon she wasn't around. And it hurt like hell. It brought home the very thing she'd worried the most about. He didn't love her. She was nothing more than a means of easing his britches. And when he left, there would always be other women to take her place. Her lips curled into a wry smile. She really couldn't complain. From the start, she'd known exactly what she was getting into with this man. She had been playing with fire; now she was going to get burned.

By the time Clint returned to his bedroom to change clothes for supper, he had come up with a theory as to how the reservation cattle were being switched. The key that made everything work was Lucas. Now all he had to do was prove it.

Clint pulled off his shirt and began sharpening his razor on the leather strop. There were no longer any questions in his mind as to what he should do about Lucas. Clint knew that if he was right, there was nothing he'd enjoy more than to put a bullet right between the cocky bastard's eyes for all the bloodshed, not to mention the damage and hurt he was inflicting on his family. The worst was yet to come. But he wouldn't shoot Lucas, not unless he was forced into it. It would only cause more sorrow.

He laid the razor down, picked up the shaving mug, then began working up a lather. He'd never wanted to hurt Kate, at least not after he'd come to know and love her. But he had a job to do. He wouldn't think much of himself if he turned his back and let Lucas and the other men involved go free without the punishment they justly deserved. As for Kate . . . He became very still. It was now at an end. If he continued making love to her until she discovered what he was up to and the deceit he had perpetrated on her and her family, her hate and pain would be twofold. As hard as it was going to be to stay away from her, for her sake he had to stick to his decision. He had a job to do, and she had a family to protect. Clint's lips twisted bitterly. He'd let his guard down and committed the prime mistake of becoming involved. Now he was going to pay dearly for it. What in holy hell ever made him think he could settle down and lead a normal life?

As Sam had said would happen, the next day cowhands began drifting in, hoping to be hired. Like Sam and Henry, Kate remained busy hiring and dispersing the men to the right areas. There was a lot of land to cover. The time had come to start gathering the two thousand steers that were needed for shipment to Chicago and the Indian reservations. The time of idleness was over.

Two weeks later, Kate sat relaxed atop Cinnamon, her leg hooked around the saddle horn, her chest filled with pride. Stretched before her were over two thousand steers grazing peacefully in the lush valley. She watched cowboys busily moving their cutting horses in and out, performing the long process of culling and checking steers. Sam had come up with the idea last year. He'd said that by making sure that only quality steers were shipped out, they'd continue getting top price and maintain their market. At first she'd disagreed, claiming it would take too much time, plus cost too much to keep extra cowhands on until the job was finished. But now she agreed with Sam that it was to their advantage. Sam's thinking always seemed to be ahead of the other ranchers. He had taught her so much. She missed their discussions and wished they hadn't drawn apart because of Clint. It seemed so useless now. Clint was no longer interested in her.

Her gaze drifted to the other side of the herd, where Lucas and Clint sat astride their mounts. Kate yearned to be a bird so she could fly over and listen to what they were saying. Since Lucas had returned to the ranch, he and Clint seemed to be thicker than thieves, which Kate found difficult to understand. They had nothing in common. Her eyes settled on the tall, muscular man she loved. Clint had hardly spoken to her since they'd last shared their passion over two weeks ago. Even a pickle brain would know he was avoiding her. He no longer came to her room at night, and if she tried approaching him he'd take off in another direction. At supper he practically refused to look at or talk to her. It had taken all the determination she possessed not to go to his room and ask why, or, worse yet, to beg him to make love to her. She wanted to feel him beside her again. To know the thrill his soft touch and warm words gave her. But that was all in the past. Now she felt like the walking dead due to lack of sleep. At night her hands roamed her body while she pretended they were his hands. But that only made her miss him more. Pride wouldn't allow her to go begging to him. After all, he was the one who had chosen to end what had been between them. It was something she would eventually come to accept, no matter how painful the process. He didn't love her, and there had never been any promises made between them. She tried straightening up in the saddle, but her body was too weary. She even thought about resting her bloodshot eyes, but that wouldn't solve anything. After all, she was out here to keep from thinking about her sorrow, yet here she sat doing that very thing. She looked out over the valley, trying to draw strength from the land she so dearly loved. When all else went by the wayside, the land would still be here. It was eternal.

Though Kate's hat was pulled low, Clint could see her head turned in their direction. His heart went out to her. She was hurting, but he was still convinced he was doing the right thing. She would get over him. Like Mattie had said, some day she'd probably marry a man more deserving. The thought of her being with another man sent a shaft of pain through him. He was tempted to draw his gun and get rid of the very person who had buried an ax between him and Kate. One way or another, Lucas's crookedness had touched everyone.

Just thinking about how difficult it had been to maintain what appeared to be a friendly attitude toward Lucas made Clint grind his teeth. But he couldn't afford to let Kate's brother have any inkling of how he really felt. Lucas was his only lead, and he was going to stick by the boy's side come hell or high water. He wasn't about to let Lucas get away from him.

The roundup had presented the perfect ploy to allow Clint to get on Lucas's good side. The same day he'd last made love to Kate, Clint had seen Lucas return to the ranch to help with the cattle. Clint had told the young man that since Kate wasn't inclined to offer information, he'd appreciate it if Lucas would teach him about the animals. Lucas had become excited, and was more than willing to prove how knowledgeable he was. The boy had even gone so far as to talk about the different methods of roping, then offered to teach Clint a few tricks, none of which were impressive. Clint had been spending his nights at the line shack, watching the homestead and waiting for the boy to take off to the Graveyard Saloon, or to meet with his cronies. But so far that hadn't happened.

Clint had soon discovered that Lucas had many faces. Since his return, the blond-headed boy had remained on the ranch instead of going out carousing. A lot of his nights were spent in the bunkhouse playing poker with the ranch hands. On those occasions, he'd insisted Clint go with him, which made it easier for Clint to keep an eye on him. It was during those poker games that Clint discovered just how good an actor Lucas was. He remained pleasant, friendly; he laughed; he asked the old-timers to tell him tales of the past; and he even acted a bit shy—an entirely different person than Clint had seen at the Graveyard Saloon. Clint knew it was all a ploy because on more than one occasion, after they had left the bunkhouse, Lucas would make a snide remark about the cowhands being so gullible. Another couple of points of interest were that Pedro and

Lucas hardly ever spoke to one another, and Lucas still never wore a hat at the ranch.

Lucas interrupted Clint's thoughts. "Take a look at that steer's horns, Clint. One's tilted up, one's tilted down."

"Yeah," Clint replied. "I'm going to go help sort the cattle. Just sitting is getting to me. Besides, Midnight and I both need the exercise."

Lucas laughed. "Hell, you sure are a glutton for punishment."

Clint flicked the reins. Seeing Kate continually glancing in their direction was more than he could handle. He didn't like the way her cheeks were hollowed, or the faint, dark circles beneath her beautiful eyes. She hadn't had the years of experience he had at not letting his feelings show. He'd learned a long time ago how to grab sleep under the worst of circumstances. All he could do was hope that once he left the ranch and she wouldn't constantly be seeing him, she'd forget. Maybe then her life would return to normal. As he moved Midnight among the steers, he came to a decision. He wasn't going to return to Maryland after this assignment. His lips twisted into a self-mocking smile. Sandoval would be pleased as hell when he received the message that Clint Morgan was once more available for assignments.

Chapter 17

～～⌒◯◯⌒～～

Clint stood among the trees surrounding the old line shack, looking down at the big house bathed in moonlight, watching, waiting for Lucas or anyone else on the ranch to sneak away. He'd stopped riding Midnight up there because he knew that if anything was going to happen, it would be soon. He couldn't take the chance now of someone finding him, as well as his horse, missing. Besides, the walk helped somewhat to relieve his need for Kate, and he had a cow pony tethered nearby just in case Lucas made his move.

At first he'd worried about Kate paying an unexpected visit to his bedroom. But he'd relied on her pride to keep her away. So far his luck had held. Should she change her mind and discover he wasn't in his room, he knew she'd start searching for him. The minute he saw her leave the house and head for the barn to check to see if Midnight was there, he'd hurry back down the mountain and circle around behind her. Then it was simply a matter of saying he couldn't sleep and had taken a stroll.

He sat on a flat rock, listening to the rustle of the trees as a breeze kicked up. When is Lucas going to make a move? he wondered angrily. He'd long since given up any hope that Lucas was innocent. Did the cattle rustling have anything to do with the reservation cattle? He shook his head. He didn't know the whole story yet, but he was convinced that Lucas was involved in both parts of it. Clint picked up a small stone and tossed it down the hillside. Gordon Vale, the government buyer, definitely had to be in on the cattle switching. If Clint had this figured out right, Vale had planned the whole thing. Lucas wasn't smart enough. It would have been easy for Vale to discover Lucas was of a greedy nature. No telling how many other nefarious dealings the man was involved in. But time was running out. Lucas would have to make a move real soon.

Clint was convinced the switching of the reservation cattle had been done somewhere on the ranch. To do it on down the line would involve too many people and reduce the amount of profit. Clint smirked. Once he found out just how it was done, and the identities of the people involved, he'd make damn sure every last man was slapped in prison. Then, Clint thought, I can get away from here.

Lucas was thinking along similar lines as he paced his bedroom floor. I'll be glad when this is over and I don't have to stay around like a damn penned-up animal! he thought for the tenth time. Suddenly he plopped down on the big four-poster bed, laughing. What was the matter with him? He had the cow by the tail. Everything was going perfectly. Yes, there had been a couple of setbacks—like Brody getting himself killed; the man he'd hired to kill Kate bumbling the job; even the failure to grab the herd during the rainstorm. But as it had turned out, nothing had caused any real problems. When he'd arrived back at the ranch that night and found out Clint had suspected a raid, it had been too late for him to call off his men.

As for Kate, there was no need to get another hired gun; he could take care of her anytime. In fact, after he'd given it proper thought, he still liked his original plan better. When she couldn't put an end to the rustling, Sam would put him in charge. Once he had control, he'd do things his way. He'd soon put a stop to checking out the herd. Hell, they already had the steers sold, so they'd just send whatever was rounded up. It was too late for the buyers to back out. Add in some scrub cattle and he'd make an even better profit. Oh, how he'd waited for the day when Kate and Sam would have no choice but to kowtow to him. And if they didn't, he'd get rid of them.

God how he hated Sam, as well as Kate, for keeping everything out of his reach and treating him like he was nothing better than horseshit! Of course as soon as he had the ranch under his thumb, he'd have to tell Vale their deal was finished, but the man couldn't do anything about it because he'd be putting his own neck in a noose.

Lucas smiled, reminiscing about how all this good fortune had fallen into his lap. When Vale had originally approached him with the idea of switching the reservation cattle and thereby putting money in Lucas's pockets, he'd backed away, saying he didn't want to get involved. But after a night of thinking it over, he'd cautiously asked Vale just what he had in mind.

It was a simple plan. Lucas was to wangle a way of having complete charge of the loading, then he could get some friends to purchase scrub cattle for five dollars a head. After those cattle were loaded onto the cars, they would drive the prime steers to Medicine Bow, where Vale knew of a buyer by the name of Riker who didn't ask questions. They'd get thirty-five dollars a head, because the buyer had to make his profit. Vale would take five thousand; Lucas could have the other ten to pay for the scrub cattle and give his men whatever he pleased. Never having had anything but cowpoke wages from his stingy father, Lucas had been quick to agree. That's when he'd gone to Kate and asked to handle the loading. At first she'd been doubtful, but he'd convinced her it was time she let him have some responsibility. When he had reminded her that Vale would be there the entire time, she'd finally consented. Brody had helped him get the men he needed. As it turned out, the men were more than happy to be able to stuff five hundred dollars in their pockets. The next time Vale arrived, he'd had everything set up. It had worked as smooth as a woman's ass.

Still enjoying how clever he'd been, Lucas reached over and pulled a cigar from the box he'd bought in town. After lighting it, he relaxed and blew smoke into the air, watching it trail up to the ceiling.

Rustling the cattle had been his idea, he thought proudly.

He tried blowing smoke rings like Clint did, but he just couldn't seem to get the hang of it.

He'd ridden to Medicine Bow and talked to Riker. The man wanted anything he could get his hands on. Lucas chuckled. He'd come up with the idea of rustling Whitfield cattle to make the old man mad—and eventually take Kate's job away because she wasn't able to put a stop to it. Though he still wanted Kate out of the way, he liked the way his pockets were soon running over with money. He especially liked the power it gave him. He could buy anything or anyone he wanted. He'd liked the thrill of holding a man's life in his hands, and the look on that man's face when Lucas pulled the trigger. It added to his feeling of power. Lucas laughed aloud. Sam and

Kate were soon going to rue the day they hadn't turned over what was rightfully his.

Deciding he still didn't like cigars, Lucas tossed what was left of the one he was holding into the spittoon.

In a couple of days he'd be meeting Horace and Oscar at the Graveyard Saloon to tell them to bring the scrub cattle into the canyon. Maybe he should take Clint with him to the saloon. Clint needed to find out what it was like to have a good woman underneath him, and the excitement at being able to make the bitch do anything he wanted. Again Lucas wondered if Clint had been sticking it to Kate. If he had, it was obviously over. But that was understandable. What joy could Clint possibly get out of being with someone like her? She was probably as stiff as a branding iron.

The next morning, Kate was about to enter the dining room when she heard Lucas and Clint talking. She stopped, remaining hidden behind the wall.

"Say, Clint," Lucas said, "I'm gettin' real bored, and before much longer, I'm going to be lookin' to have some fun. How would you like to go with me? You gotta be wantin' after all this time, and I can show you how to really enjoy the women."

Clint smiled. *You cocky little piece of shit*, he thought. *If anyone could do with some learning, it's you.* "Why not?" he said aloud. "You're not the only one who's bored."

"Good." Lucas crammed his mouth full of eggs. "Tell me something," he said before swallowing, "did you get anything going with that sister of mine?"

Clint looked up at Lucas, fighting the desire to

plant a fist in the younger man's smug face. "If I did, that wouldn't be any of your business."

"Hell, no need to get mad. I was just askin'. It don't make any difference to me."

Clint forced himself to relax. "Just between you and me, I tried, but she wouldn't have anything to do with me."

"I don't find that hard to believe," Lucas said in a worldly manner. "She's so cold I doubt she'd let any man within spittin' distance." He let his fork fall on the plate. "Gotta go watch what the men are doing with the herd. You comin'?"

"No, I thought I'd ride to town and buy a new hat. The one I have hasn't been the same since I got caught out in that rainstorm a while back."

Lucas shoved his chair back. "Come on. I'll go with you to saddle up."

Kate started to hide behind the stairs, but didn't bother when she heard them leave by way of the butler's pantry. She leaned against the wall for support, fighting the urge to go after them and give them a piece of her mind. Her hands balled into fists. Clint was bored? Well bless his *poor* soul! She wasn't good enough for him but some damn whore would do just fine! How kind of him not to tell Lucas that they had shared each other's bodies. She kicked the wall with her foot. She wanted to be mad, not hurt, that Clint was more than willing to share himself with another woman. She *was* hurt, and angry, and she wanted to cry. But she'd cried for too many nights; there were no tears left. She pulled away from the wall and squared her shoulders. She was a Whitfield, and by God, whatever it took, she wasn't going to let Clint Morgan get her down. She decided to skip breakfast. After the conversation she'd heard, she was feeling sick to her stomach.

* * *

Clint rode straight to town. After sending Sandoval a telegram to the effect that their problem could soon be solved, he crossed the street and entered the Hoof and Horn Saloon.

The place was nothing like the Graveyard Saloon. It was clean, the tables and chairs in good condition, the floor swept, and there was no stench. Even the girls eating at a back table were far more appealing than the ones he'd seen at the other place. Except for the older woman, who he immediately remembered meeting his first night in town. She was the one who had delivered the message that he was wanted out front. Violet. She'd said her name was Violet.

Clint placed the tow of his boot on the brass foot rail, pulled some coins from the pocket of his jeans, and slapped them down on top of the polished pine bar.

The bartender, who had been standing at the other end of the bar polishing glasses, immediately came forward. "What'll you have, mister?"

"A shot of good whiskey."

A big mirror covered the back of the bar, and by looking in it, Clint could see Violet talking to the other girls in the back. A couple of them giggled as they took a quick glance in his direction. Clint was sure the brassy redhead was telling them what had happened to him that first night.

The big bartender set a glass in front of Clint and filled it with a shot of whiskey. Clint noted the muttonchops along the man's jaws, and the wide, waxed mustache with the ends curled up. His hair was slicked back, failing to hide the bald spots. A red garter circled one arm of his white shirt.

"Don't I know you?" the bartender asked, setting the bottle on the bar.

Clint downed his shot of whiskey, then motioned for the bartender to pour another. "Not that I know of."

"Yeah. You're that feller that stopped the Whitfield boy that day him and his friends were raising hell in town. I hear you're related to Mrs. Whitfield. Now there's a mighty fine woman. That stepdaughter of hers could learn a few things from Mrs. Whitfield."

Clint nodded his head toward the back table. "Which one's Ellie?"

"The tall brunette that's looking your way."

Clint looked in the mirror. The woman wasn't a raving beauty by any means, but she wasn't bad-looking either. She'd probably be even better if she'd clean the paint off her face. He started to return her smile, but looked away instead. What the hell was he doing here? He couldn't tell Ellie what Star had told him, and what was the use of trying to get more information about Lucas? He'd find out what he needed to know in a couple of days. He downed his second shot.

"Care to buy a lady a drink?" a husky voice asked.

Clint's gaze darted back to the mirror, and the reflection of the woman standing beside him. He couldn't prevent a smile when his eyes met hers. Only Kate would have enough guts to enter a saloon. "Do you make a habit of coming here?"

"Depends on what I'm thirsty for. Harry, bring me a glass and I'll share Clint's bottle."

Clint arched his eyebrow. "I didn't know you had a liking for whiskey."

"As you once said about yourself, there are a lot of things you don't know about me."

Clint noticed that Harry's expression was no longer friendly. He slapped a glass down on the bar, then turned and walked away without pouring the drink.

"I don't think Harry likes you being here," Clint commented.

"He doesn't." Kate poured her drink, then took it straight down.

Her green eyes became the size of cat paws, but Clint had to give her credit, she managed not to shudder.

"Harry," Clint called to the bartender, "come pour Miss Whitfield another drink."

"This ain't no place for a lady," Harry snarled.

Clint's eyes were the dark gray of storm clouds when he turned and looked at the man. "I don't happen to agree with that. There wouldn't be a saloon—or a town, for that matter—if it wasn't for the Whitfield family." Clint hadn't raised his voice, but his words were clipped and icy cold. "Now as I was saying, because this lady here is a Whitfield and contributes considerably to your town, I don't ever want to hear you didn't pour the lady's drink, or that the lady wasn't welcomed. I mean starting right now. Because if the lady isn't treated with the respect due her, I'm personally going to come back here and shoot every one of those fine crystal glasses you have stacked up, plus the bottles and that big mirror. Don't make the mistake of thinking I'm not a man of my word. Do we have an understanding?"

Realizing her mouth had dropped open, Kate quickly clamped it shut.

Harry studied Clint for a moment, then nodded his head. "We have an understanding."

"Good." Clint tipped his hat to the women at the back table who were staring wide-eyed. "Ladies," he acknowledged. Turning back to Kate, he said, "Enjoy your drinks. There's enough money on the bar to pay for the bottle." He walked out of the saloon.

Still in a stupor, Kate moved to the nearest table, pulled out a chair, and sat.

"Hey, Harry," one of the girls called out, "if I was you, I'd be real nice to the lady."

"And if that Morgan feller returns," another one said, "I get him first."

The girls laughed at their own teasing.

To Kate's surprise, Harry came to her table and gently set the bottle and a full glass of whiskey down in front of her.

"Kate," he asked sheepishly, "was that man serious?"

"I believe so, Harry. I'll tell you one thing, you don't want him for an enemy. In all my years, I've never seen a faster draw."

"I want you to know, you'll always be treated proper any time you want to come in here."

Kate wondered if Clint knew that Harry owned the saloon. She looked up at the big man, watching the curled corners of his mustache twitch. "You know I don't like whiskey, so take the bottle away. You can keep the money."

Harry quickly complied.

Kate had half a notion to go after Clint to tell him she was perfectly capable of taking care of herself, but she didn't. Why had he defended her to Harry? Would she ever understand anything Clint Morgan did? She had just ridden into town when she'd seen him entering the saloon. Thinking he was out to get a woman, she was immediately consumed with jealousy. She'd trailed after him, not expecting to find him standing at the bar. Why had she asked for whiskey? Maybe she was still trying to prove something, but at this point she wasn't sure just what that something was. Why had she even followed him from the ranch? What had she expected to accomplish? She gave the chair next to her a hard kick, sending it toppling backwards. Look what I'm turning into, she thought bitterly. A spineless woman consumed with jealousy! The damn man's driving me insane.

Kate stood, returned the chair to its proper place, then left.

Looking out the window of the general store, Clint watched Kate ride away. He yanked his hat off and ran his fingers through his hair. He should have told her it was finished between them instead of just turning his back on her. But he wasn't sure he could look her in the eye, or that he could make her believe he no longer cared. It wouldn't have worked anyway. Had he told her it was finished, he'd have been forced to say something mean, like "You served your purpose," to make her believe him. Then, seeing the hurt in her eyes, he'd have ended up getting angry to cover his own feelings. But would that have been any worse than her looking as if life were being drained from her? There were times when anger could get you through a lot of things. If he'd made her angry she wouldn't have that lingering look of hope in her eyes.

He glanced around the store, suddenly wondering if anyone was watching him. Seeing everyone engaged elsewhere, he glanced back out the window. It was too late to change anything now. He'd made his decision. Unfortunately they were both going to have to learn to live with it. It was going to take every ounce of willpower to keep from beating the hell out of Lucas for ruining his life.

Chapter 18

Pride swelled within Kate as she looked out over the vast herd of steers with W/L branded on their hindquarters and ready for shipment. This is what's important, she reminded herself. The land and the cattle.

Though it was early, Kate turned Cinnamon around and rode away from the railroad spur. As she headed toward home, she thought about how she'd pushed herself unmercifully since seeing Clint at the Hoof and Horn Saloon four days ago. She'd helped drive the steers to the spur and into the holding pens. Lucas had helped some, Clint even more. But Clint never exchanged a word with her. He continued to act as if she weren't even around. Sam wasn't any different. Each night she entered his office to report the day's progress, then left. They had nothing else to discuss. Tomorrow they would begin loading the steers onto the railroad cars. In three more days, Vale would arrive. Shortly after that, Clint would be leaving. The end of September loomed near. Maybe it was for the best. Seeing him daily wasn't helping her to get rid of her feelings for him. She desperately needed some peace in her life.

After the punishing work she'd put herself through, Kate was bone tired. Finally she felt as if she could go to her room and get some needed sleep. She didn't know how much longer she could act as if she didn't care. She couldn't even make herself angry at the damn man!

By the time Kate reached home, she had to practically drag herself into the house. She had just started up the stairs when Mattie stepped out of the parlor.

"Kate, dear, you look terrible. Is something wrong? It's been more than a week since you've joined us for supper."

Kate groaned inwardly, but Mattie's kindly face always touched a soft spot within her. "Once the steers are shipped out and everything returns to normal, I'll be dining with the family again. I've just been too tired at night, Mattie."

"The roundup never seemed to have this effect on you before. You always welcomed it."

Kate smiled. "Maybe age is catching up with me."

Mattie flipped her hand at her stepdaughter. "What nonsense." She smiled warmly. "We've missed you, but it's been such a pleasure having Lucas back. I tell you, he's a changed boy. Sam's even acting friendlier to him."

"That's good. Maybe Lucas is growing up." Kate doubted it. He'd certainly made no effort to get his hands dirty over the last two weeks. He just sat on his horse looking the lord and master!

"Are you going to your room to rest?" Mattie asked, trying not to show her concern.

Kate nodded.

"Then when you've rested, maybe you can join us for supper tonight."

Kate took a deep breath. She couldn't keep running away from her problems. "Yes, I'll be there."

"I'm so glad. I miss not having the family together. Now you go on up. I'll have Alma bring you some hot broth. It'll help you sleep."

Mattie watched Kate slowly ascend the stairs. What am I going to do? she wondered. Sam had told her she'd made a complete mess of everything. Kate might try to hide it, but the girl was head over heels in love with Clint, and he didn't seem the least interested. After Kate's injury from the bull Mattie had been so sure. She'd thought . . . What difference did it make what she'd thought? She'd been wrong. Clint was going to leave. There wouldn't be any wedding. Sam barely spoke to anyone, and Kate and Clint no longer even so much as looked at each other. Maybe it was a good thing he'd be leaving soon, but Mattie had grown so fond of him. She just knew he'd be happier staying here than living in Maryland! She clicked her tongue and entered the kitchen. "Bessy, would you fix some broth for Kate?" she asked the cook.

"I certainly will. Is Miss Kate feeling all right?"

"Yes, she's just been working too hard. When it's ready, have Addie May take it to Kate's room."

Sam sat in his office, drumming his fingers on the desk. His door was open, and he'd heard Mattie and Kate talking. He leaned back in his wheelchair, rubbing his chin. So many times he'd wanted to talk to Kate, but his bullheaded stubbornness kept him from it. She wasn't helping matters by acting so distant. Though he hated to admit it, maybe Clint had been right about Kate needing to feel like a woman and have a life of her own. But he needed someone to watch the ranch, and he still didn't trust Lucas. The boy couldn't have changed colors this quick. He'd been furious at the possibility that Clint would take Kate to Maryland, but from the way Clint and Kate were acting now, that seemed unlikely.

Nothing had been the same since Clint's arrival. Sam had to admit that after finding out Clint was fooling around with Kate, he'd given some serious consideration to having the man tied up and put on some train heading out of Rawlins. But even as angry as he'd been, he just couldn't make himself follow through with the idea. There was a strength in Clint that Sam had seen in few other men. Clint was also the only one who'd ever had enough gumption to stand up to him. Sam's hand fell to his lap, hitting the gun he kept under his blanket. That made him think of the time he'd drawn it on Clint. The boy hadn't shown a thread of fear. I'll bet he can be a mean bastard, Sam thought. I can see it in his eyes. Of course, he'd also saved Kate's life. Sam smiled. Damned if he didn't like the man, even after all that had happened.

The soft knock on the door awoke Kate. She was surprised to find her room dark. How long had she slept? The door silently opened and Mattie stuck her head in.

"I'm awake," Kate called from her bed. She rubbed her eyes, trying to push away the laziness that still lingered.

Mattie entered, her lantern spreading light across the room. "Supper will be ready in an hour. I just wondered if you were still planning to join us."

Kate rolled onto her back, looking up at the ceiling. "Yes, I'll be there. Mattie, have Addie May come up. I think I'll dress tonight."

Mattie lit Kate's lantern. "I'll send her right up."

By the time Addie May arrived, Kate had already washed herself. Maybe Clint would be leaving soon, but she was determined to make him remember what he'd left behind. Finally, she was starting to get angry.

Kate was already in the dining room when Clint

entered. She held her head high, looking him straight in the eye. When Addie May had insisted on pulling her corset tighter, she'd come very close to changing her mind about dressing up. But seeing Clint's momentary look of admiration convinced her she'd done the right thing. She moved to her place at the table and sat herself instead of waiting for someone to pull her chair out for her.

"I'm glad to see you could finally join us, sister," Lucas remarked. "Maybe you should think about giving up running this ranch since it appears to be too demanding on you."

Kate didn't bother looking at her brother. "At least I work, which is more than I can say for you. When this ranch is too much for me to handle, I'll be the first to say so."

The corners of Clint's lips twitched with pleasure. The fire that he loved so much in Kate had returned. God knows how much she had been suffering, but like himself, she was a survivor. What a pair they would have made, he thought sadly.

Throughout supper there was a tension that could be felt by everyone. Mattie, Lucas and Sam exchanged a few words, but other than that, little else was said.

Clint tried not to look at Kate, but he couldn't seem to help it. She was absolutely magnificent tonight in her blue watered silk dress that left her milky white shoulders bare, then gathered gently just below the swell of her breasts. The light from the chandelier brought out the silver highlights in her hair. She had even applied just the right touch of rouge on her high cheekbones and full lips. He felt a deep sense of satisfaction. Never again would Mattie think of Kate as not being a lady. There was no doubt about it, Kate Whitfield was more woman than any he had ever known. A sigh escaped his lips. He had worked the devils out of his head and now accepted his fate. He was at peace with himself, or at least as much at peace as he could expect. He just wished that he could make love to Kate one more time before leaving, but that wouldn't be fair to either of them.

Pride kept Kate sitting at the table. Pride would also keep her dressing every night for supper until Clint left. She had almost asked him when he planned on leaving, but she wasn't strong enough yet to accept the answer. If she had expected Clint to pull her into his arms, to say he would never let her go, she was a fool. It wasn't going to happen. Over the years, in the quietness of her bedroom, she'd thought about love. She had even envisioned the wonderful feeling of having the man she loved always by her side. And of course, they would live happily ever after. It had never occurred to her that the man she loved wouldn't love her. Until two weeks ago, the way Clint had been acting, combined with his sweet words, had led her to believe he returned her love. He had seemed so happy and easygoing. Now he reminded her of the man he was when he first came to the ranch. He had that same underlying cold hardness she'd sensed at their first meeting. She wanted to hold him, make love to him, take care of him, make him happy again.

When supper was over, the men went out to the porch to smoke. Mattie went into the kitchen to tell Bessy the meal was lovely. When she returned, she and Kate entered the parlor to work on the puzzle they had brought back from Rawlins the week Kate had bought her new clothes. After all that time, the puzzle still hadn't been finished.

The parlor seemed overly warm, so Kate moved to the window for some fresh air.

"Yeah," Kate heard Lucas say, "I'm taking him

to the Graveyard Saloon tonight. Clint's gone too long without a woman, so I aim to fix him right up.''

A hard lump formed in Kate's chest. She wanted to hear what Clint said, but there was a ringing in her ears. She grabbed for the back of the sofa. Somehow she managed to remain standing.

''Kate, are you all right.''

Mattie's voice sounded far away. Slowly the faint that had been threatening passed, and Kate's eyes finally focused on her stepmother. ''I suddenly felt dizzy. I think Addie May laced my corset too tight.''

''The puzzle can wait, dear. Lord knows it's waited this long. Why don't you go to your room? I'll send Addie May right up. You probably still haven't had enough rest.''

''I think that's a good idea.''

Later, wearing only a nightgown, Kate stood at her bedroom window watching Clint and Lucas ride away.

As soon as they entered the Graveyard Saloon, Clint saw an immediate transformation in Lucas. There was now a jauntiness in his stride. His attitude was cocky as he waved or greeted men he seemed to know. Clint could clearly see that most of the men weren't nearly as impressed with Lucas as he was with himself.

Lucas motioned Clint to take a seat at one of the scarred, empty tables. ''I'll get us a bottle. While I'm gone, you might want to take a look at what the place has to offer.'' Lucas shoved his hat to the back of his head. ''The girls here ain't the best you've probably ever seen, but you show them who's boss and they'll give you a hell of a ride.'' He took off to the bar.

Clint scanned the room. The place was as busy

as it had been when he was last there, and the girls were hustling. Pedro was nowhere to be seen, nor was his horse tied outside.

"I seen you come in with Lucas."

Clint slowly raised his eye to the short blonde standing beside him. This time she wasn't smiling. "I haven't said a word to him about you, Rose."

"You expect me to believe that? As I remember, you said you'd only met him a couple of times. Jesus Christ! I'm goin' to get the shit beat out of me tonight."

She started to leave, but Clint grabbed her wrist. "You trusted me, now I'm going to trust you. I want you to sit beside me and cuddle, darlin'. And when Lucas returns, you work real hard at getting me upstairs. Do it right, and I'll give you enough extra money that you can stuff some of it in your stocking." Clint cocked an eyebrow, then reached over and pulled a chair next to him.

Rose hesitated, then, deciding she had nothing to lose, sat down. "Hell. This ain't work, it's pure pleasure. What's your name, precious?"

"Clint. Here comes Lucas."

"Get the hell out of here, Rose," Lucas ordered. "I'm gettin' Clint a woman that'll give him some real action."

Rose started to rise, but Clint detained her with his hand. "Let's get one thing straight, Lucas. If I take a woman upstairs, it's damn well going to be my choice."

Lucas's eyes narrowed. "Sure, Clint, whatever you say." He set the bottle and glasses down, never taking his eyes off Rose. She had wrapped an arm around Clint's shoulders and was kissing his neck. Now her other hand was disappearing beneath the table. The bitch had never treated him like that. The next time he came here she was going to pay for it. "Well, Clint, you seem to be occupied," he said, still glaring at Rose. "I just saw some friends come in, so I think I'll just mosey over there for a minute, then I'm goin' to get a woman of my own. I'm gettin' a big one on and I need a woman to take care of it." He turned and walked away.

"Son of a bitch!" Rose proclaimed as soon as Lucas was out of hearing distance. "Did you see the way he was lookin' at me? I'm dead! I know I'm dead!"

"Just calm down, Rose."

"Calm down, hell!"

Clint watched Lucas go to the bar, then he and two other men moved to a table and sat down. They were the same two Clint had seen the last time he was there. Seeing Lucas glance back at them, Clint kissed Rose's cheek. "I guarantee Lucas isn't going to lay a hand on you," he said in Rose's ear, "even if it takes me having to shoot him. Try not to be obvious, but I want you to turn and tell me if you know those two men sitting with Lucas."

"How do I know you're gonna keep your word?"

Clint leaned back, giving her an ingratiating smile. "Now, do I look like a man who wouldn't keep his word?"

Rose laughed. "I'll bet you could coax just about any woman you wanted to your bed. What the hell. You're the only hope I got of keeping that damn Lucas out of my hair." She climbed onto Clint's lap, which allowed her a clear view of where the men were sitting. "I've seen them in here off and on. The short one's named Horace, the other's Oscar. They're Lucas's friends out of Rawlins. What's goin' on here, Clint? You're actin' mighty suspicious."

Clint was feeling that old, cold excitement that he knew so well. There wasn't a doubt in his mind that Lucas was finally fixing to make a move. He smiled at Rose. "You've earned your money."

"But we ain't done nothin'."

Clint had discovered long ago that prostitutes could be relied on better than most men, and Rose definitely didn't like Lucas. "No offense, darlin', but I already have a woman, and I couldn't do you justice. I'm going to take you upstairs, but I'm going to catch some sleep."

"But I can—"

"I'm sure you can, but I'm not interested. It has nothing to do with you." He ran a long finger down her cheek. "I don't want you saying anything to anyone about what we've talked about, including the other girls. But I guarantee you, within a few days you'll never have to put up with Lucas again."

"Are you a lawman?" Rose gasped.

"No," Clint replied. "Now, let's go upstairs to make it look right."

"Damn," Lucas grumbled as he and Clint were returning home. "That Rose must a been awfully good to you. You were upstairs longer than I was."

Clint couldn't resist saying, "The right man can make a lot of difference, Lucas."

Lucas didn't say another word.

The next night, Clint waited in the trees by the line shack. Midnight was already saddled and waiting right behind him, and he had changed into his black night riding clothes.

Clint wasn't the least surprised when he saw Lucas leave the house after all the lights were out. A few minutes later, Lucas rode off, heading north. Clint flipped the reins over the stallion's head and leaped on the saddle. The clouds drifting across the moon made it almost impossible for him to be seen.

Clint followed Lucas at a safe distance, his lips spread in a crooked grin. The boy was so cocksure of himself he didn't even turn to see if he was being trailed.

For an hour, Lucas kept his buckskin at an easy lope, and Clint followed. When Lucas rode into one of the many canyons abounding in the foothills, Clint moved Midnight up the side of the mountain. He dismounted, then cupped his hand over Midnight's muzzle and looked down. He now had the answer to everything. There were at least four hundred head of cattle trying to graze on what little grass there was to offer. Lucas was talking to two men who looked like the ones he had met in the saloon. There were three other men in the canyon, but from where he stood, Clint couldn't be sure who they were. He had no trouble identifying the seventh man. Pedro's pinto pony was a dead giveaway. The men were laughing.

"Hell, Lucas," one of them said, "I'm gettin' tired of trying to round up these damn critters. Do you know what it takes to drive them here?"

"I got a feeling this is goin' to be the last time," Lucas assured the men. "Before long all you boys are goin' to be sitting around the ranch watchin' others do the work."

If they lived that long, Clint thought. Lucas would kill every one of them before he'd let that happen.

"Oscar and Horace can watch after them now," Lucas continued. "Once these critters are loaded onto the cars, all you boys have to do is drive the other cattle to Riker in Medicine Bow. Now you others get out of here before the men at the holdin' pens find you missing. Henry's already been asking about your whereabouts."

When the men had ridden off, Lucas said to Horace and Oscar, "I'll be back tomorrow night with your money."

Clint had seen and heard enough. He had a long ride ahead of him. He needed to get to the marshal in Rawlins as soon as possible.

It was late afternoon the next day when Clint returned to the house. He'd already changed out of his dusty clothes at the line shack.

"Yes, all the cattle are shipped out now, except of course yours."

Clint heard Sam's gravelly voice coming from the parlor. Knowing there would be questions, he decided to get it over with. He sauntered into the large room.

Mattie immediately rose from her chair. "Clint. Where in heaven's name have you been?"

He looked his aunt straight in the eye and smiled. "Hunting wolves."

"Wolves?" Sam barked.

"Heard them early this morning, so I took my rifle and went hunting."

Kate was more inclined to believe he'd stayed at the saloon overnight.

"Clint," Mattie said in her soft voice, "I'd like you to meet Gordon Vale. He works for the government and purchases cattle from us for the Indian reservations. Mr. Vale, this is my nephew, Clint Morgan."

The short, squat man stood and shook Clint's offered hand. Clint noticed the large diamond ring on the man's finger.

"Mrs. Whitfield was telling me you're here on a visit."

Clint nodded. Vale's double chins shook when he talked. Clint wondered how long Vale would be in prison before getting rid of them.

"I agree with you about this being mighty

pretty country." Gordon Vale looked at Sam. "But from what you've told me about the winters, I don't think I'd like that." Then Vale turned his attention back to Clint. "Clint Morgan. For some reason, that name sounds familiar. Have we ever met?"

"Not that I know of." Clint joined Mattie on the sofa. "How long will you be staying, Mr. Vale?"

"Please, call me Gordon. I'll be leaving tomorrow, as soon as I see the cattle cars headed for the switching yard in Rawlins."

"It must be a hard life having to travel from place to place," Clint commented congenially.

"I stay in Washington during the winter. But I like traveling, which helps."

"Did you shoot any wolves?" Kate asked.

Clint could see the anger dancing in her eyes. "I shot at them, but I didn't hit one." He realized he'd made a mistake the moment the words came out. Though Kate said nothing, he could tell by the way she was glaring at him that she hadn't missed his error. She was well aware of his shooting ability. "What I mean is, I was only trying to scare them away." Her expression didn't change. Clint cursed himself for being so careless.

The conversation settled down to the subject of cattle in general. Out of the corner of his eye, Clint could see Kate still staring at him, and she looked angry as hell.

Why is he lying? Kate wondered. He wasn't even carrying a rifle when he came in. Even if he'd already put it away, she didn't believe him. She didn't buy his tale about deliberately missing a wolf. So what had he been doing? Laying with some woman, making love to her? Whatever he'd been up to, he certainly didn't want anyone to know about it. He was crafty. But now that she thought about it, hadn't he always been that way?

"Kate, did you hear me?"

Kate looked at Mattie. "No. What did you say?"

"I was trying to remind you that you wanted to have a talk with Lucas about tomorrow. I believe I just saw him riding in."

Kate rose to her feet, looped her thumbs under her gun belt, took another long look at Clint, then turned and left the parlor.

She caught Lucas heading toward the back of the house. "Is everything ready for tomorrow?" she asked as she fell into step with him.

"Hell, yes. I'm damn tired of you always questionin' me, Kate. You know as well as I do that we ain't had any trouble before. Has Vale arrived?"

"He's in the parlor talking to Sam and Clint."

"Oh, you mean Clint finally showed up? I told you he would."

"He made up some cockeyed story about being off hunting wolves."

Lucas broke out in a loud laugh.

"What's so funny?"

"Well, to begin with, don't think I ain't seen how moon-eyed you been over him. Every man around knows it. I'll tell you where I think he was. Last night we were at the Graveyard Saloon, and Rose couldn't keep her hands off him. They went upstairs, and I thought he was never goin' to come back down. I think she met him in the woods. I'll bet he's been with her all this time. If you played your cards right, that could have been you in the woods with him. At least Rose knows how to please a man."

Kate stepped in front of him, her hand connecting hard with his cheek. He went for his gun, but she was too fast a draw for him. Lucas dropped his hand to his side.

"What's wrong, Kate? Can't you handle the truth?"

"I'll tell you what I can't handle," Kate said, "I can't handle a brother who thinks it's all right for his sister to take up with every man that comes along!"

"Why not? That's the only thing women are good for." His jaw tightened, his blue eyes became hard. "Now I'll tell you what *I* can't handle. It's a damn woman pointing a gun at me. Real soon, *half-sister*, you're going to be on your knees begging." He brushed past her and continued on to the house.

Kate was so furious she could feel her face turning red. She wasn't angry only at Lucas, but at Clint as well. She'd take care of Lucas later. She'd take care of Clint tonight.

Chapter 19

Kate heard the downstairs clock chime eleven times. Still she remained sitting on her bed, Indian style and fully clothed. Though she was sure the other household members were sound asleep, she decided to wait a bit longer before paying Mr. Morgan a call. Her lips twisted in a cruel smile as her hand tightened around the .45 resting on her leg. Lucas's bragging about Clint needing a *real* woman continued to drum in her head. She was through moping, feeling sorry for herself, and more importantly, telling herself Clint's desire would return. Any ninny could have figured out it was finished. Maybe if he had turned his back on her for a woman of breeding she'd have found it easier to accept. But a whore? Never! Well, tonight he was going to admit to her exactly what had been on his mind all those times they'd made love. Love? Hah! Very soon, she was going to march the weasel to the barn. Then, when no one could hear, she'd make him admit that all he'd wanted was her body, and that whores were now more to his liking. After he confessed, if he had the guts, she was going to shoot him. That was something she should have done a long time ago. She couldn't wait to see his face turn white when she pulled the trigger. But she wasn't going to kill him, she'd just leave him with a limp to remember her by. Maybe then other women wouldn't fall prey to his charm!

A half hour later, Kate slid off the bed. The time had come for the devil to receive his just reward. Kate closed her bedroom door quietly behind her, then proceeded down the hall. She was about to turn the corner, but suddenly came to a stop upon hearing a door open and close. She pressed herself against the wall and counted. One . . . two . . . three. She peeked around the corner just in time to catch a glimpse of Clint before he silently disappeared down the stairs. Curiosity prevailed. Had he just come in, or was he leaving to meet . . . Rose? Instead of taking him to the barn, she'd just follow along. If he was going to meet Rose, he was in for a big shock. After a short pause, she made her way to the stairs.

Kate wasn't surprised to see Clint heading for the barn. Naturally, if he was going somewhere, he'd want a horse. A few minutes later, he came back out leading Midnight, who was fully saddled. However, instead of mounting the stallion, he took off walking again. Why? So no one would hear him ride off. She thought about getting a horse of her own, but she didn't have time. She could always shoot him rather than let him get away.

When he disappeared, she began walking after him.

Because of Clint's long legs, he moved along at a faster clip. Kate found herself having to run at different times just to keep him in sight. She hoped he didn't decide to ride. Stealthily, she moved along the dark shadows of the buildings. When those were left behind and they'd started up into the foothills, she hunched over to make herself less visible. She was grateful that the moon was but a sliver, even though it made her progress even more difficult. At least Clint would be less apt to see her. When on several occasions Clint stopped, waited, and listened, she remained hunched over, as still as a fence post. He was being overly cautious.

Kate's breathing was already labored by the time the climb became steeper. As she made her way through the dense shrubbery, she began remembering his competent handling of the cattle before the rustlers had attacked. Just a few days after first arriving at the ranch he had stated that he knew very little about cattle. And how many times had she questioned his ready answers for any situation? Another particular bother was how he'd become so fast on the draw. But had she ever confronted him with any of this? No, she'd chosen to ignore it because she was blinded by love. Well she wasn't blinded now.

A sickening suspicion began to engulf Kate. Had she been right all along? Was Clint involved in the cattle rustling after all? If so, he'd fooled Mattie, Sam, and everyone else on the ranch, but she'd been the biggest fool of all. Though he'd saved her life the night of the stampede, she now felt sure that there had been a reason behind it. It was probably another ploy to remove all her suspicions that he was one of the bastards who had been stealing their cattle. If she was right, she had to find out who his partners were. Should it turn out that he wasn't up to anything, then this was as good a place as any to confront him about treating her like some bitch in heat. In fact it was even better than the barn. The shot would be less apt to be heard!

It finally occurred to Kate that there was only one place Clint could be headed. The old line shack. There was nothing else around. With that knowledge, she took off in a different direction. The distance was a little longer, but at least she could move faster and wouldn't have to worry about him seeing or hearing her.

As soon as Kate reached the shack, she drew her gun. Carefully she peeked around the side of the old log house. Clint must have already changed clothes in the line shack. She'd never seen him dress in such a manner. Everything he had on was black, even his hat. He was leading Midnight away from the corral. There was no longer any question that he was up to no good. Fury hammered in her head as she stepped out into the open. "You can stop right there, Morgan!"

Clint spun around, ready to go for his gun, but it was too late. Kate's revolver was pointed right at his chest. He'd been caught. There wasn't a damn thing he could do about it.

"Would you care to explain what you're up to?"

Though her voice was steady, Clint could hear the underlying anger. He knew he had to do some fast talking. He laughed. "Up to? I just wanted to go for a ride."

"And to do that you had to sneak up here and change clothes."

"Calm down, Kate. You're letting your imagination run away with you again."

"Perhaps. But I still have to ask myself why you would want to ride in the dead of night with black clothes and a black horse. So you could travel and not be seen?"

Clint knew she wasn't buying his story. He really hadn't expected her to. Still, he had to keep trying because there was no doubt in his mind that she was ready to pull the trigger. "Believe me, Kate, I simply couldn't sleep and I wanted to go for a ride. I know this looks suspicious, but if I happened to run into your rustlers I sure as hell don't want them seeing me. The last time you accused me of being up to something you found out you were wrong."

With all her might, Kate wanted to believe him. But his voice had that caressing quality to it, and he was being too friendly, especially after the way he'd been acting for the last couple of weeks. No, he was lying. Just another one of his stories to fit the occasion. Night after night, day after day, he'd used her and her family, but this time he wasn't going to get away with it. "I'll tell you what I think. I think you came to the ranch for one thing. Cattle. You've twisted everyone right around your little finger. Mattie, Sam, Lucas, and especially me. How you must have laughed after making love to me. No wonder you eventually lost interest and turned to your whores. You've killed men on this ranch and you've stolen Whitfield stock. But I might be willing to strike a deal. Tell me who your accomplices are and I'll consider letting you go."

"You're wrong, Kate."

"No, I'm not wrong. One last time. Who are the others?"

"Dammit, I'm not a rustler!"

"I don't believe you. You're nothing but a low-down, lying bastard. I'm going to make sure you pay for what you've done, Clint Morgan. I'm just sorry I can't watch you hang from a tree. Now that I know you for what you really are, I'm surprised you're not begging. Say your prayers, Morgan."

Clint kept waiting for her to move, or do anything that would allow him to disarm her. But she stood too far away for him to make a grab for her or possibly knock the gun from her hand. If he could just keep her talking, maybe she'd make a mistake he could use to his advantage. "You'd be shooting an innocent man. Besides, I'd never do anything to harm you. I love you, Kate."

"You'll try anything, won't you? Do you really think I'll believe you?" She released a harsh laugh. "You probably said the same thing to Rose last night. And if I *was* foolish enough to believe you, how could you even think I'd let that excuse what you've done to my family or the men you've killed?"

Clint took a step forward, but the bitter hate in her eyes caused him to stop. "I know you're angry," he said calmly, "but I didn't steal the cattle. You're letting what's happened between us blind you."

"For once, your sweet talking words don't have any effect on me." Kate's finger tightened on the trigger.

"You're grasping at straws." He was having difficulty hiding his anger. "You have no proof."

"I don't need proof." Thinking about how much she was going to enjoy seeing Clint get what he deserved, Kate tightened her finger on the gun. She wanted to kill him . . . but for some unfathomable . . . unforgivable reason, she couldn't pull the trigger. She tried reminding herself that he wasn't worth keeping on this earth. He'd murdered her men and used her to satisfy his lust.

Still she couldn't shoot.

She hated herself for her weakness. She hated him even more for making her this way. "Get on the horse and get the hell off this ranch," she hissed angrily. "And ride as fast as you can, because from this moment on, you'll be a wanted man. There won't be a rancher or ranch hand in the territory that won't have your description. And I assure you, your mother will also find out just what kind of a son you are, so I don't think you'll be welcomed there either. But first, take your gun out of the holster, then drop it."

"Now the rifle," she ordered when his gun hit the ground.

Clint pulled it from the saddle, then let it fall next to his revolver.

"Now mount up, and get the hell out of my sight."

Clint lifted his foot as if to place it in the stirrup, but instead he reached out and gave Midnight a hard slap across the rump. As the horse charged forward, Kate had to jump away to keep from being hit. That was all the time Clint needed to grab her gun, then jerk it from her hand. He was ready to put a hand over her mouth if she tried to scream, but all she did was square her shoulders. Her mouth was clamped shut.

Now that Clint had the situation under control, he had no idea what to do next. If she'd just waited one more day, this would never have happened. What in God's name was he going to do with her? He couldn't tie her up and leave her in the line shack; the cowhands would search every inch of the ranch looking for her. And he couldn't put her in jail until he was finished with Lucas and his cohorts because the sheriff was Sam's man and couldn't be trusted.

"You could always shoot me," Kate snarled at him. "In fact, I almost wish you would."

Clint could see no other way out. He'd have to tell her the truth, gambling that he knew her well enough to talk her into leaving with him. "I'm not going to shoot you, Kate, but I do admit you've made things difficult for me. You're wrong about my being a rustler."

"I don't believe you."

"And I don't go around checking out forts."

"Well pray tell, just what do you do?" she asked sarcastically.

"You might call me a hired gun for the government. That's how others have referred to me."

"And I suppose the next thing you're going to tell me is that the government sent you here."

He grabbed her by the arm and led her into the line shack. After shoving her down on the bed, he struck a match and lit the small candle sitting on a box. The room was suffused with dim light.

"Aren't you afraid someone will see the light?"

"No, I've already checked. The only way it can be seen is if you get way up the mountain." He sat down on a bale of hay and laid her pistol beside him. "You're not going to like what I have to tell you."

"You're right." She turned her head away, refusing to look at him.

"I was sent here because the government cattle that've been bought from this ranch are not the same cattle that're delivered to the reservations."

"If you're telling the truth, what does that have to do with us?"

"Since the shipments originate here, this was the best place to start."

"Well it's not our fault if you don't get the right steers."

"Now that's where the real problem lies. You see, you're wrong."

She flashed her eyes at him. "What are you saying? No one on this ranch switches cattle."

"Lucas does."

Kate blanched and sucked in her breath. "You're out of your mind! Lucas would never do such a thing. You're just looking for someone to take the blame, and I won't allow it."

"I respect your dedication to your family, but it doesn't have to make you blind."

"You're trying to twist my thinking with your words." Kate leaned over and rested her head in her hands. "I don't know what I believe anymore, but I'll never believe Lucas is guilty of anything other than being young and wild. He'd never hurt anyone.''

"I can prove it.''

"I still wouldn't believe you.''

"Maybe you're afraid to know the truth.''

"Are you telling me you can prove it without a shadow of a doubt?'' she whispered.

Clint nodded. He had no intention of telling her about the rustling or anything else. What she had to face would be hard enough.

"Then show me.''

"We'll have to take a ride.''

Kate's head shot up. "So that's it! You're trying to get me out of here without me making a commotion.''

"No, Kate,'' he said softly. "I wish I didn't have to prove this to you, but you've left me no choice.''

Kate could hear the sincerity in his deep voice. There was a sadness on his face she'd never seen before. Was he telling the truth, or was she so weak she felt the need to keep torturing herself until she accepted the fact that he was no damn good? "All right, I'll go with you, provided you return my gun.''

Clint considered his options. "How do I know you won't shoot a warning?''

"I give you my word.''

Clint knew he really had no choice. He had to continue gambling. "Very well, we have a deal.''

Not until they were back outside and she had the revolver in her hand did Kate start giving some credence to what Clint had told her. A crook would have more sense than to return a gun. Seeing Clint fade into the darkness with his black clothes, a thought suddenly occurred to her. When they were on the hunt for the wild mustangs she'd wondered the same thing. "Clint, did you save my life that night when White Cloud was killed?''

"Yes."

Kate still doubted him. "And what did you say to me?" She'd never told anyone the exact words.

"I said you were safe, and that there was a horse waiting for you."

Kate couldn't even force a thank-you. She wanted to run to him and have him put his strong arms around her. She needed him to say he'd told the truth about loving her, and that everything was going to be all right. But he'd turned his back on her once. She couldn't trust him not to do it again. Why couldn't she just accept that he was no longer interested? What did it take to convince her that it was finished between them? The hurt was raw pain, and dammit, couldn't he have done it in a nicer way? "Well, I guess we'd better walk back down and get a couple of horses now that Midnight has taken off. I want you to know, there's nothing you can do to make me believe Lucas is guilty of anything."

Clint whistled, and Midnight came trotting around the line shack.

"You've trained him well," Kate said bitterly, "just like you trained me to come to your beck and call."

Once mounted, Clint leaned down, lifted Kate from the ground and gently sat her in front of him. As he guided Midnight down the mountain, he desperately wanted to kiss Kate's full lips and make love to her. He didn't want to see the hurt he would be inflicting when he proved Lucas was in on the fraud. He thought about how Lucas's arrest would affect Mattie and Sam. It would be so easy to turn his back and put an end to everything with just a warning, but he couldn't do that. Kate had been right when she'd accused him of using everyone. Apparently Sandoval had been saying the same thing so long ago: "Morgan would kill his own sister if it meant getting the job done."

It didn't take long to saddle Cinnamon for Kate. Soon they were traveling at an easy gait. Kate was starting to have second thoughts. She wanted to kick herself. Again she'd allowed Clint to talk her into believing him by saying things she'd wanted to hear. Like telling her he wasn't a rustler but a government man. She'd believed him because she wanted to believe him. It was much easier than accepting the fact that she'd fallen in love with a ruthless crook. Why couldn't she make up her mind about this man? She was doing the same thing she'd done over the last two weeks. Finding excuses for his behavior, then damning herself for being a fool. It was an ongoing clash. Her heart and body said one thing, but her mind wouldn't buy it. She needed to stop thinking. Hopefully, after tonight, she'd be able to finally make positive decisions as to what kind of man Clint Morgan really was. However, if he still had any tricks up his sleeve, she was right behind him, and she had a gun. Nothing he could say would convince her that Lucas was guilty of anything. He had to know that. He probably figured that once he had her out of hearing distance, he could coax her into keeping her mouth shut. Or maybe he planned on killing her. But she couldn't make herself believe that. After all, he'd saved her life—more than once. She should have drawn her gun on him when he was saddling Cinnamon, but whether she had done right or wrong, she had to learn the truth.

She looked ahead at Clint's powerful shoulders and broad back. It had taken no effort on his part to lift her from the ground and put her on his horse. He was strong, handsome, a magnificent lover, and were circumstances different, he was everything she'd ever dreamed of in a man. She loved him. No matter what the outcome, she would love him till her dying breath. That was why she hadn't been able to pull the trigger at the line shack. But it wouldn't happen again. He'd had his chance to leave. If he tried pulling anything, she wouldn't give him another.

An hour later they made a wide circle around the railroad spur and holding pens, avoiding the cowhands on guard. Try as she would, Kate couldn't figure out where Clint was taking her. At least there was one consolation. If he'd planned on doing anything to her, he could have done so a long time ago.

When they reached the cliffs, Clint moved Midnight up the rocky side. Kate followed, wishing it were daylight so she could see better. The climb was a slow process. More than once Kate had to guide her horse back and forth around large boulders. Cinnamon stumbled several times on loose rocks, but maintained his footing.

Once they were on top of the mountain, Clint turned in the saddle and motioned Kate to be quiet by placing a finger to his lips. A few minutes later, they dismounted.

A strong foreboding clutched at Kate when Clint took her hand and led her toward the edge of the cliff. She suddenly wanted to pull back, but couldn't.

Finally Clint stopped, and Kate found herself looking down into a canyon. The silvered moon rode high, allowing a partial view of the cattle below. Bile rose in her throat at seeing protruding ribs over sucked-in sides. They all looked as if they were sick and dying, and there was practically no grass on the canyon floor to feed on. A dozen questions popped into Kate's head, but she didn't dare speak for fear the two men below would hear her. The biggest question was why the cattle were on her land. They certainly weren't Whitfield cattle, nor were they all steers. The W/L on their flanks was the Whitfield brand, but she knew there were a lot of tricks to changing brands.

Kate wanted some answers, and she wanted them now. Her cowhands weren't that far away. Once she made it back down the cliff to the holding pens, she could lead them into the canyon and capture the men. She started to leave, but Clint grabbed her and forced her to sit down. She couldn't fight him because if the men below discovered they were being watched, they could escape.

An hour passed. Kate was furious that Clint continued to detain her. What could he possibly be waiting for? Fifteen minutes later, she had her answer. Another man rode into the canyon and joined the others. Even if she wasn't able to see the color of horse he rode, Lucas's thick blond hair stood out like a beacon even in the dead of night. They were just below where she and Clint had been waiting. Getting down on her hands and knees, Kate cautiously crawled forward so as to see better. Fortunately, the men's voices carried.

"Did you bring our money, Lucas?" the man with the big hat asked.

"Sure did. Five hundred each."

Kate could see Lucas handing out something. Since the other two made no comment, she assumed it was their money. If so, where did Lucas get it? She squinted in an effort to see better, but it didn't help. Why would Lucas even get involved in something that looked underhanded? There had to be a good explanation. He'd tell her as soon as she could talk to him. Clint was trying to make her believe something that just couldn't be true. But . . . no cowhand made five hundred dollars for any job.

"I'll sure be glad when we get rid of these mangy critters."

The man with the big hat lit a cigarette, giving Kate a momentary view of his face. She didn't recognize him.

The smallest of the three men leaned back in his saddle and looked up at the sky. Kate didn't dare duck for fear the movement would catch his eye.

"Gets mighty lonely just sittin' out here," he commented. He lowered his head. "As soon as we get these crow baits loaded into the cars and the others to Medicine Bow, I'm goin' to stay on a two-week drunk and hump every woman that's willin'. Maybe even some that ain't."

"You're goin' to be mighty sore, Horace."

"Nope. Them women's the ones that's gonna be sore. When you aimin' to rustle some more of your pa's cattle, Lucas?"

Kate's heart leaped into her throat. She held her breath, waiting for Lucas to say something in denial.

"I don't know," Lucas said flippantly. "Don't worry, when I'm ready I'll send Pedro to Rawlins to get you. Made it a hell of a lot easier when I could have Brody doin' the runnin'. I don't know what the hell he thought he was gonna do at Cripple Ridge, but whatever it was the damn fool got himself killed." Lucas turned his horse around. "I'll see you boys tomorrow."

Kate fell back into a sitting position and watched Lucas ride away. Fury consumed her. Brody, Clint, and even Pedro were sheep compared to a brother who cared so little for his family, the ranch, or the men working on it that he'd stolen from them and killed others. Most of her life she'd felt sorry for Lucas. Many times she'd turned her head the other way, not wanting to believe what she'd seen all her life. He was a user, always blaming others for his faults. It was easier that way. He didn't have to account for the crimes he'd committed. He could draw his "Poor Lucas" from her and Mattie. Sam had been right all along. Maybe it was their fault. Who could say? But somewhere along the way, Lucas had turned bad. In her heart, she knew it was too late for him to change. All their hopes that some day Lucas would be able to take over the ranch were nothing more than dust in the wind.

Clint tapped her shoulder, but she couldn't move. Again Clint touched her, but this time she took a swing at him. She wanted to fight. She wanted to scream . . . she wanted to cry. Slowly she rose to her feet, wishing Clint had never brought her here. There was no longer a shred of doubt as to who Clint was. A government man. He'd used her family, and now he was ready to deliver his final blow. She hated him for it. Maybe she even hated Lucas now. But just as she couldn't shoot Clint earlier, neither could she allow her brother to be put in prison. She'd given Clint a chance, and now it was Lucas's turn, no matter what he'd done. He was her brother. He was a Whitfield.

Kate looked around and saw Clint's shadowy figure waiting by the horses. She felt his eyes on her as she slowly walked over and mounted Cinnamon.

"Clint!" Kate called in a hushed voice as he was about to climb on Midnight. "Something's wrong with my right stirrup."

Clint came back. Just as he leaned down to check the stirrup, Kate brought her boot up, kicking him hard in the jaw. As he fell backward, she jerked Cinnamon around and rode off.

Stunned, Clint was slow getting into the saddle, giving Kate a good head start.

Kate hoped to catch up with Lucas when she reached the bottom of the cliff, but the night was like a blanket and she could hardly see. Her only choice was to get to the house before Clint caught up with her.

Kate had traveled for some distance before she heard the drumming of hoofbeats approaching from behind. A quick glance over her shoulder told her Midnight was quickly closing the distance between them. She slapped Cinnamon's neck on both sides with the ends of the reins, trying for more speed, but her horse was small compared to the big stallion that continued to draw closer. When the horses were even, Clint reached out to grab her. She jerked Cinnamon to the left, causing Clint to miss. Knowing Cinnamon could turn corners quicker, she weaved him to the right, then the left. Clint proved to be too good a horseman, and Midnight too fast and powerful. Again Clint came up alongside her, and again she tried to avoid him, but she felt herself being yanked from the saddle.

"Let me go, damn you! Let me go." She pounded her fists on his head . . . face . . . body, anything she could reach. When he brought Midnight to a halt she was still flaying him, but nothing seemed to have any effect. He dismounted, carrying her with him.

"I hate you, Clint Morgan!" she yelled when he'd finally turned her loose. Angry and frustrated she started walking in circles and kicking up chunks of grass from the ground. "Do you hear me? I hate you!"

"I couldn't very well not hear you."

He sounded so calm, Kate stopped and looked at him. "Why, Clint?" Her voice cracked. "Why have you done this?"

"I had no choice, Kate. There are others involved. Vale is also one of them. Would you have me let them all go so they can rob and murder again?"

Kate stuffed her fingers in the waistband of her britches and lowered her head.

"I have a job to do, Kate, and none of these men are going to escape. I'm sorry Lucas is involved, but I'm not the cause of him turning bad."

"So what are you going to do about Lucas? Wait till he comes home, then arrest him?"

"No, if I take him in, the others will get away."

Kate looked up at him. "Then how do you plan on catching them?"

"You're going to help me."

"Oh no I'm not!"

Clint shoved his hat back. "I think you will, because it's your men that have been killed. It's also your men that have done the killing and your responsibility to see that they pay for their crimes." He pulled off his hat and slapped it against his leg. "Can't you see my hands are tied? If you hadn't caught me tonight, I wouldn't be having this problem."

"What is it you want me to do?"

"Nothing more than what you usually do. Collect the money and leave."

"And how do you plan on catching them?"

Clint had no choice but to tell her the rest. At any time, from this point on, she could foil the entire trap. "I'll be with the marshal and his men in one of the empty railroad cars. If I'm right, after you've left, the cattle in the canyon will be brought out and loaded into the cars. In the past, the good cattle have been driven to Medicine Bow and sold. The marshal has already arrested the buyer there."

"But . . . but that would mean the men at the holding pens are also a part of it."

"I found out from Sam that the same men always do the job. Add Pedro, discount the buyer, and you have eight men. With the exception of Vale, I'm sure the others have all had a hand in rustling your cattle."

Kate kicked another clump of grass. Pedro was one of the men guarding the holding pens. She'd heard Lucas say Pedro had taken Brody's place. With everyone involved, no wonder they knew when and where to strike. She doubted any of them would have been caught, at least not for a long time, and Lord knows how many cattle would have been stolen by then. And Lucas. Why? Someday all of this would have been his.

Kate looked out into the night. "I guess Lucas was smarter than we gave him credit," she said soulfully. "When will the marshal and his men get into the cars? Vale's paying tomorrow."

"Probably in about another hour, when the moon's gone down."

"And you?"

"As soon as I see you safely back to the house, I'll come back." He started to go to her, but hesitated long enough to change his mind. "Kate, whether you believe me or not, I'm sorry it has to end this way. Maybe a stretch in prison is what Lucas needs. He'll be out in a few years and he can start his life over again."

Kate had to fight back the tears. Lucas would die in prison. Never in his nineteen years had he known confinement, not with the whole valley to roam. "You haven't left me much choice. I'll do as you ask."

Clint nodded. He whistled for Midnight. "We'd better be going."

"Clint, was I just part of your plan? What we've

shared . . . didn't it mean anything to you? Was I just another woman in your life?"

Clint knew he should make the break clean and say yes, but seeing her standing there, helpless and hurting, he couldn't leave her that way. "Kate . . . it meant more to me than you'll ever know."

"Then why? Why did you turn your back on me for some trollop at the saloon?" Kate could no longer hold back the tears. Angrily, she reached up and brushed them away.

Clint took the few steps to her, gently wrapping her in his arms. "Kate," he whispered in her ear, "I haven't touched another woman since the day I met you."

"You're lying."

She tried to pull away but he held her to him. "I swear to God. Not in Rawlins. Not in Whitfield. Not at the Graveyard Saloon. How could I? I love you."

"But Lucas said—"

"Lucas was the one who lied."

She looked into the warmth of his eyes, and she believed him. His lips joined hers. His kiss was passionate, yet tender. Her arms went around his neck as he kissed her eyes, her nose, each side of her lips. "Oh, Clint," she murmured, "I thought you didn't want me. I love you so much. Please, make love to me." *Please, let me have this last moment,* she silently screamed.

With every fiber of his being, Clint wanted to, but he knew there was no future for them. One of the things he'd always admired about her was her loyalty to her family, and tomorrow he would be making her break that loyalty. She would be helping him put her brother in prison. It was something that would lie deep in her heart, and though she might try, she'd never forgive him for it.

He kissed her again, a long searing kiss that he could hold in his memories, then gently pushed her away. "We haven't time," he lied. "It's already too late for me to take you back to the house. It'll soon be dawn." He went over and pulled his rifle from the scabbard. "Here," he said, handing it to her. "Be careful."

"I will." She mounted Cinnamon. "Try to remember," she said sadly, "I love you." She rode off.

Clint stood watching her until she disappeared from view. Would she go along with his plan? He had no idea. He'd have to wait until tomorrow to find out.

When Kate reached the house, she headed directly for Sam's bedroom. Just as Clint had to do what he thought was right, so did she, even if it meant losing the only man she'd ever loved. She knocked on the door, and a moment later she heard a gravelly voice call out, "Who is it?"

"Kate."

"What do you want this time of night?" Sam grumbled. "Well, don't just stand out there, come on in."

It had been a long time since Kate had been in her father's room. He'd lit a candle, but even in the dim light she could see him clearly. She'd forgotten he slept sitting up with pillows propped behind him, or that he wore a nightcap. He looked so old.

Kate sat on the chair beside his bed. "Maybe now, Sam, you'll finally realize just how much my family, and this ranch, mean to me."

Chapter 20

❦❦

Clint impatiently waited with the marshal and his men in the second empty railroad car. The stench of old cow dung clung to the floor and to the wooden slats that boxed the sides. Sticks of straw poked into his hands and his jeans. He reached up and wiped away the sweat stinging his eyes. His shirt clung to his body as the heat continued to rise. The spaces between the slats and the open door of the cattle car afforded little relief since he and the other twelve men had to stay at the end and down low to keep from being seen. It was already past one in the afternoon.

Clint was beginning to seriously question whether Kate would arrive. She should have been here over an hour ago. Pedro, Lucas and the other three men were at the holding pen. Clint could hear an occasional laugh, but other than that they waited quietly, or kept their voices low.

Another thirty minutes passed before Clint heard horses arriving. Keeping low, he worked his way forward, looking between the slats to see who had arrived. He watched Kate and Gordon Vale dismount. After forty-five minutes of examining the steers and chatting with the men, Vale walked over to where Kate and Lucas stood waiting.

''I don't see any reason to look further, little

365

lady. You've always given me good steers." He paid Kate the money.

"We'll look forward to doing business with you next spring," Kate said as she climbed back on Cinnamon.

Clint nodded to Marshal Hawk and his men to get ready.

Kate started to ride off, but to Clint's annoyance, she turned back around. "Lucas," she called. "I forgot. Sam wants to see you at the ranch."

"Can't it wait?"

"No, he said he wanted to see you right away."

Clint cursed under his breath. Kate was getting Lucas out of there and there wasn't a damn thing he could do to stop it. She had outfoxed him. She knew he couldn't let Vale and the others know it was a trap. He had no choice now but to sit tight until he could catch the others. Then he'd have to go after Lucas. He'd probably end up having to kill the boy, and God knows who else, because there was no way anyone was going to let him just ride up and take Sam Whitfield's son away. But even though what Kate had done was wrong, he could understand it.

Lucas looked at his men and smiled. It didn't matter if he left, they knew what to do. "Very well," he said congenially. "We wouldn't want to keep dear Sam waiting." He mounted his buckskin and rode off with Kate.

Clint knew his best chance was to get to Lucas as fast as possible, before Sam and Kate rounded up the ranch hands. But precious time continued to pass. He kept wondering what the holdup was. It was nearing three o'clock when one of the men let loose with a shrill whistle. It wasn't much longer before Clint heard the bawling scrub cattle arriving. Vale hadn't left. He was watching the entire procedure.

As Clint had suspected, it wasn't the cattle in the holding pens that the men started loading into the first railroad car. He'd seen enough. He was the first one to leave the empty car, but the others were right behind him. The marshal and his men had no trouble rounding up the crooks. One of the deputies had collected their horses, and Clint leaped onto Midnight's back and took off for the house. He knew the wiser thing to do would have been to wait and have some of the marshal's men go with him, but this was something he had to do alone. In fact, it could very well end up being the last thing he'd ever do. There had already been plenty of time to fortify the ranch house.

Acting as if there was nothing wrong depleted all of Kate's energy. She had to be careful because Lucas knew her too well. If he detected anything out of the way, he'd become suspicious. Fortunately during the ride back Lucas chose not to carry on a conversation. They'd kept their horses at a slow trot, even though Kate wanted to race home. But then Lucas would want to know what was her hurry. She wanted to scream at him, demand to know why he'd committed such atrocities, then give him hell. But even though what he'd done was unforgivable, Kate also wanted to tell him she loved him. This was her brother; she had helped feed him and had rocked him to sleep when he was a baby. She wanted to take him in her arms and say everything was going to be all right, but she couldn't. Everything wasn't going to be all right.

Upon entering the house, Kate went straight to Mattie's bedroom. Mattie was sitting by the window, a lacy handkerchief in each hand, her eyes puffed from crying. Sam had already told her what he knew and how he intended to deal with it. Mattie was heartbroken at knowing she'd never see her son again.

Lucas strolled into the parlor, feeling quite pleased with himself. After this last five hundred cattle were sold, he'd be an even richer man. Sam's riling wouldn't bother him today.

"What was so important that it couldn't wait?" Lucas asked as he turned to his father, who had positioned his wheelchair in the middle of the room. "You know I'm supposed to take care of the loading."

"Slide the doors closed, boy," Sam ordered.

"You mean Kate isn't going to get to listen?" Lucas closed the doors. When he turned back around, it occurred to him that his father's weathered face was set in granite, and it angered him. "Are you fixin' to bawl me out for something again? What's wrong, haven't I been runnin' around fast enough for you?"

"You've been a thorn in my side since you were a boy. Now you've brought disgrace on this very ranch that I built with my blood and sweat. You always were a weakling."

"A weakling?" The muscles in Lucas's jaw flexed. "You're a fine one to talk. Look at you. An old man having to be pushed around in a wheelchair, still spouting orders so he can continue playing the part of the great Sam Whitfield. Don't talk to me about being a weakling."

"I know you're behind the rustling, Lucas, and you needn't try to deny it. I also know you've been switching the reservation steers and pocketing the money."

Lucas blanched. "How did you find out?"

"I didn't. Clint figured it out. He was sent here to catch whoever was responsible for cheating the government. Why did you do it, Lucas?"

Lucas's anger flared. Hell, he'd treated Clint almost like a brother! His years of pent-up anger snapped. "Why? I'll tell you why. To put money in my pocket. I'm a Whitfield, but I gotta go around working like some damn hand."

Sam's expression didn't change. "Only because you're my son, I'm goin' to let you get away. But this is the last time you can count on me for anything. There's a horse saddled out back, with provisions. I want you to get on it and ride out of here. And if I ever see you on this ranch again, I'll have you hung."

Lucas banged his fist on the side table. "Leave? Oh no. This ranch is rightfully mine, and by God not you or anyone else is going to take it away from me. I'll see you dead first. Yes, I stole cattle, but those were my cattle! It wasn't just to put money in my hand, father dear. It was to show you Kate couldn't handle a damn thing." He let out a high-pitched laugh. "But that's not the only thing I've done. I even hired a man to kill Kate, but someone came along and saved her precious hide."

"Just like you tried to kill me?"

"You know?"

"Ever since it happened, I've known that it was my own son that made me a cripple! I saw you stab that bull with your knife so he'd charge me. But I never said anything, hoping that you'd see the error of your ways, face me man to man, and become the son I've always wanted. I should have known better. But I didn't die like you expected, which must have been a great disappointment to you. Now get out of this house."

"Do you have any idea just how much I hate you? I've hated you as long as I can remember, and at last I can say it to your face." Lucas pulled his gun from his holster and rested the barrel in the palm of his other hand. He looked down at it and smiled. "Making me learn how to use this was the only favor you ever did me." Slowly he aimed the gun at Sam. "You've already lived too long, old man. Clint will probably be coming for me, and I aim to be ready to meet him."

Sam squeezed the trigger of his revolver, leaving a hole in the blanket covering his legs. Lucas's face mirrored his shock before he fell to the floor dead. The gun slipped from Sam's hand onto the floor.

Hearing the shot, Kate ran from Mattie's room and down the stairs. The servants were already gathered in front of the parlor doors, their faces white with concern. Kate slid the doors open. The first thing she saw was Lucas lying on the floor in a growing pool of blood. Her eyes shifted to Sam. He was bent over in his wheelchair, crying. Kate rushed toward Lucas to see if he was still alive.

"Don't bother checking," Sam said in a choked voice. "He's dead. My son is dead."

Kate's hand flew to her throat. "Oh my God! What have I done? If I had let him go to prison, he'd still be alive. Oh, poor Lucas. What have I done? Mattie . . . I have to take care of Mattie." Tears were running down Kate's face as she went to her father. "Are you all right?"

He nodded.

A moment later, Mattie rushed in. Her eyes grew big, then she fainted.

"Norman," Sam bellowed to the manservant. "Take Mrs. Whitfield to her room, and, Alma, you stay and attend her. Close the door behind you!"

Alma closed the door as Kate rushed to it.

"Kate, I want to talk to you before you go to her." Seeing she was in shock and hadn't heard him, Sam said gently, "Kate, come here, girl."

"Sam . . ."

"Hush, Kate, and listen to me. I can't let you

carry the burden of Lucas's death. It's not your fault.''

She went to Sam and dropped to her knees, placing her head on his useless legs.

Sam reached down and caressed her beautiful blond hair. "Lucas confessed to me that he was the one who hired the man to kill you. It's also his fault that I'm crippled.''

Kate's head jerked up.

"It's the truth, girl.''

"Why?'' Kate gasped. "Why would he do those things?''

"It was all to get the ranch for himself. As with everything else he did, he wanted it the easy way instead of working for it. He was a bad seed from my loins. Still, I also loved him. Don't blame yourself, Kate. Lucas is finally at rest.'' He stroked her head again. "Now get some of the men to take care of Lucas, then go to Mattie.''

"But what about you?''

"I want to spend a few minutes alone with my son. This isn't the first tragedy in my life, and likely not the last. I'll be all right. But I don't want to lose you too, Kate. I'm sorry for all the wrong I've done you. Now go get the men.''

As Clint neared the house, he could see Henry, Cotton and several other cowhands standing to the side of the house, but they paid him no attention, nor did they have rifles. Clint couldn't understand why the place wasn't surrounded by Whitfield men. Surely they knew he'd come back for Lucas, and they should also have expected the marshal's men to be with him.

He pulled up in front of the house and slowly dismounted. Still there was no effort made to detain him. He stepped onto the porch, trying to figure out what was going on, when Kate ran out of the door and into his arms. Tears were streaming down her cheeks.

"Oh, Clint" she muttered before burying her face in his chest.

Clint was furious that Kate had been sent out to beg for her no-account brother's life. Lucas should be out here defending himself, not his sister.

"It won't work, Kate," Clint told her in a gruff voice. "I have to take him in. Now if you don't want him killed, tell Lucas to come out peacefully."

"Lucas is dead, Clint," Kate said between sobs.

Clint didn't believe her. "Where is he?"

"In the parlor."

Clint pushed her aside and walked into the house. He stood in the doorway to the parlor and stared at Lucas lying on one of the tables, a sheet covering his body. Head bent, Sam sat in his wheelchair with Mattie standing beside him, her arm around her husband's slumped shoulders, looking down at her son. Their backs were turned to him. Seeing the hurt the family was undergoing, anger at Lucas ripped through Clint like a hot blade of steel. The boy wasn't worth it. But he'd never be able to convince the others of that, and he wasn't about to try. They'd suffered enough. And when this was all over, Clint Morgan was the one they were going to blame. He couldn't take having to see the accusing look in Mattie's eyes, and especially not in Kate's. It was time to get the hell out of there. He wouldn't even bother taking his things except what few he'd left in the line shack.

Clint left the room, walking past Kate without saying a word. He had only one thing in mind—to get on Midnight and leave.

Watching Clint leave the house and keep walking, Kate became frantic. "Clint!" she called. She ran out onto the porch. "Clint!" His steps didn't falter. Angrily Kate brushed the tears from her cheeks. "I'll be damned if you're going to say you love me and then just walk out, Clint Morgan!" she whispered.

Kate ran back into the house. After grabbing her whip from her bedroom, she ran back out.

Having changed clothes, Clint was in the line shack stuffing his things into his saddlebags when he heard Kate ride up. Next thing he knew she was standing in the doorway, her green eyes flashing with anger, her whip trailing behind her. He cursed himself because his gun belt was still lying on the bed. He made a move to grab for it when Kate cracked her whip and jerked it out of his reach.

"Get the hell out of here, Kate," he warned.

"That's something you can't make me do. You have no means of protecting yourself now."

"So what comes next? Are you going to whip the hell out of me because your brother is dead? Well, I can tell you right now that unless you plan to kill me—" The whip cracked again and his feet were pulled out from under him. "Goddammit, Kate!"

"If I decide to use the whip, it will be because you lied about loving me, or you don't have any faith in my love!"

Clint climbed back to his feet, his look menacing.

Kate's hard exterior collapsed. "Clint, I just lost a brother. I don't think I could stand losing you too. If you must leave, take me with you."

Seeing the hurt look on Kate's face destroyed the anger Clint needed to get him out of here. "Come here, Kate," he said, hoping to be able to get the whip from her.

Kate wanted to go to him, but she'd long since

learned how wily he could be. "Not until you swear you won't leave me."

Clint's sigh was heavy. "I can't do that."

"Is it because you were lying when you said you love me? Were you just trying to get me to help you after all?" She hated the tears that were again forming in her eyes.

"No, Kate," he said softly. "I could never take you away from here. This land means too much to you. And what do you think would happen to Sam and Mattie if you left? Like you, they've also lost someone they love."

"Then why can't you stay?"

Clint placed his hands on his hips and looked at the bed, unable to meet Kate's eyes a moment longer. "Because Mattie, Sam and even you could never really forgive me for Lucas's death."

"You didn't kill Lucas."

"That's not the point. It doesn't matter who did it. The question is, would he be dead if I hadn't come here?"

Kate leaned against the doorway and lowered her head. "Clint, did you mean it when you said you loved me?"

Clint wasn't about to go to Kate. If he did, he wasn't sure he could go away without her. But he couldn't leave her thinking he'd only been using her. "With all my heart."

"Then you have nothing to worry about. Sam killed Lucas."

Clint was thunderstruck. "Why?"

"I . . . I'm not sure." Tears were running down her cheeks again. It seemed as though all she'd done in the last two weeks was cry. "I was with Mattie in her bedroom. We could hear them arguing. It was so terrible. Then we heard the shot. I didn't ask what happened."

"Shh." He went to her and her arms wrapped around his waist. He stroked her back, feeling her tears soaking his shirt. "Everything is going to be all right."

She lifted her head from his chest. "I have to tell you . . . Mattie and Sam don't blame you, Clint. As hard as it's been for us to accept, we now know Lucas wasn't any good. Sam did tell me something when Mattie was out of the room. He told it to me to lessen my own guilt."

"What did he say?"

"He told me Lucas had confessed that he'd hired that man who tried to kill me." Kate felt Clint's muscles tighten, making her even more convinced of his love. "I think he tried killing Sam also. I guess he didn't remember that his father always keeps a gun under that blanket over his legs."

Clint leaned down and kissed her, savoring the taste of her lips.

"Clint," Kate said when he drew his head back, "I want you to know that last night I told Sam about Lucas and the cattle you'd shown me. It was his idea to get Lucas away."

Clint released her, then went to the doorway and stood looking out past the trees and at the beautiful valley below. "He always was a wily old man."

"Please, Clint, at least stay until after the funeral. We need your strength. Then, if you're not convinced that we all love you, I won't prevent you from leaving. But I must warn you, Sam has already started thinking of you as a son."

Clint knew he should get the hell out of there, but Kate's soulful eyes were his undoing. "All right, Kate, I'll stay. But after the funeral, I'm leaving."

It was Clint who contacted the preacher, had the casket made and the hole dug for Lucas's burial. It was a small funeral, with only the family

and ranch hands to witness it. The sky was over-
cast and the morning misty. Even Sam cried. But
each in his or her own way, the family had come
to accept Lucas's death. Clint had indeed provided the strength they needed during the ordeal,
and they all were grateful.

When the services were over, Clint lifted Sam
from his wheelchair and sat him in the front seat
of the carriage. After assisting Mattie and Kate
and making sure they were settled in the back,
Clint circled around and climbed in beside Sam.
As Clint untied the reins, Sam placed a weathered hand on his shoulder.

"You're family, boy," Sam said in a low, gravelly whisper, "and we'd like you to make this
your home. If you love Kate, don't leave her."

Clint flicked the reins. For the first time in
weeks, he felt whole again.

Two weeks later, Kate and Clint were married.

Clint stood talking to Henry about winter feed
when Kate came up and joined them.

"I thought you would like to know, darling,
I'm going for a ride." Kate smiled sweetly at her
husband. "I won't be gone too long." As she
turned to leave, she let her hand brush his crotch,
just the way Star had taught her. She had to swal-
low her laughter at hearing Clint's grunt.

"Henry, we can discuss this later. I have something I want to show Kate." He caught up with
Kate and took hold of her arm.

"So, you have something to show me?" Kate
teased.

"Indeed I do, Mrs. Morgan. Now get on your
horse and follow me."

"Where are you taking me?"

"I happen to know where there's a beautiful
warm pool near that old line shack, and I can't

think of anything I would enjoy more than showing it to you.''

Kate smiled secretly to herself, delighted that Clint knew of her special place and thrilled at the idea of sharing it with him.

''And what are we going to do at this pool?'' Kate asked with false innocence as she mounted Cinnamon.

Clint swung up on Midnight and motioned him forward. ''I'm going to show you just how much I love you, first in the water, then on the bank, and maybe in the water again.''

She laughed joyfully and followed.

Kate lay wrapped in Clint's arms, their desire temporarily sated.

''Kate,'' Clint said in a near-savage whisper, ''don't you ever try to walk out of my life.''

Now that she was married, Kate somehow felt older and wiser. She couldn't think of anything more heavenly than spending the rest of her life with the man she loved. ''I don't believe that's something you'll ever have to worry about,'' she said lovingly.

Epilogue

March 1871

The window was open and Mattie could hear Sam and Clint discussing the mare Clint had had shipped from Maryland to be bred to Midnight. Hearing Sam's gravelly, lovable voice reminded Mattie how, for the first time in years, Sam had needed her after Lucas's death. The hurt she'd felt at losing her son would be with her to her dying day, but her family was whole again. She smiled, thanking God for the blessings He had bestowed on her.

Mattie leaned forward, dipped her pen in the inkwell, and began her letter.

> Dear Sister,
>   I know Clint will be writing you soon, but I had to be the first to tell you that yesterday, you and I became the proud grandmothers of a precious baby boy. Our plan worked, Cora, though I must admit that on more than one occasion I thought it was doomed for failure.

Mattie paused. Why upset Cora by pointing out that the baby was a mite early? Unless Cora had become addle-brained, she could certainly figure it out for herself. She dipped the pen again.

You'll be happy to know Clint plans on bringing his family to see you as soon as he feels it's safe for Kate and the baby to travel. They have insisted I come with them, but I couldn't leave Sam.

Sam now lets Clint run the ranch, and swears he will never interfere, but we all know that just isn't in Sam's nature.

It's a beautiful spring day here . . .

© 1992 Coors Brewing Company, Golden, Colorado 80401 • Brewer of Fine Quality Beers Since 1873

1 Out Of 5 Women Can't Read.

1 Out Of 5 Women Can't Read.

1 Out Of 5 Women Can't Read.

1 Xvz Xv 5 Xwywv Xvy'z Xvyz.

1 Out Of 5 Women Can't Read.

*As painful as it is to believe, it's true. And it's
time we all did something to help. Coors has committed $40
million to fight illiteracy in America. We hope
you'll join our efforts by volunteering your time. Giving just a
few hours a week to your local literacy center can
help teach a woman to read. For more information on literacy
volunteering, call **1-800-626-4601**.*

LITERACY. PASS IT ON.